# BANANA CREAM PIE
# MURDER

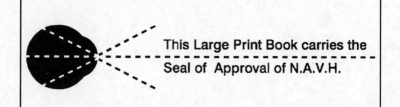

This Large Print Book carries the
Seal of Approval of N.A.V.H.

# Banana Cream Pie Murder

## Joanne Fluke

**THORNDIKE PRESS**
*A part of Gale, Cengage Learning*

POQUOSON PUBLIC LIBRARY
500 CITY HALL AVENUE
POQUOSON, VA 23662

GALE
CENGAGE Learning·

Farmington Hills, Mich • San Francisco • New York • Waterville, Maine
Meriden, Conn • Mason, Ohio • Chicago

# GALE
## CENGAGE Learning®

**LIBRARY OF CONGRESS CATALOGING-IN-PUBLICATION DATA**

Names: Fluke, Joanne, 1943- author.
Title: Banana cream pie murder / by Joanne Fluke.
Description: Large print edition. | Waterville, Maine : Thorndike Press, 2017. |
    Series: A Hannah Swensen mystery with recipes | Series: Thorndike Press large
    print mystery
Identifiers: LCCN 2016059130 | ISBN 9781410495228 (hardback) | ISBN 1410495221
    (hardcover)
Subjects: LCSH: Swensen, Hannah (Fictitious character)—Fiction. | Women
    detectives—Fiction. | Large type books. | BISAC: FICTION / Mystery & Detective /
    General. | GSAFD: Mystery fiction.
Classification: LCC PS3556.L685 B36 2017 | DDC 813/.54—dc23
LC record available at https://lccn.loc.gov/2016059130

Published in 2017 by arrangement with Kensington Books, an imprint
of Kensington Publishing Corp

Printed in the United States of America
1 2 3 4 5 6 7 21 20 19 18 17

*This book is for Doug Mendini.*
*The world was better with you in it.*

# ACKNOWLEDGMENTS

Congratulations to John and Doris Capra on their Golden Wedding Anniversary.

Big hugs to the kids and the grandkids who say that my kitchen always smells like chocolate.

Thank you to my friends and neighbors: Mel & Kurt, Lyn & Bill, Gina, Dee Appleton, Jay, Richard Jordan, Laura Levine, the real Nancy and Heiti, Dr. Bob & Sue, Dan, Mark & Mandy at Faux Library, Daryl and her staff at Groves Accountancy, Gene and Ron at SDSA, and everyone at Boston Private Bank.

Thanks to Brad, Eric, Amanda, Lorenzo, Meg, Alison, Cameron, Gabriel, Barbara, Lisa, and everyone at the Hallmark Movies & Mysteries Channel who gave us the Murder She Baked Hannah Swensen movies. What fun to see Hannah on TV!

Thank you to my Minnesota friends: Lois & Neal, Bev & Jim, Lois & Jack, Val, Ruthann, Lowell, Dorothy & Sister Sue, and Mary & Jim.

A big thank you to my patient and supportive Editor-in-Chief at Kensington Publishing, John Scognamiglio.

Thanks to all the wonderful folks at Kensington who keep Hannah sleuthing and baking so many treats.

Thanks to Meg Ruley and the staff at the Jane Rotrosen Agency for their constant support and their sage advice.

Thanks to Hiro Kimura, my wonderful cover artist for the incredibly delicious-looking covers on all the Hannah mysteries.

Thank you to Lou Malcangi at Kensington for designing Hannah's gorgeous book covers.

Thanks to John at *Placed4Success.com* for Hannah's movie and TV placements, his presence on all of Hannah's social media, the countless hours he puts in at H.L. Swensen, and for always being there for me.

Thanks to Rudy for maintaining my website at **www.JoanneFluke.com** and for giving support to Hannah's social media.

Big thanks to Kathy Allen for the final testing of the recipes. And thanks to her bowling team for taste testing. Thanks to JQ for helping with Hannah's voluminous email messages.

Grateful hugs to my talented friend, Trudi Nash, for going on book tours with me and for coming up with great new ideas for recipes.

Thanks to food stylist and media guide Lois Brown for her friendship and talented assistance with launch parties and TV baking segments.

Hugs to the Double D's and everyone on Team Swensen who helps to keep Hannah's Facebook presence alive and well.

Thank you to Dr. Rahhal, Dr. and Cathy Line, Dr. Wallen, Dr. Koslowski, Drs. Ashley and Lee, and Dr. Niemeyer *(who reminds me of Doc Knight)* for putting up with my pesky medical and dental questions. Norman and Doc Knight would be clueless without you!

Grateful thanks to all of the Hannah fans who share their family recipes, post on my Facebook page, **Joanne Fluke Author,** watch the Hannah movies, and read her mysteries.

# CHAPTER ONE

Delores Swensen typed THE END and gave a smile of satisfaction as she leaned back in her desk chair. She'd finished the manuscript for her newest Regency romance novel. She was just about to get up and open the bottle of Perrier Jouet she'd been saving for this occasion when she heard a loud crack and she fell to the floor backwards.

For one stunned moment, she stared up at the ceiling in her office in disbelief, unable to move or make a sound. She blinked several times and moved her head tentatively. Nothing hurt. She was still alive. But what had happened? And why had she fallen over backwards?

When the obvious solution occurred to her, Delores started to giggle. The loud crack had sounded when the cushioned seat of her desk chair had sheared off from its base. It was something Doc had warned her would happen someday if she didn't get around to replacing it. And she hadn't. And it had. And here she was on her back, her body effectively swaddled by soft, stuffed leather, barely able to move a muscle.

As she realized that she was in the same position as a turtle flipped over on its back, Delores began to laugh even harder. It was a good thing no one was here to see her! She must look ridiculous. That meant she *had* to figure out some way to get up before Doc came home. If he saw her like this, she'd never hear the end of it. And she wouldn't put it past him to take a photo of her stuck in the chair, on her back, and show it to everyone at the hospital.

Unsure of exactly how to extricate herself, Delores braced her hands on the cushioned arms of the chair and pushed. This didn't work the way she'd thought it, but it *did* work. Instead of moving her body backwards, her action pushed the chair forward. The part of her body that Doc referred to as her gluteus maximus was now several inches away from the seat of the chair, far enough for her to bend her legs, hook her heels on the edge of the chair seat and push it even farther away.

She was getting there! Delores pushed with her heels again and the chair slid several more inches away. By repeating this motion and squirming on her back at the same time, she somehow managed to free herself from her cushioned prison and roll over on hands and knees. She got to her feet by grasping the edge of her desk and pulling herself upright. When she was in a standing position, Delores gave a sigh of relief and promised herself that she'd buy a new desk chair in the morning.

Now that she was on her feet again and none the worse for wear, she decided that celebratory champagne was a necessity. She took the prized bottle from the dorm refrigerator Doc had insisted she install in her office, and opened it with a soft pop. Loud pops were for movie scenes. She'd learned to remove the cork slowly so that not even a drop would escape.

Delores set the open bottle on the desk and went to close the window. She liked fresh air and she always opened it when she worked in the office. She was about to close it when she heard a blood-curdling scream from the floor below.

For a moment Delores just stood there, a shocked expression on her face. Then she glanced at the clock and realized it was a few minutes past eight in the evening. The scream must have come from one of Tori's acting students.

The luxury condo immediately below the penthouse Doc had given her as a wedding present was owned by Victoria Bascomb, Mayor Bascomb's sister. Tori, as she preferred to be called, had been a famous Broadway actress. She'd recently retired and moved to Lake Eden to be closer to the only family she had left, her brother Richard, and his wife Stephanie. Unable to completely divorce herself from the life she loved, Tori had volunteered to direct their local theater group, to teach drama at Jordan High, and to give private acting lessons to any Lake Edenite who aspired to take the theater world by storm. If not the richest, Tori Bascomb was undeniably the most famous person in town. Just yesterday, Tori had told Delores that she had won the lifetime achievement award from STAG, the Stage and Theater Actors Guild, and she would receive her award, a gold statuette that resembled a male deer, at a nationally televised award ceremony soon.

Delores gave a little laugh. How silly she'd been to forget that Tori gave acting lessons in her home studio! The scream she'd heard was obviously part of an acting lesson. Smiling a bit at her foolishness, Delores reached out again, intending to close and lock the window, but a loud cry made her pause in mid-motion.

"No!" a female voice screamed. "Don't! Please don't!"

Whoever the aspiring actress was, she was very good! Delores began to push the window closed when she heard a sound unlike any other. A gunshot. That was a gunshot! She was sure of it!

The gunshot was followed by a second gunshot, and then a crash from the floor below. Something was wrong! No acting student could be that realistic. This was really happening!

Delores didn't think. She just reacted. She raced for the doorway that led to the back stairway that had been used by hotel employees before the Albion Hotel had been converted into luxury condos. The old stairway had been completely refurbished and accessible exclusively to the penthouse residents.

When Delores arrived at the landing of the floor below, she unlocked the door and rushed out into the narrow lobby that separated the two condos on the floor below the penthouse. She raced to Tori's door and only then did the need for caution cross her mind.

Delores stood there, the key Tori had

given her in her hand, and listened. All was quiet inside Tori's condo, no sounds at all. If what she'd heard had been an acting lesson, Tori should be speaking to the would-be actress, critiquing the scene she'd just performed.

As Delores continued to listen for sounds, she considered her options. She'd look very foolish if she unlocked the door and stepped inside to find that Tori and her student were perfectly fine. On the other hand, she could be walking into danger if what she'd heard was a real murder and the intruder was still there. If she called the police before she went in, they'd advise her to wait until they got there. But what if someone needed immediate medical attention?

Delores hesitated for another moment or two and then she decided to knock. She might feel foolish if Tori came to the door and said that everything was fine, but it couldn't hurt to check. She raised her hand and knocked sharply three times.

There was no answer and she heard no rushing footfalls as the intruder hurried to a hiding place. There were no sounds from inside at all. Delores hesitated for another moment and then she made a decision. She reached into her pocket, pulled out her cell phone, and dialed the emergency number for the Winnetka County Sheriff's Station.

"Sheriff's station. Detective Kingston speaking."

Delores took a deep breath. She'd been hoping to contact her son-in-law, Bill Todd, but instead she'd gotten Mike. He was a by-the-book cop and he'd tell her to stay outside the door and wait for him to get there.

"Mike. It's Delores," she said, thinking fast. "Stay on the line, will you, please? I heard a sound from Tori Bascomb's condo and I'm going in to make sure everything's all right."

"Delores. I want you to wait until . . ."

Delores unlocked the door with one hand and pushed it open. Then, holding the phone away from her ear so she wouldn't hear Mike's objections, she glanced around Tori's living room. Nothing was out of place, no overturned chairs, no strangers lurking in corners, no sign of anything unusual. But the scream she'd heard hadn't come from the living room. It had come from the room directly below her office and that was the room that Tori had converted into her acting studio.

Delores moved toward the studio silently, holding the phone in her left hand. It was still sputtering and squawking, but she ignored it. As she prepared to open the door, she spotted a piece of artwork on a table in the hallway. It was made of a heavy metal, probably silver, and it resembled a thin but curvaceous lady holding her arms aloft. Delores grabbed it. It was just as heavy as it looked and it would serve as a weapon if the occasion warranted.

The door to the studio was slightly open and Delores peeked in. The focus of the room was the U-shaped couch facing a low platform handcrafted of cherry wood. The platform was one step high and ran the length of the opposite wall, forming a stage for Tori's would-be actors and actresses. The couch served as Tori's throne. It was where she sat to observe her students. Delores had sat there one afternoon and she knew it was made of baby-soft, butterscotch-colored leather. A fur throw was draped over the back of the couch. Delores hadn't asked Tori which particular animals had given their lives to create the fur throw, but she suspected that it had been very expensive and was probably made from Russian sable.

The scene that presented itself did not look threatening, so Delores stepped into the studio. The indirect lighting that covered the ceiling bathed the studio in a soft glow. Delores glanced at the round coffee table in front of the couch and drew in her breath sharply. A bottle of champagne was nestled in a silver wine bucket next to the table and a crystal flute filled with champagne sat on the table next to a distinctive bakery box that Delores immediately recognized. It was a bakery box from The Cookie Jar, the bakery and coffee shop that her eldest daughter owned. The lid was open and Delores could tell that it contained one of Hannah's Banana Cream Pies. It was Tori's favorite pie and she'd told Delores that she often served it when she had guests.

The flute filled with champagne was interesting. Clouds of tiny bubbles were rising to the surface and that meant it had been poured quite recently. Delores knew, through personal experience, that the bubbles slowed and eventually stopped as time passed.

Two crystal dessert plates were stacked on the coffee table, along with two silver dessert forks. It was obvious that Tori had been expecting a guest.

Delores set the phone down on the couch and stared at the coffee table. The puzzle it presented was similar to the homework that her daughters had brought home from kindergarten, a photo-copied sheet of paper with a picture drawn in detail. The caption had been *What is wrong with this picture?* Something was wrong with Tori's coffee table. What was it?

The answer occurred to Delores almost immediately. Tori had set out two dessert plates and two dessert forks, but only one flute of champagne. That was a puzzling omission. Delores knew that Tori loved champagne and judging by the label that was peeking out of the ice bucket, this was very good champagne. Did this mean that Tori was imbibing, but her anticipated guest was not? Or had Tori filled her own champagne glass and carried it away to drink someplace else in the condo? And that question was followed by an even more important question. Where *was* Tori?

Delores was dimly aware that hissing and crackling sounds were coming from her phone. Mike was still talking to her, but his words were undecipherable, muffled by the fact she'd placed her cell phone down on the cushions of the couch. Delores ignored it and glanced around the studio again. Her gaze reached the floor near the back of the couch and halted, focusing on that area. The white plush wall-to-wall carpet looked wet. Something had been spilled there.

Delores moved toward the wet carpet. She rounded the corner of the couch and stopped, reaching out to steady herself as she saw a sight that she knew would haunt her dreams for years to come. Tori was sprawled on the rug, a sticky red stain on one of the beautiful silk caftans she wore on evenings that she worked at home.

The stain on the caftan glistened in the light from the tiny bulbs in the ceiling. Delores shuddered as she saw the crystal champagne flute tipped on its side on the floor, its expensive contents now permanently embedded in the plush white fibers. Thank goodness the blood hadn't gotten on the carpet! That could have permanently ruined it. She'd have to give Tori the name of a good carpet cleaning firm so that they could remove the champagne stain.

"Ohhhh!" Delores gave a cry that ended in a sob. Tori wouldn't need the name of a carpet cleaner. Tori would never need anything again. Tori was dead! Her friend was dead!

Tears began to fall from her eyes, but Delores couldn't seem to look away. Her friend's eyes seemed fixed on the ceiling and her mouth was slightly open, as if she were protesting the cruel twist of fate that had befallen her.

"It's okay, Delores. We're here."

The sound of a calm male voice released

Delores from her horrid fixation and she managed to turn to face the sound. It was Mike, and he had brought Lonnie with him. They had both come to help her. She wanted to thank them, but she couldn't seem to find the words.

"Lonnie's going to take you back upstairs and stay with you until Michelle comes."

"Michelle's still here?" Delores recovered enough to ask about her youngest daughter. "I thought she was going back to college tonight."

"She was, but she decided to stay until Hannah and Ross get back. I'll be up later to take your statement."

As Lonnie took her arm, Delores began to shake. It was as if she had been hit with a blast of icy winter wind. She leaned heavily on Lonnie's arm as he led her from the room, from the awful sight of the friend she'd never see again, the friend who wouldn't come over for coffee in the morning, the downstairs neighbor who would no longer sit by the pool under the climate-controlled dome in Delores and Doc's penthouse garden, and chat about her career on the stage. Tori would never collect her lifetime achievement award and hear the applause of her peers. Victoria Bascomb's stellar life had ended, and Delores was overwhelmed with grief and sadness.

As she entered the penthouse on Lonnie's arm and sank onto the soft cushions of the couch, another emotion began to grow in her mind. It replaced the heaviness of her sadness, at least for the moment. That emotion was anger, anger that her friend had died in such a senseless manner. How dare someone come into Tori's home and hurt her!

As Delores sat there waiting for Michelle to arrive, she was filled with a fiery resolve. She had to tell Hannah that Tori had been murdered. The moment that Michelle arrived, they had to try to reach Hannah. They needed her and she had to help them. Her eldest daughter would know where to start and what to do. Hannah had to come home to Lake Eden immediately so that they could find Tori's killer and make him pay for the horrible crime he had committed!

# CHAPTER TWO

Hannah Swensen Barton sat on the balcony of the owner's suite, a chilled glass of champagne in her hand. She gave a happy smile as she watched the sun sink lower in the sky. The gentle lapping of the waves created a rhythm of contentment in her heart and she knew that she'd never felt so joyous and fulfilled. Marriage was wonderful. She loved Ross with every fiber of her being and she truly felt one with him.

At the same time, she was happy to be alone for a few moments, to rediscover herself as a person and not half of a couple. She'd missed her alone time in the early morning, sitting at her kitchen table in her old nightgown, sipping coffee and letting her mind gather the energy to deal with the day ahead.

Early morning and late night were the times that her creative juices flourished, unchecked by the necessity of making conversation. Those were the times when she came up with ideas for new recipes, for improvements she could make at The Cookie Jar, for wonderfully personalized gifts she could make or buy for her family. Of course there were times when solitude was lonely, but she'd been with Ross for every waking moment of their honeymoon. There was no denying that it had been wonderful, but it had also felt just a bit confining, perhaps even . . . Hannah stopped herself in mid-thought and attempted to ignore the word that had flashed in her mind. That word was *stifling.* Not all of the time. Certainly not. But occasionally, she needed some room to think and to breathe.

She took a sip of her champagne. She didn't really want it, but Ross had poured it for her and he'd think that she didn't like it if her glass was still untouched. She rose to her feet, walked to the second bathroom that their butler had called the powder room, and poured half of the champagne down the drain.

On her way back to the balcony, she felt a bit disloyal. Ross had chosen the champagne especially for her. It wasn't that she didn't like it. She did. It was just that she didn't feel like drinking it now, on the last night of their cruise. She wanted to savor every moment, to stock up the memories for later, for after they'd returned to their lives in Lake Eden.

The sun was almost down and it cast a golden path across the sea, a glistening bridge between day and night. Hannah looked up and smiled as she realized the stars were beginning to appear in the sky. They seemed to be bigger and more brilliant out here on the ocean than they ever had in Lake Eden. Going on a cruise was a wonderful adventure and she hoped that they could afford to do it again sometime.

"I'm back, honey." A voice spoke behind her and Hannah almost jumped.

"Ross! I didn't hear you come in. Is everything all right with the purser?"

"Everything's fine. They just charged us for a couple of things we didn't get, like the shore excursions we canceled in Cabo."

"Oh." Hannah blushed, hoping that he couldn't see it in the twilight of the approaching night. She remembered precisely why they had stayed in their stateroom and hadn't gone on their planned shore excursion.

"I straightened it all out and while I was at it, I made reservations at the French Bistro for tonight."

Hannah began to frown. "But I thought we were just going to stay here. After those appetizers you ordered from the butler, I'm not really very hungry."

"You don't have to be hungry. Their portions are small. I checked it out when I walked by. And I made sure we have a great table by the window. Their cuisine looked really good and I thought you'd enjoy going there."

"Oh, I'm sure I will!" Hannah said quickly, realizing that Ross had sounded a bit disappointed that she wasn't more enthusiastic. "What time is our reservation? And is it a dress-up place?"

Ross glance at his watch. "We've got a half hour before we have to leave. And it's not formal, but it's something the hostess called *smart casual.* What you have on is fine, Cookie."

Hannah glanced down at her black pants and aqua blue sweater. If she changed her shoes, put on some jewelry, and covered her sweater with the black jacket she'd brought, she should pass for smart casual. "It'll only take a moment or two for me to get ready."

"We've got plenty of time." Ross picked up her half-filled glass. "I'll top this off and get a glass for myself."

Hannah watched him as he went back

inside. Ross anticipated what he thought were her needs and sometimes he was wrong. But she supposed that was better than not being concerned at all. She chided herself for being too picky. She was probably just not used to all this attention. She'd been single for years now, living alone except for her cat, Moishe, and she was used to taking care of herself. She should be grateful for the way Ross lavished attention on her.

As she sat there, waiting for the champagne she didn't really want, Hannah told herself that things would be very different when they got back to Lake Eden. Then they would have their separate careers and they wouldn't be together twenty-four hours a day. It was entirely possible she'd miss this time and regret that she hadn't been more grateful to the man who obviously loved her so much.

"Here you go, Cookie." Ross stepped out on the balcony carrying the two champagne glasses and a piece of paper. "Our butler was just here and he brought this."

"What is it?"

"A message from your sister, Michelle. The butler said it just came in."

Hannah's heart began to pound as she reached out for the paper that Ross was

28

holding.

"I hope everything's okay," he said, echoing Hannah's own thoughts. And then he noticed that her hands were shaking. "Are you all right, honey?"

"I think so." Hannah's fingers touched the paper, but she couldn't seem to grasp it and it dropped to the balcony floor.

"Do you want me to read it for you?" Ross asked, picking it up. "Your hands are shaking."

"Yes! Thank you, Ross," Hannah said gratefully, praying that nothing bad had happened to her mother, or her sisters, or Moishe, or anyone else in her extended family.

*"We're all okay, including Moishe, but Mother wanted to give you a heads-up before you get home to Lake Eden."* Ross read aloud.

Hannah realized that she'd been holding her breath and she let it out in a relieved sigh. "Thank goodness! Go on, Ross. Please."

*"Victoria Bascomb is dead. She was murdered and Mother found her body. She's shaken up, of course, and she wants you to come home right away."*

"Oh, dear!" Hannah said, beginning to frown. "We're taking the shuttle to the airport when we dock, aren't we, Ross?"

"Of course. I made those arrangements online before we left Lake Eden. Miss Bascomb was your mother's neighbor, wasn't she?"

"Yes. She lived one floor down from Mother and Doc's penthouse. I wonder if Mother heard something."

"Yes, she did. It's in the next sentence." Ross began to read again. *"Mother heard a gunshot and went downstairs to check on Tori. She says to tell you that she thinks Tori knew her killer and let him or her in, because she had one of your Banana Cream Pies and two dessert plates out on the coffee table."*

Hannah groaned. "So my baked goods were at the murder scene again?"

"I'm afraid so. I'm sorry, honey." Ross handed her the paper and then he lifted her to her feet to hug her. "Do you want me to cancel our dinner reservations?"

Hannah thought about that for a moment and then she shook her head. "No. I'm sorry that Mother had to find Tori's body, and I can understand why she's so upset. It must have been a terrible shock. And of course Mother wants me to investigate."

"But are *you* upset?"

"Murder always upsets me. The idea that one person can callously take another person's life is horrible. But if you're asking

30

if I felt a personal connection to Tori, the answer is no. I know she was Mother's friend and neighbor, but I really didn't know her that well."

Ross looked down at her searchingly. "I think I understand, honey. What I was really wondering is if you're upset that one of your pies was found at the murder scene."

Hannah took a moment to assess her true feelings. "Yes and no. While it's true that I don't like my baked goods associated with murder, Tori was crazy about my Banana Cream Pie. She bought at least two every week."

"But a lot of your baked goods have been found at murder scenes, haven't they?"

Hannah sighed as she nodded. Ross was right. Ron, their Cozy Cow delivery man, had been eating one of her Chocolate Chip Crunch Cookies when he'd been shot. And her Strawberry Shortcake Swensen had been spilled all over Danielle Watson's garage when Coach Watson had been murdered. Then there was Connie Mac, who'd been in Hannah's walk-in cooler at The Cookie Jar, filching one of Hannah's Blue Blueberry Muffins when she'd met her end. And . . .

Deliberately, Hannah pushed those thoughts out of her mind. She didn't want

to think about the number of times something she'd baked had been present at
someone's violent demise.

"You're right, Ross," she admitted. "But
that's understandable if you think about it.
I'm the only baker in Lake Eden and almost
everyone who lives there loves desserts. If
they don't make desserts themselves, they
buy them from The Cookie Jar. It's a little
like saying that clothing leads to murder
because the victim is usually wearing it at
the murder scene."

"So you don't feel bad about your Banana
Cream Pie being right there?"

Hannah sighed. Ross was like a dog with
a bone. He didn't seem capable of letting
the idea go. She could feel herself prickling
with irritation, but she pushed that emotion
back. "No, I don't feel bad . . . not really,
not if she wasn't actually eating the pie
when she was killed. It's a great pie and it's
very popular in Lake Eden."

"Then you're not going to stop baking it
just because it was there when someone was
killed?"

"No, I won't stop baking it. I refuse to
give in to superstition. I'll make as many as
my customers want to buy."

"Good!" Ross looked very relieved and
Hannah was puzzled.

"Why were you so concerned that I might take it off The Cookie Jar menu?"

"Because I've never tasted it. And Banana Cream Pie is one of my very favorite pies."

Hannah gave a little laugh. "All right then. I'll bake one for you when we get back to Lake Eden."

"Thanks, Hannah." Ross gave her another hug and then he released her to glance at his watch. "If you're going to freshen up, you'd better do it now. If we don't leave here in a couple of minutes, we'll lose our dinner res—" He stopped in mid-sentence. "Is it still okay if we go out to dinner?"

"We can go. I'll be just fine as long as you promise me one thing."

"What is it, Cookie?"

"If they happen to have Banana Cream Pie on the dessert menu, promise me that you won't order it. I want you to taste mine first!"

# HANNAH'S BANANA CREAM PIE
## Salted Pretzel Crust
## Banana Cream Pie Filling
## Whipped Caramel Topping

**Hannah's 1st Note: Make the crust first. It has to cool before you put in the filling. Once the filling is in place, the pie must "set" before you make the whipped caramel topping.**

**Salted Pretzel Crust**

Preheat oven to 350 degrees F., rack in the middle position.

2 cups finely crushed salted pretzels *(measure AFTER crushing–this will take approximately 3/4 of a 16-ounce bag of salted thin stick pretzels.) (I used Snyder's original stick pretzels.)*
1/2 cup *(4 ounces, 1 stick, 1/4 pound)* salted butter, melted
2 Tablespoons *(1/8 cup)* firmly packed brown sugar

Before you start to make the crust, prepare a 9-inch round Springform pan *(the kind you'd use to make cheesecake with a clamp on the side that you can release to lift out the bottom).* Spray the inside of the pan with Pam or another nonstick baking spray.

Mix the 2 cups of crushed salted pretzels with the melted butter and the brown sugar. Mix until thoroughly combined.

**Hannah's 2nd Note: You can crush the pretzels by putting them in a Ziploc bag and using a rolling pin, but it's a lot easier if you put them in a food processor and use the steel blade in an on-and-off motion.**

Place the crust mixture into the bottom of the pan you've chosen. Using your impeccably clean hands, press it down as evenly as you can over the bottom and two inches up the sides.

Bake your pretzel crumb crust at 350 degrees F. for 10 to 12 minutes or until lightly browned.

Take your crust out of the oven and let it cool on a cold stovetop burner or a wire rack for at least an hour. *(Longer is fine, too. I've made my crust the day before I made the rest of the pie. If you do this, cover your crust loosely, but do not refrigerate it.)*

**Banana Cream Pie Filling**
2 perfectly ripe bananas *(yellow with no black spots on the peel)*

2 packages *(4-serving size each)* instant vanilla pudding *(I used Jell-O)*
2 and 1/4 cups cold whole milk
1/4 cup rum *(I used Bacardi)*
1 cup thawed whipped topping *(I used Cool Whip)*

**Hannah's 1st Note: Use a rum that's colorless for a prettier pie.**

**Hannah's 2nd Note: If you'd like to make this recipe alcohol-free, simply use 2 and 1/2 cups of whole milk and forget about the rum in a bowl.**

To assemble the pie, slice the banana into quarter-inch rounds and place the banana slices in the bottom of the completely cooled pretzel crust.

Mix the two packages of dry instant vanilla pudding with the milk and the rum in a bowl.

Beat for 2 minutes with a whisk or a slotted spoon until the pudding has thickened.

Add the cup of thawed whipped topping to the pudding and mix it in. Don't overmix or you'll mix out all the air in the topping. The air will give your pie volume and make it look prettier.

Spoon the pudding mixture into the pretzel crust and smooth it out with a rubber spatula.

Cover your partially-completed pie loosely with a sheet of aluminum foil or with wax paper. Then place the Springform pan inside the refrigerator for 4 hours to "set".

## Whipped Caramel Topping

1 cup whipped topping, thawed *(I used thawed Cool Whip)*

1/3 cup caramel ice cream topping at room temperature *(I used Smucker's)*

Place the whipped topping in a bowl.

With a rubber spatula, fold in the caramel ice cream topping until it is well combined.

Rinse off the rubber spatula, dry it, and "frost" the top of your Banana Cream Pie with the Caramel Whipped Topping.

Once your pie is "frosted", touch the side of your rubber spatula to the top of the Whipped Caramel Topping and pull it up quickly. Use the same motion you'd use to make points in the meringue all over the top of a pie.

Let your pie sit in the refrigerator, uncovered, for another 30 minutes or longer before you prepare to serve it.

You can garnish the top of your pie by drizzling on more of the caramel ice cream topping.

Remove your pie from the pan by releasing the catch on the side and lifting off the ring. Leave the pie on the bottom of the pan and simply place it on a flat platter.

Either cut the pie and serve it at the table, or cut it in the kitchen and place the pieces on pretty dessert plates. Serve with plenty of strong hot coffee. This pie is very rich and luscious.

If there is any leftover pie, which there probably won't be, be sure to keep it refrigerated. This pie will keep for several days in the refrigerator.

Yield: 8 to 12 slices of delicious pie, depending on the width of your slices.

# CHAPTER THREE

Hannah leaned back in the cushioned chair and smiled at her new husband. Thanks to Ross, getting off the ship had been easy. Their owner's suite had entitled them to an escort and they'd been the first passengers to get off the ship. Their luggage had been waiting for them, complete with a porter and cart, and they'd gone out to the street just in time to catch a shuttle to the airport.

Once they'd gone through the airport security check, they had been escorted to the VIP lounge where a uniformed waitress had seated them at a table and taken their breakfast orders. They'd eaten the delicious breakfast, which had been followed by a pot of excellent coffee, and then they'd relaxed in lounge chairs until it was time to board their flight.

Flying couldn't have been easier, Hannah decided as she sipped the glass of orange juice that the stewardess had brought for her. Of course, Ross had prearranged every-thing for them and that was the reason they hadn't experienced the delays and frustra-tions that plagued other airline passengers. All it took was money, he'd assured her, and Hannah was beginning to believe it. So far, their journey home had been worry-free and there was no reason to expect that the rest of the trip would be any different.

The lift-off was smooth and uneventful, even though Hannah had reached for her husband's hand when the engines had revved up and the plane had begun to move down the runway.

The co-pilot had just announced that they had reached cruising altitude and they were now allowed to turn on their electronic devices. Since Hannah didn't have any electronic devices and she probably wouldn't have used them even if she'd had them, she closed her eyes and let the smooth sound of the engines lull her to sleep.

"Wake up, Cookie. We're on approach."

Ross's voice roused Hannah from a dream filled with duck appetizers quacking and spinning on the tips of the miniature waffle cones that held them. Except for the spin-ning and the quacking, it had been a replica of the appetizer they'd eaten at the ship's

French bistro restaurant the previous evening.

"I think I can make them stop quacking if I eat them," she told Ross groggily.

"Make what stop quacking?"

"The duck appetizers."

Ross reached out to hug her. "You're still dreaming, honey."

"Oh." Hannah took a moment to think about that. "You're right. I was dreaming about the dinner we had last night on the ship. Everything was delicious."

"Yes, it was." Ross reached across her and pulled a tray from the console between them. "You're probably hungry. I ordered something for you before I woke you."

Hannah looked at him in surprise. "Isn't it too late for a meal? I thought we were landing."

"We won't land for another twenty-five minutes and the stewardess is making a pot of fresh coffee for you. I thought you might need it before we landed."

Hannah smiled gratefully. "Thanks, Ross. I *do* need something to wake me up. I'm still a little groggy."

"Here you are, Mrs. Barton," the stewardess said as she delivered Hannah's coffee. "Just let me know when you need a refill."

Hannah thanked her and took a sip of her

41

coffee before she turned back to Ross. "I wonder if anyone will meet us at the airport."

"I don't think so. I ordered a car to pick us up and take us to Lake Eden, but it wouldn't surprise me if your family is waiting for us when we get back to the condo."

"You're right. They'll probably be there." Hannah gave a little sigh.

"You won't be glad to see them?"

"It's not that. Of course I'll be glad to see them. But I was looking forward to being alone with you and Moishe, and settling back into some sort of a normal routine."

"We'll do that, honey. Don't worry. But your family missed you and they'll want to welcome you home. And then there's your mother."

"Right." Hannah sighed, admitting the inevitability of having company their first night home. "Mother will want to tell me all about Tori Bascomb's murder."

"Naturally. And your sisters will want to hear all about our honeymoon cruise. That's why I was glad that you got some sleep on the plane."

"Then you knew my family would be there when we got home?"

"No, I *guessed* they'd be there. It just seemed like something they'd want to do."

"You're right, Ross. They'll probably bring dinner, or lunch, or whatever. What time is it, anyway?"

Ross glanced at his watch. "It'll be close to five by the time we collect our luggage and get back to Lake Eden."

"Dinner," Hannah said. "I hope they don't want to take us out. I'd rather just grab something at home."

"Then it'll be pizza, hamburgers, or Chinese. There's not a huge choice of take-out cuisine in Lake Eden."

"True, but that's okay. I had enough fancy meals on the ship to last me for at least a month, maybe longer. I can tell them about the meal last night. It was spectacular, especially with the view. I wish we had some photos of the ship and the shore excursions to show them. The only one I have is the photo of us that you bought from the photographer on the sailboat."

Ross smiled. "It's okay. I've got plenty. I made up a slideshow of them while you were sleeping. And I have a cable that I can hook up to your television set so that every-one can watch them. You can give them a running commentary."

"Or you can." Hannah smiled at him fondly. "You're the photographer, not me. The only photo I took was a selfie with my cell phone."

"I'm sure they'd like to see that one, too."

"No, they wouldn't. I held the phone too low and I cut off the top of my head."

Once they'd landed, retrieved their luggage and were met by the limo, the trip back to Lake Eden was uneventful and they turned in at the condo complex much sooner than Hannah dreamed was possible.

As the limo passed the guest parking area, Hannah noticed that her sister Andrea's car was there. Doc's car was parked right next to it and she was sure that her mother would be with him. Hannah turned to Ross. "Looks like you're right. Their cars are here."

"Told you," Ross said. "And there they are."

Hannah took a deep breath as she saw that her whole family was gathered at the base of the staircase that led to her second-floor condo.

"Michelle and Doc are holding takeout bags. And Andrea has something in a box."

"I guess they thought we'd be starving," Ross said as he helped her out of the limo.

"Not really. It's just that since they didn't arrange it with us ahead of time and they didn't want to impose on us, they brought

44

food for everyone. It's a very Midwestern thing to do, but you probably already know that. After all, you grew up here in Minnesota."

"Yes, but my father wasn't from the Midwest so it was different in my family. If we visited someone, we brought vodka." Ross pressed a tip into the limo driver's hand, took Hannah's arm, and walked her over to where her family was waiting. "Hello, everyone! We're home!"

"Thank goodness for that!" Delores exclaimed rushing forward to take Hannah's other arm. "There's a surprise wedding gift waiting for you inside the condo. We'll follow you, but we want you to go in first."

"Is Moishe inside?" Hannah asked, eager to see her pet.

"Not yet. Norman called to say he was on his way, and Mike and Lonnie should be here in a bit. They wanted to give you a little time to get settled before they brought the rest of the meal."

"The rest of the meal?" Hannah asked, looking at the two large takeout bags.

"Yes. Mike and Lonnie are bringing pizza, and Norman's bringing drinks for everyone. We'll do everything, dear. You won't have to lift a finger, I promise."

"I believe you," Hannah said, turning to

45

smile as her mother dropped back to follow them up the stairs.

"What do you think our surprise is?" Ross asked in an undertone as they walked up the stairs together.

"I don't know," Hannah answered in the same low tone of voice, "and I'm a little afraid to guess."

When they reached the landing, Hannah handed Ross the key. "Here. You unlock the door."

"I will. And then I'll carry you across the threshold."

Hannah laughed. "You don't have to go that far. It's not like I haven't been inside before."

"True, but I'd like to if you don't mind. Is that all right?"

"Of course it's all right," Hannah said, secretly delighted at his traditional gesture.

Ross unlocked the door and opened it. Then he lifted Hannah into his arms. "Ready?" he asked her.

"Yes." Hannah wrapped her arms around his neck and he carried her across the threshold.

"What in the world . . ." Hannah gasped. She was so amazed by what she saw, she almost lost her hold around his neck. For one brief moment, she wondered if Ross had unlocked the door to the wrong condo.

"Wow!" Ross exclaimed, and it was clear that he was just as surprised as she was. "Look at that flat-screen! It's got to be ninety inches . . . maybe more!"

"They redecorated the whole living room!" Hannah's voice was shaking with shock as Ross set her down on the floor. "Look at this beautiful new carpet!"

"And look at those couches. There's three of them, and it looks like the chairs recline. There's seating for six. We can invite your family over to watch videos."

Ross took Hannah's arm to lead her to the couches, but she pulled back. "Wait! I need to look at the kitchen!"

Hannah hurried to the kitchen doorway and flicked on the lights. Everything appeared to be exactly as she'd left it. She breathed a sigh of relief and began to smile. "It's the same."

"Did you hope they'd put in new appliances?"

"No! My kitchen is exactly the way I want it. I'm really glad they didn't decide to change it."

"You can thank me for that," a voice said behind her, and Hannah turned to see Michelle. "I told Mother she'd be taking her life in her hands if she did anything to your kitchen."

"Thanks, Michelle!" Hannah threw her arms around her youngest sister and hugged her. "I can't believe you all got together and refurbished the living room."

Delores arrived in the doorway and stood there, smiling at Hannah. "I hope you like your new living room furniture, dear."

"And your new carpeting," Andrea added, coming up behind Delores. "I picked out the color. It's called Autumn Leaves, and it's shades of browns and reds, like autumn leaves."

"It's beautiful." Hannah glanced at Andrea, who was still carrying the box in her arms. "What's in there, Andrea?"

"A new Christmas cookie for you. It's a whippersnapper cookie and Grandma McCann loves them."

Hannah smiled at her sister. If Andrea's live-in nanny and housekeeper loved Andrea's cookies, they must be superb. Grandma McCann was a great baker in her own right and Hannah had gotten several recipes from her.

"What makes them Christmas cookies?" she asked, knowing that Andrea wanted to brag about her new creation.

"They're green and red. And those are the Christmas colors. I made them with pistachio pudding and I put in a little green food coloring. I've got dried cherries inside, but I didn't think that was enough color, so I put a half maraschino cherry on top of each one."

"Sounds great," Hannah told her. "Are we going to try them tonight?"

"Yes. We're all having dinner together."

"Unless you two are too tired," Doc added quickly.

"Not at all," Hannah reassured them. "Ross? You're not too tired to have dinner with everyone, are you?"

"No. And I'm getting a little hungry."

"Then we'll eat just as soon as you see the rest of the condo, and everyone else gets here," Delores decided for all of them. She turned to Andrea and Michelle. "You girls set the table and Doc and I will show Hannah and Ross everything else."

"Wait," Hannah said, glancing down at the beautiful carpeting again and noticing that it appeared to stretch all the way down the hallway. "Did you carpet the whole condo?"

"Everything except the kitchen and the bathrooms," Andrea told her. "I had them stretch it nice and tight so that Moishe can't hide anything under the carpet anymore."

"That's good," Hannah said, remembering the old green carpeting that had come with the condo when she'd purchased it. Moishe had torn it loose in several places so that he could hide his toy mice in a nice, safe place to retrieve for later enjoyment.

"Wait until you see the master bedroom," Doc said, slipping his arm around Delores's waist. "Your mother picked out the bedroom set, but I put my foot down when she wanted to give you a delft blue bedroom with puffy white curtains and French Provincial furniture."

"That furniture was beautiful and you know it!" Delores contradicted her husband. She attempted to glare at him, but her lips turned up in a tiny smile that let everyone know she was teasing. She turned back to Hannah and Ross. "You two should be very grateful to me."

"Why is that, Mother?" Hannah asked, noticing that her mother looked even more amused.

"My dear husband wanted you to have a bed made out of logs with grizzly bears carved on the bed posts. They looked like they were ready to tear someone into little pieces and I just knew you'd have nightmares every night if you had to sleep in that bed!"

"Come on, Lori," Doc Knight gave her

arm a pat. "It wasn't as bad as you're describing it. The whole bedroom set was designed by a renowned chainsaw artist! It had acorns for knobs on the dresser drawers, squirrels chasing each other on the mirror frame, and that bed was unique, not another one like it. It was one of a kind."

"I heard the salesman tell you that, but *one of a kind* doesn't mean it's good. It just means the man with the chainsaw didn't think he could sell more than one of them!"

Doc laughed and put his arm around Delores again. "You could be right, dear. Those bears were a bit menacing." Then he turned back to Hannah and Ross. "We compromised and went for a Mediterranean look. Your mother saved you from marauding bears and I saved you from spindly chairs and gilt-edged curlicues."

"Not to mention the horrors of the French Revolution," Hannah said, getting into the spirit of things. It really was good to see her family again and the wedding gift they'd given her was truly amazing. It was almost too much to take in all at once, but she knew she'd have plenty of time to appreciate each and every thoughtful touch they'd made in the days to come. And tonight, after everyone had left, they'd sleep in a new bed, in a new bedroom, to start their new life in Lake Eden together.

## SPUMONI WHIPPERSNAPPER COOKIES

***DO NOT preheat oven yet. This dough has to chill.***

1 box *(approximately 18 ounces)* white cake mix, the kind that makes a 9-inch by 13-inch cake *(I used Duncan Hines Classic White)*

1 package Instant Pistachio pudding mix *(I used Jell-O, the kind that makes 4 half-cup servings)*

1 large egg, beaten *(just whip it up in a glass with a fork)*

several drops of green food coloring, if desired

2 and 1/2 cups of thawed Cool Whip *(measure this — a tub of Cool Whip contains a little over 3 cups and that's too much!)*

1/2 cup chopped pistachio nut meats *(measure after chopping)*

1/2 cup chopped dried cherries *(I used Mariani brand)*

1/2 cup powdered *(confectioner's)* sugar

small jar of red maraschino cherries, cut in half vertically and without stems

**Hannah's 1st Note: Notice that the**

measurement for the Cool Whip is different in this whippersnapper recipe. That's because of the added dry pudding mix. It's 2 and a HALF cups of thawed Cool Whip.

Hannah's 2nd Note: If you can't find pistachio nut meats, don't bother cracking all those pistachios. Just use chopped pecans, walnuts, or almonds instead. The taste will be different, but it will be good.

Hannah's 3rd Note: If you can't find dried cherries, you can use cherry-flavored Craisins instead.

Pour the dry white cake mix into a large bowl.

Add the dry pistachio instant pudding mix. Mix until the dry ingredients are well combined. *(I used a fork to do this.)*

Use a smaller bowl to mix the two and a HALF cups of Cool Whip with the beaten egg. Add the green food coloring, if desired. Mix until everything is combined, but don't overmix.

Fold in the chopped dried cherries and the chopped nuts. Mix well, but very gently.

Add the Cool Whip mixture to the cake and pudding mixture in the large bowl. STIR VERY CAREFULLY with a wooden spoon or a rubber spatula. Stir only until everything is combined. You don't want to mix all the air out of the Cool Whip.

Cover your bowl of dough and place it in the refrigerator for at least 2 hours. This will make it less sticky. If you try to form the cookie dough balls right now, they'll stick to your fingers and be very difficult to roll.

**Hannah's 4th Note: Andrea said she sometimes mixes whippersnapper dough before she goes to bed on Friday night, sticks it in the refrigerator, and bakes her cookies with Tracey on Saturday morning.**

**Andrea's 1st Note: If it's close to Christmastime and you're planning to make these cookies for Christmas, add a few more drops of green food coloring to the Cool Whip mixture so that your cookies will be Christmas colors, red from the cherries you'll place on top of each cookie and green from the food coloring in the dough.**

When your cookie dough has chilled and you're ready to bake, preheat your oven to 350 degrees F., and make sure the rack is in the middle position. DO NOT take your chilled cookie dough out of the refrigerator until your oven has reached the proper temperature.

While your oven is preheating, prepare your cookie sheets by spraying them with Pam or another nonstick cooking spray, or lining them with parchment paper.

Place the confectioner's sugar in a small, shallow bowl. You will be dropping cookie dough into this bowl to form dough balls and coating them with the powdered sugar.

When your oven is ready, take your dough out of the refrigerator. Using a teaspoon from your silverware drawer, drop the dough by rounded teaspoonful into the bowl with the powdered sugar. Roll the dough around with your fingers to form powdered-sugar-coated cookie dough balls.

**Hannah's 5th Note: This is easiest if you coat your fingers with powdered sugar first and then try to form the cookie dough into balls. When your fingers get covered with dough, simply wash them off under running water. It also helps if you put no more than one dough ball in the powdered sugar at a time. It gives you more room to roll and it keeps unrolled dough balls from sticking to each other.**

Place the sugared cookie dough balls on your prepared cookie sheets, no more than 12 cookies on a standard-size sheet.

If you haven't already done so, cut your

maraschino cherries in half and place one half, rounded side up, on top of each cookie ball on your baking sheet.

**Andrea's 2nd Note: Make only as many cookie dough balls as you can bake at one time and then cover the dough and return it to the refrigerator. I have a double oven so I prepare 2 sheets of cookies at a time.**

Bake your Spumoni Whippersnapper Cookies at 350 degrees F., for 10 to 12 minutes. Test for doneness by tapping them lightly with a finger to see if they're "set."

Let your cookies cool on the cookie sheet for 2 minutes, and then move them to a wire rack to cool completely. *(This is a lot easier if you line your cookie sheets with parchment paper. Then all you have to do is grab one end of the parchment paper and pull it, cookies and all, onto the wire rack.)*

Once the cookies are completely cool, store them between sheets of waxed paper in a cool, dry place. *(Your refrigerator is cool, but it's definitely not dry!)*

Yield: 3 to 4 dozen soft, chewy cookies. Your yield will depend on cookie size.

# Chapter Four

Hannah heard someone coming up the outside staircase and she hurried to open the door. It was Norman and he was carrying two kitty crates. "Hi, Norman. I'm so glad you're here! Come in!"

Norman stepped in and immediately set the two kitty carriers down on the rug. "They're not too happy about being in the carriers," he told her.

"They never are," Hannah said, noticing that both Moishe and Norman's cat, Cuddles, looked less than happy in their crates.

"You're home, Moishe!" she greeted her pet. Even though she hadn't mentioned it to Ross, she'd missed Moishe the whole time they'd been gone.

Moishe gave her a pathetic look behind the screen of his crate. Then he yowled the most plaintive yowl that Hannah had ever heard.

"Sorry about that, Big Guy," Norman said

to Moishe. "You'll be out of there in just a minute."

He waved at the others assembled at the table and turned back to Hannah. "Mike and Lonnie will be here in a couple of seconds. They were pulling in just as I reached the top of the stairs."

Moishe gave another yowl and Hannah put her hand on the crate, preparing to let him out. "Sit down, everyone," she warned her family. "Moishe wants out and I'm not quite sure where he's going to run first." Then she turned to Norman. "If you let Cuddles out at the same time, maybe it won't be as hectic."

As Hannah waited, Norman prepared to raise the wire grate on his crate. "Okay. Ready . . . set . . . go!"

Hannah and Norman raised the two screens at the same moment and the cats rushed out. To Hannah's surprise, Moishe didn't race down the hallway as he usually did when he was released from his carrier. Instead, he made a bee-line for Hannah and jumped up into her arms.

Even though Hannah was ready, she still had to take a step backwards. Luckily, she caught her balance.

"Are you all right, Hannah?" Ross asked, hurrying to her side.

"I'm fine." Hannah replied, nuzzling the top of Moishe's furry head.

"I don't know about you, but I'd say Moishe missed you," Norman commented.

"I guess he did," Hannah gasped, still recovering from the twenty-three pound orange and white bundle of feline that she'd managed to catch.

"Do you want me to take him?" Ross offered, realizing that Hannah was a bit short on breath.

"No, that's okay. Let's see how he likes the back of the new couch."

Hannah walked over to the couch and placed Moishe on the back of the closest of the new leather couches.

"Will he scratch it?" Delores asked, sounding a bit nervous about that possibility.

Hannah smiled, watching her pet settle down on the soft leather and start to purr. "I don't think so, unless it happens to be made out of mouse hide."

"Of course it's not!" Delores looked horrified at the suggestion. "These couches are made of . . ." she paused and turned to Andrea. "What did the salesman say, dear?"

"I think it was cowhide," Andrea answered, frowning slightly. "Or maybe moose hide. I really don't remember, Mother. All I remember is thinking that it was something thick and sturdy."

"I don't think we need to worry about it," Hannah told them, reaching down to scratch Moishe in one of his favorite places, under his chin. "He seems very content and comfortable."

Doc laughed. "I should hope so. The salesman said those couches were the most comfortable ones in the store."

Cuddles saw where Moishe had gone and jumped up to settle down beside him.

"Here, Hannah," Michelle said, handing Hannah the canister of fish-shaped, salmon-flavored treats that both cats loved. "These might keep them quiet while we eat."

Hannah smiled and nodded, although she really doubted that would happen. There were too many new things to explore and Moishe and Cuddles, like most cats, were curious. She shook out three treats for Moishe and three for Cuddles, when there was a knock on her door.

"That must be Mike and Lonnie," Michelle said, rushing to the door to let them in. "And Bill," she added, noticing the third person who was climbing up the steps.

"Oh, good!" Andrea said, getting up from the table and hurrying to the door to greet her husband. "He wasn't sure he could make it, but I invited him anyway."

Once greetings had been exchanged and everyone had taken a chair, there were ten people crowded around Hannah's dining room table. She glanced over at the cats as Ross passed her a piece of pepperoni and sausage pizza, and realized that both of them had disappeared.

"They're probably exploring," Ross said, noticing that Hannah's attention had been diverted.

"I'm sure you're right, unless . . ." Hannah turned to Michelle and spoke in a low voice. They were eating, after all. "Is Moishe's litter box still in the laundry room?"

"It's there," Michelle answered. "I checked it out the minute I came in. Everything's in place, Hannah. His food is in the kitchen, his water dish is full, and his litter box is clean. I got everything all ready for you to come home."

"Thanks," Hannah said, smiling at her youngest sister. There was no need to check. If Michelle said everything was ready for Moishe to come home, then everything was ready. Michelle loved Moishe almost as much as she did.

"Are you staying over tonight?" she asked Michelle. "I noticed that the guest bedroom is all ready, and it looks just beautiful."

"Not tonight." Michelle leaned closer so

that no one else could hear her. "Lonnie's driving me back to school tonight. I've got my final in directing class tomorrow."

"Are you nervous?"

"Not really. I think I'll do just fine. I've been using Mother's car to commute back and forth for rehearsals."

Hannah was shocked. "But that's a two and a half hour commute every day!"

"It was just for three days. My directing class only meets on Mondays, Wednesdays, and Fridays. I was here on Tuesday and Thursday to keep an eye on the workmen. And at night, I stayed at Mother's house. Andrea said it wasn't smart to vacate a house that was listed and had a For Sale sign in the front lawn. She said her teacher had stressed that in real estate class."

"I'm sure that's right in larger towns and big cities, but there really isn't much crime in Lake Eden . . ." Hannah paused and gave a little sigh, "except for murder, of course. Are you going to continue to commute until it sells?"

"I don't have to. It sold and the buyers are moving in today. They're going to pay rent until the paperwork goes through, but they've got the down payment, both of them work, and Andrea doesn't think there'll be any problem with the loan. Actually . . . I'm really glad it's over. It was a little scary staying there all by myself. It made me realize that I've never stayed alone before. I lived with Mother until I went off to college and I've always had roommates there. And when I come back to Lake Eden, I stay with you."

"You can still do that, you know," Hannah reassured her. "The guest room is always ready for you."

"I know, but . . . it's different now." Michelle paused and leaned a little closer. "You're still on your honeymoon. You and Ross should be alone. Or at least you should ask him how he feels about having a third person around."

Hannah was saved from the necessity of a reply when Bill asked Michelle a question. Truthfully, Hannah wasn't entirely sure how Ross felt about it. She loved to have Michelle stay with her, but Ross could feel differently. He might regard it as an intrusion. Hannah didn't think he'd feel that way, because he liked Michelle, but she'd have to check with him to make sure. And that was different too, now that she was married. She'd always made her own decisions, but now that she was married, there was her husband to consider.

The conversation flowed around her and Hannah smiled and nodded. She was fairly quiet, still trying to take in all that her family had given them for their wedding. There was what Andrea had called the "media room," with the giant flat screen, couches that provided theater seating, and all the other electronic equipment. Then there was the guest bathroom with new, plush towels in colors to complement the freshly painted walls, the guest bedroom with its new, fresh bedding that matched the color scheme that someone, probably Andrea, had chosen. And then there was the master suite, completely redone with the new Mediterranean bedroom set, bedding that looked perfect with the rest of the room, and new fixtures and color-coordinated, plush towels in the bathroom with its remodeled shower and tub.

"At least the towels aren't his and hers," Hannah said, thinking aloud.

"What was that, dear?" Delores asked her.

"Nothing. I was just thinking that I really should go and check on the cats. They're awfully quiet and Doc's about to open the container with the shrimp and snow peas."

As she pushed back her chair and headed down the hallway, Hannah experienced a very strange feeling. She loved the new carpeting. It would have been exactly what she'd chosen for herself if she'd been able to afford it. But there was something strange and unsettling about someone else buying it for her, even as a wedding present.

What was it? She tried to clarify her thoughts as she approached the bedroom. Perhaps the reason it disturbed her was because it was too much, too soon. She would almost rather have waited until they could afford to buy it for themselves. But that was terribly ungrateful, wasn't it? Shouldn't she be overjoyed that her family loved her so much that they'd done all this for her?

As Hannah stood in the bedroom doorway, the bedroom that no longer resembled hers, she heard a soft snore from the bed. That was when she gave her first spontaneous smile of the evening. Moishe was stretched out on her pillow, the pillow he always tried to steal from her in the middle of the night. And Cuddles was stretched out on Moishe's pillow, the one she'd bought to wean him away from stealing hers, sleeping the sleep of an angel kitty.

Hannah stared at them for a moment, smiling. Moishe and Cuddles appeared to be comfortable with the new furnishings. They didn't seem to find the changes upsetting in the slightest. Perhaps she should take a lesson from the wisdom of the animal kingdom and accept what had been given to her with a grateful heart. Then again, that could be a little ridiculous.

"I didn't think you'd be going to work today," Ross said, appearing in the kitchen doorway in his bathrobe the next morning.

"I thought I should. Lisa's not just an employee. She's a partner and she's been without me for over a week now." Hannah turned to smile at her husband from her seat at the table. "I made coffee if you want some."

"Later, honey. I never have coffee before my shower. I'll grab a to-go cup when I leave and get more at work." Ross walked over to kiss her on the cheek. "Do you want the shower right now? Or can I use it? I promised the boss at KCOW-TV that I'd be in early."

"You go ahead," Hannah said quickly, even though she'd been about to get up to take her own shower. "I'll just sit here and enjoy the rest of my coffee."

When Ross left the kitchen, she sat there for a moment, her morning peace disturbed. That was when she realized that she missed Michelle. It was so nice when Michelle stayed over and made coffee for her the next morning. And there was usually something wonderful to eat, a new muffin that Michelle was trying out, or some kind of new breakfast dish.

She heard the shower begin to run and she sighed. This was going to take some adjusting on her part. She was used to taking her shower whenever she wanted, but now there was another person added to the equation. Ross needed a shower before work. And they used the same master bathroom.

It shouldn't be that difficult to work out their morning schedules, Hannah told herself reassuringly. Their honeymoon had been different because neither of them had needed to leave for work at a specific time. It would be different now that they were home and both of them worked during the week. They would have to develop a routine so that they wouldn't inconvenience each other. Andrea and Bill didn't have a problem using the same master bathroom. And if her sister and brother-in-law could do it, there was no reason why she couldn't manage it with Ross. Either she'd get up earlier and take her shower first, or Ross would get up earlier. They'd work it all out. All it would take was time until they were used to living together.

As she sat there, another problem occurred to her. She wondered if she had a responsibility to make something for her husband's breakfast. Then again, perhaps she didn't. How could she know? She'd never been married before. If she made breakfast, it would have to be something quick and easy because Ross had promised to get to work early.

Hannah jumped up from the table and hurried to the refrigerator to take stock of what was on the shelves. Michelle had mentioned that she'd shopped for a few things and put them away.

There was a loaf of white bread on the second shelf of the refrigerator. She hadn't bought it so Michelle had put it there. There was also a carton of milk on the shelf in the door, another of Michelle's purchases. On the bottom shelf, Hannah found the six eggs she'd bought before she had left. The expiration date on the carton still had a week to go so she could use those. Of course there was sugar in the canister. There was always sugar in the canister. And she had nutmeg that she could grate, cinnamon she'd just bought two weeks ago, and maple syrup that hadn't even been opened yet. Those ingredients added up to one of Hannah's favorite quick breakfasts. She would make Oven French Toast for Ross and it would be ready for him when he returned to the kitchen, showered and dressed for work.

The first thing Hannah did was to open the oven to make sure that no pans were inside. She'd failed to check once and ended up incinerating two pieces of leftover pizza she'd stuck in there, intending to clear a spot in the refrigerator, but becoming distracted by a ringing phone.

Once she was certain the oven was clear, Hannah preheated it to five-hundred degrees while she gathered up the rest of the ingredients she needed. Then she got out a wide, flat bowl and began to prepare the Oven French Toast batter.

Hannah smiled as she measured ingredients, mixed them in, and found the perfect pan to use to bake her creation. She would like to cook breakfast for Ross, she thought. Since they never knew whether they could get together for lunch, and dinnertimes were equally uncertain with their fluctuating schedules, breakfast might be the only meal they could share every day. She was looking forward to researching breakfast menus and planning the meals that they could enjoy together.

"Rrrrow!"

Hannah turned to look at Moishe, who

was standing by his empty food bowl. "Sorry, Moishe. Just let me put this breakfast in the oven and then I'll feed you."

That seemed to satisfy her pet for the moment and Hannah hurried to place the bread in the pan she'd chosen, stick it in the oven, and set the timer. Then she took a can of chicken-flavored cat food out of the cupboard, and gave a fleeting thought to why it was labeled chicken *flavored*. She mixed it with some dry kitty crunchies, and spooned it into Moishe's bowl.

As she watched her cat begin to eat, Hannah wondered how busy working wives managed to juggle children, pets, and husbands at breakfast time, not to mention getting ready for work themselves. Here she was with no children and just one pet, and she'd almost forgotten to feed Moishe!

# OVEN FRENCH TOAST

Preheat oven to 500 degrees F., rack in the middle position.

**(That's not a misprint. It really is five-hundred degrees!)**

3 large eggs
3/4 cup whole milk
1 Tablespoon white **(granulated)** sugar
1/4 teaspoon salt
1/4 teaspoon ground cinnamon
1/4 teaspoon ground nutmeg **(freshly grated is best)**
8 slices white bread
2 Tablespoons **(1 ounce, 1/4 stick)** salted butter

**Hannah's 1st Note: Lisa says she sometimes uses raisin bread to make this recipe because her husband, Herb, likes it so much. I've used cinnamon swirl bread, and that's wonderful, too.**

**Hannah's 2nd Note: You don't have to use an electric mixer for this recipe. A fork from your silverware drawer will do nicely.**

Crack the eggs into a large, flat bowl. Beat

them up with a fork or a wire whisk.

Add the whole milk and mix it in. Then add the sugar and the salt.

Sprinkle in the cinnamon and the nutmeg. Mix everything up thoroughly with the fork.

Place the salted butter in a 9-inch by 13-inch cake pan. Stick it in the preheated oven for 1 minute.

Use potholders to take the pan out of the oven. It will be hot! Set it on a cold burner on your stovetop to wait for its contents, but *don't shut off the oven!*

Working quickly, dip each slice of bread in the batter mixture, flip it over to coat the other side, and transfer it to the hot, buttered cake pan.

**Hannah's 3rd Note: You can scrunch the battered bread together a bit to make room for all 8 slices in the cake pan.**

If there is any batter left in the bowl, simply pour it over the slices of bread in the pan, distributing it as evenly as you can.

Again, using potholders, return the cake pan to the oven.

Bake until the bottoms of your Oven French Toast are brown. This usually takes 5 to 8 minutes. *(Check by lifting the edge of one slice with a fork and peeking at the bottom.)*

Once the bottoms of your Oven French Toast have browned, flip them over with a fork and bake them for 2 to 4 minutes longer or until the tops *(which are now the bottoms)* are golden brown.

Remove the pan from the oven and set it on a cold, stovetop burner. Shut off the oven, and cover the pan of Oven French Toast with foil until your family comes to the table.

Serve your Oven French Toast with plenty of salted butter, syrups, and jams of your choice.

Yield: 8 one-piece servings or 4 two-piece servings, but only if you don't invite Mike. He'll eat at least 3 pieces, and sometimes 4.

**Andrea's Note: This recipe is so easy, even I can make it. Bill loves it with one of the flavored syrups, like blueberry or apricot. Tracey and Bethie want theirs buttered and spread with strawberry jam.**

**Lisa's Note: Sometimes, when I make this for breakfast for Herb, I'm in a real hurry. I just turn a stovetop burner to MEDIUM-HIGH, dip the bread in the Oven French Toast batter, and fry it on both sides. It's really good that way, too. I do this in the summer, too, when it gets really hot and muggy in Minnesota**

**and I don't want to turn on the oven and heat up my kitchen.**

# CHAPTER FIVE

"So how was the honeymoon?" Lisa asked, the moment Hannah walked in the back door of The Cookie Jar.

Hannah smiled, remembering the lazy mornings when she hadn't bothered to set the alarm clock by their king-size bed, the carafe of hot coffee that had been waiting for her just outside their stateroom door, and the table on their huge balcony where she'd enjoyed her first cup of coffee with Ross. "It was fabulous, but it's good to be back."

"Michelle told me that they refurnished your whole condo while you were gone."

"That's true. They did."

Lisa took a deep breath. And then she asked, "I'm not sure that I should open this can of worms, but . . . do you *like* it?"

"I love it! They didn't touch the kitchen. Michelle threatened Mother with dire consequences if she did anything to change the kitchen. And the rest of the place is . . . well . . . you'll have to see it to appreciate it. Andrea calls the living room a media room because of the gigantic flat screen television, the master bedroom is gorgeous with all new furniture and bedding, and the shower is totally incredible."

"They changed the shower?"

"Yes. I didn't really discover how great it was until this morning. It has all new tile, a bench you can sit on, and four adjustable jets. You can stand there and massage your back and neck."

"Wow!" Lisa looked duly impressed. "I'll bet Herb would love to have a shower like that. His neck is always stiff when he gets up in the morning and he's tried every remedy there is. We spent a fortune buying special neck pillows and creams right after we were married. Do you know how much a shower like yours costs?"

"No, but you can ask Mother. She'll be here in a half-hour or so. At least that's what she said when we had dinner last night."

"You had dinner with your family last night?" Lisa looked shocked when Hannah nodded. "But you just got back from your honeymoon yesterday. Don't tell me you cooked for your whole family last night!"

"I didn't cook. Everybody was waiting for

us when we got home and they brought takeout food."

"That's nice . . . I think. Unless you and Ross wanted to be alone."

"Not really. We were alone for a week. And it was nice to see everybody again."

"I'll bet your mother could hardly wait to tell you about . . ." Lisa stopped and swallowed hard. Then she cleared her throat. "Sorry. I get a little teary-eyed when I think about Tori Bascomb. She was so good to me, giving me acting lessons for free. She said I had real potential and I should be starring in every Lake Eden Players production."

"You should be if you can find the time. Maybe I should stay late and let you go early when they have rehearsals and . . ."

"No," Lisa said firmly, cutting off the rest of Hannah's offer. "I'd much rather tell stories here. Tori taught me a lot about good storytelling."

"I think you do just fine right now."

"I do okay and it sure brings in the business. I'll be telling the story about Tori today, and that's one of the reasons I'm here early. We always sell out of cookies and so I'm baking more this time."

"Is that what smells so good?" Hannah smiled as she sniffed the air. "Do I smell chocolate and orange?"

"You do. It's a new recipe I just made up last night. I call them Orange Fudge Cookies. I just put them in the oven and . . ." Lisa glanced at the clock on the kitchen wall, ". . . they've got a few more minutes to go. Tell me what your mother said about the murder."

"Not a word. I think Andrea and Michelle managed to convince her that she shouldn't bring it up on my first night home."

"That must be it. She didn't waste any time telling me about it. As a matter of fact, she was waiting for me when I unlocked the back door at five o'clock yesterday morning."

"Really?" Hannah was amazed. "Mother was here at five in the morning?"

"On the dot. And it was before I'd even baked anything with chocolate."

Hannah laughed. Delores was, and had always been, a real chocolate lover. "She's going to love your Orange Fudge Cookies."

"I hope so. She was pretty upset when she told me about finding the body, Hannah. Her voice was shaking and she had to sit down. I really don't know how you do it."

"Do what?" Hannah was puzzled.

"I don't know how you stay so calm when you find a murder victim." Lisa stopped and thought about that for a moment. "I guess it's because it's happened to you so many times in the past. After a while, you must almost . . . well . . . expect it."

Hannah thought about it. "Sometimes I do expect it. There are times when I just know there's something wrong. I hope against hope that it's not what my instincts tell me it is, but my instincts are usually right. But even if I'm almost expecting it, it's still a shock."

"Maybe, but you always do everything right. You call the sheriff's department, you wait for Mike or another detective to arrive, you're coherent when you tell them what happened, and you seem so in control. I think I'd fall to pieces if I ever found . . . well, you know."

"No, you wouldn't. You'd do what you had to do. Everyone's stronger than they think they are. And it's not that I'm used to finding murder victims. It's just that I don't show my emotions right away, that's all."

Lisa looked thoughtful. "It must be that way with Mike, too."

Hannah took a moment to consider it. "You could be right, Lisa. It probably bothers him when he's at home alone."

"There's the timer," Lisa said, reacting to the electronic beeping that had just begun.

"I'll take the cookies out of the oven. As soon as they cool a little, you can taste one and see if your mother will like them."

"They have chocolate, don't they?"

"Yes. Both baking chocolate and chocolate chips."

"Then she'll love them. Mother thinks chocolate is a food group."

"These are wonderful cookies!" Delores said to Lisa, who was placing sheets of unbaked cookies on the racks in their industrial oven.

"Thank you, Delores," Lisa responded to the compliment. "I'm glad you like them."

Delores took a sip of her coffee and reached for a third cookie. "I love the combination of chocolate and orange."

"I know you do, Mother." Hannah said and smiled at her. "You'd love the combination of chocolate and absolutely anything."

Delores thought about that for a moment. "Maybe not chocolate and pickles, although there is that wonderful chocolate sauerkraut cookie you make, dear."

"Thank you." Hannah reached for another one of Lisa's cookies, even though she'd intended to limit herself to one. Although she hadn't stepped on the scale to validate her suspicions, she was quite certain she'd gained at least five pounds on the honey-moon cruise. "Go ahead, Mother. Tell me about finding Tori Bascomb's body."

Delores took a deep breath and another bite of her cookie before she began. Then she launched into her account of the evening before Hannah and Ross had come back to Lake Eden. Hannah knew that her mother had given the account at least two times before. Certainly Mike had heard it when he'd interviewed Delores, and she'd told Lisa so that the story could be told at The Cookie Jar. Andrea and Michelle must have heard all about it right after it had happened, but her mother's hands were still trembling slightly and Hannah slid the cookie plate closer to her.

Long moments passed while Delores spoke. Hannah listened carefully, occasionally asking questions she hoped would help her mother recall certain details.

"And that's it," Delores concluded, looking up to meet her daughter's eyes. "Doc said I was very brave."

"Very," Hannah agreed. "You did everything just right, Mother."

"Mike doesn't think so. He didn't like me going into Tori's condo all by myself."

"Of course he didn't."

"Do you think it was foolish of me to do it?"

"Without a doubt it was," Hannah said with a smile as she prepared to use one of her grandmother's favorite phrases. "*That was about as foolish as foolish can get.* But honestly, Mother . . . if I'd been there, I would have done exactly the same thing."

Delores laughed and then she stopped abruptly. "I think Mike was a little angry with me."

"Of course he was. Mike's a by-the-book cop and he likes to take charge. He probably told you to wait until he got there."

"I did," Mike said from the doorway, startling both of them. "She disobeyed a direct order from a police officer. Do you know that's actionable, Delores?"

"I didn't disobey your direct order. I didn't *hear* you. The phone was squawking, but I couldn't make out the words because I was busy trying to find Tori."

"And now she's telling me I squawk. Parrots squawk. Police officers don't." Mike reached out to pat Delores's shoulder to show that he was teasing and then he took the stool next to hers. "I was just concerned for you, Delores. It could have been dangerous."

"I know. If I'd thought it through, I might

not have gone in alone. But I didn't think. I was too worried about Tori to think. All I cared about was finding out if she was hurt and if she needed my help."

"Water over the bridge, or under the bridge, or whatever that is," Mike said, dismissing the subject. Then he thanked Lisa as she brought him coffee and reached over to take a cookie. "I don't know about your mother, Hannah. First she disobeys my direct order and now she's hogging the cookies. If there isn't a statute on the books against that, there ought to be."

The three women laughed and Mike took a bite of his cookie. He finished it in three gulps and reached for another. "There ought to be a statute against these cookies, too."

"Why?" Hannah asked, knowing full-well that Mike was teasing again.

"Because not only are they criminally deli-cious, I can testify that they're definitely ad-dictive."

"I'll get more," Lisa said, grabbing the empty platter and heading off to the bakers rack to refill it.

"Story time today?" Mike asked Hannah.

"Yes. Lisa told it yesterday, too." She turned to her mother. "Did you hear Lisa yesterday?"

Delores shook her head. "No. I couldn't bear to hear it. The whole thing was still too fresh in my mind. I'll listen today, though. The audience might like to ask me a couple of questions."

"I'm sure they will," Mike said, standing up. "It's been fun chatting with you ladies, but my coffee break's over, and I have to get back to work." He turned to Hannah. "Will you be home later?"

Hannah was surprised by the question. "Yes, of course I'll be home."

"What time will you get there?"

Hannah frowned slightly. It was a strange question for Mike to ask. "I'm not sure. I might have to stop at the store, but I should be home by five-thirty. Why?"

"Because Norman and I bought you a wedding present and we need to bring it out to you. Will Ross be there, too?"

"He should be. He told me he'd be home by six at the latest. Would you and Norman like to stay for dinner? I'm trying out a new recipe in the crockpot."

"You bet! Whatever it is, it's bound to be good. I'll check in with Norman later today and we'll come out together."

Mike hesitated and Hannah knew he wanted to say something else, but he must have thought better of it because he headed directly for the back door. He turned to give her a wave, and then he went out into the frosty early morning.

"I wonder what they bought for you and Ross," Delores said. "Neither one of them asked me for suggestions."

Hannah shrugged. "I have no idea, but I'll tell you tomorrow, Mother."

"That's fine, dear. And I have to leave, too. I'm opening at Granny's Attic this morning. Donald Meyers called and he wants to take a look at the hand crank sewing machine I have in the front window. He says he thinks it might be perfect for the leather work he does."

Lisa set a full cookie bag in front of Delores. "Take these cookies, Delores. You can have them on your coffee break."

"Thank you!" Delores smiled as she took the bag. "These cookies are going to be a real winner for you. I just know it. And, Lisa?"

"Yes, Delores."

"I'm going to come in at noon to hear you tell your story."

Hannah got up to escort her mother to the door. She opened it, expecting Delores to step out and hurry through the chilly morning to her antique store, but Delores stood there with her hand on the door.

"I have something to give you, Hannah. I didn't want to do it in front of Mike. Andrea said she's coming in this morning for coffee so I want you to bring her over to Granny's Attic. Will you do that, dear?"

Hannah was puzzled. What did her mother have for her that she didn't want Mike to see? "What's this about, Mother?"

"I'll tell you when you get to Granny's Attic. I have to go now, dear. I need to call Michelle and wish her good luck with her play. She's been rehearsing her cast for a month now."

"When I talked to her last night, she mentioned that she had a final for her directing class."

"That's right. Everyone in the class had to stage a one-act play. They're performing them today."

"I'll text her and wish her success," Hannah promised. She still didn't know what her mother wanted to show her, but she knew that asking for the second time would do little good. Instead, she gave her mother a parting hug. "Okay, Mother. Andrea and I will see you later."

## ORANGE FUDGE COOKIES

DO NOT preheat the oven yet. This dough must chill before baking.

1 and 1/2 cups butter *(3 sticks, 12 ounces, 3/4 pound)*

1 ounce unsweetened baking chocolate *(I used Baker's)*

1 and 3/4 cups white *(granulated)* sugar

1/2 cup orange juice concentrate *(I used Minute Maid)*

2 beaten eggs *(just whip them up in a glass with a fork)*

2 teaspoons baking soda

1/2 teaspoon salt

4 cups flour *(don't sift it — pack it down in the cup when you measure it)*

1 cup miniature chocolate chips *(I used Nestlé)*

1/2 cup white *(granulated)* sugar in a small bowl for rolling the dough balls

Melt the butter and the one ounce of unsweetened baking chocolate in a large microwave-safe bowl. Heat it on HIGH for 1 minute. Leave the bowl in the microwave for another minute and then check the butter and chocolate to see if it's melted. If it's not, give it more time, in 20-second increments followed by 20 seconds standing time, until it is.

Take the bowl out of the microwave and mix in the white sugar. Mix until it's well combined.

Add the frozen orange juice concentrate to the bowl and mix it in. Mix until it's thoroughly incorporated.

Let the butter, chocolate, sugar, and orange mixture sit on the counter while you get out the eggs.

Break the eggs into a small bowl or a large glass and whip them up with a fork from your silverware drawer.

Add the eggs to the large bowl with the chocolate mixture and stir them in thoroughly.

**Hannah's 1st Note: Lisa and I use a stand mixer to mix up this cookie dough down at The Cookie Jar. You can do it by hand at home, but using an electric mixer makes it a lot easier.**

Sprinkle in the baking soda and salt. Mix until all of the ingredients are well combined.

Add the flour in one-cup increments, mixing after each addition.

**Hannah's 2nd Note: You don't have to be painstakingly precise when you add the four cups of flour. No one's going to**

know if one cup is a little bigger than the next one. Just make sure you mix after each addition of flour.

The dough will be quite stiff after you add the flour. This is exactly as it should be.

Add the miniature chocolate chips and mix them in by hand. Your goal is to get them evenly distributed so there will be chips in every cookie.

Cover the dough with plastic wrap and refrigerate it for at least two hours. *(Overnight is even better.)*

When you're ready to bake, take the cookie dough out of the refrigerator and let it sit, still covered with the plastic wrap, on your kitchen counter. It will need to warm just a bit so that you can work with it.

Preheat your oven to 350 degrees F., rack in the middle position.

While your oven reaches the proper temperature, prepare your cookie sheets. You can either spray them with Pam or another nonstick cooking spray, or line them with parchment paper. *(The parchment paper is more expensive, but easier in the long run. If you use it, you can simply pull the paper over to the wire cooling rack, cookies and all.)*

Prepare a shallow bowl by filling it with the half cup white sugar. This is what you'll use as a coating for the cookie dough balls you'll roll.

Take off the plastic wrap and roll the cookie dough into walnut-sized balls with your impeccably clean hands. Roll each dough ball in the bowl with the white sugar, one ball at a time, and place it on your prepared cookie sheet — 12 dough balls to a standard-sized sheet.

Press the dough balls down just a little so they won't roll off when you carry them to the oven.

**Hannah's 3rd Note: If you form the dough into smaller dough balls, the cookies will be crisper. If you choose to do this, you'll have to reduce the baking time. If I roll smaller balls, I start checking the Orange Fudge Cookies after 8 minutes in the oven.**

Bake the walnut-sized cookie balls for 10 to 12 minutes or until they're nicely browned around the edges. The cookies will flatten out, all by themselves. Let them cool for 2 minutes on the cookie sheets and then move them to a wire rack to finish cooling.

**Hannah's 4th Note: Orange Fudge Cookies freeze well. Roll them up in foil, the same way you would roll coins in a wrapper, put them in a freezer bag, and they'll be fine for 3 months or so.**

Yield: 8 to 10 dozen tasty chocolate-orange cookies, depending on the size of your dough balls.

# CHAPTER SIX

"What did you want to give me, Mother?" Hannah asked when they were all seated at the antique, red oak table on the second floor of their mother's shop.

"It's this." Delores pulled out a leather tote bag that was decorated with the initials *V.B.*

"Tori Bascomb's tote?" Andrea guessed.

"That's right. And wait until I show you what's inside!" Delores drew out a black leather book with the word *Appointments* written on the outside in fancy gold script.

Hannah was almost afraid to ask, but she did. "Did Tori have anything written for the night she was killed?"

"Yes." Delores turned to the proper page. "The page is divided into time slots from eight in the morning until five at night. And Becky Summers was written in for a five o'clock appointment. After that, there's a space for evening appointments, but there are no indications of time."

"Becky?" Hannah was surprised. "I didn't know Becky had an interest in acting."

"She doesn't," Delores told them. "Becky was helping with the props for the Jordan High class play. Her son has the lead. Tori told me all about it. They need all sorts of old-fashioned props that are difficult to find so Becky's helping the class locate some period pieces."

"And you're helping Becky." Hannah came to the obvious conclusion.

"That's right. I've already found an old hand pump and I'm currently working on the rest of the rigging for a well. Let me tell you, that's not easy. Most of the farms around here did away with their old wells fifty or more years ago."

"It's very nice of you to help them, Mother," Hannah said before her mother could go into even greater detail. "Did you happen to talk to Becky to ask her if Tori seemed upset about anything, or if she mentioned any appointments she had that night?"

"Of course I did, dear. Becky met Tori in her office at Jordan High and they talked about the props for about ten minutes. Then Tori said she had to rush home because she had a couple of evening appointments at her studio. She didn't mention any names and Becky didn't ask. I did ask Becky if Tori seemed nervous or anything like that, and Becky said that Tori was in a good mood and she appeared perfectly normal."

"Are there any names written in that space for the evening?" Andrea asked.

"Tricia Barthel is listed for six o'clock. Tori wrote in the time. Tricia has the lead in the play the Lake Eden Players are performing at Thanksgiving. And there's one more name," Delores said with a sigh. "But I don't think it'll be of any immediate help."

"Why do you say that, Mother?" Andrea asked.

"Because the last name listed is M. Dumont."

The two sisters exchanged puzzled glances and Andrea was the first to speak the thought that had crossed their minds. "I've never heard of a Dumont family around here."

"Neither have I," Delores admitted, "and that's why I told you that I didn't think it would help us. But it's right here in Tori's handwriting and she had beautiful penmanship. It's M. Dumont. There's no mistaking it. And there's even a time in front of the name. M. Dumont was due to arrive at

Tori's condo at seven forty-five on the night that she was murdered."

When Hannah returned to The Cookie Jar through the back kitchen door, she hung her coat on a hook and headed straight to the kitchen coffeepot to pour herself a decent cup of coffee. Delores had served them herbal tea and Hannah had dutifully sipped it, but she needed something to jolt her into high gear so that she could bake more cookies for Lisa's remaining afternoon performances.

As she sat down at the stainless steel workstation and took her first sip of strong coffee, Hannah realized that she heard no buzz of voices or friendly chatter drifting in from the coffee shop. Usually, she could hear voices, laughter, and the clinking of coffee cups and spoons. She got up and walked closer to the swinging restaurant-style door, but the coffee shop was silent, as if all the customers had left and the chairs and tables were completely deserted. Had Lisa closed early for some reason? Surely her partner would have called or left her a note if there had been some sort of emergency.

Hannah looked around the kitchen. There was no note on the counter by the phone, nothing at all to explain the silence. She was about to open the swinging door to look when she heard Lisa's voice.

*"There Delores stood, in front of her downstairs neighbor's door, panting a bit from the exertion of her headlong rush down the narrow staircase. She was here and quite suddenly, she wasn't sure what she should do."*

Hannah breathed a sigh of relief. Lisa was giving another performance, telling the story of the murder. All of their customers were perfectly silent, no coughing, no clearing of throats, not even the rustling of clothing as people moved in their chairs. Everyone there was so enthralled by Lisa's rendition of Delores finding the murder victim that they didn't want to miss a word.

*"Delores knew she had to do something. But what? She considered her options. She knew that Victoria Bascomb gave acting lessons in her condo. Could the screams, the sharp bangs, and the crash she'd heard be part of a very realistic rehearsal? She would feel very foolish if she pulled Victoria away from her rehearsal because she'd overreacted. But wasn't that better than doing nothing if something was dreadfully wrong?"*

"I would have knocked," a male voice said and Hannah recognized Gus York's nasal twang.

"I'm with you, Gus! Better to feel foolish than to ignore a friend in distress." The female voice was forceful and Hannah began to smile. Grandma Knudson had been the first customer in the door this morning when Lisa had opened the coffee shop for business and she was still here.

"That's exactly what Delores did, Grandma," Lisa said. "She raised her hand and knocked as loudly as she could. But there was no answer."

Hannah heard several gasps from the audience even though she was sure that everyone there had heard about Tori Bascomb's murder. Lisa knew exactly how to get the audience involved. Tori Bascomb had been right. Lisa had real acting potential.

*"Delores knocked again. And again. Someone must be there. The sounds she'd heard had come from Victoria Bascomb's condo. Was there a reason why her friend wasn't answering the door? Should she use the key that Victoria had given her for emergencies?"*

"Yes," several voices chorused.

"No way," a male voice objected, and Hannah recognized Mike's official tone. "She should call the authorities immediately."

"And that's exactly what Delores did,"

Lisa continued the story. "She called the sheriff's office for help. She spoke to you, Mike."

But before she could continue telling the story, Mike's voice broke in.

"She spoke to me, but she didn't listen to my advice. She asked me to stay on the line and she told me she was going in. And then she stopped listening to me. And that's when Lonnie and I rolled."

Hannah's lips lifted in a smile. There was nothing that Mike hated more than someone refusing to listen to him.

*"Delores knew what Mike would tell her, so she put the cell phone in her pocket and used her key to unlock the door."*

There were several more gasps and Hannah knew that Lisa had them on the edges of their chairs. Since she'd heard Lisa's story once this morning, she ceased to listen and headed for the recipe book to bake more cookies for the crowd that was bound to grow larger and larger as the day wore on.

Hannah paged through their laminated recipe book, but nothing struck her fancy. She should bake something different, something new. She thought about it for a moment and then an idea popped into her head. Everyone loved their meringue cookies. Perhaps it was time for a new variety.

She walked to the pantry and stared up at the shelves, searching for inspiration. She'd never made a meringue cookie with coconut. And there was a bag of dried pineapple pieces. Coconut and pineapple were wonderful together. Since all of their meringue cookies had the word *angel* in the title, she'd call these cookies Tropical Angels.

Less than thirty minutes later, Hannah was slipping the second batch of her new creation on the revolving racks in her preheated industrial oven. Once she'd finished, she set the timer and headed straight for the kitchen coffeepot to pour herself a pick-me-up cup of hot caffeine. She was just about to sit down on a stool at the stainless steel work island when someone knocked on the back door.

Hannah smiled as she hurried to open the door. She recognized that knock. Norman was here.

"Coffee?" she asked.

Norman nodded as he hung his coat on the rack by the door. "That would be good. It's cold out there."

Hannah set a mug of coffee in front of the stool where Norman always sat. "How about trying my newest cookie? I'm calling them Tropical Angels."

"You won't have to twist my arm for that!" Norman gave a little laugh. "I missed lunch today."

"Problems?" Hannah went to the bakers rack to fill a plate with some of the Tropical Angel Cookies she'd already baked.

"You could say that. Hal McDermott broke his appliance again, and I . . ."

"Hold it!" Hannah interrupted him. "I think you told me once, but I forgot. What's an appliance?"

"In Hal's case, it was a partial. You've heard of a bridge, haven't you?"

Hannah squelched the urge to remind him of the Mississippi River Bridge that was only a few miles away from Lake Eden, and simply nodded. She knew what a bridge meant in dental parlance.

"Well, Hal broke his and there were sharp edges. I had to remove it, file the sharp edges, and make him a temporary."

"Hal's broken it before, hasn't he?" Hannah set the cookies in front of Norman and took the stool across from him.

"Oh, yes. He keeps crunching ice. He says it's a habit he's had for years and he just can't seem to stop doing it. This is the second time he's broken it this month. I've been patching it up, but this time I had to send it back to the lab."

"How long will that take?"

"At least a week."

"So Hal won't have teeth for a week?"

Norman shook his head. "He'll have teeth, but they're temporary."

"That's good."

"It could be. But unless the ice machine in their restaurant breaks down, that temporary I made won't survive much more than a day or two at the most." Norman reached out for a cookie and took a bite. Then he began to smile. "These are good, Hannah. They taste like a vacation in the tropics. Your name for them is perfect."

"Thanks," Hannah said, smiling back. "It's probably the coconut and dried pineapple. They taste like a tropical drink."

"A piña colada. Back when I was still drinking, that used to be one of my favorite drinks."

Hannah remembered the day, several years ago, when Norman had told her why he no longer touched a drop of alcohol. "Should I warn you when I put liquor in something I bake?"

"No need. Alcohol in food doesn't bother me. I just don't want to drink it straight. And that reminds me . . . do you have any beer at your place?"

"*You* want to drink beer?"

"Not me. But I would like you to try a recipe I got from one of my former dental school colleagues. He's a cook and he sent it to me online."

"What is it?"

"Beer muffins. He says he makes them every time he puts up a pot of chili."

"That sounds interesting. Do you have the recipe with you?"

"No, but I can forward his email to you. Or I can bring it when we come over tonight."

"Send it to me and I'll look at it on my phone. Then I'll pick up what I need at the Red Owl and make your beer muffins for dinner tonight."

"Great!" Norman looked delighted. "The recipe's easy and it just sounded good to me. Thanks, Hannah. I can hardly wait to taste them."

## TROPICAL ANGEL COOKIES

Preheat oven to 275 degrees F., rack in the middle position.

**(Yes, that's two hundred and seventy-five degrees F., NOT a misprint.)**

6 large eggs
1/4 cup dried pineapple, finely chopped **(measure AFTER chopping)**
1/4 cup dried mango, finely chopped **(if you can't find it, double the dried pineapple — measure AFTER chopping)**
1 cup coconut flakes, finely chopped **(measure AFTER chopping)**
1/4 teaspoon cream of tartar
1/2 teaspoon vanilla
1/4 teaspoon salt
1 cup white **(granulated)** sugar
2 Tablespoons **(1/8 cup)** all-purpose flour **(Pack it down when you measure it.)**

Separate 6 large eggs and put the whites in one container and the yolks in another.

Cover the container with the yolks and put it in the refrigerator. You can use it to make yolk-rich scrambled eggs for breakfast in the morning, or you can use the yolks to make a Chocolate Flan with Caramel Whipped Cream.

Set the egg whites on your kitchen counter until they've come up to room temperature. *(This will give them more volume when you whip them up into a meringue.)*

While you're waiting for your egg whites to warm to room temperature, use your food processor with the steel blade *(or a chef's knife with a cutting board)* to finely chop your dried pineapple, dried mango, and coconut flakes into very small pieces.

Prepare your cookie sheets by lining them with parchment paper *(this works best)* or brown parcel-wrapping paper. Spray the paper with Pam or another non-stick cooking spray and dust it lightly with flour.

**Hannah's 1st Note: You can also use Pam Baking Spray or another brand of baking spray that has the flour already in it.**

**Hannah's 2nd Note: These cookies are a lot easier to make if you use an electric mixer because you must beat the egg whites until they form soft peaks and, ultimately, stiff peaks. You can use a copper bowl and a whisk, but it will take some time and muscle.**

Beat the egg whites with the cream of tartar, vanilla, and salt until they are firm enough to hold a soft peak. Test this by shutting off the mixer and dotting the egg whites with the side of a clean rubber spatula. When you pull up the spatula, a soft peak should form.

**Hannah's 3rd Note: For those of you who haven't made meringues before, soft peaks slump a bit and bend over on themselves. That's what you want at this stage. A bit later on in the recipe, you'll want stiff peaks. Those stand straight up and do not slump or bend over.**

With the mixer running on MEDIUM HIGH speed, sprinkle the egg mixture with approximately one third of the sugar. Turn the mixer up to HIGH speed for ten seconds. Then turn the mixer down to MEDIUM HIGH speed again.

Sprinkle in half of the remaining sugar, turn the mixer up to HIGH speed for ten seconds, and then back down to MEDIUM HIGH speed again.

Sprinkle in the remaining sugar and follow the same procedure, turning the mixer OFF when you're through.

Sprinkle in the flour and mix it into the egg white mixture at LOW speed. *(You spent all this time whipping air into your meringue. Now you don't want to whip any air back out!)*

Take the bowl out of the mixer and, using your rubber spatula, carefully fold in the chopped dried pineapple, mango, and the finely chopped coconut.

Use a spoon to drop small mounds of meringue onto your cookie sheet, no more than 12 mounds to a standard-sized sheet. *(If you make 4 rows with 3 meringue mounds in each row, that should be perfect.)*

Bake your Tropical Angel Cookies at 275 degrees F. for approximately 40 minutes *(forty minutes)* or until the meringue part of the cookie is slightly golden and dry to the touch when you tap it lightly with your finger.

Cool the cookies on the paper-lined baking sheet by setting it on a cold stovetop burner or on a wire rack.

When your Tropical Angel Cookies are completely cool, peel them off the paper and store them in an airtight container in a cool, dry place. *(Unfortunately, your refrigerator is NOT a dry place. A cupboard shelf will do just fine as long as it's not near your stove.)*

Yield: 3 to 4 dozen crunchy, melt-in-your-mouth cookies with a delightful tropical flavor. Warning: Tropical Angel Cookies are like potato chips. You can't eat just one!

# CHAPTER SEVEN

Hannah stood in the adult beverage aisle, staring at the display on her cell phone. Norman had sent her the recipe and it was the reason she was here at Florence's Red Owl grocery store. Once she'd read through the recipe, she'd decided that the beer muffins would go perfectly with the Chicken Stroganoff she'd made for tonight's dinner. As always, she'd made extra just in case anyone dropped by and she was glad that she'd invited both Mike and Norman to have dinner at the condo with them.

"One sixteen-ounce bottle of pale lager," Hannah read the ingredient aloud, but it still didn't make sense. Of course she knew that a lager was a type of beer, but what kind was it? For the first time in her life, she wished that she were more familiar with beer terms. Did "pale" mean the same as "light," the way it did with skin color? According to the ad she'd seen on television, a light beer had less calories than regular beer. Perhaps that was it. Or did "light" refer to the alcohol content? She seemed to remember Michelle saying something about three-two beer having less alcohol than regular bottled beer. But this recipe called for a sixteen ounce bottle of beer, so that couldn't possibly be the answer.

Hannah reached out to take down a bottle of beer from the shelf. It was Coor's Light and "light" might be "pale." But was it a lager? She wasn't sure so she grabbed one of the six-pack holders that Florence provided for mix and match beer samplings. She unfolded the holder, stuck the Coor's Light in one of the six divisions, and put the holder in the bottom of her shopping cart.

The next beer she examined was Newcastle Brown Ale. If it was brown it couldn't be pale, so it lost out on that count. And if it was ale, it might not be a lager. She put it back on the shelf.

The next beer was a total mystery. It said *Pilsner Urquel.* Was a pilsner a lager? She just wasn't sure. But she could see that the liquid inside the green bottle wasn't brown, so she stuck it in the six-pack holder. A bottle of Budweiser was next and that made three different bottles in her cart. There were three more spaces in the six-pack holder and Hannah found another beer that said *Lagunitas IPA*. Perhaps the *P* stood for "pale" so she added that to the mix. A bottle of Corona was the next beer she took, followed by a bottle of Beck's. She was just getting ready to push her cart to the next aisle when she heard voices coming from the baking aisle.

"Hello there! I haven't seen you for ages! Of course I see Tricia at every rehearsal. She's doing very well, Helen."

Hannah recognized the high-pitched voice of Irma York. And since she'd mentioned Tricia, the other shopper must be Tricia's mother, Helen Barthel.

Hannah went on full alert. This was a real stroke of luck! Tricia's name had been in Tori's appointment book and if she stayed quiet and listened to Irma and Helen's conversation, perhaps she'd hear something that might help her investigation.

"I'm glad we ran into each other, Irma," Helen said. "Do you know who might be taking over as the director of the Lake Eden Players? Tricia's worried that the play might be canceled and it's her first starring role."

"I'm not sure, Helen. We've been talking about finding another director, but we haven't come to a decision yet."

110

"It's a terrible shame. Tricia worked so hard at her acting lessons, not to mention learning all those lines."

There was a moment of silence and then Irma spoke again. "I guess Tricia is very upset about Tori."

"Of course she is. She was there earlier that night, you know."

"I *didn't* know! What did she say about Tori?"

"She wasn't happy when she dropped by my place at six-thirty. Tori cut her lesson short because she got a phone call. And Tricia heard Tori tell the person to come over."

"Does she know who was on the phone?"

"No. She did overhear something else, though. She told me about it."

Irma drew her breath in so sharply that Hannah could hear her gasp. "What was it?"

"She heard Tori's part of the conversation. Tori took the call in her living room and she told Tricia to go straight to the studio and go over her lines. So Tricia did. But the door wasn't closed all the way and she could hear what Tori was saying."

"What did Tori say?"

"Tricia only caught a couple of phrases when Tori raised her voice and almost shouted at the person on the other end of the line. She knew that Tori was angry because Tori said that she wasn't about to put up with it any longer. And then Tori slammed the phone down so hard it jangled."

"What happened then?"

"Tori came into the studio and told Tricia that something had come up and she had to cut her lesson short, but she'd give her a longer lesson next week to make up for it."

"And then?"

"And then Tricia left."

"Thank goodness! What if . . ." Irma stopped speaking and gave another little gasp.

"What is it, Irma?"

"I was just thinking that if Tricia had stayed longer, she could have run straight into the killer!"

"I know, and I don't want to think about that. It's just too frightening!"

"It certainly is! Did Tricia see anyone on her way out of the building?"

"I asked her the very same thing! She said no, that she took the elevator down to the lobby and it was completely deserted. She went out to the parking garage, got into her car, and drove straight to my place."

"So she didn't see anyone lurking in the parking garage or anything like that?"

"No. She said there were lots of cars coming in because the Red Velvet Lounge was serving Reuben sandwiches that night and everybody in town loves those. But nothing she saw was unusual and she didn't really pay any attention to the other cars. She was still mad at Tori for cutting her acting lesson short and she was in a hurry to drive to my place to tell me all about it."

"Maybe it's a good thing that Tori cut her acting lesson short."

"It was a good thing, in hindsight." Helen stopped speaking and gave a little sigh. "That's all I know, Irma. You won't tell anyone, will you?"

"Of course not! I never gossip. I know how to keep a confidence, especially when it's this important."

Hannah almost laughed out loud. She'd never heard anything so silly. Irma York was a charter member of the Lake Eden Gossip Hotline and Hannah had no doubt that Irma would be on the phone, telling her friends, the moment she got back home.

"Let's talk about something more pleasant," Helen suggested. "Which cake mix should I buy for Ned's birthday? I'm having his favorite chili and garlic bread, and Tricia promised to make the three-bean salad he's so crazy about. That's why I bought all this jarred garlic and a whole bag of onions. Ned lost most of his sense of smell after that horse kicked him in the head and everything tastes bland to him unless we put in lots of spices. The doctor warned us that it could affect his taste buds, but I didn't know it would last this long."

"Ned got kicked six or seven years ago, didn't he?"

"That's right. He was trying to shoe Tricia's horse himself and Sable didn't cotton to it. That's the last time he tried to be his own blacksmith! Now we call the blacksmith from Annandale to come out to the farm for things like that."

"Did the doctor say when Ned's sense of smell and taste would come back?"

"He said it could happen anytime, but I don't hold out much hope for it. Now I'm resigned to buying all my spices in bulk because Ned can't taste them unless they're overpowering."

"Oh, my!"

Hannah realized that Irma sounded more than a little shocked, and that was totally understandable. It would be a terrible thing to lose your sense of taste.

"If you use all those spices, doesn't it ruin meals for the rest of the family?"

"Not really. I just take out a double portion for Ned and spice it up for him. The pies are the hardest part. You can't spice up just one piece of a pie. I bought some of those little disposable pans for things like chicken pot pies. Florence carries them for me. Then I make Ned's pies separately."

"But that's a lot of extra work for you."

"Not really. I always make too much pie filling anyway, and I just mix up a little extra crust. I bake a separate pumpkin pie for Ned every Thanksgiving that's loaded with cinnamon and cloves. That first year, I tried to put the extra spices in just one place and poor Tricia got the wrong piece."

"What happened?"

"She started to choke and she had to drink lots of water to wash it down. I tell you, Irma, there are times when it's a three-ring circus around my house."

Irma laughed. "I've got an idea. Why don't you make a spice cake for Ned? You could divide it up into cupcakes and add more spice to his batter. And you could stick a couple of toothpicks into his cupcakes before you bake them."

"That's a wonderful idea!" Helen sounded pleased. "I could even put some of those little birthday candles on his so we could tell them apart after I frost them."

Hannah felt someone tap her shoulder and she whirled around to see Florence standing there.

"Do you need some help, Hannah?"

"Uh . . . yes, Florence. Yes I do." Hannah recovered quickly. "I'm serving Chicken Stroganoff tonight and I need to choose a wine that'll go well with it."

"I'd suggest beer, but I see you already have six mix and match bottles." Florence examined the beer in Hannah's holder. "Good choices, Hannah."

Hannah began to smile. "I don't know much about beer. Are any of mine pale lagers?"

"Why yes, the Corona is. And . . . Let me see."

"That's okay, Florence. All I need is one. It's for a recipe."

Florence looked interested. "What kind of recipe uses a pale lager?"

"A recipe for beer muffins that Norman gave me."

"Interesting! If they turn out to be good, will you give me the recipe?"

"Of course."

"Thanks, Hannah. Now, for the wine, I'd suggest a dry white with a hint of a fruit finish."

Hannah half-listened as Florence described the characteristics of various wines. She already had a jug of white wine from

CostMart in her refrigerator, the kind she called Chateau Screwtop, but she'd buy a bottle from Florence, just to be nice.

As Florence continued to extoll the virtues of the wines she carried, Hannah realized that she'd learned a lot by simply coming to the Red Owl grocery today. If you weren't in a hurry, and you stood in an aisle long enough and listened to the conversations that were all around you, you might overhear an important clue. She would call this phenomenon the "unseen shopper trick." It was almost as good as the invisible waitress trick, when Hannah and Lisa walked around The Cookie Jar, refilling coffee cups, and their customers didn't seem to notice that they were there and went right on talking about private matters.

*If only Michelle were here!* Hannah thought as she accepted the wine that Florence had chosen for her and stood in the checkout line. Tricia and Michelle had stayed in touch, and Hannah's youngest sister would be the perfect person to elicit information from Tricia about exactly what she'd seen and heard in Tori's condo on the night of the murder. But Michelle was back at Macalester College and she wouldn't be back in Lake Eden until Thanksgiving vacation.

■ ■ ■ ■

As Hannah climbed up the outside staircase to her second-floor condo, she noticed that the living room window was open slightly. That was odd. She was almost certain she'd closed it this morning when she'd left for work, and Ross had left even earlier than she had.

Had someone broken into her condo? Should she call Mike or Bill? Hannah considered it for a moment and then shrugged off the idea. If someone had broken into her condo through the window, the window would be broken, or it would, at least, have been opened wide enough to admit a human body. A burglar certainly wouldn't have taken the time to replace the screen, and since Moishe didn't have opposable thumbs and couldn't open the window, either Ross had come home in the middle of the day and opened it, or she had left it open this morning.

As she approached the vicinity of the open window, a delicious aroma floated out to greet her. Chocolate. It just had to be melted chocolate. She was sure of it. And under the heady chocolate aroma was a hint of chicken and onions from the Chicken

Stroganoff she'd started in the crockpot this morning. How very strange! It was almost as if someone was inside her condo, working in her kitchen, making something for dessert!

"Rrrowww!"

Hannah started to smile as she heard Moishe yowl inside the condo. He must have spotted her coming up the stairs. It didn't sound like a frightened or anxious yowl, so she stopped worrying about intruders or break-ins.

When she reached the landing, she pulled out her keys and was just moving forward to unlock the door when it opened and Moishe jumped out, nearly knocking her over.

"Sorry!" a familiar voice said. "I should have warned you that I was going to open the door. I hope you don't mind, but I used the key you gave me and came right in."

It was Michelle and Hannah began to smile. "Of course I don't mind. That's why I gave you the key in the first place. When did you get here?"

"About an hour and a half ago. I had Lonnie drop me off here and I hope that's all right. I can stay with Mother and Doc if you don't want company."

Hannah stared at her youngest sister in

surprise. "Why wouldn't I want company?"

"I told you last night. You just got married and I thought you might want to be alone with Ross."

"Don't be silly. We have a guest room and you're a perfect guest. You're more than welcome to stay with us."

"That's great, but . . . maybe you'd better check with Ross to make sure he feels the same way? Mother and Doc have all sorts of empty bedrooms and I really don't want to cause any problems."

Hannah thought about that for a moment. "I'm sure Ross will want you to stay with us, but if it makes you feel better, I'll call him to make sure. What are you doing here in Lake Eden? I thought you weren't coming home until Thanksgiving break."

"I wasn't, but my one-act was a smash hit with the audience and with my professor, too. He was so pleased, he gave me permission to come back and direct the Lake Eden Players. They've only got a couple of weeks before they open their Thanksgiving play and with Tori gone, they're going to need someone to direct them."

Hannah began to smile. "I think I see Mother's fine touch in that idea. Am I right?"

"You're right. Mother called my professor

and asked him if I could come back here to direct the Thanksgiving play for the Lake Eden Players. He checked with the college and he called me a couple of hours ago to tell me that I could get independent study credit if I wanted to do it."

Hannah reached out to hug her sister. "That's just wonderful, Michelle. I'm sure you'll do a really good job."

"That's not all." Michelle gave a smug smile. "From what I've heard about Tori's abrasiveness from a couple of my friends in the Lake Eden Players, there are bound to be suspects in the group."

Hannah laughed. "So you want to be my mole by directing the Lake Eden Players?"

"Don't call me a mole. Dad showed me one once, and they're ugly with those big feet and those tiny little eyes. I prefer to think of myself as an undercover agent. I know that I'm a good director, Hannah. I promise you that I'll do a good job with their play."

"I never doubted that for a moment."

"Then call Ross and make sure it's okay if I stay here. Mother says I can use her car so transportation won't be a problem. And don't try to talk Ross into it. I don't want to stay here if he doesn't want me."

"I'll check with him right after I taste one

of those chocolate goodies you're baking," Hannah promised. "They smell delicious."

"I hope so. I got the recipe from the mother of a student in my one-act play. She sent a box of them to our dress rehearsal and they were really good! They're a no-bake dessert so they're really easy to make."

Hannah followed Michelle to the kitchen and sighed as Michelle took a pan from the refrigerator. "Are they like brownies?"

"A little. I'd describe them as a cross between brownies and candy. They're not really firm enough yet, but I can cut one from the edge of the pan."

A moment later, Hannah took her first bite of the brownie that was like candy. "Decadent!" she pronounced as she sat down at the kitchen table. "Now the only thing I'm missing is . . ."

"No, you're not," Michelle interrupted Hannah by setting a mug of black coffee down in front of her.

"Perfect. Thanks, Michelle," Hannah took a sip and smiled in enjoyment. "This dessert is so rich, I really needed coffee."

"That's what I thought the first time I tasted it. And it's so easy to make." Michelle gestured toward the slow cooker on the counter. "What are you making? And who's coming for dinner?"

"It's a chicken dish I decided I'd try. I'm calling it Chicken Stroganoff and I just hope it's going to be good."

"It smells great and I know it'll be good if you made it."

"Thanks for the vote of confidence. If it's not good, will you run out to the Corner Tavern for burgers? Mike and Norman are joining us for dinner. They said they had a wedding present to give us. And now that you're here, Mike will probably bring Lonnie, too."

"Great. If Lonnie comes, that'll make six. And of course I'll run out to the Corner Tavern for burgers, except I'm pretty sure we won't need them. Do you think you have enough of your Chicken Stroganoff for six? Or is that a stupid question?"

"I have enough. I'm going to serve it over egg noodles, and I picked up ingredients for a salad. I'm also making Cheesy Beer Muffins and we'll have your Brownie Candy for dessert."

"Beer muffins?" Michelle sounded puzzled. "I've never heard of muffins with beer before."

"Norman sent me the recipe. He got it from a dentist friend of his and I thought I'd try it."

"Is Norman bringing Cuddles?"

"I'm not sure."

"Why don't you call him and make sure he does. I picked up a big bag of salad shrimp and we'll never use all of them in your salad. And don't forget to touch base with Ross."

"I'll do it now," Hannah said, heading for the bedroom. Her conversation with Ross had to be private. If he didn't want Michelle to stay, they could think of some kind of excuse together so that she wouldn't feel rejected.

As Hannah shut the door and prepared to make her call in private, she crossed her fingers for luck. Then she uncrossed them again, punched in the number for Ross's cell phone, and crossed them again.

"Hannah!" Ross answered on the second ring. "Do you miss me?"

"Of course," Hannah said quickly, "but that's not why I called. Michelle's here. She took the bus to Lake Eden and I wondered if it was all right if she stayed in our guest room."

"Of course it is!"

The answer came immediately and Hannah breathed a sigh of relief. "Then you really don't mind? Michelle thought we might want to be alone."

"I don't mind at all, if you don't."

Hannah felt a little pang. Ross didn't mind if they weren't alone. Was that good? Or was that bad? She just wasn't sure. Before she could think better of it, she asked, "Don't you *want* to be alone with me?"

"Of course I do, Cookie!" Again the answer came immediately. "It's just that we have the rest of our lives to be alone with each other. Eventually, Michelle will get married and have children. And then she'll have her own family and she won't be able to spend as much time with you. I just think that you should enjoy your time with her while you can."

Hannah wanted to ask Ross if that's what had happened with his own family, but that was a conversation for another time. All she really knew about Ross's family was that he said he'd called them and they'd been unable to come to the wedding.

"Okay then," she said quickly. "If you're sure you don't mind, I'll tell Michelle that she's welcome to stay."

"I don't mind. As a matter of fact, I like having her stay with us. She takes some of the workload off you at The Cookie Jar and I know you want her to stick around so that she can help you find out who killed the mayor's sister."

"That's true. I could use Michelle's help. As a matter of fact, there's a friend of hers who could answer some of my questions. If Michelle goes with me to talk to her, we might learn more than I would alone."

"How long can Michelle stay in Lake Eden before she has to go back to college?"

"Two weeks and maybe a little more. Michelle's filling in as the interim director of the Lake Eden Players. She's currently enrolled in an advanced directing class and her professor is giving her college credit for helping out here."

"That's even better. The mayor's sister was the director, wasn't she?"

"That's right. Tori Bascomb directed the Lake Eden Players and she also directed the plays at Jordan High."

"If Michelle is working with the same people, she'll probably be able to find out some things about Tori Bascomb as a director. If she was tough on anyone in particular at rehearsals, if she had favorites, how she got along with the crew, that sort of thing. Oops. I'm needed for something. Hold on for just a second or two, Hannah."

Hannah frowned slightly as Ross put the phone down with a thunk and said something she couldn't quite hear to a colleague.

Then the phone thunked again as he picked it up.

"Sorry about that. I've got to go, Hannah. I'll be home around six."

"Good. Mike, Norman, and maybe Lonnie are coming to dinner. Mike and Norman are bringing a wedding present for us."

"Okay, sounds good. I love you, Cookie."

And then, before Hannah could tell him that she loved him too, Ross ended the call with a click.

# BROWNIE CANDY

DO NOT preheat oven. This dessert needs NO baking!

1 cup *(2 sticks, 8 ounces, 1/2 pound)* salted butter, softened

1 cup cashew butter

1 pound powdered *(confectioners)* sugar

1 and 1/2 cups finely crushed vanilla wafers *(I used Nabisco Nilla wafers)*

1 cup semi-sweet or milk chocolate chips *(6-ounce by weight bag is fine)*

**Hannah's 1st Note: Take the 2 sticks of butter out of the refrigerator, unwrap them, and put them in a covered mixing bowl the night before you want to make this Brownie Candy. They'll be nice and soft in the morning.**

**Hannah's 2nd Note: I chop my vanilla wafers in the food processor with the steel blade in an on-and-off motion. If you don't have a food processor, put them in a sealable plastic bag and crush them with a rolling pin. Just make sure they're finely crushed.**

In a medium-size mixing bowl, mix the salted butter with the cashew butter. A wooden spoon works well for this. Continue to mix until the mixture is smooth, creamy, and thoroughly incorporated.

Add the powdered sugar to your bowl. There's no need to sift unless it's got big lumps. Stir until the powdered sugar is thoroughly incorporated.

Measure out a cup and a half of crushed vanilla wafers and add them to your bowl. Mix until you have a homogenous mixture.

Spray the bottom of a 9-inch by 13-inch cake pan with Pam or another nonstick cooking spray. Alternatively, you can line the pan with heavy duty aluminum foil and spray that.

Dump the butter, cashew butter, powdered sugar, and crushed vanilla wafer mixture into the cake pan and pat it out as evenly as you can in the bottom.

Melt the chocolate chips in the top of a double boiler over MEDIUM heat or in a heavy metal saucepan on LOW heat, stirring constantly.

Alternatively, you can melt the chips in the microwave by placing them in a small microwave-safe bowl or Pyrex 2-cup measuring cup and heating them on HIGH for 1 minute. At the end of that time, let them stand in the microwave for 1 minute and then try to stir them smooth. If there are still lumps, heat them in 20-second intervals with 20-second standing times until you can stir them smooth.

With a heat resistant spatula, spread the melted chocolate on top of the mixture in the cake pan. Spread it out as evenly as possible.

Place the pan in the refrigerator until the Brownie Candy is firm. This will take at least 2 hours.

When your dessert is firm and the chocolate on top has hardened, take the cake pan out of the refrigerator and cut your dessert into brownie-sized pieces.

Yield: Approximately 24 to 36 pieces, depending on cutting size.

# CHAPTER EIGHT

Hannah was smiling as she carried the crockpot to the table. She'd tasted the Chicken Stroganoff and Noodles and it was delicious. The Cheesy Beer Muffins had also turned out to be very tasty and they had gone perfectly with the salad that Michelle had made for a first course.

Michelle followed Hannah with the huge bowl of egg noodles. They'd cooked them in boiling water and four chicken bouillon cubes to add extra flavor. Michelle had drained and buttered them so the noodles wouldn't stick together in the bowl and the entrée part of their dinner was complete.

"This is a real feast, honey," Ross said after he'd taken the first bite. "Please don't tell me that we're going to eat like this all the time."

Hannah frowned slightly. "Why? Is there something you don't like?"

"I like absolutely everything, and that's

the problem. If I eat like this every night, I'm going to gain hundreds of pounds."

Everyone at the table laughed and so did Hannah. At first she'd thought Ross might be serious, but he was only teasing her.

"Just wait for dessert," she told him. "Michelle made it and it's delicious. You might have to change to your sweatpants after dinner if you don't limit yourself to three pieces."

"What's for dessert?" Lonnie asked Michelle.

"Something we named Brownie Candy. One of the girls in my directing class brought it to rehearsal and I asked for the recipe."

"Sounds dangerous," Mike commented, ladling another helping of noodles on his plate. "I may have to stop with this helping or I'll be too full for dessert."

"Very funny," Hannah said with a smile. "You've never been too full for dessert in your whole life, have you?"

"My sister says she remembers the time I refused ice cream. And it was chocolate, my favorite flavor."

"Really?" Hannah asked.

"At least that's what my sister says. I was so young, I don't remember it."

That earned Mike a laugh, but Hannah

noticed that Norman was quiet. "Is there something wrong, Norman? You haven't said much all evening."

Norman shook his head. "It's probably nothing, but I'm going to take Cuddles to Doctor Bob's office tomorrow. She's been sleeping a lot lately."

"Maybe Cuddles is recovering from all that chasing she did with Moishe," Hannah suggested. "She's not used to having another cat in the house and they probably played all day while you were gone."

"Maybe. But I'm going to take her in anyway. Cuddles likes Dr. Bob. She's due for her annual checkup anyway and I'd feel terrible if something were wrong and I ignored the warning signs."

"You're right," Hannah agreed. "I wouldn't want to take any chances with Moishe, either. He means the world to me."

"I thought *I* meant the world to you!" Ross jumped into the conversation. "Don't tell me that I come in second to a cat!"

Hannah turned quickly to look at him. He'd sounded slightly upset, but there was the hint of a grin on his face and she assumed that he was kidding. "Moishe's not just a cat. He's a fur person. And you mean the world to me, too. But don't ask me to choose between you and Moishe. That's something that I would never do."

Slightly too late, Hannah caught the pained expression on Norman's face. She knew that he was remembering how she had given Cuddles a home when his fiancée, Doctor Bev, had pretended to be allergic to cats. She reached out to squeeze his hand to show him how sorry she was that she'd spoken without thinking, and he gave her a smile to say that all was forgiven.

"I'm going down to the car to get your wedding present out of the trunk," Norman announced, standing up and heading for the door.

"Wait and I'll come with you," Mike said quickly. "It's pretty heavy."

"Did you bring us a popcorn machine?" Hannah asked, remembering the one Norman had bought for his own media room.

Norman shook his head. "No, but it's something just as good. I think you're really going to like it."

Ross and Lonnie cleared the table while Hannah put on the coffee and Michelle cut her Brownie Candy for dessert. By the time Mike and Norman came back in, everything was ready for the final course.

"Wow!" Ross exclaimed as the two men carried in a large box. "It's huge!"

"It's not as big as it looks," Mike told him

as they set the box in the middle of the living room.

"Mike's right," Norman agreed. "A lot of it's packing. It had to be shipped here from a warehouse in California. Why don't you open it now, Hannah? Then Mike and I can tell you more about it over dessert."

Hannah turned to Ross. "Come on. Since it's our wedding present, we should open it together."

She cut the tape and Ross pulled up the flaps on the large cardboard box. Together, they lifted out mounds of packing material until they reached the smaller box inside. Ross lifted it out and set it on the rug, and Hannah bent down to read the legend on the side. "RoboVac," she read aloud. And then she turned to Mike and Norman with a puzzled expression. "Now I know what it's called, but I still don't know what it is."

"I do," Ross said, smiling at her as they returned to the table. "It's a robotic vacuum cleaner." He turned to Mike and Norman. "I'm right, aren't I?"

"You are," Norman told him. "I know how Hannah hates to vacuum, so Mike and I got you this. Now she'll never have to vacuum the rug again."

"I didn't know you hated to vacuum," Ross said to Hannah.

"I've *always* hated to vacuum. I don't mind other housekeeping chores, but vacuuming is so boring."

"That's exactly how I feel about it," Norman said, smiling at her. "And that's one of the reasons that I bought a RoboVac for myself." He got up to get the owner's manual out of the bottom of the box and handed it to Ross. "You can program it for any time of day and any combination of days. The only problem I have with it is that my house is two stories and I have to carry it upstairs."

"Why don't you get another one that you keep upstairs?" Ross suggested.

Norman considered that for a moment. "Actually . . . that's a very good idea. I could run them both simultaneously and be done with the vacuuming in half the time. Thanks for thinking of that, Ross. I'll order a second one tomorrow."

"How about you, Mike?" Ross turned to him. "Do you have a RoboVac?"

"Not me. I hired Marjorie Hanks to clean my place and she brings her own vacuum."

"How about you, Lonnie?" Ross asked.

Lonnie shook his head. "I don't need to clean my place. I still live with my parents." He turned to look at Michelle. "I'm thinking about getting my own apartment,

136

though."

Hannah glanced at her sister. Michelle was beginning to blush. Since her youngest sister wasn't the type to show her embarrassment, Hannah decided she'd better have a heart-to-heart with Michelle later to find out exactly what was going on.

Of course everyone loved the Brownie Candy and all of them complimented Michelle for making such a delicious dessert. Hannah put on a second pot of coffee and when that was almost empty, Norman turned to Ross. "I'll help you with the vacuum settings if you want me to."

"Me, too," Mike offered.

"Sounds good to me." Ross pushed back from the table and stood up.

"You're only having two pieces of Brownie Candy?" Hannah asked Ross.

"Yes, for now. Don't take them off the table, Cookie. Just as soon as we take care of the RoboVac settings, I'll have another with a second cup of coffee." Ross stopped at Michelle's chair and gave her a little hug. "They're really good, Michelle. You and your sister are incredible bakers!"

Hannah smiled at Ross, even though his back was to her and she knew he couldn't see it. Ross really did like Michelle and he said that he didn't mind at all if she stayed with them. Since Hannah loved having her youngest sister stay with her, the fact that Ross approved of the arrangement made her very happy.

"I'd better cut some more of that Brownie Candy," Michelle said.

"And I'll help you," Lonnie replied, "I'll bet you that Ross eats more than one more piece and I figure Mike is good for two."

"How about you?" Michelle asked him.

"I'll have another one for sure. Ross is right. You and Hannah are incredible bakers."

"Just sit and relax, Hannah," Lonnie told her as Hannah made a move to get up from the table. "Michelle and I have got this covered. Besides, those three," he gestured toward the three men huddled over the RoboVac, "might need a referee if they start arguing about how to set the vacuum."

"Do you think it's a case of *Too many cooks spoil the broth*?" Hannah asked him, repeating one of her great-grandmother Elsa's favorite sayings.

"It could be," Michelle said quickly. "You know how men are with tools and Mike just picked up the wrench that came in the tool pouch."

"The box says, SOME ASSEMBLY REQUIRED," Lonnie pointed out, "and Norman just dumped out some vacuum parts on the rug."

"Then I'm right," Hannah admitted. "Ross just picked up a wheel and now Norman is paging through the instruction book. I'd better keep an eye on them to make sure we don't have a replay of Dad, Uncle Ed, and the ten-speed bicycle."

"What did they do?" Lonnie asked Michelle.

"I don't know. I was probably too young to remember. Ask Hannah."

Hannah chuckled a bit at the memory. "Andrea wanted a ten-speed bike for her birthday and Mother and Dad decided to get it for her. Dad owned the hardware store at the time, so he ordered the bike through one of his vendors. Unfortunately, he didn't order it assembled."

"Uh-oh!" Lonnie shook his head. "I did that once and tried to put it together myself."

"What happened?" Michelle asked him.

"I ended up paying the guy at the bike shop fifty bucks to take it apart and put it together the right way for me. And I could have ordered it assembled for only twenty-five dollars more."

Michelle laughed. "So you paid an extra twenty-five because you tried to save money?"

"That's right." Lonnie turned to Hannah. "Did the same thing happen with your dad and your uncle, Hannah?"

"In a way, but it was much worse. Michelle and Andrea were upstairs sleeping and Mother and I went into the den to watch television while the men worked on the bike."

"And they couldn't assemble it?" Michelle guessed.

"Oh, they could. And they did. It took them hours and several pots of coffee, but when they called Mother and me in to see it, it looked beautiful. It was pink and it had something in the paint that made it glitter. It was exactly what Andrea had wished for."

Michelle looked puzzled. "Then it worked out all right?"

"Not exactly. It was perfect until Andrea tried to ride it. That was when she discovered that she couldn't change gears while the bike was moving."

"But . . . that's when you want to change gears," Lonnie pointed out.

"I know. Dad returned the bike to the vendor and asked for a replacement."

"Assembled?" Michelle asked, beginning to grin.

"Oh, yes. This time it was assembled. And

it wasn't until years later that Mother showed me the parts that she took out of the garbage the next morning, the parts that Dad and Uncle Ed had decided weren't necessary to install."

"But didn't Mother ever say anything to Dad about it?" Michelle asked.

"No, never. She only showed the parts to me after Dad died. She said she didn't want to embarrass him."

"She must have loved him a lot," Lonnie said.

Michelle nodded. "You're right. It had to be love. We all know Mother, and it must have just about killed her to keep quiet about it for all those years."

After Lonnie and Michelle had gone into the kitchen, Hannah turned to watch the three men again. The wheels were on the RoboVac, but they were still working on something else that connected to the bottom of the machine.

As she watched them work, Hannah began to smile. It was good to see Norman, Mike, and Ross get along so well together. Everything was working out perfectly between her three favorite men.

# SLOW COOKER CHICKEN STROGANOFF AND NOODLES

(This recipe is for a 5-quart slow cooker.)

1 medium onion, diced *(I used a Maui sweet onion)*

3 pounds boneless, skinless chicken half-breasts *(9 or 10 pieces)*

1 can *(8 ounces)* mushroom stems and pieces, drained

1/2 teaspoon garlic salt

1/2 teaspoon onion salt

1/2 teaspoon regular salt

1/4 teaspoon ground black pepper *(it's always better if you grind it yourself)*

1 can *(10 and 1/2 ounces)* condensed cream of mushroom soup *(undiluted — I used Campbell's)*

1 can *(10 and 1/2 ounces)* condensed cream of celery soup *(undiluted — I used Campbell's)*

1 packet *(1 ounce)* dry Ranch Dressing mix *(I used Hidden Valley Original Dressing Mix)*

8-ounce package cream cheese, cut into cubes *(not whipped cream cheese — I used Philadelphia brick cream cheese in the silver package)*

1 cup *(8 ounces)* sour cream *(to add right*

**before serving)**

Hot cooked and buttered noodles of your choice *(cook right before serving)*

Spray the inside of the slow cooker with Pam or another nonstick cooking spray. *(This will prevent sticking and make it easier to wash the crockpot later.)*
Place the diced onion in the bottom of the crockpot.
Arrange the chicken on top of the diced onion.
Plug in the crockpot, turn it on LOW heat and let it cook for 5 to 6 hours.
When the chicken is fork tender, turn off the crockpot, put on potholders, and lift the crock out of the crockpot. Set it on a cold burner on the stovetop.
Take the top off the crockpot and let the chicken cool for a few minutes.
Remove the chicken breasts, one by one, and place them on a platter.
Set a large strainer in a bowl and, again using potholders, pour the liquid and onions into the strainer.
Reserve the liquid for later use and return the onions caught by the strainer to the crock.
Cut the chicken on the platter into bite-

size pieces.

Open the can of mushroom stems and pieces, drain off the liquid and add it to the onions in the crockpot.

Return the pieces of chicken to the crockpot.

Sprinkle the chicken with the garlic salt, onion salt, regular salt, and black pepper. *(You'll taste this later to see if you have to further adjust the seasonings.)*

Open the can of condensed cream of mushroom soup. Use a rubber spatula to remove the soup from the can and add it to the crockpot.

Open the can of condensed cream of celery soup. Again, use the spatula to add it to the crockpot.

Sprinkle the packet of dry Ranch Dressing mix over the top.

Add the cubes of cream cheese.

**Hannah's 1st Note: No, I didn't forget the sour cream, but if you add it now, it will lose its texture. You will add the sour cream right before you serve the stroganoff.**

Using your rubber spatula, stir everything up.

Return the top to the crock, replace the crock in the base, and turn it on LOW heat.

Let this yummy mixture cook for 30

144

minutes or longer. At the end of that time, taste the sauce and adjust the seasonings. If you think the sauce is too thick to pour over noodles, stir in enough of the cooking broth you saved to make it the right consistency.

**Hannah's 2nd Note: Don't worry if your company is late. This stroganoff will keep on low for 2 hours or longer.**

When your company comes, fill a large pot with water, saving room for that cooking broth you reserved earlier. It will add flavor to the noodles. If you want even more flavor, add a couple of chicken bouillon cubes to the water.

Follow the directions on the noodle package to cook your noodles.

When your noodles are cooked, drain them and toss them with butter. Then transfer them to a serving bowl.

Add the cup of sour cream to the crockpot, stir it in, and you're ready to serve.

**Hannah's 3rd Note: If you don't feel like dishing up plates for everyone, let your guests serve themselves from the noodle bowl and the crockpot.**

Yield: 8 to 10 servings unless you plan to invite Ross, Norman, Mike, and Lonnie. Then you'd better double the recipe and prepare two crockpots.

# CHEESY BEER MUFFINS

Preheat oven to 350 degrees F., rack in the middle position.

4 cups flour-based muffin mix *(I used Bisquick)*
12-ounce bottle or can of pale lager beer *(I used Budweiser)*
1 cup finely shredded sharp cheddar cheese *(I used Tillamook sharp cheddar)*

**Hannah's 1st Note: I've used finely-shredded Kraft Mexican cheese or Kraft finely-shredded Italian cheese in these muffins when I didn't have the cheddar cheese. It works just fine.**

Measure the muffin mix by filling the cup measure and leveling it off with a knife. DO NOT pack it down in the cup when you measure it.

Place the muffin mix in a large mixing bowl or the bowl of an electric mixer.

**Hannah's 2nd Note: I usually use my stand mixer to make these muffins, but you can also mix them up by hand.**

Pour in the bottle or can of beer, wait a bit for it to stop foaming, and then mix it in on LOW speed. Make sure that the muffin mix and the beer are combined, but don't worry if your mixture has a few lumps.

**Hannah's 3rd Note: If the beer you're using is cold, let it warm up a bit before you pour it into the muffin mix. If you add it cold, the baking time will be longer by several minutes.**

Take the mixing bowl out of the mixer and stir in the half-cup of cheese by hand.

Spray two 12-cup muffin or cupcake pans with Pam or another nonstick cooking spray. Alternatively, you can line the muffin cups with double cupcake papers.

Fill the muffin cups three-quarters full, distributing the muffin batter as evenly as you can.

**Hannah's 4th Note: Sometimes, when I bake these muffins, I add a 4-ounce can of well-drained Ortega diced green chilies to the batter before I stir in the cheese. If Mike is coming to your house for dinner, you can also add a couple squirts of Slap Ya Mama hot sauce.**

**Hannah's 5th Note: If I have any shredded cheese left over, I sometimes sprinkle a little on top of the muffins before I bake them. Don't sprinkle on too much cheese. Just sprinkle a bit to add visual interest.**

Bake your Cheesy Beer Muffins at 350 degrees F. for 15 to 18 minutes or until the tops are golden brown and a long toothpick or thin skewer inserted in the center of a muffin comes out clean with no muffin batter clinging to it. *(Mine took exactly 16 minutes.)*

Remove your muffins from the oven and set the muffin pans on a cold stovetop burner or a wire rack. If you sprayed your muffin cups, let them cool in the pan for 1 to 2 minutes and then tip them out of the muffin cups and place them on a wire rack to cool for another 5 minutes. If you used double cupcake papers to line the muffin cups, let them cool in the muffin pan for 1 to 2 minutes. Then pull them out of the pan by the edges of the paper liners, place them on a wire rack, and let them cool for an additional 5 minutes.

You can serve these muffins warm or cold. *(I think they're better warm, but Mike also likes them cold and spread with cream cheese for breakfast the next morning.)* If you serve them warm, place them in a napkin-lined basket, cover them with a second napkin, and serve them with plenty of softened, salted butter.

**Lisa's Note: Herb loves these muffins with homemade chili or beef stew. He also enjoys eating them with tomato soup. Sometimes I brush the top with**

**butter and garlic salt while they're warm.**

Yield: 2 dozen beery, cheesy muffins that your guests will love.

# CHAPTER NINE

Hannah said good night to their guests and joined Michelle in the kitchen. She glanced up at the clock and realized that it was only eight-thirty. "Do you think Tricia is still at work?"

"Tricia?" Michelle asked, looking puzzled. "I think so. I talked to her about a week ago. She said she was on nights and her shift didn't end until they closed."

"And she's still working out at the Lake Eden Inn?"

Michelle nodded. "She really likes it. She says Sally's a dream to work for and Dick's always really good about giving her breaks when she needs them."

"She's a cocktail waitress isn't she?"

"Yes. She used to work as a waitress in the restaurant, but she says the tips for cocktail waitresses are even better. Why do you want to know Tricia's schedule?"

"Because I need to talk to her and I think

it'll go better if you're there. I'm not even sure if she remembers me."

"Of course she does. She mentioned your Butterscotch Crunch Cookies the last time I talked to her."

"Great! I've got some in the freezer. I'll get them out and then let's go and talk to her."

Michelle grabbed Hannah's hand as she headed for the freezer. "Wait!"

"What?"

"How about Ross?"

Hannah felt an immediate stab of guilt. She'd forgotten all about the fact that Ross was in their bedroom, changing into comfortable, television-watching clothes. "I'll go ask him if he wants to go for a drink at the Lake Eden Inn with us."

Ross was sitting on the bed, putting on his slippers, when Hannah opened the door to the master bedroom. "Hi, honey," she said, coming in and closing the door.

"Hello, Cookie. I took a quick shower and I'm almost ready to vegetate in one of those reclining couch chairs in front of our incredible home theater."

"I can see that," Hannah said with a smile, noticing that he was wearing one of his monogrammed sweatsuits.

Ross frowned slightly. "That's what I told

151

you I was going to do. It's okay with you, isn't it?"

"Of course it's okay!" Hannah said quickly. "I'd change too, but . . ." she stopped speaking, not exactly sure how to go on.

"But what, honey?"

"But I have a chance to talk to a friend of Michelle's who might know something about Tori Bascomb's murder."

"Right *now*?"

Hannah noticed that the frown on her husband's face had grown a bit deeper. "Yes, but that's okay. It can wait until tomorrow. I just thought you might want to go out to the Lake Eden Inn for a drink. She's a cocktail waitress out there and she doesn't get off shift until they close."

"Oh, Cookie! I'd go with you in a flash, but I've got an early call tomorrow. And to tell the truth, I can barely keep my eyes open. It's a little hard to get back into the work routine after that wonderful week we had together on the cruise."

"I know," Hannah told him. "I feel the same way. I got really tired at work today, but then I got my second wind. Don't worry about it, honey. I can always talk to her sometime tomorrow."

Ross nodded, but he didn't look happy.

"Yes, but this *is* a *murder* investigation. I really should be helping you with things like that, but . . . to tell you the truth, I'm just too beat tonight and I'm afraid I wouldn't be any help to you at all. Of course I'll go with you if you really need me, but . . ." he stopped speaking and began to look worried. "Tell me the truth, Cookie. This person you want to see isn't a suspect, is she?"

"No, not at all!" Hannah hurried to reassure him. "She's got an air-tight alibi. It's just that she may have some information I need."

"You said she's a friend of Michelle's?"

"Yes. They went to high school together."

"I hate to ask this, I know Michelle's had a long day, too. But . . . will she go to see her friend with you?"

"Absolutely. She's already offered. I just thought that you might like to go along with us."

"Then you won't be upset if I stay here and fall asleep in front of our TV?"

Hannah laughed. "I won't be upset. I used to fall asleep in front of the television all the time. I'd start a movie, fall asleep in the middle, and when I woke up there'd be something else on." She sat down on the bed next to Ross and put her arms around

153

him. "It's okay, Ross. You stay here and relax. Michelle and I will drive out there, find out what we can from her friend, and be home as fast as we can."

"No hurry. I'll probably fall asleep the moment you two leave. Those couches are really comfortable. Drive safe, Cookie. Will you promise to wake me when you get home?"

Hannah smiled. "It's a promise."

"Good. I'll probably be sleeping through some late-night movie with Moishe."

That comment earned Ross another hug. It was good to know that she wasn't leaving Moishe alone. Ross seemed to genuinely like Moishe and it was clear that Moishe liked him, too.

A country-western song was playing on the speakers when Hannah and Michelle entered the bar at the Lake Eden Inn. The stools at the bar were fully occupied, but that was fine with Hannah. She wanted a table anyway, so that Tricia could wait on them. She gave Dick, who was shaking some colorful cocktail, a wave of greeting and headed for the table in the corner with Michelle following closely behind her.

It took a moment, but then Tricia saw them. She smiled, picked up an order pad, and hurried to their table. "Hi, Michelle." And then she turned to Hannah. "Hello, Hannah. I didn't get a chance afterwards, Hannah, but I've got to compliment you on your wedding. It was the most exciting wedding I've ever been to. I really enjoyed it!"

"Thank you, Tricia," Hannah said politely, not mentioning that she'd rather not remember the state she'd been in when she'd arrived at Holy Redeemer Lutheran Church.

"So how's married life?" Tricia asked her.

"It's good, Tricia," Hannah responded, giving her a smile.

Tricia looked only slightly older than the Jordan High student Hannah remembered, the girl Michelle had brought home from school for Hannah's cookies. The only change Hannah noticed was that that now, Tricia wore her hair piled up in a loose knot on the top of her head and she was wearing makeup. She was no longer the freshly-scrubbed high school student whose mother didn't allow her to wear any makeup except lipstick to school.

"You look really good, Tricia," Hannah complimented her, "but you're making me feel old. You're all grown up."

"So is Michelle," Tricia pointed out.

"Yes, but it happened gradually. I was

around to see her grow up. I don't think I've spent any time with you since you two graduated from high school. How's the world treating you, Tricia?"

"Good. Very good. I'm engaged, Hannah." Tricia pulled an engagement ring from the pocket of her cocktail waitress apron and placed it on her left hand. "I don't usually wear it at work because if the guys know I'm engaged, the tips aren't as good."

"Who's the lucky guy?" Hannah asked her.

"Lonnie Murphy's cousin, Sean. We met last year and things . . ." Tricia paused to smile. "Well, you know how it goes. We haven't set a date yet, but maybe next year when both of us make enough money to afford a really nice place."

"Sean's working for Cyril as a mechanic," Michelle explained to Hannah. "I introduced them and they hit it off right away." Michelle reached for the package of cookies that Hannah had brought with her. "Look what Hannah brought for you, Tricia. They're your favorite Butterscotch Crunch Cookies."

"Oh, wow!" Tricia gave Hannah a huge smile and Hannah could see the kid lurking behind the grown woman. "Thanks, Hannah! I just love these cookies! My mom calls me every time she buys them at The Cookie

Jar, and I drive right over to get some before they're gone. Thanks a lot for bringing them for me."

"You're welcome," Hannah said, and then she made an executive decision. The interlude for small talk was over and it was time to get down to business. "On a serious note, I really need to talk to you about Tori."

"Okay. Just let me ask Dick if I can take my break now. Then maybe I can come and sit with you. Did you want something to drink? Or did you just come for information?"

"We want something to drink, too," Michelle told her. "I'll have a glass of white wine."

"The same for me," Hannah said quickly.

"How about an appetizer? Sally made Cheese Pops."

"Cheese Pops?" Hannah was immediately interested. "What are those?"

"They're little cheese balls made out of bleu cheese and cream cheese. Sally rolls them in minced bacon and then she sticks in a salted pretzel as a handle. Would you like to try some?"

"I would," Hannah responded quickly. "Sally's appetizers are always wonderful."

"I would, too." Michelle added. "Thanks for asking, Tricia."

When Tricia hurried off to the bar, Hannah turned to Michelle. "Did you play matchmaker with Tricia and Lonnie's cousin?"

"In a way, I did. I usually don't do anything like that, but Tricia broke up with the boyfriend she'd been seeing since high school and I thought she needed to meet someone new. Sean's nice. He went to a couple of places with Lonnie and me, and he didn't have a girlfriend, so . . . well, they're both really hardworking people and they were both single and . . . well . . . you know."

"I *do* know, and it seems to have worked out just fine. Tricia looks good, almost the same as she did in high school except for her hairstyle and makeup."

They both watched as Tricia came back to their table with a tray of drinks. She had white wine for Michelle, white wine for Hannah, and water for all three of them.

"Your appetizers are almost ready. They're just rolling them in the bacon pieces and then they'll be up. And Dick says I can take my break as soon as I deliver them."

"Can you sit with us then?" Michelle asked her.

"I'm not supposed to sit with the customers, but Dick says it's okay because it's you guys. I just have to keep my eye on the two other tables and serve them if they need anything while we're talking. I stopped at my tables to tell them where I'd be and I told them to just wave at me and I'd come right over."

"I'll help you watch your tables," Michelle offered. "I can see them from where I'm sitting."

"Thanks, Michelle."

Tricia left for the kitchen and Hannah took a sip of her wine. She hoped that Tricia could give her more information about her visit to Tori's condo on the night of her murder.

"Tricia was glad to see you," Michelle commented. "I'm almost positive that she'll tell you everything she knows."

"I hope so. I really want to catch Tori's killer for Mother. She's terribly upset about losing Tori."

Tricia came back almost immediately with a tray of Cheese Pops. "Aren't they darling?" she asked.

"They are," Hannah agreed, reaching for one of the Cheese Pops. She took a bite and chewed happily as the flavors of bleu cheese, cream cheese, and bacon bits exploded in her mouth. They were the perfect complement to white wine and she made a mental note to tell Sally just that the next time she saw her. Sally was good about sharing recipes and Hannah firmly intended to ask her for this one!

"I can tell you like the Cheese Pops," Tricia said, watching as Hannah took another bite. "They're experimenting with different cheeses in the kitchen. Sally told me that the cream cheese is a constant because it adds the smooth texture to the inside, but they've also made them with cheddar. The ones rolled in bacon bits look red, don't they?"

"They do. They're redder than I'd expect them to be."

"That's because Sally mixes in some Hungarian paprika with the bacon bits. Not enough to give it too much flavor, but just a little. And she rolls the cheddar ones in chopped parsley and that makes them green on the outside. She told me she does that so her customers can tell them apart."

"Makes sense to me," Hannah said. "I hope she has a tray of them at her Christmas party. The red and the green would be nice."

Tricia began to look excited. "You're right! Red and green are the Christmas colors and they'd be perfect for the party! Do you mind if I tell her?"

"Please do. Sit down, Tricia. I really need

to talk to you."

Tricia pulled out a chair and sat down. "I know you want to ask me about Tori. Since your mother found her, you're probably investigating her murder."

"That's right," Hannah said. "I heard you were there earlier that night for an acting lesson."

Tricia sighed heavily. "I was, and I guess all that work I did will be wasted now. Without Tori, the Lake Eden Players won't be able to put on their Thanksgiving play."

"Oh, yes they will!" Michelle announced. "That's why I'm here, Tricia. I'm a theater major at Macalester and I just finished an advanced class in directing. My professor sent me here to help you out."

"You mean, *you'll* be our director?"

"That's right."

"Fantastic! At least you'll be a lot nicer than Tori was. She could be really nasty if she didn't like your reading of a line."

Michelle laughed. "I've heard that . . . and I promise I won't be nasty. Critical, yes. Nasty, never. Can you get everyone to come to a rehearsal tomorrow?"

"You bet I can! But it has to be at one in the afternoon. Everybody in the play re-arranged their work schedule so they had from one to three free."

"That sounds fine with me," Michelle said, turning to Hannah for confirmation. "You won't need me at The Cookie Jar during that time, will you?"

Hannah shook her head. "That's not a problem, Michelle. I've got Lisa, Marge, Jack, and Aunt Nancy. You don't need to work at The Cookie Jar at all if you don't want to."

"I want to. It's fun. But I know it's generally slow between the lunch rush and the afternoon coffee break rush."

"The timing couldn't be better," Hannah agreed, "but it really doesn't matter what time you schedule rehearsals. We can get along whenever you choose. The play is very important to the community. It's practically a tradition to go to a performance during the Thanksgiving holidays." She turned to Tricia. "Now that we have *that* settled, will you tell me about the last time you saw Tori?"

"Sure thing. I feel a little guilty, you know? I was so mad at her for cutting my lesson short. And now . . ." she took a sip of her water, ". . . and now I realize that I was probably saying awful things to my mother about Tori when she was being murdered!"

"You had no way of knowing that was going to happen," Hannah said quickly. "And

162

I don't blame you for being angry. Do you know why Tori did that?"

"I . . . um . . ." Tricia stopped speaking and glanced around to make sure she wasn't being overheard. Since there was no one except Hannah and Michelle within earshot, she continued in a slightly lower voice. "I do know why, but I haven't told anybody except Mom."

"You can tell us," Michelle reassured her.

"OK, but please don't tell anyone else. He could really hurt me in this town, you know?"

"Start from the beginning, Tricia," Hannah advised. "And no, Michelle and I won't tell anyone what you're going to tell us."

"Not even Mike?"

"If it pertains to the investigation and if I think that Mike has to know, I'll have to . . . but I won't tell him *you* told me."

Tricia thought about that for a moment. "Okay. That's fair enough."

Hannah reached out to pat Tricia's hand. "I want you to start by telling me who you think could hurt you."

"It's . . ." Tricia stopped to glance around again. When she turned back to face them, there was real fear in her eyes. "It's Mayor Bascomb. *He* could hurt me!"

"Why?"

"Because I know he was going up to Tori's condo. And I know that Tori was really mad at him."

"Okay, Tricia," Hannah said, "Tell me how you know all this."

Tricia took another swallow of water and drew a deep breath. "I got to Tori's condo at exactly six o'clock. I know because I had my cell phone with me and I looked at the time before I knocked on her door. Tori didn't like it if I was early and she hated it if I was late so I always made sure that I was exactly on time for my lessons. Anyway, I knocked and she came right to the door. She told me to come in and we were just walking through the living room on our way to her studio when the telephone rang."

"What did she do then?" Michelle asked.

"She answered it and then she started to frown. *'Hold on!'* Tori said in that voice she used to order everyone around. She covered the mouthpiece of the phone, turned to me, and said that she had to take the call."

"But you didn't know who Tori was talking to at that point?" Hannah asked her.

"No, not then. Tori told me to go into the studio and rehearse my lines while she took the call."

"Is that what you did?" Michelle asked her.

"Well . . ." Tricia stopped and looked slightly guilty. "Not exactly. I did go in the studio and I even opened my play book to the right page, but then I heard her voice."

"You could hear her voice from the living room while you were in the studio?" Hannah questioned.

"Yes, because I'd left the door open a little. Maybe I shouldn't have, but she didn't tell me to close it. And that's when I realized that she was very angry with whoever was calling her."

"How close is the studio to the living room?" Hannah asked.

"It's just a couple of steps down the hall. I mean, it's not directly across the hallway, but close enough."

"Close enough for you to hear what Tori was saying?"

"Yes. You see, I probably shouldn't have, but she sounded so mad that I moved all the way to the door and listened. I didn't go out in the hall or anything, but I was right by the open door."

"And what did you hear?" Hannah queried.

"I heard Tori tell her caller to get lost, that she wasn't going to bail him out again. She said that she'd done it too many times before, and this time he could grow up and

165

handle things on his own."

"And you knew who it was then?" Michelle asked her.

"I didn't *know,* but I guessed. Everybody in town knows that Mayor Bascomb goes to his sister for help when his wife catches him with another woman."

"What else did you hear?" Hannah asked, being very careful not to censor Tricia in any way for eavesdropping on a private conversation.

"Mayor Bascomb must have argued with her, because Tori blew up. I mean, she really let him have it. I don't even want to repeat some of the things she said to him, but the upshot of it was . . . um . . . ."

"He ought to have more self-control?" Hannah provided the polite phrase.

"Yeah. That was it. She didn't put it quite that way, but that's what she meant."

"What happened then?" Michelle leaned forward because Tricia's voice had dropped even lower.

"She said, *'Listen to me, Ricky.'* And that's when I knew for sure who was on the other end of the line. *'You've cheated on Stephanie from the very beginning and this has got to stop!'* And then Mayor Bascomb must have said something, because Tori was quiet for a couple minutes."

166

"That was it?" Michelle asked. "Was that all you heard?"

"Oh, no." Tricia shook her head. "Tori told the mayor that she was putting a stop to his little escapades once and for all, except she didn't say escapades. She said . . . something else."

Hannah realized that even in the dim light in the bar, Tricia's face was turning bright pink with embarrassment. "It's okay, Tricia," she hurried to reassure her. "We don't need to know the exact words Tori used."

"Oh, good. But anyway, Tori told him she'd already taken steps to stop the drain on her life savings. She said he'd already used all of his inheritance on his little . . . um . . . escapades, and that she had already taken steps to cut him off."

"Oh, boy!" Michelle gasped. "Do you think she was serious?"

Tricia shrugged. "I don't know. I couldn't see her. And even if I'd been right there in the room with her, I might not have been able to tell. Tori was an award-winning actress. She could make anybody believe anything. She did say she'd seen a lawyer, though. And she told him that she'd drawn up a new will." Tricia stopped and gulped. "Do you think that's a motive for . . ."

Since Tricia seemed unable to complete

her sentence, Michelle jumped in. "Murder?"

"Yeah." Tricia sounded scared as she turned to Hannah. "Do you think I'm in danger, Hannah?"

Hannah reached out to pat her hand again. "No, you're fine, Tricia. No one's going to know that you're the one who told us this. The mayor doesn't know you overheard Tori's side of the conversation. Just don't tell anyone else and you should be fine."

"I won't tell another soul! The only reason I told you was because I felt guilty about being mad at Tori when she had all these problems. That wasn't very nice of me."

"You don't have to feel guilty," Michelle told her. "Tori doesn't know you were angry with her. And really, Tricia, it was a natural reaction. I would've been angry, too."

"Did Tori say anything else before she ended the conversation?" Hannah asked, bringing them back to the important matter at hand.

"She told the mayor to come over if he wanted to discuss it further, even though it wouldn't do him any good. And he must have said he was coming because she told him she'd cancel her acting lesson with me. And then Tori said that she could only see him for thirty minutes because she had another appointment that night."

"Do you think she did have another appointment?" Michelle asked.

"I don't know. I guess it could have been an excuse so the mayor wouldn't stay any longer than that."

Hannah nodded, but she had other suspicions. Tricia had left in time to be at her mother's house by six-thirty and the Barthels' farm was approximately twenty minutes from town. If Mayor Bascomb had visited Tori the night she was murdered, he would have left her condo by seven. Tori's appointment with M. Dumont was scheduled for seven forty-five that evening. It was possible the mayor had stayed longer than his allotted half hour and the screams and gunshot that Delores had heard had been caused by Mayor Bascomb. Of course, it was also possible that Tori had been alive when the mayor had left her and M. Dumont was the killer.

Hannah decided to think about all that later, and she turned to Tricia with a smile. "Thank you, Tricia. You've been very helpful. There's only one more thing I'd like to know."

"What's that?"

"Did you notice anything unusual in the studio that night?"

"Not really," Tricia said. "The studio looked the same as it always does and the stage was set up with a straight-back chair and a couch at the side."

"That wasn't unusual?" Hannah asked her.

"No. It's always that way . . . I knew Tori would want me to rehearse my scene the moment she came in, so I took my script down to the couch where she always sits and put it on the coffee table." Tricia stopped and sighed. "Tori's really tough about memorizing your lines. She doesn't want to see anyone even glancing at a script. I wanted her to know that I'd memorized everything, so I left my script down there."

"You said you put your script on the coffee table," Hannah repeated what Tricia had told her. "Was there anything else on the coffee table?"

Tori looked at her blankly for a moment and then she nodded. "Yes. Tori's clipboard was there. She has this clipboard with a battery-operated light on it to take notes while I rehearse."

"There was nothing on the table except Tori's lighted clipboard and your script?" Hannah asked, just to be certain.

"That's right. And right after I put down my script, I went over to the doorway so I could hear what Tori was saying on the phone." Tricia paused and looked up at Hannah. "Does what I told you help?"

"Yes. Thank you, Tricia."

"Then you know who did it?"

"Not yet," Hannah answered quickly. "But don't worry, Tricia. Sooner or later, I'll know."

# BUTTERSCOTCH CRUNCH COOKIES

Preheat oven to 350 degrees F., rack in the middle position.

The following recipe can be doubled if you wish. Do not, however, double the baking soda. Use one and a half teaspoons — 2 teaspoons is too much.

1 cup softened butter *(2 sticks, 1/2 pound, 8 ounces)*

2 cups white *(granulated)* sugar

3 Tablespoons molasses

2 teaspoons vanilla

1 teaspoon baking soda

2 beaten eggs *(just whip them up in a glass with a fork)*

2 cups crushed salted potato chips *(measure AFTER crushing) (I used regular, thin, unflavored, salted Lay's potato chips)*

2 and 1/2 cups all-purpose flour *(pack it down in the cup when you measure it)*

1 and 1/2 cups butterscotch chips *(I used Nestlé, a 10-ounce by weight bag, not quite 2 cups, but you can use the whole bag if you like lots of chips)*

**Lisa's 1st Note: The butter in this recipe should be at room temperature**

unless you have an un-insulated kitchen and it's winter in the Midwest. Then you'd better soften it a little.

**Hannah's 1st Note:** 5 to 6 cups of whole potato chips will crush into about 2 cups. Crush them by hand in a plastic bag, not with a food processor. They should be the size of coarse gravel when they're crushed.

Mix the softened butter with the white sugar and the molasses. Beat them until the mixture is light and fluffy, and the molasses is completely mixed in.

Add the vanilla and baking soda. Mix them in thoroughly.

If you haven't already done so, break the eggs into a glass and whip them up with a fork. Add them to your bowl and mix until they're thoroughly incorporated.

Put your potato chips in a closeable plastic bag. Seal it carefully *(you don't want crumbs all over your counter)* and place the bag on a flat surface. Get out your rolling pin and roll it over the bag, crushing the potato chips inside. Do this until the pieces resemble coarse gravel. You can also crush them with your hands if you prefer.

Measure out 2 cups of crushed potato chips and mix them into the dough in your bowl.

Add one cup of flour and mix it in.

Add the second cup of flour and mix thoroughly.

Add the final half cup of flour and mix that in.

Measure out a cup and a half of butterscotch chips unless you want to use the whole bag. Add the chips to your cookie dough. If you're using an electric mixer, mix them in at the LOW speed. You can also take the bowl out of the mixer and stir in the chips by hand.

Let the dough sit on the counter while you prepare your cookie sheets.

Spray your cookie sheets with Pam or another nonstick cooking spray, or line them with parchment paper, leaving little "ears" at the top and bottom. That way, when your cookies are baked, you can pull the paper, baked cookies and all, over onto a wire rack to cool.

Drop the dough by rounded teaspoons onto your cookie sheets, no more than 12 cookies on each standard-sized sheet.

**Hannah's 2nd Note: I use a 2-teaspoon cookie scoop at The Cookie Jar. It's faster than doing it with a spoon.**

Bake your Butterscotch Crunch Cookies at 350 degrees F. for 10 to 12 minutes or until nicely browned. *(Mine took 11 min-utes.)*

Let the cookies cool for 2 minutes on the cookie sheet and then remove them with a metal spatula. Transfer them to a wire rack to finish cooling.

Yield: Approximately 5 dozen wonderfully chewy, salty and crunchy cookies that are sure to please everyone who tastes them.

**Lisa's 2nd Note: These cookies travel well. If you want to send them to a friend, just stack them, roll them up in foil like coins, and cushion the cookie rolls between layers of styrofoam pea-nuts, or bubble wrap.**

# CHEESE POPS

8-ounce package brick-style cream cheese **(NOT whipped! I used Philadelphia Cream Cheese in the silver package.)**

8 ounces bleu cheese, crumbled

8-ounce by weight package bacon pieces **(I used 6-ounce Hormel Real Bacon Bits — it worked just fine)**

2 teaspoons ground paprika

Small bag of medium thin salted pretzel sticks **(I used part of a 16-ounce bag of Snyder's Family Size Stick Pretzels)**

**Hannah's 1st Note: Since you only use a dozen pretzel sticks in this recipe and I bought a family-size bag, I had a lot left over. Ross ate some when he watched one of the TV movies he made and so did I. Then I made Pretzel Patties with the rest and both of us took them to work.**

Unwrap the package of cream cheese and place it in the bottom of a medium-sized microwave-safe mixing bowl.

Crumble or cut up the bleu cheese in small bits and put it on top of the cream cheese.

Place the bowl in the microwave and heat on HIGH for 30 seconds.

Leave the bowl in the microwave for 1 minute, then take it out and try to stir the cream cheese in with the bleu cheese. *(I used a heat-resistant spatula to do this.)*

If the cheeses are too stiff to combine, return them to the microwave and heat on HIGH for an additional 20 seconds. Repeat as often as necessary until the mixture is well combined and there are no big lumps.

Set the bowl on the counter and cool to room temperature. Then place the bowl in the refrigerator for 2 hours to chill thoroughly.

Once the cheese mixture has chilled, take the bowl out of the refrigerator and set it on the kitchen counter.

Set a flat pan with sides on the counter next to the bowl with the cheese mixture. *(I used a rectangular plastic container.)* Line that container with a layer of wax paper.

Divide the cheese mixture into four equal parts.

**Hannah's 2nd Note: Each quarter of the cheese mixture will make 3 cheese pops. You will have a dozen Cheese Pops when you finish assembling them.**

Divide each quarter of the cheese mixture into thirds. You will have twelve parts in all.

Wash your hands thoroughly. Then wet them again and partially dry them on a clean towel. You will be rolling cheese balls and this is easier with slightly moistened hands.

Roll the cheese balls and place them on the piece of wax paper in the pan or container. Leave at least an inch of space surrounding each ball. If you don't do this, they'll stick together.

**Hannah's 3rd Note: My container was not that large and I needed a second layer to contain all my cheese balls. If this happens to you, simply tear off another piece of wax paper and place it between the layers.**

Refrigerate the cheese balls for another 2 hours. *(Overnight is fine, too.)*

Once your cheese balls have re-chilled, take them out of the refrigerator.

Put your bacon crumbles or bits into a small shallow bowl and mix in the 2 teaspoons of paprika.

Working with one ball at a time, roll the cheese balls in the bacon and paprika mixture and place them back in the container on fresh sheets of wax paper.

Refrigerate your bacon and paprika coated cheese balls until fifteen to twenty minutes before you want to serve them.

When you're ready to finish your Cheese Pops, simply insert a pretzel stick into the middle of each ball and place them on a platter.

**Hannah's 4th Note: You can also make these Cheese Pops with sharp cheddar cheese. Simply substitute finely shredded sharp cheddar for the bleu cheese and proceed as directed. If you make both types of Cheese Pops, roll the bleu cheese ones in the bacon and paprika, and roll the cheddar cheese balls in finely chopped parsley.**

Yield: 12 Cheese Pops that will delight your guests.

**Hannah's 5th Note: This recipe can be doubled or tripled for large parties. Use different kinds of cheese with the cream cheese and experiment with different coatings. I've used sesame seeds, ground nuts of various types, and even finely chopped coconut mixed with finely chopped dried pineapple.**

# PRETZEL PATTIES

**(These can be made from leftover salted pretzels from Cheese Pops.)**

Approximately 8 ounces of salted stick pretzels
2 cups *(12-ounce package)* of semi-sweet chocolate chips
2 Tablespoons *(1 ounce, 1/4 stick)* salted butter
Several handfuls of miniature marshmallows

Break each pretzel stick into small pieces and put them into a bowl.

**Hannah's 1st Note: The kids can help you with this, but you'd better put some extra pretzels into the bowl when they're through! I can almost guarantee that some pretzels will be eaten during the breaking process.**

Tear off several sheets of wax paper and stretch them out on your kitchen counter.

Put the chocolate chips in a large microwave-safe bowl.

Put the ounce of salted butter on top of the chips.

Melt the chocolate chips for 1 minute in the microwave on HIGH heat.

Let the chips sit in the microwave for 1 minute to rest.

Try to stir the chips and butter smooth with a heat-resistant spatula. If you can, you're done. If you can't, heat for an additional 20 seconds in the microwave, let the bowl rest in the microwave for 1 minute, and try again. Repeat as often as necessary until you can achieve a smooth mixture of butter and chocolate chips.

Stir the broken pretzels into the melted chocolate and butter mixture.

Stir in the miniature marshmallows.

Use a Tablespoon from your silverware drawer to drop patties of Pretzel Patties onto the sheets of wax paper.

Let the candy harden to room temperature. Then peel it off the wax paper and store it in layers, separated by more wax paper, in a plastic container in your refrigerator.

Yield: Several dozen Pretzel Patties, depending on patty size.

# CHAPTER TEN

When Hannah woke up the next morning, she rolled over to give Ross a kiss. It was a promise they'd made to each other during their honeymoon. The first to wake up in the morning would kiss the other awake. But Ross wasn't there! And, at that moment, she realized that the reason she'd awakened in the first place was because she'd heard the shower running.

Ross had gotten up without kissing her awake and he was already in the shower. No doubt he thought he was being considerate by letting her sleep a bit longer. And, quite honestly, Hannah wasn't sure what her reaction to this change in their morning routine should be. Should she be grateful or disappointed that Ross hadn't kissed her awake? And should she let Ross know how she felt?

Hannah thought about that for a moment and decided that it was best to forget the whole thing. Ross had already been in bed when she'd come home with Michelle last night after their talk with Tricia. She knew he'd been tired after his first full day back at work. Since she was also very tired, she'd simply prepared for bed, slipped under the covers beside him, and gone to sleep. Perhaps he'd been upset this morning when he'd realized that she hadn't awakened him with a goodnight kiss, another one of their promises to each other. She had kissed him, but it hadn't roused him. And since he'd been sleeping so peacefully, she'd decided not to wake him by kissing him again. That was another factor to consider.

As Hannah sat up and dislodged the last wisps of sleep from her consciousness, she became aware of a delicious scent in the air. Black coffee, certainly. And something else . . . perhaps cheese and breakfast sausage. Michelle must have gotten up earlier to make breakfast for them.

Her slippers were on her side of the bed and Hannah thrust her feet into them. Then she stood up and took her robe from the hook on the back of their bedroom door. It was a new robe, one of the robes that her mother and sisters had given her. So, instead of the old chenille robe she'd rescued from a lonely existence in a bin at the Helping

Hands Thrift Shop, she donned a beautiful, fluffy, powder-blue silk robe. She gave a fleeting thought to that comfortable old robe that had been her companion on so many mornings and wondered what had happened to it. Perhaps she should drop by the thrift store this afternoon to find out if Delores or Hannah's sisters had returned it to its former home.

Hannah glanced at the bed. Moishe was still sleeping, but now he was asleep on Ross's pillow. Usually Moishe preferred hers, but since she'd been using it, he'd probably decided that any other pillow would do. She reached down to pet him and he opened one eye, and began to purr. "Daylight in the swamps," she told him, the morning phrase she used every morning. Hannah watched Moishe, bemused, as he yawned, stretched, and then jumped down from the mattress to follow her to the kitchen.

As she passed the living room windows, Hannah realized that it was still dark outside. Well, of course it was . . . it was November already with Thanksgiving on the way. The days were short-lived in the Minnesota winters. There were several weeks, in the dead of winter, when she didn't see the sun unless she happened to look out the window or the back kitchen door of The Cookie Jar. She got up in the dark, drove to town in the dark, and when she'd finished work for the day, she drove home in the dark. But even though the days were short, the temperatures were multiple degrees below zero, and icy winds defeated even the warmest parka, Hannah enjoyed the transitions of a four-season climate.

"Whatever you made smells delicious," Hannah said to Michelle as she entered the kitchen.

Michelle gestured toward the counter where a cake pan was cooling on a wire rack. "I made my Cheese and Sausage Breakfast Bake. It'll be cool in a few minutes if you want to try some."

"Of course I want to try some!" Hannah walked over to look at the breakfast dish. "It looks divine and it smells really heavenly."

"It sure does!" Ross appeared in the doorway, wearing a velveteen robe and the leather bedroom slippers they'd bought in Puerto Vallarta on their honeymoon.

"Sit down and I'll get you both some coffee," Michelle promised, pointing to Hannah's kitchen table. "I know it's black for you, Hannah, but you take cream, don't you, Ross?"

"That's right," Ross responded. "It's your fault I cut my shower short, Michelle. It smelled so good out here that I could hardly wait to see what was cooking for breakfast." He gave her the grin that Hannah loved to see, reaching out to take Michelle's hand once she'd delivered his coffee. "I don't suppose you'd consider dropping out of college and coming to live with us so you could cook us breakfast every day, would you?"

"Thanks for the offer, but not right now. I'd like to graduate and earn a living for myself first. Then you can come to visit me."

"It's a deal," Ross said, smiling at Hannah. "What time do you have to be at work, Cookie?"

"Soon," Hannah said, smiling back. "I'll eat my breakfast, take a quick shower, and go off to work. What time do you think you'll be home tonight, Ross?"

"Six at the earliest and eight at the latest. It depends on how much time P.K. takes to edit the footage we're shooting this afternoon. If it's going to be later than eight, I'll call you."

"That's fine," Hannah said. She'd known that their schedules would differ, but Ross was trying to give her a ballpark figure. "I should be home by six, too. And if something comes up and we're not here, I'll leave you a note, or text you to let you know."

Michelle brought over plates with pieces of her Cheese and Sausage Breakfast Bake while they were sipping their coffee. "I hope you like it," she said.

"I do," said Hannah after the first bite. "It's delicious, Michelle."

Ross nodded. "It really is. It's almost like a quiche, except not quite, isn't it?"

"In a way," Michelle told him. "Quiche doesn't usually have bread in it and this does, and a standard quiche is made in a round pan with straight sides that's a lot like a pie pan, but it's really the same concept. It's basically an egg and cheese pie whether it's round or made in a cake pan."

"We should take a piece of this to Lisa," Hannah recommended. "She could make it for Herb for breakfast. I'm willing to bet that it would be almost as good cold as it is warm."

Michelle glanced at the cake pan that had only three pieces gone. "I think we're going to find out if you're right, Hannah. I made two pans and there's not a lot left. Unless we finish it this morning, we may have to eat it for breakfast tomorrow, too."

"What a pity," Ross said, winking at Michelle. "I guess we'll just have to suffer through it."

"Indeed," Hannah agreed, taking another bite of her piece. Breakfast with Michelle and Ross was fun and it was wonderful to have her sister there. She was sure that Ross had been kidding when he'd asked Michelle to drop out of college to live with them, but right now, with a bite of Michelle's breakfast bake in her mouth, it sounded like a really good idea to Hannah.

"So who are we interviewing this morning?" Michelle asked as Hannah drove them to town.

"I'm not sure. I think we should go over that appointment calendar of Tori's and see if there's anyone who might tell us more."

"I have a rehearsal of the Lake Eden Players at one this afternoon," Michelle reminded her. "Maybe I'll learn something there. Everyone in the play is bound to be talking about Tori's murder and speculating about who might have done it."

Hannah turned off the highway and took Main Street to Third. Then she turned the corner and went down the alley to The Cookie Jar parking lot.

"There's Mike," Michelle pointed out, although Hannah had already noticed the black and white cruiser parked in the spot next to hers. "Do you think he's in the kitchen pumping Lisa for information?"

"Maybe. Lisa did take acting lessons from Tori. There's no way she's a suspect, but she could provide some background on Tori and everybody else from Lake Eden who took private acting lessons from Tori at her studio."

"Hurry up, Hannah," Michelle said, opening her door and getting out the moment Hannah had stopped the truck. "We'd better get in there and rescue Lisa."

"Rescue?" Hannah asked, dropping the keys in her purse and getting out of the driver's side.

"That's right. You know how Mike is when he's digging for information. If he's grilling Lisa too much, we can always distract him with a cookie or two."

"True," Hannah agreed, heading for the back kitchen door. "It's a good thing we baked Double Fudge Brownies before we left The Cookie Jar last night. Mike loves those, and he has to stop asking questions if his mouth is full of chocolate."

# CHEESE AND SAUSAGE BREAKFAST BAKE

Preheat oven to 350 F., rack in the middle position.

1 pound breakfast sausage patties *(I used Farmer John's)*

8 to 10 slices of bread of your choice *(I used white, Michelle uses rye from the bakery near her house just off campus at Macalester.)*

Enough salted butter, softened, to cover 8 to 10 slices of bread

8-ounce can mushroom stems and pieces, drained

3 cups sharp cheddar cheese, shredded *(about 12 ounces)*

6 large eggs

2 cups half-and-half or light cream

2 Tablespoons *(1/8 cup, 1 ounce, 1/4 stick)* salted butter, melted

1 teaspoon salt

1 teaspoon Dijon-style stone ground mustard

1/2 teaspoon ground paprika

Several dashes of hot sauce *(I used Mike's favorite Slap Ya Mama)*

1 cup chopped, fresh parsley

Spray a 9-inch by 13-inch cake pan with

Pam or another nonstick cooking spray and set it on the counter.

Using a large frying pan, fry the breakfast sausage patties over MEDIUM heat until almost all of the fat is rendered out and the sausage is nice and brown.

Remove the sausage from the pan and place it on paper towels on top of a large plate or platter to soak off any excess fat.

Cut the crusts from the slices of bread and spread one side with the salted butter.

Place the bread slices in the bottom of your prepared cake pan, buttered side up. *(If necessary, you can cut them to make them fit.)*

Place the breakfast sausage patties on top of the buttered bread in the cake pan. Distribute it as evenly as possible.

If you haven't already done so, drain the mushroom stems and pieces and pat them dry with a paper towel.

Sprinkle the mushroom stems and pieces on top of the breakfast sausage.

Sprinkle the sharp, grated cheddar cheese over the top of the ingredients in the cake pan as evenly as possible.

Crack the 6 eggs into a medium-sized bowl and beat them until they're thoroughly mixed.

Add the half-and-half to the bowl with

the eggs and mix it in until everything is thoroughly incorporated.

In a separate small bowl, mix the melted butter with the salt, mustard, and paprika.

Add several dashes of hot sauce and mix them in thoroughly.

Stir in the butter, salt, mustard, paprika, and hot sauce mixture into the egg and half-and-half mixture. Stir until everything is thoroughly combined.

Pour the resulting mixture into the baking dish, making sure to cover everything as evenly as possible.

Sprinkle the chopped, fresh parsley over the top of the pan.

Bake, uncovered, for 55 to 60 minutes, or until a table knife inserted one-inch from the middle of the cake pan comes out clean and without any milky egg mixture clinging to it.

Remove the cake pan from the oven and set it on a cold stovetop burner or on a wire rack on the counter.

Let your Cheese and Sausage Breakfast Bake cool for at least 10 minutes. Then cut it into pieces, remove them from the cake pan with a metal spatula, and serve them to your guests.

Yield: At least 10 servings of a delicious breakfast dish that your guests will love and ask you to make again and again.

**Michelle's Note: When I make this breakfast dish for my roommates at college, I prepare everything the night before and place it in the cake pan. Then I cover the cake pan with aluminum foil and put it in the refrigerator overnight. Then all I have to do in the morning is preheat the oven and bake it. If you decide to do this and you bake your Cheese and Sausage Breakfast Bake cold, baking time could be increased by as much as 10 or 15 minutes. Be sure to test for doneness before you take it out of the oven.**

**Hannah's Note: I've made this breakfast bake with ground sausage rather than sausage patties. It works just fine as long as you fry it to reduce the amount of fat.**

**Andrea's Note: I made this for Bill on his birthday. Tracey helped me do it. Since I didn't have any breakfast sausage, we used slices of ham. Bill loved it and it was delicious that way.**

# CHAPTER ELEVEN

"Hannah!" Mike greeted her the moment she and Michelle came in the door. "Just the person I wanted to see."

*Wish I could say the same,* Hannah's mind made a sharp retort, but of course Hannah didn't voice it. Mike was sitting on his favorite stool at the stainless steel work station, drinking a cup of coffee. "Good morning, Mike," she greeted him pleasantly. "I see Lisa gave you coffee. Where is she?"

"Lisa had to straighten up in the coffee shop. She said you hadn't had time to do it after you closed last night and it was a mess. She told me she'd come back as soon as she could, but there were a lot of things she had to do before she'd be ready to open."

Somehow, Hannah managed to keep the delighted grin off her face. Absolutely nothing needed to be done in the coffee shop and Lisa knew it. They'd straightened up and prepared for opening before they'd left for the night.

*Smart move on Lisa's part!* Hannah thought, but again, she said nothing of the sort. She'd compliment Lisa on her quick thinking after Mike had left. Then she'd be able to find out what Mike had asked her.

"How about a couple of Double Fudge Brownies?" she offered.

"Chocolate for breakfast?" Mike asked, looking pleased when Hannah nodded. "Sounds good to me." He turned to Michelle. "I heard you two went out to the bar at the Lake Eden Inn after we left Hannah's place last night."

"Yes," Michelle replied, giving Hannah one of their silent but communicative sisterly glances that said, *I don't know how you want to play this, so you'd better get me out of it.*

Hannah interpreted Michelle's meaningful look and responded immediately. "That's right. We were there. Michelle, why don't you get the brownies out and cut some for Mike? And heat up his coffee a bit, will you?"

Michelle gave Hannah a grateful smile and went off to do as her sister had suggested. When she'd poured more coffee for Mike and given Hannah a cup, she walked to the walk-in cooler to get the brownies. When she came out of the cooler with the brownies and passed behind Mike, she gave Hannah a wink.

"Dick said Ross wasn't there with you," Mike continued.

"That's right. We were only there for a short while and Ross wanted to watch something on the giant flat screen."

"Wasn't it a little late for you two girls to go out for a drink?"

"Of course it was, but that's not why we went out there." Hannah stopped speaking and did not explain further. Perhaps it was a bit mean, but she knew that not being completely forthcoming about last night's visit to the Lake Eden Inn would drive Mike crazy. Now Mike would have to dig for the information, and it served him right for waylaying her the moment she'd come in the kitchen door.

Mike looked up as Michelle set a plate of brownies on the worktable. "Those look really good!"

"They are," Michelle told him. "I cut one a little crooked so of course I had to eat it."

"Of course you did," he said with a grin.

Michelle turned to Hannah. "I'll put the rest of these back in the cooler, Hannah. And then I'll put on some more coffee. The kitchen pot's almost empty."

"Thanks, Michelle." Hannah watched her sister walk back to the cooler. She had no doubt that Michelle would take her time about putting the brownies away and making another pot of coffee. She waited just long enough for Mike to take a huge bite of his brownie, and then she asked, "So how is the investigation coming along, Mike?"

"Mmmmff," he said, waving aside her question and indicating that he'd answer her in a moment or two.

"Poor Mother's still very upset over Tori's death," Hannah continued. "I probably should have invited her to join us for dinner last night since Doc had a staff meeting at the hospital, but I just didn't feel like discussing Tori's murder and I knew she'd ask you a bunch of questions."

Mike swallowed and took another sip of coffee, so Hannah went on. "Mother's going to want to know how you're doing on the investigation, Mike. What should I tell her?"

"Just. . . . well. . . . just tell her it's going as well as possible. How about you, Hannah? Is that why you were out at the Lake Eden Inn last night?"

"No, we went to see Michelle's friend, Tricia Barthel. She works out there and we wanted to catch her before she was through with her shift."

"Do you know that Tricia was one of the last people to see Tori alive?"

"Yes, she mentioned something about having an acting lesson at six that night, but that Tori had cut it short. Of course we asked her if she'd seen anyone who might have been going up to Tori's condo, but she said she hadn't met anyone on her way out of the Albion."

"Yes. That's what she told me. What is Michelle doing here, Hannah? I thought she was going back to college."

"She did, but she came back to direct the Thanksgiving play."

Mike looked over at Michelle, who was filling the display cookie jars at the far end of the kitchen. "Do you think she can do it?"

"I'm sure she can. Michelle's very capable. She can do anything she sets her mind to."

"And you think she'll be able to help you investigate Tori's murder?"

Hannah sighed. All the misdirected talking she'd done hadn't done any good. Mike had gone straight to his goal.

"Hannah?"

"If Michelle does find out anything, I'm sure she'll tell me."

"And will you tell me?"

He'd zeroed in again! There were times when Hannah wished that Mike didn't have such a one-track mind when it came to solving crimes. "Yes, Mike. I'll tell you."

"You'll tell me right away? Or will you put off telling me until I uncover it myself?"

"I'll tell you right away," Hannah said, crossing her fingers under the table in the childish gesture they'd always used to negate a promise.

"Okay, then." Mike finished his coffee in one swallow, grabbed another brownie, and stood up. "Thanks for the brownies, Hannah. I'd better get back to work . . . unless there's anything you want to tell me right now?"

"I can't think of anything," Hannah said, deliberately steering her thoughts away from the subject of Mayor Bascomb and whether or not he'd gone up to Tori's condo to confront her about her will.

Hannah had just taken the last two pans of Citrus Sugar Cookies out of the oven and slipped them onto shelves in the baker's rack when Michelle came into the kitchen, carrying an empty display jar.

"We need more cookies," she announced. "I'll fill this and take it out to Lisa and then I'll help you bake. Aunt Nancy came in

199

early, and Marge and Jack are due in an hour, so Lisa said I could stay in the kitchen and help you."

"That's good news! I can't believe how many cookies we went through in the past two hours. Every time I turned around, you were here with a display jar, filling it from the racks."

"I know. If Lisa gets any better at telling murder stories, you'll have to hire more kitchen help," Michelle laughed.

"That or come in two hours earlier," Hannah said, brushing back a curl that had escaped her baker's cap.

"That might put a real crimp in your marriage," Michelle warned. "You're tired enough as it is. I'd suggest more help."

"I agree. The way I feel right now, I could use a four-hour nap. And it's not even noon yet."

"Sit down and I'll get you a cup of coffee," Michelle offered. "You're going to need some caffeine."

"Caffeine may not help. I think my get up and go, got up and went."

Michelle came over to the workstation with two cups of coffee and plunked one down in front of Hannah. "Do you know there's a country-western song like that?"

"Like what?"

"My get up and go, got up and went. I can't remember the name of it, but it has a line like that."

"That figures." Hannah took a sip of her coffee. "Did you know that a lot of country-western songs that were popular in the fifties and sixties were written by a lady who lived in the country in Minnesota?"

"No, but that makes sense. If you live in the country, there's not much to do in the winter. And in Minnesota, you can get snowed in for weeks unless the county plow happens to come through. And that was before they probably had cable or satellite out in the country. And there were only one or two television stations to watch."

"That's true. At times like that, you had to rely on your family for entertainment. It's possible that lady entertained her husband and children by singing the songs she wrote."

"Maybe," Michelle said, sounding doubtful. "But if that woman made it big and sold a lot of songs, the whole family probably moved to a big house in Minneapolis and went out to dinner and a movie whenever they wanted." Michelle was silent for a moment and then she abruptly changed the subject. "What cookies did you bake, Hannah? I'm getting a little hungry and they smell really good."

"I'm calling them Citrus Sugar Cookies. They have lemon and orange zest in them and I rolled them in sugar and baked them. The pans at the bottom of the bakers rack came out of the oven first and they should be cool enough to try if you want to taste them."

Michelle didn't wait for a second invitation. She jumped to her feet and rushed to the bakers rack to put some cookies on a plate. "Here you go," she said, arriving back at the workstation slightly breathless.

Hannah took a cookie and smelled it. It still had a lovely scent of lemon and orange. She bit into it and began to smile. "Not bad," she said, taking another bite.

"Not bad?" Michelle questioned, looking a bit dumbfounded. "*Not bad?* Think again, Hannah. They're fabulous!"

Hannah preened slightly. She always loved it when a new recipe worked the first time around. "You're right. I'm happy with them."

"And everybody else will be happy with them, too. Are we going to serve them today?"

"We might as well. You can fill a couple display jars with them and carry them out front, but save at least a dozen for me to take to Lorna. I have to catch her at the office before she goes to lunch."

"Lorna Kusak at Howie's law office?"

Hannah nodded. "Howie goes to lunch first and then he comes back to relieve Lorna so she can go. I need to catch her after Howie leaves and before he comes back."

"You're going to find out about Tori's will," Michelle said and it was a statement rather than a question.

"That's right. It might not matter if Mayor Bascomb believed it, but I'd like to know if Tori really changed her will, or if she was simply making an empty threat to try to bring the mayor back in line."

# CITRUS SUGAR COOKIES

DO NOT preheat the oven. The dough must chill before baking.

2 cups salted butter, melted **(4 sticks, 16 ounces, 1 pound)**

2 cups powdered sugar **(don't sift unless it's got big lumps and then you shouldn't use it anyway)**

1 cup white **(granulated)** sugar

2 large eggs

1 teaspoon lemon extract

1 teaspoon orange extract

Zest of 1 lemon

Zest of 1 orange

1 teaspoon baking soda

1 teaspoon cream of tartar **(critical!)**

1 teaspoon salt

4 and 1/4 cups all-purpose flour **(don't sift — pack it down in the cup when you measure it)**

1/2 cup white sugar in a small, shallow bowl **(for later — you'll be using the sugar to coat dough balls after the dough has chilled)**

**Hannah's 1st Note: Just in case you don't know, zest is the finely shredded**

**colored part of the peel on citrus fruit. Use the colored part of the peel only. The white part under it contains pectin and it's very bitter.**

If you haven't already done so, melt the butter in a microwave-safe bowl. 60 seconds on HIGH should be enough.

You can also melt the butter in a saucepan on the stovetop at LOW heat. If you do this, stir the butter with a spoon to make sure the butter doesn't brown.

Pour the butter into a large bowl or the bowl of an electric mixer.

Add the powdered sugar and the white *(granulated)* sugar and mix it in thoroughly.

Let the mixture cool to room temperature before you proceed further.

When the butter and sugar mixture is cool, turn the mixer on LOW. Add the eggs, one at a time, mixing after each addition.

With the mixer running on LOW speed, mix in the lemon and orange extracts.

Mix in the lemon zest and the orange zest.

Add the baking soda, cream of tartar, and salt. Mix until everything is thoroughly combined.

Add the flour in one-cup increments, mixing well after each addition. *(You can mix the quarter-cup at the end in with the fourth full cup of flour.)*

Give your dough a final stir by hand and cover the bowl.

Chill the covered dough in the refrigerator for at least one hour. **(Overnight is fine, too.)**

When you're ready to bake, preheat your oven to 325 degrees F. with the rack in the middle position.

Prepare your cookie sheets by spraying them with Pam or another nonstick cooking spray, or lining them with parchment paper.

Prepare a shallow bowl with the half-cup of white sugar.

Take your chilled Citrus Sugar Cookie dough out of the refrigerator and set it on the counter. Remove the cover.

Use your impeccably clean hands to roll the dough into walnut-sized balls. Roll only a half-dozen dough balls or so to start. Then cover the bowl again so that it will remain chilled.

One at a time, dip the dough balls into the bowl of sugar and roll them around until they're coated.

Place the sugar-coated dough balls on the cookie sheets you've prepared, 12 dough balls to a standard-sized sheet. Flatten the dough balls with the back of a metal spatula.

Bake the cookies at 325 degrees F. for 10 to 15 minutes. **(The cookies should have a** *tinge of gold around the edges when they're fully baked, but they should not be brown.)*

When the cookies have baked, take them out of the oven and set them on cold stovetop burners or on wire racks to cool. Leave them on the cookie sheets for 1 to 2 minutes.

**Hannah's 2nd Note: If you remove the cookies from the cookie sheets right away, they may break into pieces. The reason you cool them on the sheets for a minute or two first is so they will "set" and not crumble when you move them.**

After the cookies have cooled slightly, remove them from the cookie sheets to a wire rack to finish cooling.

**Hannah's 3rd Note: If you used parchment paper, just pull it off the cookie sheet and onto the rack. The cookies can finish cooling on the paper and you can peel them off later.**

Yield: approximately 10 dozen crunchy, buttery, citrus-infused sugar cookies that children and adults will love.

**Michelle's Note: I bet that you can't eat just one!**

# CHAPTER TWELVE

Michelle had agreed to come with Hannah and thirty minutes later, they were entering Howie Levine's law office. The person Hannah wanted to see was Lorna Kusak and, as she'd explained to Michelle, if Howie had decided not to go to lunch today, it would be extremely helpful if Michelle could ask Howie a few questions about legal procedure to keep him busy while Hannah talked to Lorna.

"Oh, my!" Hannah exclaimed as they entered Howie's outer office. It had been completely redecorated and it was gorgeous.

"Hi, Hannah," Lorna, who did double duty as Howie's receptionist as well as his legal secretary, greeted her. Lorna then turned to Hannah's sister, "Hello, Michelle. I thought you were still in college."

"I was, but I'm doing work-study here in Lake Eden. I'm taking over as director of the Lake Eden Players for their Thanksgiving play."

"That's great! Everybody was afraid that it wouldn't happen now that Tori's gone." Lorna sighed heavily, and then she turned back to Hannah. "You're late."

"What?"

"I said, you're late. Mike was here when we opened this morning at nine."

It was Hannah's turn to sigh. "I should have figured he'd beat me to it. I suppose he asked you about Tori's new will."

Lorna shook her head. "Nope. He said he needed to talk to Howie, and when Howie got here a couple of minutes later, he took Mike into his office and shut the door."

"So you didn't hear their conversation?" Michelle asked her.

"No, but Howie buzzed me on the intercom and asked me to bring in a copy of Tori's new will."

"Did you type it up?" Hannah asked, hoping that Lorna was privy to its contents.

"Yes. It's a computer form and all I have to do is fill in the blanks and print it out."

"Did Howie make out Tori's previous will?" Michelle asked her.

"Oh, yes. She came in right after she moved to town. I prepared that one, too."

"Since there's a new will and that other one is now null and void, can you tell us what was in it?" Hannah asked her.

Lorna shook her head. "I wish I could, but I can't. That will is now the will of record."

"You mean Tori never got in here to sign the new will?" Michelle guessed.

"That's right. She had an appointment to sign all the paperwork at ten o'clock on the day *after* she was murdered."

"Who was the new beneficiary?" Hannah asked her.

"That's a somewhat tricky ethical question," Lorna said. "But since Tori's revised will is now null and void, I don't think I could be faulted for telling you what Tori intended."

"Please tell us," Hannah said, taking out the bag she'd brought with the Citrus Sugar Cookies inside. "And before I forget, I brought you some of the new cookies I made."

"Ooooh!" Lorna took the bag and looked inside. Then her eyes narrowed. "You're not trying to bribe me with cookies, are you, Hannah?"

"Of course not! I'm just delivering a little gift to a friend and neighbor of mine."

Lorna began to smile. "Well . . . since you put it that way, I don't see how I could object. And I'm even more certain that it wouldn't be unethical to tell you that Tori's new will, the one she didn't sign, divided her inheritance between the drama department at Jordan High and the Lake Eden Players."

"Oh, boy!" Michelle said, looking shocked. "Do you think anybody in town knew that?"

Lorna shook her head. "They didn't know it from me. And I'm ninety-nine percent certain they didn't know it from Howie. Unless Tori told someone that she'd changed her will, nobody knew it except Tori, Howie, and me."

Michelle and Hannah exchanged meaningful glances and Hannah knew that both of them were thinking the same thing. There were two other people who knew about the new will before Tori had been murdered. And those two people were Tricia and Mayor Bascomb.

Hannah had dropped Michelle off at the Jordan High auditorium where the Lake Eden Players rehearsed. She'd intended to go straight back to The Cookie Jar, but she decided to drop by the antique shop that Delores owned with Carrie Rhodes Flensburg before she returned to work. She parked behind The Cookie Jar and hurried across the parking lot to the antique store.

"Hi, Mother," she called out as she followed the narrow path past the stored antiques in the back storage room and entered the store.

"Hello, Hannah!" Luanne Hanks called out. Luanne was Delores and Carrie's assistant and Hannah doubted that her mother or Carrie could have made a success of their business without her.

"Is Mother here?" Hannah asked, arriving at the counter in the front of the store where Luanne was studying a page in a ledger.

"She's up in the break room with Carrie. Go on up, Hannah. I'm sure they'll be glad to see you."

"I will," Hannah said with a smile. "What are you doing, Luanne?"

"Figuring out the profit margin on the antiques I bought at the estate sale last weekend. I don't want your mother and Carrie to price them too low."

"And they tend to do that?"

"Yes. Both of them want to give everyone a break. That's very nice of them, but they have to make a profit to stay in business."

"You're right, Luanne."

"I know. You used to do the same thing, Hannah. You'd give away cookies for free. Generosity must run in your family."

"Either that or poor business sense."

Luanne laughed. She had the best laugh Hannah had ever heard. It started off softly and grew in volume until it died off into a series of soft giggles.

"Go on up, Hannah," Luanne told her pointing to the stairway in the center of the shop. "They'll both be happy to see you. I know your mother wants to ask you about how your investigation is going."

"Hannah!" Delores greeted her as she came in the door of the coffee room. "Thank goodness you're here! I called The Cookie Jar, but Lisa wasn't sure where you'd gone."

Her mother looked highly agitated and Hannah felt a stab of concern. "What's the matter, Mother?"

"I need you to go to lunch with me! I can't go with Carrie because she's meeting Earl at Bertanelli's, and I can't take Luanne because someone has to keep Granny's Attic open."

Hannah was puzzled. Her mother was in a real state and she didn't understand why. "You need me to take you to lunch because you don't want to go alone?"

"No, that's not it! I need you because you know how to ask questions. I need to have lunch at the Red Velvet Lounge before Georgina Swinton finishes her waitress shift!"

Hannah still didn't understand, but she nodded. "All right. Let's go then." She gave Carrie a wave that served as both greeting and departure, and was gratified when Carrie winked at her. Her mother's best friend knew just how demanding Delores could be.

"You drive," Delores ordered, heading across the parking lot at a trot that was only a few paces slower than a gallop. She glanced behind her to make sure that Hannah was following and arrived at Hannah's cookie truck quite breathless. "Get in, Hannah! And step on it! We have to be there in twenty minutes if we want to get Georgina as our waitress. Otherwise, it's all for naught!"

*All for naught?* Hannah's mind repeated the phrase. Her mother must have started working on her new Regency romance. "Don't worry, Mother. We'll get there in five minutes or less," she promised.

Three and a half minutes later, Hannah pulled into her mother's extra parking spot right next to the entrance to the Albion Hotel. True to her word, they slid into a booth at the Red Velvet Lounge with fifteen seconds to spare.

"Please tell me what all this is about," Hannah said, reaching for the menu on the

214

table. She hadn't been planning on having lunch, but now that they were here, it would be foolish not to sample the food that her mother had told her was very good.

"In just a minute," Delores said, gesturing toward the busboy who was heading for their table with two glasses of water. "Is Georgina working?" she asked him before he even had time to deliver their water.

"She's here. Do you want her to wait on you?"

"Yes, please," Hannah answered for her mother. She still didn't know why Delores had asked her to come here and insisted that Georgina be their waitress.

Delores took a sip of water and sighed heavily. "That's better," she said.

When the busboy had left, Hannah turned to her mother. "Will you please tell me now?"

"Yes. I talked to Irma York. Georgina is her cousin. Irma said that Georgina told her that Mayor Bascomb was in here having drinks with his wife on the night that Tori was killed."

"Okay. So you want me to ask Georgina about Mayor Bascomb?"

"Of course I do. But there's more. Irma said that Georgina said she overheard the mayor say something about having to go up to Tori's place to straighten her out about something important. And then he told Stephanie to order another drink for him because it wouldn't take long for him to set Tori straight."

"That's interesting," Hannah said, not mentioning that she already knew that from the one-sided conversation Tricia had overheard. "Do you happen to know what time that was?"

"No. Georgina didn't say, so Irma didn't know."

"And you'd like me to find out when that was?"

"Of course I would." Delores turned to give Hannah a questioning look. "Wouldn't you like to know?"

Her mother seemed to be waiting for something more than a simple answer, and for a moment, Hannah was puzzled. Then she realized what Delores wanted. "It certainly might be helpful. Thank you for bringing this to me, Mother."

Delores smiled and Hannah knew she'd given the correct response. "You're welcome, dear."

A moment later, a woman with obviously dyed black hair swept up in a tight knot on the top of her head came over to their booth. "Hello, Hannah," she said with a smile. "It's good to see you again."

Hannah's mind went into high gear, searching her memory banks. She knew she'd seen the woman before and her name was obviously Georgina, but where, exactly, had that been?

One by one, in rapid succession, she eliminated the possibilities. Not a customer at The Cookie Jar. Not a relative or a friend of a relative. Not at her mother's Regency Romance Reader's Club. Her synapses flew through the other venues and came up with a possible winner. But it wouldn't hurt to double check the accuracy of her assumption.

"I didn't realize you worked here, Georgina," Hannah said, fishing for information.

"Only a couple shifts a week," Georgina responded with a smile. "It gets really busy when we have a special on Reubens or Patty Melts. We get very crowded then."

The voice was right, Hannah concluded, remembering the last time Georgina had asked her if she wanted onion rings or fries with her burger. Her memory for faces might be faulty and of course the uniform was different, but her initial assumption was correct. "You're still working at the Corner Tavern, aren't you?"

"Yes, on the weekends," Georgina confirmed it. "What would you and your mother like to have for lunch, Hannah?"

"I'll have the Cobb Salad," Delores said, "and could you put the dressing on the side, Georgina?"

"I sure can. Do you want the salad mixed together in the kitchen, or do you want it with the meat, cheese, hard-boiled eggs, sliced avocados, and chopped tomatoes arranged in nice little ribbons on the top of the lettuce?"

"They can toss it in the kitchen," Delores told her. "I've seen it the other way and it's really pretty, but I always make a mess when I toss it at the table myself."

Georgina gave a little laugh. "Don't feel alone. A lot of people order the pretty version the first time around, but after they discover how full that bowl is, they decide to have it tossed in the kitchen. Anything to drink with that, Delores?"

"Mango iced tea. I had some sent up to me last week and it was delicious!"

"It's one of my favorites, too." Georgina made a note on her order pad and then she turned to Hannah. "How about you, Hannah?"

Hannah motioned her a little closer. "Are the burgers as good as they are at the Corner Tavern?"

218

"Well . . ." Georgina paused to glance around to make sure no one was listening to their conversation. "In a word? That would be a big no! They're not nearly as juicy and the fry cook doesn't seem to know how to fix them any way except well done. And the fries that come with them aren't very good either."

"Then what else would you suggest?" Hannah asked.

"Nothing deep fried and that leaves sandwiches. We've got a really good Turkey Stack on whole wheat."

"What's in a Turkey Stack?" Hannah asked her.

"Two slices of roast turkey. We roast it fresh every day from a turkey grown right here in the turkey barns outside of Lake Eden. You know it's fresh because it's home-killed meat."

Hannah gave an involuntary shudder. She knew where the meat she ate came from, but she really didn't like to think about how it got from the farm to the meat counter in Florence's Red Owl Grocery. "What else besides roast turkey?"

"I'll explain the whole thing. I watched the sandwich guy make one yesterday. As a matter of fact, that's what I had for lunch. He starts with two slices of whole wheat bread. We get it from a bakery in The Cities that delivers every day."

Hannah found herself wondering if that bakery was where Michelle got the wonderful rye bread she bought, but she didn't ask. Right now she was more interested in how the sandwich she'd already decided to order was made. "Two slices of whole wheat bread," she repeated. "What's next, Georgina?"

"He spreads both slices of bread with a mixture of mayo and stone ground mustard. Then he sets one to the side and assembles the sandwich on the other slice. First, he puts on a slice of Emmentaler."

"What's that?" Delores asked her.

"Swiss cheese. The sandwich guy says it's the best Swiss cheese you can buy. I think he said it comes from Emmental, a town in Switzerland." Georgina turned back to Hannah. "Then he puts one slice of roast turkey on top of the cheese. And that gets topped with whole berry cranberry sauce that we make right here."

Hannah began to smile. "So far it sounds great. What goes on top of the cranberry sauce?"

"Another slice of roast turkey. And on top of that turkey is a little layer of coleslaw, not enough to make it really wet, but enough to add a good crunch."

"Coleslaw!" Delores repeated, sounding a bit shocked.

"It's really not that unusual," Hannah told her mother. "The deli down the block from Michelle's house uses coleslaw on top of their corned beef sandwiches."

"Do they now?" Georgina sounded as if she'd just discovered the key to something that had been puzzling her. "So *that's* where he got it!"

"He who?" Delores asked.

Hannah bit her lip to keep from laughing out loud. Her mother almost always used impeccable grammar and the question, *He who?* coming from her mother's mouth was hilarious.

"I'm talking about the sandwich guy. And now I know why he puts on coleslaw. He told me he used to work in St. Paul and I'll bet he worked at that deli!"

"That could be," Hannah agreed with a smile, although she suspected that more than one deli made their sandwiches with coleslaw. "Is that it for the sandwich, Georgina?"

"Almost. He puts on another slice of Swiss cheese. He told me that the cheese acts like a moisture barrier so he puts that on top of the stack. And then he picks up the other slice of bread that's already spread with the mayo and mustard, and slaps it on top. That's the whole sandwich. To cut it, he pushes it down on top so it won't fall apart when he slices it. And he serves it with a cup of our Special Corn Chowder."

"Special Corn Chowder?" Delores looked interested. "What makes your corn chowder special?"

"There's nothing special about the chowder itself. It's so easy to make, I even do it at home when my grandkids come over for lunch. The special part is a little dollop of jalapeño jelly on the top of the bowl with a half dozen or so pieces of salted popcorn sprinkled over it."

"Good heavens!" Delores exclaimed. "I'm not sure if that sounds appetizing or not, but it certainly does sound intriguing." She turned to look at Hannah. "I've never heard of anyone serving corn chowder like that before, have you?"

"Never, but I think we owe it to the Red Velvet Lounge to try some. I'll have the Turkey Stack, Georgina, with mango iced tea and a cup of your Special Corn Chowder." She turned to Delores. "You can taste mine if you want to, Mother."

"No thank you, dear," Delores said firmly. "Please cancel my previous order, Georgina.

I'm going to have my own Turkey Stack and Special Corn Chowder. It sounds like the most interesting lunch I've had in years!"

"Good choice, Delores," Georgina complimented her. "I'll put in your orders and bring your drinks. And then I'll sit down and talk to you on my break. I didn't get one this morning, so I'll tell the manager I'm taking it now." She turned to Hannah. "When I get back, you can do what you came here to do."

Hannah frowned slightly. "You mean . . . eat?"

"No, I mean you can start asking me questions about Tori and Mayor Bascomb. I know you're investigating. You always do. And I know that's why you came in today for lunch. But I know even more than that. You're just lucky I was working the afternoon shift when Tori came in here with Stan Kramer. Those two had a very interesting conversation and I heard the whole thing. Let me tell you, I wouldn't be surprised if what I'm going to tell you leads you straight to Tori's killer!"

# TURKEY STACK SANDWICH

2 medium-thick slices of firm whole wheat bread

1/8 cup mayonnaise *(I used Best Foods Mayonnaise)*

1/8 cup stone ground mustard *(I used Dijon)*

2 sandwich-size slices of Swiss cheese *(I used Kraft)*

2 sandwich-size slices of roast turkey breast

1/8 cup whole berry cranberry sauce *(I made my own from fresh cranberries)*

1/8 cup coleslaw made from finely shredded cabbage

Place the two slices of wheat bread on a cutting board.

Mix the eighth-cup of mayonnaise with the eighth-cup of stone ground mustard.

Spread the mayonnaise and mustard mixture on the surface of the two slices of bread.

Push one slice of bread to the side *(that's the top of your sandwich)* and work with the other slice.

Start by topping your bottom slice of bread with a slice of Swiss cheese.

Place one sandwich-size slice of roast turkey on top of the Swiss cheese.

Spread the turkey with the cranberry sauce.

**Hannah's 1st Note: If there's any cranberry sauce left over, feel free to eat it along with your sandwich after it's assembled.**

Place the other slice of roast turkey breast on top of the slice with the cranberry sauce.

Drain the coleslaw and pat it dry with a paper towel. *You don't want a leaky sandwich!*

Arrange the coleslaw on top of the turkey slice in a thin layer.

**Hannah's 2nd Note: Don't use too much coleslaw. In this case, less is more. The slice of turkey doesn't have to be completely covered with coleslaw. Your goal is simply to get a little bit of crunchy coleslaw in every bite.**

Top the coleslaw with the second slice of Swiss cheese.

Cover your Turkey Stack Sandwich with the top slice of bread, mayonnaise and mustard side down.

Press your sandwich down slightly with a wide spatula or with the palm of your impeccably clean hand. This will keep it from falling apart when you slice it.

Slice your sandwich into two pieces crosswise and place the pieces on a plate.

Serve your sandwich with a cup of Special Corn Chowder if you made it. If not, you can substitute corn chips or potato chips.

**Hannah's 3rd Note: If you have leftover cranberry sauce and leftover coleslaw, don't forget to put them on the table for your guests who would like more.**

Yield: One delicious sandwich. This recipe may be doubled, tripled, quadrupled, or repeated for the number of people you've invited to lunch.

# SPECIAL CORN CHOWDER
(Made on the stovetop)

1 cup whipping cream
2 chicken bouillon cubes *(or enough dry bouillon crystals or beads to make 2 cups of chicken broth)*
1/2 stick *(2 ounces, 1/4 cup, 1/8 pound)* salted butter
10-ounce bag frozen whole kernel corn
2 sixteen-ounce cans cream style corn
1 Tablespoon brown sugar
1/4 teaspoon grated nutmeg *(freshly grated is best)*
1/2 teaspoon onion salt
1/2 teaspoon garlic salt
1/2 teaspoon ground black pepper
Hot sauce to taste *(I used Slap Ya Mama)*
1/4 cup instant potato flakes *(if needed to thicken the chowder)*

One jar of jalapeño jelly
1 package microwave buttered popcorn

On the stovetop, using a 3 to 4 quart saucepan over LOW heat, warm the cup of whipping cream with the chicken bouillon cubes and the salted butter. Stir constantly. You don't want the cream to scorch. Continue to heat and stir until the bouillon cubes and the butter have dissolved.

Add the bag of frozen corn kernels and stir until the corn has cooked. This will take about 6 minutes.

Add the cans of cream-style corn and stir them in.

Add the Tablespoon of brown sugar and the grated nutmeg. Mix well.

Add the onion salt, garlic salt, black pepper, and hot sauce to taste. Heat everything until your Special Corn Chowder is piping hot.

Check the chowder to see if it's thick enough. If it's too thick, add a little more whipping cream. If it's too thin, sprinkle in a few of the instant potato flakes until it's the right consistency.

Add more salt, pepper, or hot sauce to suit the tastes of your family.

**Hannah's 1st Note: Careful if you decide to add more hot sauce. Don't forget that you'll be topping each bowl with a teaspoon of jalapeño jelly, which will add its own "heat" to the dish.**

Turn the stovetop burner down to SIMMER and prepare your jalapeño jelly and popcorn for serving.

Place approximately 3 Tablespoons of jalapeño jelly in a small, microwave-safe bowl.

Heat the jelly on HIGH for 20 seconds to melt it. Stir to see if it's melted and if not, give it another 10 to 15 seconds on HIGH in the microwave.

Set the melted jelly on the counter.

Follow the package directions to pop your buttered popcorn in the microwave. When it's popped, and after it's cooled enough so that you won't burn yourself, open the bag and pour the popcorn into a bowl.

Give your Special Corn Chowder another stir and ladle it into bowls.

Top each bowl with a teaspoon of melted jalapeño jelly placed in the center of the bowl. It will spread out in a little puddle.

Top the jalapeño jelly with a half-dozen or so perfect pieces of hot popcorn and serve immediately.

Yield: 4 generous bowls of Special Corn Chowder that everyone will enjoy. Almost everyone who tries it will never be satisfied with regular corn chowder again!

**Hannah's 2nd Note: Save the rest of the popcorn for later and give the bowl to the kids after they've done their homework.**

**Michelle's Note: When I was little, Hannah used to make microwave popcorn for Andrea and me. She always poured it into a bowl, picked out the un-**

popped kernels so we wouldn't bite down on one and hurt our teeth, and mixed the popcorn with M&Ms. It was a real treat to have the salted popcorn with the sweet, chocolate candy even though Andrea always made me eat the brown ones. She told me that the colored ones weren't good for me because I was too young. Of course I didn't believe that, but I never told her I didn't mind because I counted a whole bag of M&Ms once when she was at cheerleading practice, and I discovered that there were a lot more brown M&Ms than colored ones!

# CHAPTER THIRTEEN

Georgina was back in less than two minutes, carrying a tray with three tall glasses. She set it on the table, delivered theirs, and pulled up a chair to join them. "I decided to have a mango iced tea, too."

Scores of questions had occurred to Hannah as they'd waited for Georgina to reappear, but somehow she managed to quell them until their waitress had taken a sip of her iced tea.

"Go ahead, Hannah," Georgina told her. "I can see you're just about bursting to ask me all those questions."

"You're right. I am." Hannah decided to get to the most important question first. "I know that Mayor Bascomb was here with Stephanie on the night that Tori was murdered. And I know that he said he was going up to her condo to straighten her out on something important."

"I figured you'd know all that. It's one of

the reasons I told my cousin, Irma. She's the biggest gossip in town."

"Maybe," Hannah agreed, deliberately not glancing at Delores, the cofounder of the telephone tree Hannah always referred to as the Lake Eden Gossip Hotline. "Do you know what time Mayor Bascomb got back here to the lounge?"

"Not exactly, but I can give you a time frame. He left right before I went on my break at seven-thirty and he was back here, sitting with his wife when I got back at ten to eight. The night manager's real strict about our breaks so I always watch the time."

Hannah sighed heavily. The mayor was in the clear if Delores was right about the time she'd heard Tori scream. Right then and there, Hannah decided to go up to her mother's condo after lunch to check the time on her office clock.

"Disappointing, isn't it?" Georgina said, reading Hannah's expression. "I call him the Teflon Mayor, you know. No matter what kind of trouble that man gets into, nothing ever sticks to him."

"You're right, Georgina," Delores said. "Ricky-Ticky gets away with a lot in this town, but so far he hasn't murdered any-body. It's mostly just trouble with . . ." she paused, trying to think of an appropriate word.

"Trouble with remembering that he's married," Georgina finished the sentence for Delores. "There's a lot of that going around lately. Kitty Levine was in for lunch a couple of weeks ago and she told me that Howie takes her to this big Winnetka County trial lawyers Christmas party every year. I guess those lawyers know how to get loose once they've had a couple of drinks. She snapped a picture with her phone at the party two years ago while everybody was dancing and not one single guy was dancing with his own wife. And when they went to the party this last Christmas, all those lawyers had gotten divorced and had remarried the women they were dancing with in Kitty's picture. That photo predicted the whole thing."

"That's funny," Hannah said, but once the words were out of her mouth, she amended it. "I mean, it's funny that the picture predicted the future, but it probably wasn't funny for the divorced wives."

"That's what I thought, but Kitty said that once she'd looked around, most of those former wives had new husbands, too."

Hannah glanced at her watch as unobtrusively as she could, but Georgina saw her and laughed.

"Okay, Hannah. I'll get to the point. We can talk *after* I tell you about the last time I saw Tori."

Both Hannah and Delores leaned a bit closer to Georgina.

"Go ahead, Georgina," Delores prompted her.

"It was exactly a week ago today and I was working the lunch shift. Stan Kramer came in and asked me for a nice, quiet booth. He said he was meeting Tori for lunch and they had some business to discuss. I gave him that booth over there." Georgina pointed to a four-person booth in the corner. "I figured they might need to spread out papers and things."

"That was nice of you, Georgina," Delores said.

"I try to please." Georgina gave a dry little laugh. "Besides, the tips are better when my customers are satisfied."

"That booth looks fairly isolated," Hannah commented as she concentrated on the booth in the corner. "The only one that's close is that huge one on the wall."

"I know, and we don't have many big groups for lunch. Mostly, it's just the people who work in the area, a few clerks from city hall, some of the condo residents who don't feel like cooking, and locals who want something fancier than what they can get at Hal and Rose's Café."

"So how did you hear their conversation?" Delores asked her.

"I needed to clean the big booth so I sat there for my break and then I made sure it was spotless for the party of ten coming in for dinner that night. I put out a RESERVED sign and then I slid over into the corner and just sat there until my break was over."

Hannah gave an amused smile. "You mean you just sat there and listened to Tori and Stan, don't you?"

"Well . . . yes, I did. And it's a good thing for you that I was so nosy. It might turn out that I was listening to Stan and Tori talk about the man who killed her!"

"Who were they talking about?" This time it was Delores who asked the pertinent question.

"Tori's business manager. She called him her *money man.* Did you know that Tori got an allowance every month from him? And she had to ask him if she needed more than what he gave her."

"That's not all that unusual," Hannah told Georgina. "A lot of people who have investments with a money manager get monthly allowances."

"But it was *her* money! She earned it, not him! What right did he have to say how much of it she could have? Not only that, but she *paid* him for keeping her money! I heard her tell Stan that she sent him a check every month."

Georgina sounded outraged and Hannah could understand that. For people who'd always handled their own money, hiring a money manager seemed like an unnecessary expense. Hannah understood that and she tried to explain it to Georgina.

"It's seems strange to you and me, but Tori earned a lot of money when she was at the top of her profession. And when you earn a lot of money, it's hard to exercise self-control and not run right out to spend it. Tori knew her acting career wouldn't last forever and she wanted help to make some sound investments so that she'd have enough to last for the rest of her life."

"I guess I get it," Georgina said, but she still looked a bit dubious. "Why didn't Tori just put it in the bank? That's what a lot of people do."

"Because the bank doesn't pay much interest and Tori wanted her money to work for her and earn more money. She probably didn't know that much about the stock market and investments, so she hired an expert to handle it for her."

"Okay. That makes some kind of sense," Georgina conceded.

"Why was Tori talking to Stan about her money man?" Hannah asked.

"Because Stan's an accountant and he went through all her financial papers for her. From what I could hear, it sounded like Stan found a bunch of things wrong with the way the business manager was handling Tori's money."

"That's troublesome," Delores commented. "Did it sound like he was deliberately cheating Tori?"

"That's what Stan said. He said some stocks that Tori had were missing from her portfolio and there was no record of them being sold and reinvested someplace else. And some money was missing from one of the savings accounts she had in a New York bank."

"Did Stan say how much money was missing?" Delores asked.

"He said he couldn't tell to the penny what was missing without doing a full accounting, but that he could give her a preliminary ballpark figure."

"And that figure was . . ." Hannah held her breath. This could be very important.

"Close to sixty thousand dollars. And that

237

was just for the current year."

"What did Tori say to that?" Delores asked.

"She said that she'd get the rest of her financial records to Stan by the end of the day so that he could give her a full accounting. And she asked how long that would take. Stan told her he could probably finish it in a couple of weeks now that he knew what he was looking for. And then he warned her that a full accounting could be expensive."

"Did Tori ask how expensive?" Delores looked interested.

"Yes. And Stan said it might be as high as five thousand dollars."

"Did Tori agree to that?" Hannah asked.

"Oh, yes. It didn't seem to faze Tori at all because she just laughed and said that since her money man had already cheated her out of sixty thousand this year, another five grand sure wouldn't kill her." Georgina stopped and shuddered. "And that's what I keep thinking about. That's just it. That's why I told you all this. It *could* have killed Tori if she ignored Stan's advice!"

Hannah was confused. "What advice?"

"Stan's advice came a little later, right after the waitress that was taking over for me delivered Tori's second vodka martini.

Tori told Stan that she had a good notion to call her money man before he left his office for the day. She was going to tell him that she knew he'd cheated her. And that if he didn't pay her back every penny by the end of the month, she was going to contact every single one of his clients and tell them exactly what he'd done to her and urge them to get their own independent accounting the way she'd done."

"That sounds like Tori," Delores said, looking as if she really missed her outspoken friend.

"Well, Stan told her not to do it, that she would be cutting off her nose to spite her face. He pointed out that if her business manager knew that Tori was onto him, he might grab all the money he could from all of his clients and take off for parts unknown. And if he did that, they'd never get their money back."

"Good point!" Hannah said.

"Tori thought so, too. She said that Stan was right, that she wouldn't do anything to alert her money man until Stan had finished his full accounting. But . . ."

"But what?" Delores asked her.

"But what if Tori didn't keep her word? That would be a motive for her money man to kill her before she could tell any of his other clients, wouldn't it?"

"Oh, yes," Hannah said, exchanging glances with her mother. They both knew how impulsive Tori could be. If she'd done what she'd threatened and called her business manager, that would be a compelling motive for her murder.

By the time Hannah got back to The Cookie Jar, she was thoroughly frustrated. Mayor Bascomb had been her prime suspect, and in light of what Georgina had told them, he was cleared. She'd checked the clock in her mother's office and it was actually a few minutes slow. If Delores had glanced at the clock and thought the screams and gunshot had come at a few minutes past eight, it could have been closer to eight-fifteen or even eight-twenty.

Of course, she did have a new prime suspect. It was Tori's business manager, but Georgina hadn't known his name. Hannah knew that she could ask Stan Kramer, but he would never tell her. That would be violating a client's confidence and Stan prided himself on his integrity. Of course Stan would have to tell Mike if Mike asked him, but Georgina had said that Mike hadn't contacted her. And if Mike didn't know that Tori's business manager had been skimming money from Tori, Hannah wasn't about to tell him . . . at least not until she'd exhausted all avenues to attempt to find him by herself.

The Cookie Jar kitchen was deserted and Hannah was glad. She really didn't feel like talking to anyone right now. She had to figure out how to get Stan to reveal Tori's business manager's name. She poured herself a cup of coffee, sat down on her favorite stool at the work island, and rummaged around in her saddlebag purse for the stenographer's pad she referred to as her murder book.

"You didn't do it," she said to no one in particular since there was no one to hear her as she flipped to the suspect page and crossed off Mayor Bascomb's name. "I don't like it, but you're in the clear."

"Who's in the clear?" Lisa asked, coming into the kitchen with an empty display jar.

"Mayor Bascomb. I really thought he did it, but he's got an alibi for the time of Tori's murder."

"Don't sound so depressed, Hannah. You always eliminate suspects in your murder investigations. Who else do you have on your suspect list?"

"Someone, but I can't write him down because I don't know his name."

241

"The unknown suspect with an undiscovered motive?"

Hannah shook her head. "I know his motive. He was stealing money from Tori. But I don't have a name. All I know is his occupation. He was Tori's business manager."

"Why don't you ask Mayor Bascomb? He's out there having his afternoon coffee."

"Because he'll ask why I want to know and if I tell him, he might tell Mike."

"I get it. You want to follow this lead without any interference from Mike. Is that right?"

"That's it exactly. This might sound a little crazy, but I want to solve this case for Mother. She worked so hard planning my wedding and redecorating the whole condo for me. Now she's depending on me and . . . well . . . I owe her, Lisa."

"I understand. Calm down, Hannah. You're under a lot of stress and you're just not thinking clearly. If you relax, the solution will come to you. There are ways around every problem."

Hannah sighed. Lisa was right. There was simply too much on her mind, and she couldn't seem to think clearly. She had to work out a morning routine for showering and dressing, figure out some easy and fast things to make for her husband's breakfast, write out all the thank-you notes for their wedding gifts, spend quality time with Ross and be a good wife, *and* solve a murder case.

"I think I've got it, Hannah."

"A way for me to ask Mayor Bascomb for the name of Tori's business manager?"

"You can't ask, but your mother could."

"My mother?"

"Yes. Have your mother ask Mayor Bascomb for the name. She can say she needs someone to help her with her investments and Tori mentioned that she had someone really good, but she didn't give Delores his name."

Hannah thought about that for a moment. "Thanks, Lisa! It might just work. Mother's very good at getting information out of people. But what if Mayor Bascomb doesn't know?"

"You can cross that bridge if and when you come to it." Lisa walked over to the nearly-empty baker's rack and took off a pan of bar cookies. She tipped them out, cut them into pieces on the kitchen counter, and brought two to Hannah on a paper napkin. "Here. Eat these with your coffee. You sound tired and the sugar will give you some energy. Besides, they're delicious. Aunt Nancy baked them right after you left. She said she got the recipe from her friend,

Lynn, and everybody out front loves them."

"What are they?"

"Salted Caramel Bar Cookies. I had one for lunch and they're wonderful! The combination of sweet caramel and salt is just perfect."

Hannah picked up one and bit into it. Then she started to smile. "You're right. I like these a lot!"

"So does everyone who tasted them. Just as soon as Michelle gets back, I'll send Aunt Nancy back here to bake some more. We're almost out of cookies."

"I can bake them if she left the recipe," Hannah suggested. "I always think better when I bake."

"It's in the back of the book. She brought it in this morning." Lisa glanced at the kitchen clock. "Uh-oh! Time for another performance. Happy baking, Hannah."

Hannah was smiling as she finished the rest of her coffee and the second Salted Caramel Bar Cookie. She'd call Delores later this afternoon to ask if she'd try to get the name of Tori's business manager from Mayor Bascomb. Right now, she wanted to start baking. Lisa was right. There were ways around every problem if you calmed down enough to think of them.

# SALTED CARAMEL BAR COOKIES

Preheat oven to 325 degrees F., rack in the middle position.

## The Crust and Topping:

2 cups *(4 sticks, 16 ounces, 1 pound)* salted butter softened to room temperature

1 cup white *(granulated)* sugar

1 and 1/2 cups powdered *(confectioner's)* sugar

2 Tablespoons vanilla extract

4 cups all-purpose flour *(pack it down in the cup when you measure it)*

## The Caramel Filling:

14-ounce bag *(approximately 50 pieces)* square Kraft caramels, individually wrapped *(If the kids help you unwrap the caramels, better buy 2 bags!)*

1/3 cup whipping cream

1/2 teaspoon vanilla extract

1 Tablespoon sea or Kosher salt *(the coarse-ground kind)*

Before you begin to make the crust and filling, spray a 9-inch by 13-inch cake pan with Pam or another nonstick baking spray.

**Hannah's 1st Note: This crust and filling is a lot easier to make with an electric mixer. You can do it by hand,**

**but it will take some muscle.**

Combine the butter, white sugar, and powdered sugar in a large bowl or in the bowl of an electric mixer. Beat at MEDIUM speed until the mixture is light and creamy.

Add the vanilla extract. Mix it in until it is thoroughly combined.

Add the flour in half-cup increments, beating at LOW speed after each addition. Beat until everything is combined.

**Hannah's 2nd Note: When you've mixed in the flour, the resulting sweet dough will be soft. Don't worry. That's the way it's supposed to be.**

With impeccably clean hands, press approximately one-third of the sweet dough into the bottom of your prepared cake pan. This will form a bottom crust. Press it all the way out to the edges of the pan, as evenly as you can, to cover the entire bottom.

Wrap the remaining sweet dough in plastic wrap and put it in the refrigerator *(or out on the back porch if it's winter and you live in Minnesota)* to chill.

Bake your bottom crust at 325 degrees F., for approximately 20 minutes or until the edges are beginning to turn a pale golden brown color.

While the crust is baking, unwrap your

caramels and place them in a microwave-safe bowl on the counter. *(Count them as you go to make sure that there are 50 caramels.)*

When the edges of your crust have turned pale golden brown, remove the pan from the oven, but DON'T SHUT OFF THE OVEN! Set the pan with your baked crust on a cold stovetop burner or a wire rack to cool. It should cool approximately 15 minutes.

While your crust is cooling, sit down and have a cup of coffee. You need the rest after unwrapping all those caramels.

**Hannah's 3rd Note: If the kids have helped you unwrap the caramels, you'd better count them to make sure there are still 50 of them in the bowl. If not, unwrap enough to make up the difference from that 2nd bag of caramels you bought, just in case the inevitable happened.**

After your crust has cooled approximately 15 minutes, get out the whipping cream and pour 1/3 cup over the unwrapped caramels in your microwave-safe bowl.

Place the bowl in the microwave and heat the caramels and cream for 1 minute on HIGH power. Let the bowl sit in the microwave for an additional minute and then try to stir the caramel and cream mixture smooth with a heat resistant spatula or a wooden spoon. If you cannot stir it smooth, heat it for an additional 20 seconds on HIGH power, let it sit in the microwave for an equal length of time, and then try again. Repeat as often as necessary alternating heating and standing times until you can achieve a smooth mixture.

Once your caramel mixture is melted, add the half-teaspoon vanilla extract and stir until smooth. DO NOT ADD THE SALT YET.

Pour the caramel, cream, and vanilla mixture over the baked crust in the pan as evenly as you can.

**Here comes the salt!** Sprinkle the Table-spoon of sea salt or Kosher salt over the caramel layer in the pan.

Take the remaining sweet dough out of the refrigerator and unwrap it. It has been refrigerated for 35 minutes or more and it should be thoroughly chilled.

With your impeccably clean fingers, crumble the dough over the caramel layer as evenly as you can. Leave a little space between the crumbles, so the caramel sauce can bubble through (this will not change the taste, but it will look very pretty.)

Return the pan to the oven and bake for

25 to 30 additional minutes, or until the caramel layer is bubbly and the crumble is light golden brown.

**Hannah's 4th Note: Your pan of Salted Caramel Bar Cookies will smell so heavenly, you'll want to cut it into squares and eat one immediately. Resist that urge! The bubbly hot caramel will burn your mouth. Instead, eat one of your extra caramels and let the bar cookies cool on a cold stovetop burner or a wire rack until they reach room temperature. Alternatively, if you live in Minnesota and it's winter, you can move the wire rack to a table on the back porch and set the bar cookie pan out there to cool.**

When your Salted Caramel Bar Cookies are completely cool, cut them into brownie-size pieces, place them on a pretty plate, and serve them to your guests.

Yield: A cake pan full of brownie-sized Salted Caramel Bar Cookie delights!

If you've invited Mother, you'd better have a large plate of these bar cookies. I've seen her eat six at a sitting!

# CHAPTER FOURTEEN

"Oh, good! You're here!" Michelle came bursting through the back kitchen door, a huge smile on her face.

"Hi, Michelle. How did rehearsal go?"

"Just great! The woman playing Tricia's mother is fantastic. And the rest of the cast isn't bad, either. There's some work to do, but I don't see a problem in mounting a good show by Thanksgiving."

"So everything is going to work out fine without Tori?"

Michelle frowned slightly. "Well . . . I didn't say that. The reason I'm a little late getting back from rehearsal is I stayed at the school and took some time in Tori's office to go over the books."

Hannah heard the worried note in Michelle's voice. "And . . . ?" she asked.

"Tori spent an awful lot of money on costumes and makeup. And the play they did on the Fourth of July didn't make much money. She left a note reminding herself to write a check for a thousand dollars to the Lake Eden Players bank account, and I stopped to check with Doug Grierson to make sure the money was there. Doug wasn't in so I asked to see Lydia Gradin, instead. She knew I'd taken over for Tori as director because her niece is in the play. And she checked the balance on the account for me."

"And Tori never got around to writing that check?" Hannah guessed.

"That's right."

"So the Lake Eden Players are broke?"

"Pretty close to it. There's only eighteen dollars in their account and Tori hadn't sent in the money they owe for the performance rights to the Thanksgiving play they're doing. It's only fifty dollars, but there's not that much money in the account. We need to have a fundraiser."

"It sounds like that's the answer. What kind of a fundraiser did you have in mind?"

"I'm not sure. A car wash works well here, but it's cold! Nobody's going to want to stand out in the cold and wait for us to wash their car. I guess we could have a rummage sale in the school auditorium, but the marching band just had one two weeks ago to fund their new uniforms."

Hannah thought about it for a moment. "You could always have a bake sale," she suggested. "The people in Lake Eden always turn out for that."

"A bake sale might work," Michelle agreed, beginning to look a bit excited about the idea. "And maybe we could team it with something else."

"Like what?"

"I don't know. Maybe we could sell tickets to some kind of show, or hold a raffle, or something that would make the bake sale even more fun. We're the Lake Eden Players, after all. It should be bigger than a bake sale, more entertaining and more fun. What can you do with a bake sale that's fun, Hannah?"

"Buy something good and eat it," Hannah answered immediately. "But that's not exactly what you mean. Maybe you could . . ." she stopped speaking and began to smile.

"What?" Michelle asked her.

"A pie eating contest! They have them at the state fair every year. It's a huge attraction and they sell tickets to get in to watch. There's no reason why you couldn't have a pie eating contest right here in Lake Eden and sell tickets to watch it happen."

"You're right! And if people knew the

contestants ahead of time, they'd come to see who was going to win."

"You'll need publicity," Hannah pointed out.

"That should be easy. Rod is always looking for a good story and he'd take pictures of the contestants for the paper. I know he would."

"He would if you managed to get some well-known Lake Edenites to agree to be contestants."

"Like who?"

Hannah thought for a moment. "I'll bet Mayor Bascomb would do it. He loves to get his picture in the paper."

"You're right, Hannah. Mayor Bascomb would draw a crowd. Do you think Ross could talk the people at KCOW into taping the contest and airing a segment on the evening news?"

"There's only one way to find out. Call Ross and ask him." Hannah gestured toward the phone on the wall. "Be persuasive. He's in charge of their extra programming. Convince him that this would be good for the community and also good for KCOW's ratings."

"Okay, I will. Can I tell Ross that you'll be making the pies for the pie eating contest?"

Hannah chuckled. Her youngest sister didn't miss a trick. "Yes, you can tell him that."

"And can I say that you've agreed to be on the stage, helping me with the contest?"

This time Hannah laughed out loud. "Yes, Michelle. You can tell him that."

"What's Ross's favorite pie?"

"He loves Banana Cream Pie. He mentioned it when we were on our honeymoon."

"And will you make Banana Cream Pies for the pie eating contest?"

"Sure."

"Great! I'll tell Ross that, too. Everybody in the KCOW area knows you and your pies and it'll add a little human interest." Michelle headed for the kitchen phone, but she stopped and turned when she got there. "Can I tell Ross that the whole thing about the pie eating contest was your idea?"

"Yes, Michelle," Hannah said, the amusement clear on her face.

Michelle obviously thought that Ross would do anything to please his new wife and she was counting on that. Hannah wasn't so sure that was the case, but for her sister's sake, and hers too, she hoped that Michelle's assumption was correct.

"What's next?" Michelle asked Hannah,

who was sitting across from her at the stainless steel worktable, holding yet another cup of coffee. "We're almost out of cookies again."

"Bar cookies. They're faster and easier to make. And everyone loves bar cookies. Which ones shall we make?"

"I don't know. They're all good, but I'm in the mood for trying something new and different. Maybe we can find some way to tweak one of your recipes with a new ingredient. Why don't you look through the recipe book and pull out all the bar cookies. I'll duck into the pantry and see what you have on hand. If I can find some interesting ingredient, that'll give us some ideas." Michelle brought the recipe book to the worktable and left to take stock of the pantry.

Hannah cupped her hands around her mug of coffee and sighed. She knew exactly which bar cookies were in her recipe book and she really didn't need to page through them. It had been a busy day and she was tired. She sat there longing for the lazy days she'd spent on the ship and the wonderful feeling that she had no responsibilities. It was different now that she was back at home and her personal Shangri-La had vanished. Now she had a whole truckload of duties and responsibilities. It seemed as if everyone in Lake Eden was depending on her for one thing or another, and she hadn't even thought about what she could make for her husband's dinner. Her to-do list was so long, it was mentally tripping her, and all she could do was sit there and feel guilty about all the things she hadn't accomplished today.

*Feeling guilty is a waste of time,* her mind said, *and even worse, it's counterproductive. You won't accomplish anything at all if you continue to sit there and feel sorry for yourself.*

"You're right," Hannah said aloud. Then, when she realized that she was talking to herself, she clamped her lips shut.

*Call Stan Kramer's office,* her mind instructed. *Even though you don't think he'd divulge any information about a client, you can at least exhaust that possibility.*

It was good advice and Hannah got up from the workstation to walk to the phone on the wall. She dialed Stan's office, but instead of getting Stan or his secretary, she got a recording. **We are not in the office this week,** the message informed her. **We will be back the following Monday at nine in the morning. If this is an emergency, please call . . .**

Hannah didn't bother writing down the number given on the recording. An accountant in another town wouldn't know anything about Stan's current business. She hung up and was about to walk back to the workstation when she remembered that she hadn't yet spoken to Delores about Lisa's idea.

Hannah picked up the phone again, punched in her mother's number and took a deep breath for courage. She was about to ask Delores to do something that she might not want to do.

"Hello, Mother," Hannah said when Delores answered. "Are you home?"

"Of course I am. I answered the phone, didn't I?"

"Yes, of course you did. Sorry, Mother."

"That's all right, dear. What's wrong?"

"I really don't want to mention it over the phone, but would you mind if Michelle and I dropped over in an hour or so?"

"That would be lovely, dear. Is there anything you can tell me now about why you girls want to see me?"

Hannah's mind went into high gear and landed on something that was true and would also please her mother "Actually . . . yes, Mother. There's one reason that I can't discuss right now, but Michelle and I really need your advice on another matter that concerns the Lake Eden Players. Michelle wants to hold a fundraiser and we need your expert advice about that."

"Of course, dear!" Delores sounded very pleased. "And I'm always happy to see both of you. And if you don't mind my asking, does that other matter you can't discuss right now concern Tori's murder?"

"Yes, it does. We'll see you in an hour or so, Mother. And thank you so much."

There was a silence and then Delores spoke again. "You're thanking me for what, dear?"

"For being there. And . . . for being my mother. We'll see you soon, Mother."

"What was all that about?" Michelle asked, coming out of the pantry in time to hear the last of Hannah's conversation.

"I have to talk to Mother about something sensitive," Hannah told her.

"Is it too sensitive for me to know?"

"Of course not," Hannah replied with a little laugh. "It's just that Mother and I learned about a meeting Tori had with Stan Kramer, who'd discovered that Tori's business manager was cheating her out of money."

"Whoa!" Michelle's eyes widened. "I've heard of that happening before. My drama professor, the one who used to be a stage actor, said he had several friends who were taken to the cleaners by their business managers."

"Well, it seems that Tori was in the same boat. And she promised Stan that she wouldn't call the guy and alert him in any way, but from everything Mother's said about Tori, she was a bit of a hothead and she might just have done it."

"And her business manager killed Tori to keep her from turning him in or telling anyone else about it?"

"Something like that. At least it's a possibility and I have to check it out."

"So you're going to ask Mother if she knows the name of Tori's business manager."

"No, I already did that at lunch today and she doesn't. I'm thinking of asking her if she'll ask Mayor Bascomb."

Michelle began to frown. "Isn't that a little insensitive? I mean, his sister was just murdered."

"I know. I just thought maybe Mother could think of some roundabout way to work it into a social conversation. Something like, 'Tori once told me she had a wonderful investment manager. You don't happen to know his name, do you?' "

Michelle's frown deepened. "Mother's very good in social situations, but I think that one is doomed to failure. How about asking her to invite Stephanie Bascomb over for tea? Mother might be able to find out from her."

Hannah considered that for a moment. "Good idea! By *tea,* you do mean champagne, don't you?"

"Of course. Mother told me about the last time Stephanie came up to the penthouse for tea. Mother served her favorite champagne and Stephanie spilled the beans about all sorts of things."

"You're right, Michelle. And asking Mother to find out from Stephanie wouldn't break any social rules. It's not like Stephanie and Tori were friends. They got along because of the mayor, but they certainly weren't close. I doubt that Stephanie is too upset that her husband inherited all that money."

"It sounds like a plan to me. Let's bake and then we'll run up to Mother's and ask her if she'll try to get the information we need from Stephanie. I already told her that we wanted to come up to talk to her. And you can ask her advice about the bake sale and pie eating contest. She could probably suggest some people you could try to get for contestants and judges."

"Perfect. We'd better take something for

Mother to serve to Stephanie. Stephanie's got a real sweet tooth and she loves everything you bake. What's her favorite flavor, Hannah?"

Hannah took a moment to think about that. "I'm not sure, but she seems to love things with fruit. And that reminds me, did you find any interesting ingredients in the pantry, Michelle?"

"I did." Michelle gestured toward the workstation where a huge can sat in the center of the stainless steel surface.

Hannah walked over to look. "Orange marmalade? I didn't even know I had that! I wonder what possessed me to buy a can that large! I don't think I was planning on making anything with orange marma . . ." Hannah paused and an amused expression crossed her face. "I remember now! I won it. Florence got it from a friend of hers who brought it all the way back from London. It's very popular over there. Florence told me she likes it, but she said she'd never use up a can that big, even if she lived to be a hundred. She took it to Grandma Knudson at the parsonage for their white elephant Christmas drawing and I won it."

"Does Stephanie like oranges?" Michelle asked.

"I think she does. I know she was wild

about my Citrus Sugar Cookies. Lisa told me she had six, all by herself."

"That's good enough for me. And it's good enough for Stephanie, too. Let's make Orange Marmalade Bar Cookies."

"With a shortbread crust?"

"Yes, but let's modify the crust by adding shredded coconut."

"That sounds good to me. Coconut and orange are great together. Shall we use the crust from my Lovely Lemon Bars?"

"Yes. I think it would be even better with coconut in it. You'll have to cut the coconut up really small though. A lot of people don't like to get coconut stuck between their teeth."

"You're right. And I will. I'll put shredded coconut in the food processor and use the steel blade the way I do when I make Rose's Coconut Cake."

A little over an hour later, Hannah and Michelle stepped into the elevator in the Albion Hotel. Hannah was carrying an almost cool pan of Orange Marmalade Cookie Bars. "Can you get out your key card?" she asked Michelle.

"I've got it." Michelle pushed the card into the slot and pressed the proper button for the penthouse.

"What time is it?" Hannah asked her.

"A quarter after three. I just hope it's not too late for Mother to invite Stephanie over for tea."

"It's not too late. The mayor has a council meeting scheduled for six tonight. I read it in the *Lake Eden Journal.* They're hearing concerned citizens speak about the new parking garage the mayor wants to build to handle city vehicles."

"Where does he want to build that?"

"On the way out to the cemetery, but August Rahn is objecting because it's right next to one of his pastures and he says the traffic will upset his cows and reduce the volume of his milk. From what I heard in the coffee shop this morning, August has several of his neighbors to back up his claim about milk production and it could be a long meeting."

"Stephanie doesn't go to the meetings, does she?"

"Of course not. It's beneath her." The elevator doors opened and Hannah got off to find Delores waiting for them.

"Oh, good! You're here. Come in, girls." She turned back to look at Hannah. "What are you carrying, dear?"

"Orange Marmalade Bar Cookies. I'm hoping you'll serve them when Stephanie comes over for tea at five this afternoon."

Delores stopped short to look at Hannah in confusion. "Stephanie Bascomb? But I haven't invited Stephanie to tea!"

"Not yet," Michelle took over. "But Hannah and I are hoping you will. You're wonderful at getting information out of people, Mother. And Hannah really needs some information from Stephanie."

Delores laughed. "Flattery will get you everywhere, dears. I think I know exactly what you need, Hannah. You want me to ask Stephanie if she knows the name of Tori's business manager."

"Precisely, Mother. If anyone can get that name, it's you. And there's no one else who knows it except Stan Kramer and he's out of town until Monday."

"I see." Delores led the way to the climate controlled garden and gestured toward a table and chairs. "Sit down, girls. I have a nice bottle of white wine for you . . . unless, of course, you'd rather have coffee."

"Hannah will have a glass of wine with you, Mother," Michelle spoke for her older sister. "She needs to relax a little. I'll have coffee it it's made. Or water. Either will do just fine. I'm going to drive us back to Hannah's condo when The Cookie Jar closes and I'd rather not drink."

"I raised very smart girls," Delores said, preening a bit. "You'll like this wine, Hannah. Dick Laughlin recommended it highly. Doc and I had it the last time we went out to the Lake Eden Inn and it was superb. And there's bottled water in the cooler, Michelle . . . unless you'd rather have coffee."

"Water's better when you're thirsty. And I am," Michelle said, opening the cooler and taking out a bottle.

"Would you like a glass for your water, dear?"

"No, thank you, Mother. The bottle's plastic and it's perfect for out here."

"I know. Doc makes sure the cooler is full every morning. He says I need to stay hydrated. When you reach a certain age . . ." Delores stopped and looked slightly embarrassed. "Of course I'm not there yet, but I humor him anyway."

"Do you have any champagne chilled?" Hannah asked her mother as she accepted the glass of wine.

"Of course, dear. I always have a bottle in the refrigerator. And it just happens to be Stephanie's favorite. I'll call her right now and invite her for five. I believe Ricky-Ticky has a council meeting tonight."

"He does," Hannah said. "Thank you, Mother. If anyone can find out who Tori's business manager was, it's you."

Delores looked determined as she went off to make the call while Hannah and Michelle waited in the penthouse garden under the dome. "I wish we had time to go swimming," Michelle said. "It's so nice to swim in Mother's pool."

"I know. It's especially wonderful in the winter when you're relaxing in the pool or the Jacuzzi and snow is falling outside on the dome. This is a gorgeous place to live."

"It really is. And Mother deserves it. I know how much she enjoys it and she does a lot of entertaining out here."

The two sisters sipped in silence for a moment and then Michelle began to laugh.

"What is it?" Hannah asked her.

"I just had the craziest thought. I wonder if Mother and Doc ever go swimming out here without bathing suits."

"Really, Michelle!" Hannah was shocked, but she did her best to cover her reaction. "To tell the truth, I'd prefer not to think about that."

Michelle looked slightly ashamed of herself. "You're right. I shouldn't have said that. But I'd really like to know if . . . never mind."

Hannah felt tremendously relieved when Michelle changed the subject and began to talk about the kinds of cookies they could mix up before they left work for the night. They were just discussing the advisability of baking something fancy, like Christmas Lace Cookies, when Delores came back to the garden.

"Is Stephanie coming?" Hannah asked, resisting the urge to cross her fingers for luck.

"Yes. She told me she really needed to get out of the house and she'd love to have tea with me. And she was very interested in the new bar cookies you'd baked. Would you cut them for me before you leave, Hannah? I never know how large to make the pieces."

"I'll do it," Michelle offered, getting up to go inside to the gourmet kitchen in her mother's condo.

"You'll find a silver serving platter in the cupboard," Delores called after her. "It has filigree handles and Grandma Knudson gave it to me when I married Doc. She said it had been in her family for almost a hundred years. I think the cookie bars would look lovely on that."

"I think *anything* would look lovely on that!" Hannah said, smiling at her mother. "I remember that platter and it's gorgeous."

"Shall I leave it to you when I die?" Delores asked.

"Mother! Don't talk like that!" Hannah gave an involuntary shiver. "I don't like to think of things like that."

"But why? Everyone dies eventually. Life is lethal, Hannah."

"I know that, but I don't like to talk about it. The only purpose that serves is to make living life less enjoyable. We should savor every moment and live life to the fullest . . . shouldn't we?"

Delores blinked several times and then she nodded. "Yes, I think we should. And you have a valid point, Hannah. Dwelling on the inevitable does nothing except keep us from enjoying what we have now."

Michelle came back to the garden just in time to hear her mother's comment. "That sounds like a deep discussion for such a nice afternoon. It's a good thing I brought you something to lighten the mood."

"Oh, good!" Delores said, accepting the small plate that Michelle handed to her. "I've wanted to taste these ever since you told me what they were."

"Me, too," Hannah admitted, reaching for one of the bar cookies. "Dig in, Michelle. Let's see if these are good enough to serve to Stephanie with her first glass of champagne, or whether Mother should wait until she has poured the second or third glass."

Delores laughed and took a bite. And then a beatific expression spread over her face. "These are wonderful, dears!"

"I thought so," Michelle said. "I made one just a little too large, so I had to cut off the excess. I certainly didn't want to throw it away, so I took one for the team and ate it."

"Nice!" Hannah agreed, taking a second bite. "I think the coconut was a great idea, Michelle."

Hannah was about to reach for her second bar cookie when her cell phone rang. She pulled it out of her pocket, glanced at the display, and smiled. "It's Ross. Do you mind if I take this?"

"Go ahead," Delores said. "He probably wants to tell you what time he's going to be home from work."

"Hi, honey," Hannah answered the call. She listened for a moment and then she said, "You're *where*?"

As the conversation went on, both Delores and Michelle noticed that Hannah's eager expression faded away to be replaced by a resigned look.

"Of course," she said. "I understand completely. I'll see you when you get home, honey." Hannah ended the call and looked up to see her sister and her mother looking concerned.

"Is something wrong?" Delores asked her.

"No, not really. I'm just disappointed, that's all. Ross and P.K. are at the airport in Minneapolis and they're flying out to New York tonight. KCOW wants Ross to do a bio on Tori and he needs to interview some of the people she worked with on Broadway."

"Of course you're disappointed, dear," Delores did her best to console Hannah. "You're a new bride and your husband is going away."

"I just wish he'd told me earlier. He could have called me on the way to the airport, or even when he was at home, packing. But he didn't."

"He was probably in a rush," Michelle made an effort to explain Ross's actions.

"They're staying at the Weston in the theater district!" Hannah swallowed with some difficulty. She had no idea why she was holding back tears, but she was. "That's where we stayed when we went to New York for the dessert contest. And he didn't even think to . . . to . . . invite me to go with him!"

"I'm sure Ross knew that you couldn't have gone anyway," Delores said hurriedly. "He knows that you have to work. And he also knows that you're investigating Tori's

270

murder."

"That's . . . true," Hannah spoke past the lump in her throat. "I'm just being silly, I know. I would have told him that I couldn't go, but . . . I really wish he'd asked me anyway!"

Michelle gave her a sympathetic look. "Of course you do, but look on the bright side."

"There's a bright side?" Hannah managed to get part of her equilibrium back.

"You bet there is! Now you don't have to rush straight home after work to fix dinner for Ross."

"You're right." Hannah managed a smile. "And I didn't have any idea what I was going to make."

"Now you two girls can join Andrea and the kids for dinner with me!" Delores said. "Doc has a consultation at the hospital and he thinks it might run late. Bill's working tonight so I invited Andrea and the children to join me at the Lake Eden Inn for dinner. You haven't seen Tracey and Bethie since you got back from your honeymoon, have you, Hannah?"

"No, I haven't," Hannah said, realizing that her mother was right. She hadn't seen her nieces since the night of her wedding reception, and that had taken place over a week and a half ago. It was a diversion and she welcomed it. If she went straight home from work, she'd probably just dwell on the fact that Ross was gone. "I'll have to run home to feed Moishe, but I'd love to join you, Mother."

"Good." Delores turned to Michelle. "And you'll come too, won't you, dear?"

Michelle laughed. "It's not in my budget to miss a free meal. And dinner at the Inn is always wonderful. Of course I'll come, Mother. Thank you for inviting me."

"Excellent. Andrea and the children are going to meet me there at seven. Grandma McCann is giving Bethie a long afternoon nap so she won't be too tired. Can you two girls come a little earlier than that?"

"Of course we can!" Hannah said quickly, realizing that her mother wanted a private conversation with just the three of them. "Michelle and I will leave The Cookie Jar at five, go straight back to my condo to change clothes and feed Moishe, and drive right out to the Inn. Will you be there by six-thirty?"

"I'll be there and six-thirty is perfect," Delores told them. "I reserved one of the curtained booths, and I'll be waiting for you. That will give me plenty of time to tell you both everything that I managed to pry out of Stephanie."

# ORANGE MARMALADE BAR COOKIES

Preheat oven to 350 degrees F., rack in the middle position.

**Coconut Shortbread Crust and Topping:**

1 and 1/2 cups shredded coconut flakes

1/2 teaspoon ground cinnamon

1/2 cup powdered sugar *(not sifted)*

1/2 cup brown sugar *(pack it down in the cup when you measure it)*

1 and 1/2 cups cold butter *(3 sticks, 12 ounces, 3/4 pound)*

2 cups all-purpose flour *(don't sift — pack it down in the cup when you measure it)*

1 teaspoon vanilla extract

1 teaspoon coconut extract *(If you don't have coconut extract, use a total of 2 teaspoons of vanilla extract)*

**Orange Marmalade Filling:**

18-ounce *(by weight)* jar of orange marmalade *(I used Smucker's – if you can only find 10-ounce jars, use two jars)*

Prepare your baking pan by spraying a 9-inch by 13-inch cake pan with Pam or another nonstick cooking spray. You can also line it with heavy-duty aluminum foil, leaving "ears" of foil on the top, bottom, and sides, and then spray the foil. *(If you do this, you may not have to wash your cake pan!)*

## To make the Crust:

Put the shredded coconut in the bowl of a food processor with the steel blade in place.

Add the cinnamon, powdered sugar, and brown sugar.

Process in an on-and-off motion with the steel blade until the coconut is finely cut and the cinnamon and sugars are mixed in thoroughly.

Cut each stick of butter into 8 pieces.

Place eight pieces on top of the shredded coconut mixture.

Sprinkle one cup of flour on top of the butter.

Place the 8 pieces from the second stick of butter on top of the flour.

Sprinkle HALF of the remaining flour on top of the butter.

Place the 8 pieces from the final stick of butter over the flour.

Sprinkle the rest of the flour on top of the butter.

Sprinkle the vanilla extract and the coconut extract on top of the flour.

Process in an on-and-off motion with the steel blade until the resulting mixture is the size of coarse gravel.

Spread HALF of the crust and topping

mixture out in the bottom of your prepared 9-inch by 13-inch cake pan.

Pick up the cake pan and shake it back and forth a couple of times until it looks as if the crust mixture is spread out evenly.

Pat the crust mixture down with the palms of your impeccably clean hands or with a wide blade off-set metal spatula.

Open the jar(s) of orange marmalade and place puddles of it all over the crust in the pan.

Spread the puddles of marmalade out evenly with a rubber spatula.

Sprinkle the remaining crust and topping mixture over the top of the marmalade filling.

Bake your Orange Marmalade Bar Cookies for 45 to 50 minutes, or until the crumble topping is golden brown.

Take the pan out of the oven and place it on a cold stovetop burner or a wire rack to finish cooling.

Refrigerate the bar cookies after they're cooled so the orange marmalade filling will "set".

When you're ready to serve, cut the bar cookies into brownie-size pieces and place them on a pretty platter.

**Hannah's 1st Note: If you lined your cake pan with foil, this is easy. You**

simply lift up the bars by the foil "ears" and place them on a cutting board. Then flatten the top and the sides of the foil, and cut your **Orange Marmalade Bar Cookies.**

Yield: One cake pan full of brownie-sized, Orange Marmalade Bar Cookies fit for a King (or a Queen).

**Hannah's 2nd Note: Everyone loves these bar cookies. Mother says that Stephanie Bascomb told her they were especially good with champagne.**

# CHAPTER FIFTEEN

The first thing Hannah did when she got back to the condo was feed Moishe. The second thing she did was to go off toward the bedroom to take a quick shower and get into the clothing her mother would deem suitable for a fancy family dinner.

She entered the bedroom, glanced around, and began to frown. It was fairly obvious that Ross had not been in a hurry to pack. She turned on her heel, and hurried to the guest room where Michelle was changing into something dressier than jeans and a sweatshirt. "Can you come out for a second? I've got something to show you."

"Sure! I'm ready!" Michelle opened the door and frowned slightly as she noticed that Hannah hadn't yet changed clothes. "You look upset. What's wrong?"

"Follow me." Hannah led the way inside the master bedroom. "Look around. I think you were wrong about Ross being in too much of a hurry to call me."

Michelle stepped into the room and her frown deepened. "He took a shower. I can smell the soap."

"That's just one thing he did. Go see what's in the wastebasket." Hannah gestured toward the wicker wastebasket that matched the wicker clothes hamper and the wicker tissue holder.

"Dry cleaning bags," Michelle announced, plucking something from the contents of the wastebasket. "Here's a receipt. And it's date-stamped with the time of pickup."

"I missed that," Hannah said, mentally chastising herself. "What time did Ross pick up his dry cleaning?"

"One twelve this afternoon."

Hannah thought back to her activities of the day. "I was at work, baking in the kitchen. He must have known he was leaving. Otherwise, he would have picked up his dry cleaning after work. But he knew by then and he didn't call me!"

"That appears to be the case," Michelle said carefully. "Perhaps he didn't have his phone with him."

"Ross always carries his phone. He calls it his electronic leash and he says he doesn't like it, but he has to keep in constant touch with the television station."

"Maybe he was on his lunch hour then and he just happened to pick up his dry cleaning," Michelle suggested another possibility.

"No. I called to check on it yesterday, Michelle. It wasn't ready then, but they told me that I could pick it up any time after three today."

"Did you mention that to Ross?"

"No. I was planning to pick it up after work today, but Ross beat me to it. And he didn't even know if it was ready. He must have called them and told them to rush it, that he needed it right away."

"That means he knew he was leaving before one today?"

"You got it." Hannah sighed deeply. "There's only one conclusion I can draw, Michelle. Ross simply didn't bother to tell me that he had to go to New York until he was actually leaving and that means he didn't think that I was important enough to tell."

Michelle took a moment to digest that, and when she did, she shook her head. "You could be wrong, Hannah. He might have wanted to tell you earlier, but he was too busy rushing around, trying to get everything that he needed to take with him. Not to mention that he had to coordinate with

P.K. That might have taken a while."

"Maybe . . ." Hannah knew she sounded doubtful, "but how much time does it take to make a phone call? It could have been as simple as, *Honey, I've got to fly to New York for a special assignment. I just wanted you to know right away. I'll call you back later to explain.* That would have taken him just a few seconds and then I'd have known."

"That's true." Michelle conceded the point. "Maybe he just didn't want to upset you and he was putting off calling you."

"Upset me?" Hannah stared at her sister in shock. "Telling me wouldn't have upset me. *Not* telling me did!"

"Okay, but he might not have known that. You've only been married for a little over a week. And you got married in a real rush. I realize that you knew each other in college, but you didn't really know each other as adults."

Hannah thought about that for a moment. "Okay. That's true, I guess."

"Ross might have been afraid that he'd have to spend a long time on the phone explaining things to you, and he simply didn't have that kind of time. And no husband wants to tell his wife something that'll make her angry with him."

"True . . . but, Michelle, I don't resent

280

the fact that he had to leave on business, and I thought Ross knew that. I'm sure he realizes that I have my own life to run, and he has his own life to take care of. We're married, yes, but it's not like we're joined at the hip."

Michelle laughed. "Maybe not at the hip, but . . . never mind. Maybe he *did* try to call you earlier and you didn't answer."

"If he had called, Lisa or Aunt Nancy would have told me."

"Yes, if he called The Cookie Jar. But maybe he didn't want to bother you at work, and he tried to contact you on your cell. Did you check your cell phone to see if you missed any calls?"

"No. Tracey didn't teach me how to do that."

"Let's do that now. You get your cell and I'll check it for you. And then I'll show you how to do it yourself."

A few short minutes later, Hannah had her answer. Ross had attempted to call her three times. He'd even tried to text her to tell her that he was leaving.

"I feel like a real fool!" Hannah admitted, once Michelle had shown her the missed calls and the unread text message from Ross. "No wonder Ross couldn't reach me! I left my cell phone in the truck when I went in to have lunch with Mother at the Red Velvet Lounge."

"You forgot to bring it in with you?"

"No. You know how Mother is about taking phone calls during social occasions. She thinks that answering calls in front of other people is rude. And since I didn't expect any calls or text messages, I decided not to carry in my phone."

"And when you got back to your truck, you didn't check it?"

"That's right. I turned it back on, but that was all I did. Thanks for showing me how to check it, Michelle. Tracey probably taught me how when I first got my phone, but there were a lot of new things I had to learn and I must have forgotten that one."

"I'll show you how to put your phone on vibrate. Then all you have to do is put it in your pocket and it won't disturb anyone else by ringing. When you feel it vibrate, you'll know that a call or a text came in, and you'll remember to check it later."

Hannah watched carefully as Michelle showed her how to go to the OPTIONS program and put her phone on vibrate, and how to take it off vibrate when she wanted it to ring. "I think I've got it," she said gratefully.

"Good. Now you've got one more thing to do."

"What's that?"

"You'd better get changed. You already know how irritated Mother gets with people who take phone calls during social engagements. And she gets even more irritated with people who arrive late."

When Hannah and Michelle arrived at the Lake Eden Inn, two minutes before the allotted time, Dot Larson was working at the hostess stand.

Dot greeted them with a smile. "Your mother requested a private booth and I gave her the one on the far end. She said you'd be here at six-thirty and you're even a little early."

"We figured we'd better be on time," Michelle said as Dot picked up two menus and stepped out from behind the stand.

"You're right," Dot began to smile. "Delores and Mrs. Chambers, my first grade teacher, have something in common. They both hate it when someone is late."

Hannah and Michelle exchanged smiles. Dot had been working at the Lake Eden Inn since she was a senior in high school and she knew everything about everybody who came in regularly.

"Just follow me," Dot told them. "I'll take you to your mother's booth. And congratulations for being on time. Your mother's going to be happy."

Michelle poked Hannah gently in the back as if to say *I told you so!* and then she followed Hannah as Dot led them up the three, carpeted steps that led to the raised area with five private booths.

"How are Jimmy and Jamie?" Hannah asked Dot on their way past the other booths.

"They're both just fine. Jimmy got a promotion. They really like him at work. And Jamie's just as active as ever. I don't know how we'd manage without Jimmy's mother to babysit. We'd have to hire a Jordan High track star to keep up with Jamie. Somehow he must have missed learning how to walk because it's nothing but run, run, run."

"But your mother-in-law can handle that?" Michelle asked.

"Yes. She says it keeps her in training and she loves it."

"In training?" It was Hannah's turn to ask the question.

"Yes. She runs the Minneapolis Marathon every year and next year she wants to run the Boston one. The whole family is very athletic."

When they arrived at the last booth on the end, the privacy curtain was drawn. Each booth had a lace curtain for semi-privacy, and another heavier curtain for total privacy.

"They're here, Delores," Dot announced, pulling back the curtains and ushering Hannah and Michelle inside the enclosure.

"Wonderful!" Delores greeted them, and then turned to Dot. "Could you please ask our waitress to serve the wine now?"

"Of course, but I'll be happy to do that," Dot offered, and napkin in hand, she extracted a wine bottle from the silver cooler next to Delores.

*Uh-oh!* Hannah mind warned. *It's not champagne. And it would be champagne if Mother had learned the name of Tori's business manager from Stephanie.*

"Just a half-glass for me," Michelle told Dot. "I'm the designated driver tonight and it looks like it's going to snow."

Dot laughed. "It's November in Minnesota. Of *course* it's going to snow."

All three of them laughed and Dot looked pleased. "It's not going to be a storm, Michelle. Jimmy always puts on the weather before he goes to work and they were predicting light snow and no winds to speak of. You shouldn't have any trouble driving home."

"In that case, I'll have a whole glass," Michelle said. "But only one. After that, I'd like soda water."

"I'll tell your waitress," Dot said with a smile. "You're having wine, aren't you, Delores?"

"Yes. Doc dropped me off on his way to his consultation and he's going to pick me up later. I don't have to worry about driving home."

Once the glasses were filled and Dot had left to go back to her hostess station, Delores gave a little sigh. "I'm afraid I have bad news, girls."

Hannah guessed. "Stephanie wouldn't tell you the name of Tori's business manager?"

"Stephanie didn't *know* the name of Tori's business manager. She called Ricky-Ticky to ask him, and he didn't know, either."

Hannah felt her spirits fall. "So the only person who knows is Stan Kramer and he won't be back until Monday."

"I'm afraid that's right, dear. I even called Nina Reinke to get Alma's number."

Hannah knew that Alma Reinke had been the former director of the Lake Eden Players and Tori had worked with her for several months before Alma had moved out of state.

"First, I had to track Nina down. She got married last summer and she lives in Brainerd now. She gave me Alma's number so that I could call her."

"Alma's in Chicago now, isn't she?" Hannah was amazed at her mother's determination.

"Yes, dear."

"Did Mrs. Reinke know anything?" Michelle asked.

"She knew quite a few things. Alma's neighbor is having an affair with a repairman and he parks his truck in their driveway from noon to one on Mondays and Wednesdays. She's trying the latest low-everything diet and she still hasn't lost an ounce, her sister had a gall bladder attack last Thursday, and her television set is broken. She must have been terribly bored, because she kept me on the phone for a solid fifteen minutes. And I still had to get dressed for dinner."

"So you didn't learn anything helpful from her at all," Michelle said sympathetically.

"Nothing," Delores said with a sigh, "but it was worth a shot. Alma and Tori used to spend a lot of time together, and I thought Tori might have mentioned her business manager. I'm sorry, girls. I'm afraid we've reached a dead end until Stan comes back to town."

"Unless we can learn the name of Tori's business manager from another source," Hannah corrected her.

Delores nodded in agreement. "You're right, Hannah. But how can we do that?"

"Do you still have the key that Tori gave you?"

"No. Mike asked me to give it to him when he interviewed me on the night she was murdered. And of course I did. I believe in complying with law enforcement."

"You gave him the original key, is that right?"

"That's correct, dear."

Michelle laughed and Hannah knew she'd caught on immediately. "You always told us to make a copy of important keys right after we got them."

"Yes, indeed. It's good policy, dear."

"So you made a copy right after Tori gave you her key, but you didn't give the copy to Mike. That's right, isn't it, Mother?" Hannah exchanged smiles with Michelle.

"That's right, dear. I complied with everything Mike asked of me, but Mike didn't ask me if I had more than one key, and it never occurred to me to tell him."

Michelle laughed. "You would have made an amazing trial lawyer, Mother. You're very sneaky."

"I prefer to think of it as literal, dear. It sounds so much nicer. Am I right in assuming that you want to search Tori's condo to look for the name of her business manager?"

Hannah gave a little nod. "That seems to be our only option, Mother. We need that name so that we can find out if he was in Lake Eden the night of Tori's murder."

"That seems reasonable, dear. You can't very well investigate his whereabouts if you don't know his identity. Tori could have it written down somewhere in her condo."

"That's what I'm hoping. Michelle and I will come to get the key right after dinner tonight. We'll go through Tori's condo as quickly as we can and bring the key back to you when we're through."

"No, dear."

"No?" Hannah repeated, and she exchanged puzzled glances with Michelle.

"No," Delores repeated.

"But why, Mother?" Michelle asked her.

"Because I promised Tori I wouldn't let anyone else use that key. The authorities, of course, were an exception. I had to comply with Mike's order."

The urge to roll her eyes was strong, but Hannah knew it would do no good. Instead, she'd play her mother's game. "I understand, Mother. I know you promised Tori that you wouldn't let anyone else use the key she gave you. But you didn't promise her that you wouldn't make a copy, did you?"

"No, I did not."

"So you made that copy and you still have it."

"That's right, dear."

"So you have a *copy* of Tori's key, but you didn't promise her that you wouldn't let anyone use that *copy,* did you?"

"Of course not! And I see where you're going with this, Hannah. Your line of questioning is shrewd, but I still won't let you use the key."

Hannah was stymied. "Why not?"

"Because if Tori had known I had a copy, she would have asked me not to let anyone else use it. Yes, it's an implied promise, but I keep my promises. So if you can't use the key and Michelle can't use the key, it simply means that I'll just have to come along with you so that *I* can use the key myself."

"I'll have the mini quiche appetizer," Andrea said, after Michelle had ordered a salad appetizer. "And the pork with Calvados. I practically never have pork at home and Sally's pork dishes are always superb."

"I'll tell her you said so," the waitress responded and then she turned to Hannah.

"I'm torn between Sally's cocktail meatballs with two different sauces and the Cheesy Pepperoni Bites. I've never seen those on the appetizer menu before."

"That's because they're new and Sally's trying them out on the appetizer menu tonight."

"Can you tell me about them?"

"Of course. They're cute little packets of cheese, pepperoni, and olive, wrapped in puff pastry dough. We came in early to taste them and they're just great. They're nice and salty because of the olive and the sea salt Sally sprinkles on top of the packet and the cheese is melted because Sally bakes them in the oven."

"What kind of cheese does Sally use?"

"Gouda. She's got the kind that comes in little balls that are covered in red wax."

"How about the olives? What kind are they?"

"Kalamata olives. They're my favorites."

Hannah remembered the wonderful, salty taste of the olives and began to smile. "I really like them, too."

"Where do they come from, Aunt Hannah?" Tracey asked.

"Most of them are grown in Kalamata."

She was interrupted by a giggle from Tracey.

"What?" Hannah asked.

"That figures that Kalamata olives would come from Kalamata. I should have guessed that."

"Not really. Green olives don't come from Greenland, do they?"

Tracey made a face and began to laugh. "You're right, Aunt Hannah."

Everyone around the table laughed, including their waitress, and Hannah waited until the mirth had quieted a bit before she continued. "A lot of them come from Messenia. That's in the Peloponnese Peninsula. And some are grown in Laconia. That's close to Kalamata."

"Kalamata is a better name than Mess . . . whatever you said," Tracey commented.

"I think so, too. The olives are dark purple and they have to be picked by hand so they don't bruise."

"I'll bring you a couple to try," their waitress offered.

"Thank you!" Tracey looked delighted at the offer. "We need a new tree in our back yard. Daddy said our old tree has to come out because it's dying. Isn't that sad?"

"That's very sad," Hannah commiserated, "but you won't be able to grow a Kalamata olive tree, Tracey."

"Why not?"

"Because Kalamata olive trees are intolerant of cold weather. Intolerant means . . ."

"I know, Aunt Hannah!" Tracey said quickly. "It means they don't like cold. And it gets cold here in Minnesota."

"It sure does!" their waitress agreed.

"I'll try the Cheesy Pepperoni Bites," Hannah told her. "They sound really interesting."

"And for you, Ma'am?" The waitress turned to Delores.

"I'll have the shrimp cocktail. I always have the shrimp cocktail. Sally gets the best jumbo shrimp I've ever tasted."

"That's one of my favorites, too," the waitress admitted. And then she turned back to Andrea. "And for your girls?"

"They're going to order all by themselves," Andrea told her. "You go first, Tracey."

"Thank you, Mommy," Tracey said politely. "Could I please have one slider with the little shoestring potatoes?"

"Of course," the waitress said, giving her a smile before she turned to Bethie. "And for you, young lady?"

Bethie giggled. "No lady. I am the baby."

The waitress managed to retain a perfectly sober expression, but Hannah could tell she was close to breaking into laughter. "I see. And what would you like, pretty baby?"

"Fank you for *pretty*," Bethie said, and then she glanced at Tracey, who nodded. "Please I want . . ." she stopped and sighed as she attempted to remember. "I forgot. But I would like . . . what she said!" Bethie pointed to Tracey and smiled. "It sounds very . . . 'licious."

"It is," the waitress told her. "I'll put in your order right away and I'll be back in a couple of minutes."

Hannah noticed that the waitress's shoulders were shaking slightly as she hurried away and headed toward the kitchen. Hannah had no doubt that there would be laughter in the kitchen when their waitress recounted Bethie's conversation. "Good job, Bethie!" she said, slipping her arm around her youngest niece. "You ordered just beautifully."

"Gamma 'Cann teached me. But I forgot."

"You did just fine anyway," Delores told her. "Our waitress knew exactly what you wanted to order."

"Fank you, Gamma Dee," Bethie said, and she looked very proud of herself.

"I printed out the menu for Grandma Mc-Cann," Tracey told them. "And she taught Bethie what to say. I thought she did very

294

well. And that was a good save when she forgot a word, wasn't it?"

"It was very smart," Michelle said, and then she turned to Bethie. "What are you having for dinner, honey?"

"Hadog!" Bethie said, giving Michelle an excited smile. "I love hadogs! Mommy puts hadogs in the machine for me."

"The microwave," Andrea explained. "Bethie's crazy about hot dogs this week. Last week it was mac and cheese. And before that, it was bologna sandwiches."

As Hannah watched the interplay between Bethie and Andrea, she found herself hoping that she'd have children with Ross. It would be difficult juggling motherhood with work, but plenty of other women had done it successfully. Andrea was a case in point. She was still working and she was a good mother. Of course she had Grandma McCann to help her. Would they be able to afford a wonderful nanny like Grandma McCann? That was something she'd have to discuss with Ross. And, actually, she didn't even know if Ross *wanted* children since they'd never discussed the possibility. Was it possible they'd rushed into marriage a bit too soon, without really knowing each other's wishes and needs?

Just then their appetizers materialized on

a tray carried by their waitress. As they were distributed, one by one, Hannah found that she was very relieved to have something less serious to think about.

"This quiche is wonderful," Andrea said after she'd taken the first bite.

"So is my salad," Michelle commented. "I love a salad with radishes. They add so much color and unique flavor."

Delores just smiled and dipped her jumbo shrimp into Sally's special shrimp cocktail sauce. The smile on her face was a testament to Sally's culinary ability.

"My hamboo is bery good," Bethie said, joining in the conversation. "I wan to eat it all up."

Hannah sampled her first Cheesy Pepperoni Bite and nodded. Sally's new appetizer was absolutely delicious, a wonderful combination that caused the taste buds to sit up and beg for more. Perhaps she could make them at home for her next dinner party. She knew they'd be a huge hit, and Ross was crazy about olives. She'd learned that about him on their honeymoon. Perhaps it might even be possible to make them ahead and freeze them right in their packets. Then all she'd have to do was stick them in the oven and bake them.

"What are you thinking about, Hannah?"

Michelle asked, noticing Hannah's preoccupation.

"This appetizer. I think Ross would love them and they'd be great at a dinner party. I need to get the recipe from Sally. Remind me before we leave, will you, Michelle?"

"Of course." Michelle looked over at Bethie and then she leaned closer to Hannah. "Bethie's counting her shoestring potatoes and putting them in piles, but she's eating one for every pile she makes on the side of her plate. Do you think she's too young to point out that she'll lose count if she keeps on eating them?"

"She's definitely too young. Remember when Mother took us to Winnie Henderson's farm to pick strawberries?"

"Vaguely. I was pretty little, wasn't I?"

"You were about four years old, I think. And you did exactly the same thing when you put a berry in your pail. Every time you got to ten, you ate one."

"Did you point that out to me?"

"Oh, yes. I tried to tell you that for every group of ten, you'd have to add one strawberry if you wanted to know the total strawberries you'd picked."

"And did I do that?"

"No. You just told me to leave you alone because you were hungry, and you loved strawberries, and you were working so hard to pick them, you deserved to eat one whenever you wanted."

"I wasn't interested in learning the math?"

"Not at all. And Bethie's more than two years younger than you were at the time."

"Lesson learned," Michelle said. "I won't say a word. I'll just watch Bethie enjoy eating her shoestring potatoes."

# CHEESY PEPPERONI BITES

**Hannah's 1st Note:** I tried making my own puff pastry dough once and, quite frankly, it wasn't worth the time and effort. You can buy perfectly wonderful frozen puff pastry dough at your favorite grocery store. I usually keep a package at home in my freezer. The brand I buy contains two large sheets of pastry, individually wrapped. It's fun to thaw a sheet, wrap leftovers inside, and bake them. I also use puff pastry packets to make fruit turnovers or to make little fruit tarts by using pieces of puff pastry to line the cups in a cupcake pan.

## The Crust:

17.5-ounce package frozen puff pastry dough *(I used Pepperidge Farm – it contains 2 sheets)*

1 egg

1 Tablespoon water in a cup

Kosher salt or sea salt to sprinkle on top *(I used Morton's Kosher salt)*

## The Filling:

Baby Bell cheese balls in the cute little nets *(I used Baby Bell Gouda, 6 cheese balls to a package - you can also use Baby Bell*

Brie, or Baby Bell Cheddar if you want a variety of cheeses)

1/4 pound thinly-sliced pepperoni *(the kind you'd put on homemade pizza — or if you'd prefer, you can use any other fairly dry sausage, and cut it to fit the cheese)*

6 Kalamata pitted olives *(I got mine at the Whole Foods Grocery olive bar, but they also come jarred or canned in the grocery store)*

Thaw the frozen puff pastry dough according to the package directions.

While your puff pastry dough is thawing, open the package of Baby Bell cheese and start taking off the wax covering on each small ball of cheese.

If you used jarred olives, drain them and reserve the juice in case you don't use all the olives and want to store them in a jar with juice.

Pat the olives dry with a paper towel and place them in a bowl on the counter.

When your puff pastry dough is thawed, preheat your oven to 400 degrees F., rack in the middle position.

Prepare a sheet cake pan or a cookie sheet by covering the bottom with parchment paper.

Lay one sheet of puff pastry out flat on a

very-lightly floured board.

Use a rolling pin to "erase" the folds from the puff pastry, but don't apply very much pressure.

When the fold marks have been erased, dust a little extra flour over the dough and roll it into an 8-inch by 12-inch rectangle. *It helps to have a ruler or tape measure handy.*

Cut the short side *(8-inch side)* into two equal pieces that will turn out to be 4 inches by 12 inches apiece.

Cut each 12-inch side into thirds, making six squares with 4-inch sides.

Break an egg into a cup. Add the Tablespoon of water and whisk it up briskly. This will be your egg wash.

Cut a Baby Bell cheese ball in half horizontally, so you have two pieces. You will use one piece for every Cheesy Pepperoni Bite.

Place half of the cheese ball in the center of a piece of puff pastry, the cut side of the cheese facing up.

Place a piece of pepperoni on top of the cut side of the cheese.

Cut a Kalamata olive in half and place one half on top of the pepperoni, cut side down.

Use a pastry brush to brush the inside

edges of the puff pastry square with the egg wash. This will make the edges stick together when you fold the dough over the cheese ball.

Use a sharp knife to cut a line from one corner of the puff pastry in until it almost reaches the cheese ball.

Repeat this action for the three other corners.

Pick up one side of the puff pastry and fold it up over the cheese ball, pepperoni, and olive.

Fold the opposite side of the puff pastry up over the top and press it down on the other piece that is already there. It should stick because of the adhesive properties of the egg wash.

Repeat with the other two sides of the square, pulling them up and over the top and making sure that they stick to each other.

Brush the top of the cheese, pepperoni, and olive packet with the egg wash.

Sprinkle on a little Kosher salt or sea salt and place it on the parchment paper in your prepared pan or cookie sheet.

Repeat for all 6 squares.

Prepare the second sheet of puff pastry the same way you prepared the first, cut it into 6 squares and make 6 more appetizers.

When all the Cheesy Pepperoni Bites have been filled, sealed, brushed with egg wash, and sprinkled with Kosher or sea salt, it's time to bake them.

Bake your appetizers at 400 degrees F. for 20 to 25 minutes, or until they're golden brown on top.

Remove the pan or cookie sheet to a wire rack and let the Cheesy Pepperoni Bites cool for 5 to 10 minutes.

Serve your Cheesy Pepperoni Bites immediately on a pretty platter for a delicious party appetizer.

Yield: 12 crowd-pleasing appetizers.

# Chapter Sixteen

"Here we are," Michelle said, pulling into the empty parking spot reserved for penthouse guests.

"Sorry it took so long to get that recipe from Sally," Hannah said. "She was really busy and had to wait for a break so she could copy it for me."

"That's okay. I wanted an extra cup of coffee anyway. I just wish I'd asked you to get a copy for that wonderful cheesecake I had. It was really fantastic."

"You had the Peanut Butter Cheesecake with Chocolate Sauce, didn't you?"

"Yes, and I was going to let you taste it, but my fork kept right on digging into it until it was gone. Really, Hannah. It was fantastic. I need to find out how hard it is to make."

"I'll get the recipe tomorrow while you're at rehearsal," Hannah promised. "I have to go back out there anyway. Sally said she had something to tell me, but the kitchen staff kept interrupting her. She said it was confidential and asked me to come out and have lunch with her so we wouldn't be interrupted."

"That's intriguing. I wonder what Sally knows."

"I'll find out tomorrow and I'll let you know as soon as I know. And now, before we go in, I've got to bring up another problem."

Michelle paused with her hand on the door handle. "What problem is that?"

"How do we keep Mother from going down to Tori's apartment with me?"

"With *you*?" Michelle noticed the singular rather than the plural, just as Hannah had expected she would.

"Yes. I've been locked up in jail before and I don't want it to happen to you. I know that Doc is going to try to prevent Mother from going with me, and I know he could use your help to keep her in their penthouse while I'm searching for Tori's business manager's name."

"No way, Hannah!" Michelle said firmly. "I'm going with you and that's that! It'll go much faster with two of us searching and that means the risk to both of us will be minimized. You can't argue with that."

"True," Hannah admitted, "but you're my baby sister. I have a duty to protect you from harm."

"Maybe you did when I was three but, just in case you haven't noticed, I'm an adult now. That means I make my own decisions and I've decided to go with you."

"But . . . I want to protect you."

"And I want to protect you. That's how sisters feel about each other. I'm positive that if we'd told Andrea what we'd planned to do, she would have moved heaven and earth to go with us."

Hannah couldn't deny the truth in Michelle's statement. "I think it's a good thing we didn't tell Andrea. Just think of what it would do to Bill's career if the Winnetka County Sheriff's wife was caught removing crime scene tape and searching a murder victim's apartment."

"That would be bad," Michelle agreed.

"That would be a *disaster*! There's no way Bill would be re-elected and he might even be kicked out of the department, leaving him without a job and with two kids to support."

"True," Michelle admitted, "but I'm not in that position. The college wouldn't kick me out unless they prosecuted me. And even then, they probably wouldn't. I'm going with you, Hannah, and I'm not going to change my mind about that. Let's stop arguing about it and start working out a game plan."

Hannah considered that for a moment and then she nodded. "Okay. What do you think we should do first?"

"First we get the key from Mother. And then we take the back stairway down to Tori's condo, so no one sees us use the elevator."

"Good."

"Then we search, room by room. How many rooms are in Tori's condo?"

Hannah thought back to the night she'd seen the condos on Tori's floor. "Three bedrooms — she used one as her acting studio — two baths — a guest and a master — a powder room, the large living room, a den, and a large kitchen."

"Nine rooms in all?"

"Yes. The other condo on that floor is exactly the same size, but the order of the rooms are reversed."

"Tori didn't have a patio?"

"She *did* have a patio right off the living room and the master bedroom. It's on the side of the building that faces city hall."

"How big is it?"

"Not that big. It's long, but it's not very

deep. And it's doubtful that Tori would have stored any papers out there."

"Why not? Isn't it a covered patio?"

"It *is* a covered patio, but the sides are open to the elements. There's no way Tori would have put a filing cabinet, or a desk, or anything that could be ruined by the weather out there."

"Okay. That's ten rooms including the patio, but that's a quick walk-through. We'll take four rooms apiece and check out the patio and the living room together. If we divide it that way, we'll be through in half the time it would take you to search alone."

Hannah sighed and then she nodded. There was no arguing with Michelle's logic.

"Which room do you think is the most likely to contain the papers we need?"

"The den. Mother told me that Tori has a desk and filing cabinet in there and she used it for her home office."

"Okay then," Michelle said. "I'll search the den with you and you can do the living room alone. The filing cabinet and desk will be the most labor intensive and it'll help to have two sets of eyes."

"That's true," Hannah told her. What Michelle had said made perfect sense.

"Okay. Let's go!" Michelle grabbed a take-out box from the back seat and opened the driver's side door to get out.

"What's that?" Hannah asked, noticing the Styrofoam box in Michelle's hand.

"A slice of Sally's Peanut Butter Cheesecake with Chocolate Sauce. While you were talking to Sally, I ordered dessert for Doc. Mother was in such a hurry to go, he didn't even get a chance to have coffee."

Both sisters got out of the cookie truck and walked through the parking lot. As they neared the door to the Albion Hotel, Hannah reached out to take Michelle's arm to stop her before she could open the door. "Do you think we should use the penthouse staircase so no one sees us go up in the elevator?"

"I don't think that matters. If people see us go up, they'll just assume that we're visiting Mother and Doc. And we are, before we go down to Tori's apartment."

"You're right. I guess I'm getting a little paranoid."

Michelle shrugged. "It doesn't hurt to be a little paranoid when you're about to do something illegal."

"I guess that's true," Hannah agreed, but her mind was saying, *You're jumping into jeopardy again, Hannah Swensen. You'd better be very careful, because this time you're taking your baby sister with you!*

Delores answered the door at the first chime of the doorbell, and Hannah knew that her mother had been waiting for them.

"Bad news," Delores said, and then she put her finger to her lips. "Doc's out in the garden with Norman."

"Norman's here?" Hannah was surprised.

"Doc called him and he came right over. He was working late, doing paperwork at the dental clinic."

"Why did Doc call Norman?" Hannah asked, getting right to the heart of the matter.

"Because he didn't want me to go down to Tori's apartment with you. He said it might trigger my nightmares again."

Hannah was surprised. "I didn't know you had nightmares! Are they about finding Tori?"

"Yes. I had them for the past three nights, and last night was the first night I didn't have one. I kept seeing Tori down on the floor with her spilled champagne glass and all that blood. It was awful! Doc said I woke up, screaming her name."

"I'm sorry, Mother," Hannah told her, wishing that there were some way to console her. She'd had nightmares about her milk-man, Ron LaSalle, being shot on the front seat of his Cozy Cow milk truck. Tori had also been shot and seeing her must have been a horrible shock for Delores.

"I think Doc is right and you shouldn't go with us," Michelle said quickly. "Having nightmares is probably an occupational hazard when you find a murder victim. It happened to me after I found Judge Du-quesne in Sally's cooler. I haven't been able to go into a walk-in cooler since then without taking a deep breath and telling myself that lightning doesn't strike in the same place twice, and it won't happen again."

"Thank you for understanding, dears," Delores sighed deeply, "I wish I could, but I do think it's best if I don't go down there with you. Doc told me that if I went, he'd have to schedule a pre-frontal lobotomy for me. He was just teasing me, wasn't he, dear?"

"Yes, Mother, I'm sure he was," Hannah said.

"You still haven't told us why Norman's here," Michelle pointed out. "Why did Doc call him?"

"Doc wants Norman to go down there with you. When I told him that I had to go with you because it would go faster if three people searched, he went straight to the phone and called Norman. And when Norman agreed to go to Tori's condo with you, Doc told me that I was no longer needed and that he wanted me to stay home with him."

"He strong-armed you," Michelle remarked.

"Yes, in a way. But he was only trying to protect me. Or perhaps he was trying to . . ."

"What, Mother?" Hannah asked her.

"Perhaps Doc was simply trying to get a good night's sleep. Every time I had a nightmare about finding Tori, he sat up with me until I calmed down."

Hannah laughed. "You could be right. But it's okay, Mother. Norman's very good at searching for things. He's done it before. We think it's fine if you stay right here with Doc, don't we, Michelle?"

"Of course we do," Michelle agreed immediately. "Norman can go with us. And you can make coffee for Doc, I brought him a piece of Sally's Peanut Butter Cheesecake with Chocolate Sauce."

"Oh, my!" Delores said, beaming at her. "How very nice of you, dear. Come to think of it, I was torn between ordering that and the chocolate soufflé. This way I'll get to taste it anyway."

"Maybe not," Michelle warned her. "It's so good, Doc may not want to share."

"He'll share," Delores gave a little smile. "Either that, or I'll simply sneak a little in the kitchen before I serve it to him."

Michelle handed the takeout container to Delores and both daughters followed their mother to the garden. There they found Norman seated in a lounge chair next to Doc.

"Hi, Doc," Hannah greeted her stepfather and then she turned to Norman. "Hello, Norman."

"Hi, Hannah." Norman smiled and turned to Michelle. "It's good to see you again, Michelle."

"You, too." Michelle gave a little wave to Doc. "We'll see you later, Doc," she told him, and then she turned to Norman again. "Mother told us why Doc called you."

"Good. Then no explanations are necessary." Norman retrieved a small, black zippered pouch from the table by his chair and stood up. "I'm ready. Let's go down there and find those papers you need."

"We're going to need the key from Mother," Hannah told him.

"That's not a problem." Norman patted the black pouch. "I've got what we need in here. Let's go."

Hannah and Michelle followed Norman to the entrance of the penthouse staircase, where he grabbed the key that hung from a hook by the door and opened it. They hurried down the steps to the floor below and Norman used the key to open the door to the lobby of that floor.

"Follow me," he said leading the way across the lobby to Tori's door. "Your mother called Tori's neighbors to invite them up for a drink. She wanted to make sure that we didn't run into them. They told her they'd love to come up another night, but that they were just leaving for the mall to see a movie at the multiplex."

"That was a very smart move for Mother to make," Michelle commented. "She's very devious. I think she'd make a really good criminal."

"Don't tell *her* that!" Hannah cautioned. "It's not exactly a compliment."

Both sisters watched as Norman removed the crime scene tape, then opened the zippered pouch. They expected him to take out the duplicate key to Tori's door that their mother had made, but instead of a key, he pulled out several dental tools of various sizes.

"What are you doing?" Hannah asked as

he inserted the point of one in the lock.

"Picking the lock. I told Doc I could do it after I looked at theirs. It's a four-tumbler system and it's not very complicated. I'll have it open in just a few . . ."

A clearly audible click interrupted the rest of Norman's sentence.

"There it is," he said, turning the handle and opening the door.

"I guess Mother's not the only one who could lead a successful criminal life," Hannah said, following Norman into Tori's living room.

"I can pick a padlock, but not a lock like that," Michelle admitted. "Will you teach me how, Norman?"

"No!" Hannah said, grabbing Norman's arm. "Michelle doesn't need that particular skill."

"But what if I lock myself out of the house?" Michelle argued.

"Then you call a locksmith, show him your ID to prove that you live there, and get *him* to do it."

"But that costs money!"

"So does a lawyer if someone catches you and doesn't believe that you live there."

"How are we going to do this?" Norman asked them, closing and locking Tori's door. "And what, exactly, are we looking for?"

"We're looking for the name of Tori's business manager and financial advisor, the guy she called her money man," Hannah told him.

"You're sure it's a man?"

"Yes. His name could be in a lot of different places. It might be on a financial record, a bank statement, Tori's checkbook register if she wrote him a check for his services, her will if she kept a copy of that, her address book if she had one, a list of telephone numbers, or . . . what else, Michelle?"

"A note he sent her on letterhead, or maybe a check stub that she deposited."

"Good! I didn't think of those."

Norman looked thoughtful. "How about a stack of mail that hasn't been opened yet? There could be an unopened bank statement."

"You're right, Norman. And that could be anywhere in this condo. That means we'll have to search the whole place."

"Do you know if she had a computer?" Norman asked.

"I don't know, but almost everybody does."

"You didn't for a while," Michelle pointed out.

"I know, but I was stubborn. And now I couldn't get along without it. But how can

316

we access Tori's computer if we don't know her password? And if she had a computer, don't you think that Mike already found it and took it down to the experts at the sheriff's station?"

"He probably did, but it won't hurt to look. We're going to be searching everywhere anyway. Now . . . where do we start?"

"We start right here. I'll search Tori's living room while Michelle searches the patio. You start with the powder room, Norman. And then move on to the other two bathrooms. After Michelle finishes the patio, she'll search Tori's acting studio. There are a lot of cabinets in there and it should take a while."

Norman looked a bit disappointed. "It won't take long to search the bathrooms. Where do you want me to go next?"

"Tori's master bedroom is huge and there are two walk-in closets. You'll probably be done with the bathrooms before I finish in the master bedroom. You can join me in there."

"That's the best offer I've had in years!" Norman quipped and then he chuckled at the shocked expression on Hannah's face. "It's okay, Hannah. I was just teasing you. I knew perfectly well what you meant."

"How about Tori's home office?" Michelle

asked. "You said that was the place we'd be most likely to find what we needed."

"That's why I think we should search that together. If one of us misses something, somebody else might catch it. When Norman and I are through in the bedroom . . ." Hannah stopped speaking and sighed. "Let me rephrase that. When Norman and I are through *searching* the bedroom, we'll head for Tori's office. You can meet us there, Michelle."

Fifteen minutes later, Hannah entered Tori's master bedroom. She'd found nothing related to Tori's business manager in the living room and she was eager to start going through the closets. Some people stored important documents in banker's boxes and Tori could have stacked them in a corner of one of her walk-in closets.

"I'm here," Norman announced, coming in the bedroom door. "I finished the bathrooms."

"And you didn't find anything?"

"Nothing except the fact that Tori used Charmin Ultra Soft bathroom tissue, and was very fond of scented soap." Norman walked over to Hannah. "Do you have your phone on vibrate, Hannah?"

"Uh . . . I think so."

318

"Where is it?"

"In my purse in the living room. I know I shouldn't have brought it with me, but I feel naked without it."

Norman made a choking sound. "I'm not touching that one," he said. "I'll go get your purse and bring it back here. It's so big, it would be the first thing anyone saw if they came in the door."

"But who would come in the door?"

Norman shrugged. "A detective from the sheriff's department who came around to check that their crime tape was still up? If he saw that it wasn't, he'd come in here right away."

"Right," Hannah said quickly. "I didn't think of that when you took it down."

Norman was back in a moment with her purse and Hannah handed him her cell phone. "I think it's on vibrate, but you'd better make sure I did it right."

Norman checked Hannah's phone settings. "It's on vibrate. Now, what shall we do with your purse?"

"We could put it on the floor of the closet. I noticed that there were other purses there. It won't look out of place if someone does happen to come in. But what are *we* going to do if that happens?"

"Hide." Norman walked over to the bed

and knelt down, looking beneath the bed-skirt. "There's room for us under here," he said, flipping the bedskirt back into place and standing up straight again.

"How about Michelle?"

"We already discussed it. She's going to hide in one of Tori's costume wardrobes. There are three of them against the wall in back of the stage area and one's almost empty."

Hannah was impressed. Norman had everything all worked out, even an emergency plan. She hoped they wouldn't need it, but planning ahead was a lot better than trying to find a hiding place at the last moment.

"I'm glad you're here, Norman," she said, smiling at him. "Let's start in the closet and maybe we'll hit pay dirt."

After twenty minutes in the first walk-in closet, they had nothing to show for their efforts except a tangle of multicolored yarn that had yet to be rolled into balls, fuzz from a stack of blankets they'd unfolded, a box of old grocery receipts that Tori had kept for some unknown reason, and a torn veil that had fallen off a hat they'd been unable to identify.

"Nothing here," Norman said lifting another box of useless receipts and putting them back on the closet shelf. It's got to be somewhere . . ." He stopped in mid-sentence and gripped Hannah's arm. "Listen!" he whispered.

"I don't hear . . ." Hannah drew in her breath sharply as she heard the distinctive creak of the hinges on Tori's front door. "Someone's here!"

"Under the bed. Quick!" Norman pulled her to her feet and both of them raced for the side of the bed. They'd just managed to squirm underneath when the sound of footfalls on thick carpeting approached the master bedroom.

Hardly daring to breathe, Hannah gripped Norman's hand. Would the intruder find them? Was Tori's condo being burglarized? Or was the person who'd broken into Tori's condo the person who'd killed her?!

Heart beating so frantically in her chest that she was afraid the intruder might hear it, Hannah shut her eyes and hung on to Norman's hand. She was grateful she wasn't alone. If she'd been under the bed, all by herself, her terror might have escalated even more rapidly. Norman's presence steadied her, made her body remain perfectly motionless, listening for any sounds that would tell her what the intruder was doing.

A drawer in Tori's bedside table opened.

The intruder was searching for something, rummaging around in its contents. Hannah found herself wishing that they'd started their search with the bedside tables. Then she might have known what the intruder was searching for.

"Ah-ha!" a low voice exclaimed, a man's voice. "I knew you wouldn't throw it away and now I've got it back!"

There was a creak as the man sat down on the bed, immediately above her, and Hannah held her breath again. He wasn't going to stretch out and go to sleep here, was he?

Something was happening. He was panting slightly.

Hannah turned her head and took a chance she would not have taken if she'd thought it through before she acted. She lifted the bedskirt and peeked out of the opening she'd made.

Black tennis shoes with silver shoelaces. And there was a silver stripe on the side, about an inch up from the sole. They looked as if they were new, or almost new, and the tip of the lace she could see was shiny, as if it were made of real silver.

"I knew you'd save it," the voice said, and paper rustled above Hannah's head. "You said you'd thrown it away, but I knew you wouldn't do that. It meant too much to you, and you kept it. You would have changed your mind about me, Tori. I know that. But you never got a chance to tell me so. Who did this to you? I just wish there were some way you could tell me! Who could do something so horrible to you?!"

The bed creaked as the man got up, and Hannah dropped the bedspread and let it whisper back into place. And then, as he moved toward the door, his footfalls grew softer. He was heading down the hallway with whatever he'd taken from Tori's bed table.

"Shhhh!" Norman warned in a whisper, squeezing her hand. "Not a word until he leaves."

They remained there, stretched out on their stomachs, motionless and still until both of them heard the sound of the outer door opening and then shutting again.

"He had a key!" Hannah whispered.

"Maybe. Or maybe he's as good as I am at picking locks. Don't get up, Hannah. If he forgot anything, he might come back."

And so they remained there, under Tori's king-size bed, until they heard the sound of the elevator descending.

Norman released Hannah's hand. "Okay," he told her. "You can get out now. Let's go see if Michelle's okay. I don't think he went into Tori's studio at all."

Hannah squirmed out of her uncomfortable confinement and stood up to brush off her clothes. She was covered in dust and it was obvious that Tori's cleaning woman hadn't bothered to vacuum under her bed.

"Did you see him?" she asked as she followed Norman to the bedroom doorway and down the hall to the studio.

"No, did you?"

Hannah shook her head. "No, but I saw his shoes. And I'll recognize them if I see them again. They were black with silver laces. And they had a stripe on the side."

"That's something," Norman said, turning back to give her a friendly hug. "You did fine, Hannah. I'm positive that he didn't know we were there."

"Me, too." Hannah followed Norman into Tori's studio and both of them hurried to the standing wardrobes. "Which one?" Hannah asked him.

"This one." Norman lifted the catch and opened the wardrobe. He pushed aside several period dresses from the turn of the last century to reveal Michelle, crouching there.

"Boy, am I glad to see you!" she said, holding out her hands so that Norman could help her to her feet. "I forgot to look, but these things don't open from the inside. I would have been in there until Mother and Doc came looking for me. I think I would have been frozen in that crouch for the rest of my life!"

# CHAPTER SEVENTEEN

"Did you find anything?" Delores asked as her daughters and Norman arrived back at the penthouse.

"Maybe," Hannah told her. "We found a bill from a business management service in New York."

"Then you know Tori's business manager's name?"

"Not exactly," Norman admitted. "The bill has the name of the management firm on top, and it lists four of the principals below it."

"Then one of those four people was Tori's business manager?" Delores asked them.

"Not necessarily." Michelle answered. "If it's the same as a big law firm, we have to assume that more people work at that firm than the principals who are listed."

Delores sighed. "Of course you're right. So how are you going to tell which one was Tori's money guy?"

"I'm not sure," Hannah told her. "Do you and Doc have any suggestions for us?"

"Let's go ask Doc." Delores led the way to the garden area. "We're enjoying a glass of champagne. Would you like one?"

Hannah shook her head. "No, thanks, Mother. I'll just have cold water, if you have any left in the cooler."

"There's always plenty of bottled water in the cooler. I also have iced tea and iced coffee."

"Then I'd love iced coffee!" Hannah told her.

"Me, too," Michelle echoed the request.

Norman nodded when Delores turned to him. "I agree with the Swensen sisters. Iced coffee would be wonderful. But if you don't have enough, iced tea will do just fine for me."

"I'll have plenty in just a minute," Delores told him, picking up the phone on the table next to her chair. "This is a direct line and I'll simply order it. That's one of the wonderful perks about living in the penthouse. We can order anything we want from the Red Velvet Lounge in the lobby. They send it right up and all I have to do is meet them at the elevator."

Hannah remembered the nights on the cruise ship when Ross had ordered drinks, or food from their butler. It was a convenience most people didn't have in their lives.

"Doc and I decided that we were hungry at midnight last night," Delores went on, "and all we had to do was call down to the lounge and they brought up grilled cheese sandwiches and ice cream." She turned to Doc. "You liked it, didn't you, dear?"

"You know I did. I ate half of your grilled cheese and all of mine. And the homemade strawberry ice cream was great." Doc slipped his arm around Delores's shoulders and gave her a little hug. "You're a much better cook than you used to be."

Delores laughed good-naturedly, and Hannah realized that her mother would have bristled at the remark from anyone else. Delores really loved Doc and that was proof of it.

As her mother ordered their iced coffees, Hannah thought about rich people in luxury apartments who ordered from restaurants whenever they wanted and didn't even know how to turn on their expensive, gourmet stoves. In her mother's case, it was a very good thing if she *didn't* turn on her stove. And her daughters would be the first three people to testify to that! Her favorite two entrees, perhaps her *only* two entrees, were Hawaiian Pot Roast and EZ Lasagna. They were certainly edible, but no one could eat the same thing every other night. Perhaps that was the reason that their father had made lunch and dinner for them every time Delores was gone. And perhaps it was also the reason that Hannah had learned to cook and bake. That meant she ought to be thanking Delores for falling short in the meal preparation department.

As their mother's new husband, Doc deserved good cuisine when he came home from the hospital. It was a very good thing that her mother and Doc were living in a place where they could order good food by simply picking up the telephone.

*Could that be one of the reasons why Doc had purchased the penthouse condo and given it to Delores as a wedding present?* Hannah's mind latched onto the idea, and she gave what she thought was a silent chuckle. As it turned out, it wasn't so silent.

Norman turned to give her a quizzical look. "What's so funny?" he asked her.

"Nothing at all," she responded. "I was just thinking about having a good restaurant a few floors below me and being able to order anything I wanted at almost any time."

"A few floors below you would be the sub-basement below the parking garage," Norman pointed out. "I don't think you'd want

329

to order food from there."

"Rat-toui," Michelle said, and everyone laughed except Hannah, who bit her lip in order to maintain a sober expression.

"I don't know about that," she said, rising to the challenge. "I think Moishe would love it. Lizard with *Mole*-A sauce could be good. I might even *gopher* it."

Doc groaned and so did everyone else. That made Hannah feel justified that she hadn't lost her touch. "And then there's always *mouse*-sakka if you want to go Greek, or that traditional American standard, ground beef-*snake*."

"What's going on out here?" Delores asked, arriving with a tray of drinks. "I heard you groaning."

"Hannah's punning again," Michelle complained. "Make her stop, Mother!"

"That's like asking the wind to stop blowing," Delores said. "It does no good whatsoever. Hannah won't stop and you know it. It's much easier if you stop listening."

Norman took a sip of his coffee and smiled at Delores. "This is really good iced coffee."

"It's vanilla mocha," Delores told him. "They make it fresh when you order it. They have all sorts of flavors."

"But it has caffeine, doesn't it?" Hannah

asked her.

"Of course, dear. I wouldn't order anything for you without caffeine. Doc always says that decaffeinated coffee is a waste of good water."

Hannah laughed and took a big sip of her iced coffee. "It's really good," she said, and then she turned to Doc. "How would you go about getting Tori's business manager's name if you knew the name of the firm, but not the name of the person who handled her investments?"

"I'd probably call and try to convince them that Tori had referred me," Doc said. "That might not work, though."

"Why not?"

"They'll attempt to contact Tori to make sure that she referred you. If she's been with them for years, the person who handled her is probably a senior member of the firm by now and only takes select clients. My guess is that they'll ask you questions about how much money is involved, who handled that money for you in the past, and request a bank reference. And if you can't answer those questions to their satisfaction, they're likely to refer you to a junior member of their firm."

"Oh," Hannah said with a sigh. "Isn't there any way around that?"

Doc thought for a moment. "You could go there in person. It's always more difficult to say no to a person face-to-face. But you'd have to be very convincing."

Hannah felt gloom settle over her like a shroud. "I can't go to New York so I guess I'll just have to wait until Stan Kramer gets back from his convention and try to convince him to give me the name."

"Sorry, Hannah," Doc said, slipping an arm around her shoulder. "That does seem like your best bet. Stan knows you and you can be honest with him. I know you want the name right now and I'd call that firm myself to try to get it, but I don't think I'd have any better luck than you would."

Hannah was silent all the way back to her condo as she attempted to think of a way to get Tori's business manager's name. By the time Michelle pulled into the underground garage and parked in Hannah's designated space, she had to admit that no viable plan had occurred to her.

"Come on, Hannah," Michelle said, shutting off the engine and opening the driver's door. "Let's go up and I'll make you a cup of hot chocolate."

Hannah nodded and got out the passenger's side. She was disheartened about the way her investigation was progressing. Very little had gone right so far and she was out of suspects. The only new clue that had materialized was the man with black tennis shoes and silver laces, and she doubted that he was Tori's killer. All he was doing in Tori's condo was retrieving a letter or a note that he shouldn't have written to her in the first place.

"But how did he get in?" Hannah said aloud as she followed Michelle up the covered, outside staircase to her unit on the second floor.

"The man with the black tennis shoes?" Michelle asked, catching Hannah's cryptic meaning immediately.

"Yes. Norman locked the door behind us after he picked the lock. And that means the intruder must have had a key. Norman agreed that it was either a key or the man knew how to pick locks, but I really doubt that the man had professional tools like Norman brought. The man must have had a key."

"You're right. Do you think he might be the killer?"

Hannah shook her head. "I really don't think so. He just didn't seem like the type. He was too broken up over Tori's death and he sounded more sad than mad when he found the letter in Tori's bed table."

"A former lover?"

"Perhaps. I just don't know, Michelle. I know he fits in the picture somehow, but I'll have to identify him to find out exactly where he fits."

"You unlock the door and I'll catch Moishe," Michelle offered. "And right after we get inside, I want you to go straight to your bedroom and change into something comfortable. Then come back out here to the couch. You've been working all day and you're tired and depressed. A cup of hot chocolate will pick up your spirits and then you'll be able to sleep tonight."

"Yes, Mother," Hannah said, only half joking as she unlocked the door and opened it to release the orange and white ball of fur that hurtled into Michelle's arms by way of greeting. For the umpteenth time today, she was grateful that Michelle was staying with her. She was so tired, she probably would have fallen over if she'd tried to catch Moishe herself.

Ten minutes later, after a hot shower, Hannah reappeared in the living room and joined Michelle on one of the new sofas. She picked up her cup of hot chocolate, took a sip, and smiled at her sister. "Thank you for being here, Michelle."

"You're welcome."

"I was just thinking about how lonely I'd be with Ross in New. . . ." She stopped and gasped, suddenly remembering what Doc had said about how refusals were more difficult if you spoke to people face to face.

"What is it?" Michelle asked her.

"Ross is in New York! Do you think I should ask him if he could do a little legwork for me?"

"Of course you should ask him! You know Ross loves to help you investigate."

"Do you think it's too late to call him?"

Michelle glanced at her watch. "It's ten o'clock here and that means it's eleven in New York. Is Ross a late night person?"

Hannah thought back to their honeymoon. "He's probably still awake."

"Then call him. Use your cell phone so he'll know who it is and then put it in the charger. You keep leaving it on the table overnight and forgetting to charge it."

"Yes, Mother," Hannah said for the second time in less than an hour. "I'll call Ross right now."

Fifteen minutes later, Hannah ended the call with the phrase they'd promised to use every night before they went to sleep. "I love you too, Ross."

Michelle, who'd been busy in the kitchen during Hannah's call, walked back into the living room carrying two dessert plates.

"What's this?" Hannah asked her.

"Half of a piece of Sally's Peanut Butter Cheesecake with Chocolate Sauce. I was going to save it for our breakfast, but I wanted you to have sweet dreams."

Hannah laughed. "Sweet dreams," she repeated. "I get it. I was wondering what was in the bag you carried upstairs."

"From the look on your face as I walked through the living room to go to the kitchen, I figured you might want to celebrate. I'm guessing that Ross agreed to help you with the business management firm?"

"He did. And he told me he was almost positive that he could get the name of Tori's business manager for me."

"Then he probably can. Try the cheese-cake, Hannah. It's really good."

Hannah took a bite of her cheesecake and smiled in pure enjoyment. "Wonderful! I'll get the recipe for this cheesecake from Sally tomorrow. If Ross is successful about getting the money man's name for us, we can serve it to him when he comes back home."

"How about if he's not successful?"

Hannah thought about that for a second or two and then she laughed. "We'll serve it anyway. This is so good, I want another piece!"

# Chapter Eighteen

It had to be Georgia, because she was up on a ladder that was leaning against a peach tree, reaching for a perfectly beautiful peach that was above her head, but just out of her reach. Of course they had peach trees in many states other than Georgia, but Hannah was almost certain that Georgia was where they must be.

"Can you reach it?" Ross asked her, and Hannah looked down to smile at him. Ross was with her and he was steadying the ladder so that she wouldn't fall.

"I can almost reach it," she replied, climbing up another step.

But the elusive peach, the most beautifully ripe peach she'd ever seen, was just out of her grasp.

"I can't reach it," she told him, feeling small and inadequate. "I'm sorry, Ross, but I can't do it."

"Sure you can. Stand on the top of the ladder."

"But . . . you're not supposed to climb up higher than the top step. There's a warning right on the ladder."

Ross laughed. "There's a warning on everything, Cookie. It's true you're not supposed to stand on the very top, but that's when you're all alone. I'm here and I'm holding the ladder for you."

"But what if I fall?"

"Then I'll let go of the ladder and catch you. I'd never let you get hurt, Cookie. I love you."

"I love you, too." Hannah took a deep breath and stepped up on the top of the ladder. It wobbled a bit, but she steadied herself against the tree trunk and tried to grab the peach, but it was still impossible to grasp. Her fingertips brushed the bottom of the perfectly formed fruit, but she wasn't quite high enough to curl her fingers around it to pick it.

"Stand on tiptoe," Ross advised. "That should do it."

Hannah tried to do as he asked, rising up on her toes and stretching as far as she could. But the beautiful, prized peach was still just slightly out of her reach.

"Jump a little," Ross told her. "That ought to do it."

Hannah jumped, but the peach seemed to

be rising higher and higher on the branch.

And then another voice spoke from below. "Never stand on the top of a ladder," that person said, and Hannah recognized her father's voice. "How many times have I told you that, Hannah?"

"I'm sorry, Dad. I wouldn't have done it, but my husband wants this peach and I need to get it for him."

"People in hell want ice water," her father said. "But that doesn't mean you have to go down there to bring it to them."

It was one of his favorite phrases and Hannah laughed. And when she laughed, she began to fall.

She fell slowly, very slowly, so slowly that she could see every leaf pass her eyes. She saw other peaches, peaches she could have reached, but it was too late for that. All she could do was hope, blindly, that Ross would catch her.

But he'd stepped away to film her instead, to document her fall for his next movie.

The ground approached, faster and faster, and she screamed in terror. She was going to die, broken into pieces by the parched earth below. She screamed once. Twice. And then . . .

"Hannah! What is it, Hannah?"

Someone was touching her arm and Hannah's eyelids flew up.

"Where . . . ?" she began to ask, but suddenly it was all clear. She'd been dreaming and she was still in the lovely bed that Doc and Delores had bought for her wedding present. There was no hard, lethal ground below her, no fallen ladder, no peach tree laden with beautifully ripe peaches.

"What in the world were you dreaming?" Michelle asked her, sitting down on the side of Hannah's bed.

"I was picking a beautiful peach, from a tree, I fell off the ladder, and . . ."

"And you scared Moishe half to death!" Michelle interrupted, lifting up the dust ruffle on the bed and leaning down to peer underneath. "When I ran in here to see what was wrong, the first thing I saw was Moishe diving under the bed."

"It's okay, Moishe," Hannah said, attempting to reassure her pet. "You can come out now. It was just a bad dream."

Michelle rose to her feet and headed toward the bedroom door. "Put on your robe and come out to the kitchen," she said. "Moishe will follow you if you don't tie your robe. You know he loves to chase the ties. And once you get out there and I've poured you a cup of coffee, I'll show you why you were dreaming about falling out of a peach tree."

By the time Hannah washed the sleep from her eyes and donned her robe and slippers, Moishe was out from under the bed. He eyed her warily as she put on her robe, but when she didn't tie it, he came closer to bat at the ties.

*Michelle was right,* Hannah thought to herself, as she walked down the carpeted hallway. "Coffee," she breathed as she entered the living room and the enticing smell drew her like a magnet. Coffee in the morning was the most wonderful gift a sleepy body and mind could give to itself. It woke the senses, spurred on mental function, and engaged the phenomenon that most people referred to as their *get up and go.*

The scent of ripe peaches grew more enticing with every step that Hannah took toward the kitchen. Once inside the doorway, she drank in the heady scent. "I'm here," she announced.

"I see that." Michelle turned to smile at her. "Sit down at the table, Hannah. Your coffee is waiting for you."

Hannah sat. And Hannah drank. And Hannah sighed in wonderful contentment. Nothing in the world was more superb than coffee in the morning. "Thank you, Michelle," she said gratefully. "You may have just saved my life."

"The coffee is *that* good?" Michelle asked with a laugh.

"Yes, but it's not just the coffee. You woke me up before I hit the ground. Someone once told me that if you die in your dream, it means that you'll die in real life before you wake up."

"That's very interesting," Michelle said, walking over to the wire rack on the counter, "but it smacks of superstition to me. I really doubt that it's true. Because, if it were true, and whoever dreamed it did die, how would they let you *know* that they'd dreamed it and it was true?"

"I don't know, but at least we don't have to find out this morning. You came in to wake me before that happened."

"Good. Tell me your schedule for today."

"I'll be at The Cookie Jar until eleven-thirty and then I'm driving out to the Lake Eden Inn to meet Sally for lunch. Don't worry, Michelle. I'll get that recipe for Peanut Butter Cheesecake for you."

"Good. How about after that?"

"I'll check in at work and if they're okay, I'll drop by Jordan High to watch your rehearsal. If that's okay with you, that is."

"It's great. How about after that?"

Hannah shrugged. "It's back to work, I guess. I wish I could identify the man who came into Tori's condo last night, but I can't very well go door-to-door, looking through everyone's closet for black sneakers with silver laces and a silver stripe down the sides."

"Right. If they don't need us at The Cookie Jar, will you go to Mayor Bascomb's office with me? I'll call and make an appointment at three o'clock if that's okay with you."

"I'll go, but why do you need to . . . never mind," Hannah thunked the side of her head with her hand. "I get it, Michelle. You're going to tell him that you're holding a bake sale as a fundraiser for the Lake Eden Players and you'd like him to be a contestant in the pie eating contest?"

"Exactly right."

"Do you have a game plan? Mayor Bascomb likes to be thought of as a dignified public official. And getting whipped cream and pudding all over his face isn't exactly very dignified."

"Don't worry, Hannah. I've got a plan. I worked it all out this morning. I'm going to tell him that his sister was going to write a check to cover some of the expenses for the makeup she'd ordered, but she didn't get around to it before she died."

Hannah began to frown. "He's going to think you're asking him for money."

"That's exactly what I want him to think. And then I'll tell him about the fundraiser we're having, and he'll be so relieved that he doesn't have to honor his sister's wishes that he'll agree to be a contestant in our pie eating contest."

Hannah thought about that for a moment. "That's not bad, Michelle. As a matter of fact, it's really good! I think it might just work."

"It's worth a try. Are you curious about the reason I want you to go to his office with me?"

"Yes. I was wondering about that."

"I figure he'll sweat bullets about turning me down with a third person there, especially since he knows it'll get out that he reneged on his sister's obligation."

"Very clever, Michelle. And I think it might work, especially on a man with an ego as big as Mayor Bascomb's. You have the mind of a politician."

"I hope not! That's practically an insult!"

"Sorry. I meant it as a compliment." Hannah began to smile. "I'm really looking forward to seeing the mayor squirm."

"Me, too." Michelle came back to the table with a crock of soft butter and two muffins. "Try these and tell me what you think. They're peach muffins. And that's probably why you dreamed about picking peaches."

Hannah removed the cupcake paper and took a deep breath of the delicious-smelling air. "Nice aroma. And your assumption is absolutely right. Do I smell almonds, too?"

"Yes. I thought almond extract would be better than vanilla extract with the peaches. They just seemed to go together."

"They do. I put almonds in my Peach Bread." Hannah took a bite of the muffin without even bothering to butter it.

"Well?" Michelle asked eagerly.

Hannah took the time to take a second bite, chew it, and swallow. Then she smiled at her youngest sister. "Perfect!" she said. "These could just be the best breakfast muffins you ever made for me."

"Better than the strawberry?"

"Well . . ." Hannah thought it over for a moment. "I'm not really sure, since they're not side by side. Maybe you'd better make both tomorrow morning so that I can give them both a fair test."

"I can do . . ." Michelle stopped, her eyes narrowing, but Hannah noticed that they were also sparkling with laughter. "You almost had me there, Hannah. You just want both, don't you."

It was more of an accusation than a question and Hannah nodded. "You're right. And while you're at it, you can make all the muffins in your repertoire. I can freeze them down at The Cookie Jar and you can use them for your Lake Eden Players bake sale."

"Sounds great!" Michelle agreed quickly. "I'm assuming that you'll want to taste one of every kind to make sure they're worthy of being offered for sale?"

"You got it," Hannah told her with a smile. "That's purely in the interests of being impartial, of course."

"Of course. Purely." Michelle broke open one of her muffins, buttered it, and then frowned slightly. "You won't forget to ask Sally for that Peanut Butter Cheesecake recipe, will you, Hannah? I really want it."

"I won't forget, but . . ." Hannah stopped, not sure quite how to phrase her question without being insulting. "Look, Michelle. I know you'd never do this intentionally, but . . . you're not going to bake it for the Lake Eden Players bake sale, are you?"

"Of course not! That's Sally's recipe and I'd never use it for anything commercial or public without her permission! But . . ."

"But what?"

"Sally supports the Lake Eden Players. She even hires them to do a little one-act play in the restaurant for special occasions. Do you think I should ask her if she'll contribute a cheesecake for our bake sale? I could make a sign saying that it was Sally's cheesecake and she serves it for dessert at the Lake Eden Inn."

Hannah smiled. She'd been worried for nothing. Michelle understood that she should give credit where credit was due. "I'll ask Sally when I see her for lunch. And I'll tell her about the sign you're going to make. I'm almost certain that she'll be glad to help out."

Two Peach Muffins later and Hannah was ready to go in for her morning shower. She was just getting up from the table when there was a knock at her front door.

"Ross?" Michelle asked.

"No. He's not due back yet and he has a key. If it's not Ross, it's got to be . . ."

"Mike." Both sisters spoke at once and then they began to laugh.

"He was driving by and he smelled your muffins," Hannah offered an explanation.

"You could be right. Mike does have Foodar."

The two sisters exchanged smiles at Michelle's use of the phrase they'd coined for Mike's uncanny ability to arrive just as they were about to serve food. *Foodar* was a takeoff on his label — *Slaydar* — for Hannah's proclivity for finding murder victims. He'd first used *Slaydar* for this phenomenon, comparing it to the Winnetka Sheriff's Department's use of radar for locating speeders, in an interview about Hannah for the *Lake Eden Journal.*

"I'll get the door while you shower," Michelle said. "Then you can talk to him while I get ready for work. I'll give him a couple of muffins, but I'm going to hide two for Lisa. I want her to taste them, too."

Less than fifteen minutes later, Hannah was showered and dressed. She could hear Mike and Michelle talking as she walked down the carpeted hallway to the kitchen.

"Hannah should be out any . . ." Michelle was saying as Hannah appeared in the doorway. "And here she is!" Michelle turned to her. "Ask Mike about Tori's condo. He says he thinks someone got in there last night."

Hannah put on her most innocent expression. Truth be told, two separate parties had broken into Tori's condo last night. They'd gone in first, and the man with the black

349

tennis shoes had come in next. "Really?" she asked, looking directly at Mike.

"That's what it looked like to me this morning."

"Did they steal anything?" Hannah asked the obvious question.

"Not that I could tell. Of course we didn't go through every closet and drawer to catalogue the contents."

"Then why would they . . ." Hannah stopped speaking and assumed a shocked expression. "You think *I* did it?"

"The possibility did cross my mind. You don't have a key, do you?"

"Of course not. I barely knew Tori. There's no way Mother would go down there, not after finding Tori's body, but she has a key, doesn't she?"

"Not anymore. I asked her to give it to me on the night that Tori was murdered. And she did."

"But you locked it up after the crime scene people left, didn't you?"

"Of course I did. It's police procedure." Mike stared at her with the same expression that Hannah assumed he used to interrogate suspects. "Are you sure you didn't have a key?"

"I'm absolutely positive. And I can't believe you suspect me. Do you want me to

350

take a lie detector test?"

"No." Mike sighed heavily. "I'm sorry, Hannah, but I had to ask. Somebody was in there and we need to find out who. And they were smart enough to replace the crime scene tape."

"How can you tell if nothing was taken?"

"It didn't smell vacant anymore when I went in there this morning." Mike noticed the disbelief on Hannah's face. "I know. That sounds a little crazy, but there's a certain . . ." he stopped, at a loss for words.

"Smell?"

"Yeah! That's part of it. When you go into a place that's been vacant for a day or two, it smells . . . vacant."

"Okay. I understand."

"You *do*?"

"Yes. It's stale, like nobody's been breathing the air there. No smells at all, except closed-up and stale. Airless and almost dusty, like no one's walked on the rug or the floor."

Mike just stared at her. And then he blinked several times. "How could you know something like that? It's something I can't even teach my detectives."

Hannah shrugged. "It's a feeling. A sixth sense. An empty deserted place. You know if someone's been there recently, even if they've just been walking around and not touching anything. Then it feels . . ." she stopped, unable to find the words.

"More alive."

"Yes! That's it, exactly. And Tori's condo felt that way?"

"Yeah." Mike let out his breath in another sigh and then he took another sip of his coffee. "So who do you have for suspects, Hannah?"

"Only one. I had another, but I had to eliminate him."

"Who did you eliminate?"

"Mayor Bascomb. The word around town was that Tori was getting ready to cut him out of her will because he borrowed money from her to buy Stephanie things every time he . . . well, you know, and Tori was fed up with his . . ."

"Philandering. I heard that, too. So how did you eliminate him as a suspect?"

"I found out that the mayor and Stephanie were in the Red Velvet Lounge that night for their Reuben sandwiches. The mayor did go up to Tori's condo, but he was back in the lounge with Stephanie long before the time of her murder."

"Okay. That corresponds with what I have. Who's your other suspect?"

"The as yet unidentified suspect with the

352

unknown motive and he or she is always on my list. That's it. How about you?"

Mike shook his head. "Nothing much, either. I've got theories, but none of them have proved out yet. Somebody killed her, that's for sure, but I can't tell you who."

They sat and talked about other things for several minutes while Mike ate another two muffins. Hannah didn't know exactly how many he'd consumed before she came into the kitchen, but judging from the stack of cupcake papers on the table it had to be at least two or three.

"Tell Michelle I really like her muffins," Mike said, getting up from the table. "I've got to go, Hannah. I'm meeting a couple of my guys for breakfast."

Hannah glanced over at the wire rack with the muffin pan. There was one muffin left. She had eaten two, Michelle had eaten two and said that she was going to hide two for Lisa. Including the one left, that was a total of seven. There were twelve muffins in a batch and that meant Mike had eaten five Peach Muffins!

*You're going to eat breakfast after five muffins?* Hannah's mind prompted her to ask. But of course Hannah didn't comply with the suggestion. She knew that Mike was like a camel when it came to tanking up on food. He'd eat great quantities in one sitting and then he wouldn't eat again all day. If he was going to the Corner Tavern for breakfast, he'd probably have three eggs, and ham, and a side of bacon, and pancakes, and hash browns, and buttered toast. And then he wouldn't eat again all day long.

Mike got up from the table and Hannah walked him to the door. When they got there, he turned to look at her searchingly. "You'll let me know if you discover anything, won't you?"

"I will," Hannah promised. It was an easy promise to make since she hadn't told him exactly when she'd let him know. This was not the time to mention Tori's business manager, or the man with the black tennis shoes with silver stripes and laces.

"Okay. Keep safe, Hannah. I know there's something you're not telling me. I can just sense it. But please don't get into any trouble. If you even think you might be getting into danger, call me, or text me, or let me know somehow. I . . . well . . . I worry about you."

"I know," Hannah said softly. "And I worry about you too, Mike. You're a cop and you could face a dangerous situation at any time."

"Yeah, but I know how to handle it." *And*

*you don't* was his implication.

Hannah heard his unspoken meaning and she began to bristle. She'd managed to get herself out of several dangerous situations in the past and she'd do so again if the occasion arose. But Mike was concerned about her and that meant he cared. And even though she was a bit angry that he didn't trust her to use good judgment, his concern for her made her feel good.

"Thanks for caring, Mike," she said. "And don't worry. I'll let you know if I think I'm walking into anything I can't handle."

Mike looked like he wanted to say something else, but he restrained himself and didn't. Instead, he simply patted her on the shoulder, thanked her for the breakfast treats, and went out the door.

As she closed the door behind him, Hannah was left feeling conflicted. She didn't know whether she should feel irritated with him, or grateful for his concern. And then, before she could settle the question in her own mind, Michelle came out of her bedroom, handed Hannah her parka, and they went out the door to start a new workday.

# PEACH MUFFINS

Preheat oven to 375 degrees F., rack in the middle position.

## The Batter:

15-ounce *(net weight)* can of sliced peaches *(I used Del Monte)*

1 Tablespoon all-purpose flour

3/4 cup salted butter *(1 and 1/2 sticks, 6 ounces)*

1 cup brown sugar *(either light brown or dark brown — it really doesn't matter — pack it down in the cup when you measure it)*

2 large eggs

2 teaspoons baking powder

1/2 teaspoon salt

1/2 teaspoon cinnamon

1 teaspoon almond extract

2 cups all-purpose flour *(pack it down in the cup when you measure it)*

1/2 cup whole milk

1/2 cup peach jam *(I used Smucker's)*

## Crumb Topping:

1/2 cup brown sugar

1/3 cup all-purpose flour *(pack it down in the cup when you measure it)*

1/2 teaspoon cinnamon

1/4 cup cold salted butter *(1/2 stick)* cut into 8 pieces.

Grease the bottoms only of a 12-cup muffin pan *(or line the cups with double cupcake papers)*

Drain your peaches in a strainer. *(You can save the juice to drink later if you wish.)*

Pat the peach slices dry with a paper towel and put them in the bowl of a food processor with the steel blade in place.

Cut up the peaches by processing in an on-and-off motion. Continue processing until the peaches are in small pieces.

Measure out 1 cup of the diced pieces and put them in a bowl on the counter. Sprinkle them with the Tablespoon of flour and stir until the peaches and the flour are thoroughly combined.

Place the butter in a microwave-safe bowl and heat it on HIGH for 60 seconds. Let it sit in the microwave for 60 seconds and then stir it. If it's melted, take it out and put it in a mixing bowl or the bowl of an electric mixer.

**Hannah's 1st Note: You can mix up these muffins by hand or with an electric mixer.**

Place the brown sugar in the mixing bowl and mix until it's thoroughly combined with the melted butter.

Add the eggs, one at a time, mixing after each addition.

Mix in the baking powder, salt, cinnamon and almond extract. Continue mixing until everything is thoroughly incorporated.

Add half of the flour to your bowl *(1 cup)* and mix it in with half of the milk *(1/4 cup)*. Mix thoroughly.

Add the rest of the flour and the rest of the milk. Mix that in thoroughly.

Add the half cup of peach jam to your bowl and mix it in thoroughly.

Shut off the mixer *(if you used one)* and remove the bowl. You will be finishing the rest of the muffin batter by hand.

Remember that bowl of diced peaches on your counter? It's now time to fold them into your batter.

Fold in the peaches and then give your batter a final stir.

Fill the muffin cups three-quarters full of muffin batter.

If you have peach muffin batter left over, grease the bottom of a small tea-bread loaf pan and fill it with your remaining batter.

## Crumb Topping

Layer the sugar, flour, and cinnamon in the bowl of your food processor.

Place the pieces of chilled butter on top. Process **with the steel blade in an on-and-off motion until the mixture resembles coarse gravel.**

Fill the remaining space in the muffin cups with the crumb topping.

Bake the muffins in a 375 degrees F. oven for 25 to 30 minutes. **(If you made tea bread, it should bake about 10 minutes longer than the muffins.)**

When your muffins are baked, set the muffin pan on a wire rack to cool for at least 30 minutes. **(The muffins need to cool in the pan for easy removal.)** Then just tip them out of the cups and enjoy.

**Hannah's 2nd Note: Lisa and I like to use cupcake papers when we bake muffins. It makes them easier for our customers to handle, and they look prettier on display.**

**Hannah's 3rd Note: These muffins are wonderful when they're slightly warm, but the peach flavor will intensify if you store them in a covered container overnight.**

Yield: 12 pretty, tasty muffins.

# CHAPTER NINETEEN

Hannah arrived at the Lake Eden Inn five minutes early and waved at Dick Laughlin as she walked past the bar.

Dick was racking glasses and arranging bottles behind the long polished red oak bar, but he saw her and motioned for her to come closer. "Sally's waiting for you in her office," he said.

"Okay. Thanks, Dick."

Hannah turned to go, but he stopped her with a gesture. "Sit down for a second, Hannah. I need to talk to you about something."

"What is it?" Hannah sat down on the closest bar stool and looked at him questioningly.

"I know something about what Sally's going to tell you."

"What's that?"

"She's going to tell you that Tori was out here the Saturday before she was murdered. And she was with a man in one of the curtained booths."

Hannah took a moment to digest that fact and then she asked, "Who was the man?"

"I don't know. All I can do is give you a description of what he was wearing when he left. I saw him walk past the bar, but didn't see his face." Dick gestured toward the doorway. "See how the swinging doors cut off my view of the upper part of everyone's body?"

Hannah turned around to look. As she did, a waitress passed by and all Hannah saw was her uniform from the waist down and her shoes.

"I see what you mean," she said, turning around to face Dick again.

"As I told you, I couldn't recognize the man, but I'd recognize his shoes if I saw them again. It was pretty obvious he'd hung up his coat and changed to shoes in the cloakroom before he went past here on his way to the dining room, because he was wearing sneakers and it was snowing that night."

Hannah felt her heartrate increase tenfold. "Anything unusual about his shoes?"

"Yes. They were black with silver laces and a silver stripe on the sides. I'd never seen sneakers like that before."

"And you haven't seen them since?"

Dick shook his head. "I haven't. Of course, he could have been in here wearing different shoes."

"Thanks for telling me, Dick. It could be important."

"I hope that helps, Hannah. I'm going to really miss Tori. She used to come out here quite a bit with the mayor and Stephanie. She'd have a couple of vodka martinis and then she was the life of the party. You should have seen her on Karaoke Night. It figures, since she was on the stage, but Tori could really belt out a song."

"Come in, Hannah." Sally stood up, grabbed some papers, and came out from behind her desk. "I've got a curtained booth reserved for us. Dot's working lunch today so she'll be our waitress. I told her it was important and she's going to make sure our conversation doesn't go any further than the two of us."

"Great. Thanks, Sally."

"Here." Sally handed her the papers. "These are for you."

"What are they?"

"The recipe for Peanut Butter Cheesecake. Since Michelle ordered three pieces, I figured she'd want it."

"You figured right. She reminded me to

362

ask you for the recipe this morning. I had half of her slice last night. It's a great cheesecake, Sally."

"Thanks. Dick likes it, too." Sally led the way down the hall and into the main dining room where Dot was waiting to show them to their booth.

Sally waited until they were seated and Dot had left and then she leaned forward toward Hannah. "Tori called to reserve this booth every time she made a reservation. And that was at least three times a week."

"Dick said she was in the bar quite often. And she enjoyed singing on Karaoke Night."

"Tori was good. Usually I was too busy to duck in there to hear her, but I saw her perform a couple of times. The mayor's not bad, either. They did a duet one night that would knock your socks off. It was 'I Got You, Babe,' the song that made Sonny and Cher famous."

"I didn't know Mayor Bascomb could sing!"

"Neither did Stephanie from the look on her face. I've seen freshly caught trout that looked less surprised than she did."

"Was she angry with the mayor for getting up to sing?"

"Oh, no! Stephanie loved it, once she re- alized he had a good voice. He even coaxed her up there to do one song with them."

"Sounds like a fun-filled night."

"It was, but not until Tori got rid of the man she met for dinner. Their waitress told me that they were fighting all the way through their meal. And Tori wouldn't let her come in to serve their food. She just told her to leave it on the stand outside the curtains and they'd bring it in themselves."

"Did your waitress recognize the man?"

"No. She said she never got a good look at his face. Every time she pulled back the curtain, he turned his face away from her. And she probably wouldn't have recognized him anyway. She lives twenty miles away and drives in to work here. She described his shoes, though. Did Dick tell you he saw the man come in?"

"Yes, he did. Did the waitress tell you anything else about the fight they had?"

"She did. She said Tori told him to get lost, that she never wanted to see him again, and that it had been a mistake in the first place. He tried to bring her around, but she didn't want to hear it, and he ended up leaving halfway through the entrée."

"Did Tori go after him?"

Sally laughed. "Heavens, no! The waitress said she looked relieved that he was gone. She ordered another vodka martini, chatted with the waitress for a few minutes, and ate her dinner. As a matter of fact, she even ordered dessert, so I guess she couldn't have been too upset about breaking up with him, if that's what it was."

"What did Tori do after she finished her dinner?"

"She used her cell phone to call the mayor and Stephanie and ask them to join her in the bar. I checked the bill and she'd had three vodka martinis by that time and she was pretty sloshed. And that's what I wanted to tell you about. It might not have anything to do with Tori's murder, but you never know."

"You're right. You never do. Thanks for telling me, Sally."

"You're welcome. I ordered for you, if that's all right. I've got a new warm duck salad that I want you to try."

"Perfect!" Hannah said, and she meant it. She loved duck and Sally prepared it beautifully.

The salad was every bit as wonderful as Hannah expected it to be, and they chatted about inconsequential things over lunch.

Hannah thanked Sally again for the lunch, the information, and the cheesecake recipe, waved at Dick on her way out, and went to the cloakroom to change into her boots and put on her parka.

Since she'd parked in a spot very close to the entrance, it didn't take Hannah long to start her cookie truck and drive back to town. Once there, she went straight to Jordan High to see if Michelle was through with her rehearsal.

"I told you he'd break your heart!"

"But Mother . . . I know he loves me! And he promised me that he'd never . . ."

"Men always promise," the woman playing Tricia's mother interrupted her. "Believe me, dear. It means nothing."

"But I know he means it, Mother."

"Of course he does . . . right now. But just wait. Another one will come along. And then another. And then another. And each time he'll promise, and each time he may very well mean it. But . . . listen to me carefully, dear."

Hannah watched as the older woman she didn't recognize stepped closer to Tricia. In the bright lights from the stage, she could see the tears glistening in the older woman's eyes.

"I love you, dear. And I'd never lie to you. He can promise and promise, but that won't stop it from happening again. Once they

366

cheat, they'll cheat again."

"But, Mother. I love him. What can I do?"

The older woman stepped away and sighed deeply. "Nothing, dear. You can do nothing. But I can. There's only one thing that'll stop him. And I'll take care of that for you!"

As the curtain closed on the scene, Hannah felt a chill run down her spine. Even though the words were never actually spoken, she knew exactly what the older woman was going to do in the next act of the play.

"Good!" Michelle said, standing up and motioning for the house lights to go on. "That was much better, Tricia. And Vivian? I really didn't think there was any way you could improve on your performance yesterday, but today was even better. You really ought to be on the stage."

"Thank you," the older actress responded.

"Act Three tomorrow," Michelle told the cast that was now sitting on the apron of the stage. "If everyone comes on time, we can get through Act Three and even have time to break for lunch."

"When will we rehearse all three acts together?" Tricia asked Michelle.

"That'll be next week on Monday. Or perhaps on Sunday if Act Three goes well tomorrow." Michelle glanced down at her notebook. "I need everyone here at noon Saturday with everything they're bringing for the bake sale. I have the list, and when you get here, we'll price everything and set it out. The bake sale will take place right after the pie eating contest."

"And the pie eating contest begins at one?" Trudi Schumann asked.

"That's right. I talked to Rod Metcalf this morning. He's going to run a feature article on the contest and the bake sale in tomorrow's paper. And he also agreed to sell tickets to the contest for us at the newspaper office."

"Who are the contestants?" Becky Summers asked her.

"One is Rose McDermott. She said she loves Hannah's Banana Cream Pie. Not only that, Rose and Hal are going to sell contest tickets at the café."

"Too bad you couldn't talk your mother into being a contestant," Tricia said. "Everyone in town would have turned up for that!"

Michelle laughed right along with everyone else. "You're right, Tricia. I'm a fast talker and I'm pretty convincing, but I'm not *that* convincing! I don't think anyone could talk my mother into getting pie on her face in public."

"Who else are you planning to ask?" Trudi

wanted to know.

"I'm talking to Mayor Bascomb about it this afternoon."

"Good luck!" Trudi looked amused. "Our mayor thinks of himself as dignified. I don't think he'd want to be seen with pie on his face either."

"I'll try to convince Mayor Bascomb," Michelle promised. "Do any of you have suggestions for the other contestant?"

"How about Al Percy?" Loretta Richardson suggested. "Everyone in town knows Al. He's president of the Lions Club, he supports all the athletics at Jordan High, and he was the Grand Marshal of the Fourth of July parade last year."

"That's a good idea!" Trudi said. "Al would be perfect. And he prints his own flyers down at the real estate office. I bet he'd do some for us for the play."

"Thanks, Loretta!" Michelle said. "Since Andrea works there, I'll drop by and ask her to ask Al."

"Perfect!" Trudi said with a smile. "Andrea can talk anybody into anything."

"I have a favor to ask of you, Trudi," Michelle said. "Do you think you could get Cliff to sell tickets to the pie eating contest at the hardware store?"

"I'll do that and I know he will. I'll run

over there this afternoon and ask him."

"Thanks, Trudi." Michelle gave her a smile, and then she turned to the rest of the group. "Thanks, everyone. That was a really good rehearsal and this is going to be a great play. I want all of you to pick up tickets on the way out. They're on a table in the lobby in packs of twenties. Take as many as you think you can sell and get out there tomorrow and sell them. And don't forget to tell everyone that there'll be a bake sale after the contest and we'll have a drawing for one of Hannah's pies."

"I wish we knew if the mayor was going to be a contestant," Loretta said. "That would make it a lot easier to sell tickets."

"You're right. I'll call Trudi if I'm successful at getting the mayor to agree, and she'll pass the word to all of you. And I'll check with Andrea about Al." Michelle picked up her things and smiled. "Okay. That's it for today. I'll see you all here tomorrow for Act Three."

Michelle glanced around and caught sight of Hannah standing at the back of the auditorium. She gave a little wave, and hurried to join her older sister. "Hi, Hannah," she said when she arrived at her side. "I didn't see you come in."

"I've been here for a few minutes." Hannah moved a bit closer so she wouldn't be overheard by the Lake Eden Players who were leaving. "Vivian is a really good actress."

"I know. And Tricia told me that Tori never complimented her on her performance. She also said that Tori never complimented anyone else, either. They all mentioned that Tori was a good director, but I don't think anyone liked her very much."

Hannah's mind snapped into high gear. "Did any one of the Lake Eden Players really dislike Tori?"

"Not really. And believe me, I asked that question!" Michelle gave a little laugh. "I'm learning how your mind works, Hannah. I knew you'd ask me that."

"Just checking," Hannah said. "For a minute there, I thought I'd have another suspect."

"No such luck. Did Sally tell you anything useful, Hannah? And did she give you the cheesecake recipe? And did Ross get back to you about Tori's business manager?"

"Yes, yes, and no. Let's go talk to the mayor, Michelle. I'll tell you all about it when we get back to The Cookie Jar."

# PEANUT BUTTER CHEESECAKE WITH CHOCOLATE PEANUT BUTTER SAUCE

**The Crust:**

2 cups chocolate wafer cookie crumbs *(measure AFTER crushing — I used Nabisco chocolate wafers)*

3/4 stick melted butter *(6 Tablespoons, 3 ounces)*

1 teaspoon vanilla extract

Pour the melted butter and vanilla extract over the cookie crumbs. Mix with a fork until everything is evenly moistened.

Cut a circle of parchment paper *(or wax paper)* to fit inside the bottom of a 9-inch Springform pan. Spray the pan with Pam or another nonstick cooking spray, set the paper circle in place, and spray that.

Dump the moistened cookie crumbs in the pan. With impeccably clean hands, press the moistened cookie crumbs down over the paper circle and one inch up the sides.

Stick the pan in the freezer for 15 to 30 minutes while you prepare the rest of the cheesecake.

## The Baked Topping:

2 cups sour cream
1/2 cup white *(granulated)* sugar
1 teaspoon vanilla extract

Mix the sour cream, sugar, and vanilla together in a small bowl. Cover and refrigerate. You will put on this topping right after the cheesecake comes out of the oven.

## The Chocolate Peanut Butter Sauce:

11.75-ounce *(by weight)* jar of hot fudge ice cream topping *(I used Smucker's)*
1/4 cup peanut butter *(I used smooth Jif, not the crunchy)*

In a separate microwave-safe bowl, spoon out the hot fudge ice cream topping and add the quarter cup of peanut butter on top.

Stick the bowl in the microwave and heat it on HIGH for 30 seconds. Let it sit in the microwave for an additional 30 seconds and then stir. Let it cool on the counter, cover the bowl with plastic wrap, and refrigerate it.

Preheat the oven to 350 degrees F., rack in the middle position, while you mix up the cheesecake batter. By the time you're through, the oven should be up to temperature and ready for you to bake.

## The Cheesecake Batter

1 cup white *(granulated)* sugar

3 eight-ounce packages brick cream cheese at room temperature *(total of 24 ounces — I used Philadelphia Cream Cheese in the silver box)*

1/4 cup peanut butter *(I used Jif smooth peanut butter)*

1/2 cup mayonnaise

4 eggs

2 cups peanut butter chips *(I used Reese's in an 11-ounce bag)*

2 teaspoons vanilla extract

1 cup miniature chocolate chips *(I used Nestlé — approximately half of an 11 or 12 ounce package)*

Place the sugar in the bowl of an electric mixer. Add the blocks of cream cheese, the peanut butter, and the mayonnaise. Mix it at MEDIUM speed until the batter is smooth and creamy.

Add the eggs, one at a time, beating after each addition.

Melt the peanut butter chips in a microwave-safe bowl for 1 minute. Let them sit in the microwave for one minute and then try to stir them smooth. *(Chips may retain their shape, so stir to see if they're actually melted. If not, microwave in 20-*

*second increments followed by 20 seconds of standing time until you can stir them smooth.)*

Cool the melted chips for a minute or two on a cold stovetop burner or on a towel on the kitchen counter.

Mix the peanut butter chips into the batter gradually at LOW speed.

Add the vanilla extract and mix it in thoroughly.

Scrape down the bowl and take it out of the mixer.

Stir in the miniature chocolate chips by hand.

Pour the batter on top of the chilled crust, set the pan on a cookie sheet to catch any drips, and bake it at 350 degrees F. for 55 to 60 minutes. Remove the pan from the oven, but DON'T SHUT OFF THE OVEN.

Starting in the center, spoon the sour cream topping over the top of the cheesecake, spreading it out in a circle to within a half-inch of the rim. Return the pan to the oven and bake your cheesecake for an additional 8 minutes.

Take your cheesecake out of the oven and cool it in the pan on a wire rack. *(This time, you can shut off the oven.)* When the Springform pan is cool enough to pick up with your bare hands, place it in the refrigerator and chill it, uncovered, for at least 8 hours.

To serve, run a knife around the inside rim of the pan, release the Springform catch on the side, and lift off the rim. Place a piece of waxed paper on a flat plate and tip it upside down over the top of your cheesecake. Invert the cheesecake so that it rests on the paper.

Carefully pry off the bottom of the Springform pan and remove the paper from the crust.

Invert a serving platter over the crust of your cheesecake. Flip the cheesecake right side up, take off the top plate, and remove the waxed paper.

Take the bowl with the hot fudge peanut butter mixture out of the refrigerator, uncover it, and microwave the contents for 30 seconds on HIGH power. Let it sit in the microwave for 30 additional seconds and then spread the chocolate peanut butter sauce over the sour cream topping on your cheesecake. If the sauce hardens too fast when it touches the chilled cheesecake, simply microwave the sauce for another few seconds for ease in spreading. You can drizzle a little down the sides if you wish.

Yield: The number of pie-shaped pieces

you can cut from this cheesecake depends entirely on you. If your guests love cheese-cake, cut the pieces a little larger. If you've just had a big meal and your guests are too full to appreciate a large piece, cut smaller pieces. If you invited Mother to join you for dessert, you can depend on her to have a second piece, even if you decided to cut large pieces!

# CHAPTER TWENTY

"Thank you for seeing us, Mayor Bascomb," Michelle said as they were ushered into his office.

"It's always a pleasure to see you, Michelle. How's college?"

"Good, Mayor Bascomb. You probably heard that I'm doing work-study for college credits here in Lake Eden for the rest of the semester."

"That's wonderful, Michelle. I'm sure your family is glad to have you back in Lake Eden for a while. Isn't that right, Hannah?"

"Yes it is, Mayor Bascomb."

He gave Hannah the smile she always thought of as *smarmy* and turned back to Michelle. "Are you working at The Cookie Jar for your sister?"

"Yes, but that's not work-study. That's because I love Hannah, and I love to bake."

"Admirable." Mayor Bascomb nodded and turned back to Hannah. "And how are you, Hannah?"

"Just fine, thank you. I'm not sure you know this, but Michelle is working for the Lake Eden Players. The college has sent her here to direct the Thanksgiving play."

"Wonderful!" Mayor Bascomb smiled at Michelle. "I'd forgotten that you were a drama major. I'm happy to hear that our traditions will be upheld. Lake Eden has had a Thanksgiving play for the past twenty-seven years."

"And the play is the reason I came to see you today, Mayor Bascomb," Michelle said quickly. "Your sister did such a wonderful job with the production that it shouldn't really be a problem to wrap up a few loose ends and perform it."

"I'm glad to hear that." Mayor Bascomb assumed an expression that was both grateful and sorrowful.

Hannah knew it was mean of her to even think it, but she wondered if he had practiced that same expression in front of the mirror to make sure it reflected the emotions that he wanted to convey.

"My older sister, Victoria, was a very talented and generous person."

"She certainly was!" Michelle agreed, and Hannah knew that her youngest sister had glommed onto the word *generous* and would use it to the advantage of the Lake Eden Players.

"Her generosity is certainly something I've encountered in the short time I've been their director."

"How so?" Mayor Bascomb asked.

Hannah felt like cheering. Ricky-Ticky had waltzed right into Michelle's trap.

"She ordered new makeup for the production and it's the best that money can buy. It's even more expensive than the makeup we use in Macalester College theatrical productions."

"Well, I'm glad to hear that. The Lake Eden Players deserve the best."

Hannah wanted to cheer for a second time. The teeth of Michelle's trap had just clanged shut.

"They certainly *do* deserve the best. They're working so hard on this production, Mayor Bascomb. I'm very proud of them. But we do have a slight problem."

"What's that, Michelle?"

"Your sister promised to write a check for the makeup invoice and she . . . well . . . she didn't get to it before she . . ." Michelle stopped and brushed a tear from her cheek.

Hannah stared at her sister in shock when she realized that a very real tear had begun to roll down Michelle's other cheek.

"It's so very sad," Michelle concluded.

"Well . . . yes, it's very sad. And I'd love to help you out . . . but there's a slight problem." Mayor Bascomb paused and Hannah could see him go on the defensive. "I'm sorry about this, Michelle. I'd write a check immediately, but probate has to be settled before . . ."

"Oh no, Mayor Bascomb!" Michelle looked properly shocked. "I didn't mean *that* at all! We're holding a bake sale to pay for the makeup, and we're even selling tickets to a pie eating contest on Saturday afternoon."

Hannah could see Mayor Bascomb visibly relax and he smiled at Michelle kindly. "What a good idea! I'll be sure to pass the word to everyone, Michelle."

"Thank you, Mayor Bascomb! I was hoping you'd say that. If you mention it, I'm sure that people will come. And perhaps I shouldn't even ask, but . . ."

Hannah watched in amazement as Michelle stopped speaking and a blush rose to her cheeks.

"What is it, Michelle?" Their mayor smiled at her kindly.

"Well . . . I know it's a lot to ask, but . . . would you possibly consider being a contestant in our pie eating contest?"

"I . . . well . . . I'm really not . . ." Mayor Bascomb equivocated.

"Wait!" Michelle interrupted what was sure to be a refusal. "Let me tell you about the contest before you say anything else. It's not going to be one of those pie-in-your-face awful contests you see on television. And by the way, KCOW will be televising it."

"Really?" Mayor Bascomb began to smile. "Tell me more about this contest, Michelle."

Hannah bit the inside of her cheek to keep from chuckling, as Michelle continued. "There won't be any hands tied behind your back or anything undignified like that. Each contestant will be given a spoon and they'll have one to two minutes to eat as much pie out of the pie plate as they can. Then the judges will inspect the pie plates and declare the winner. Of course, the winner will be featured on the front page of the *Lake Eden Journal* in their Sunday edition."

"Really! A spoon, you say? And no hands behind the back?"

"That's right. I certainly don't want to embarrass any of our Lake Eden citizens."

"Of course not. That's very perceptive of you, Michelle."

He still hadn't agreed and Hannah held

her breath. Had Michelle planned for this?

"There's something else, Mayor Bascomb. The Lake Eden Players are planning a small tribute to your sister right after the Thanksgiving play. It'll take place during our curtain call and . . ." Michelle stopped and sighed. "I know it's a lot to ask, but would you and Mrs. Bascomb consider announcing the names of the players as they come out, one by one, to take their curtain calls? It'll be something like an award show with both of you standing at the podium and calling out the names."

"They've never done *that* before!"

"I know. It's always been a regular curtain call when the whole cast comes out, people applaud, and the curtain goes down again. This time I thought we should make it special. And if you and Mrs. Bascomb announce the names of the players, it would be just wonderful! I'll be happy to prepare a script with all the character names and the names of the people who play them. And then, if you'll agree to do it, you could give a short speech about what a wonderful actress and director your sister was and how proud she'd be that the Lake Eden Players are dedicating their performance that night to her."

"That's very nice!" Mayor Bascomb

looked impressed. "Do you think that KCOW Television will be there for the curtain call, too?"

"Absolutely. I've already talked to them about that. Everyone loves to see you on television, Mayor Bascomb. And Mrs. Bascomb is a celebrity, too."

Michelle had said the perfect thing and Hannah came very close to losing it. Mayor Bascomb was a media hound. It was like Ross had told her. Whenever there was a camera, you could count on Mayor Bascomb to give a sound bite.

"You can count me in, Michelle. And I'm sure Stephanie will agree to stand at the podium with me. After all, we've always been patrons of the arts. And not only that, it'll give me a chance to practice the speech I'll be giving when I accept the award honoring Tori at the Stage and Theater Actors Guild the following week in New York."

"That's wonderful, Mayor Bascomb. Please be sure to mention that on the night of the play. I'm sure everyone in Lake Eden will watch you accept your sister's award."

"I'm sure they will."

Hannah bit the inside of her cheek again to keep from laughing. Their mayor was definitely not humble.

"I think this will be an excellent fundraiser

for the Lake Eden Players," Mayor Bascomb continued. "Stephanie and I will be delighted to help in any way we can."

"Thank you, Mayor Bascomb!" Michelle looked properly grateful. "This is so kind of you. I'm going to rush right out and tell everyone how wonderfully supportive you've been."

"Good heavens!" Hannah said on their way out the front door of city hall.

"Good heavens what?"

"Just *good heavens*! Your performance in the mayor's office deserved an Academy Award. Are you sure you don't want to be an actress instead of a director?"

Michelle turned to look at Hannah in surprise. "I don't want to be a director, or a producer, or an actress. I want to own and manage a theater. That's why I've been taking business classes in addition to my drama major."

"But why? I saw you in there and you're very good. That tear was amazing."

Michelle shrugged, but Hannah could tell she was proud of herself. "It amazed me, too. I wasn't sure I could do that on command. But think about it, Hannah. Everyone wants to be a performer. And everyone wants to be a director or a producer. Unless you're really good and you happen to hit it at just the right time, you can't earn a decent living that way. I'd rather do something more business oriented. It might be a dinner theater, or a cabaret, or some kind of niche thing that attracts a lot of customers. And if that doesn't fly, I can always make a living with my business degree."

"I understand," Hannah said. "That's very level-headed of you, Michelle."

"Thank you. I'm a dreamer, Hannah. If something big came my way, I'd take it. But I'm also a realist."

"Yes you are," Hannah said. And then she realized that she no longer had to worry about Michelle's future. Her baby sister had her head on straight. "By the way, Michelle . . . were you just hoping when you told Mayor Bascomb that the pie eating contest and the curtain call would be televised? Or did you actually call KCOW and get them to agree?"

"I went straight to the top. I called P.K. in New York and asked him to ask Ross and let me know. I figured Ross would be the one to make that decision because he's the head of special programming."

"So you already talked to Ross about it?"

"No, just P.K. He got back to me during rehearsal and told me it was a go."

"Do you know if Ross got a chance to visit the business management firm that Tori used?"

Michelle shook her head. "Sorry, Hannah. I didn't even think to ask him that. Ross will call you, won't he?"

"I'm sure he will." Hannah approached her cookie truck and hesitated. "Are we going back to The Cookie Jar now?"

"I guess so. Since Marge and Aunt Nancy are there, I'll stay with you in the kitchen and help you bake."

"Sounds good to me." Hannah smiled at her. "How do you feel about trying something new?"

"New is good. What did you have in mind?"

"I've got an idea for a cookie using Cheerios. There's no reason they wouldn't work. Cheerios are made with oats and we use oatmeal in some of our cookies. I thought I might use Cheerios with cherries and call them Cheery Cherry Cookies."

"Catchy." Michelle began to smile. "I like it."

"Great. You can help me in the kitchen today and then, tomorrow, we'll bake a bunch of cookies for your bake sale and you can help me make the Banana Cream Pies for the pie eating contest. I have no idea how to do it. Most of those pies I've seen on televised contests don't seem to have crusts."

"That's right. Why don't we just put the filling in a disposable pie pan and cover it with your caramel whipped cream. Then the contestants can eat it with a spoon."

Hannah considered it for a minute. "Good idea. That'll be really easy to make and to transport to the school. How long shall we give them to eat it?"

"I told the mayor it would last between one and two minutes, but I really don't know how long it should be. What do you think?"

"I think you were right on track. It shouldn't last any longer than two minutes, and it could be as short as one minute. That's a long time to eat banana pudding and whipped cream as fast as you can, and that's all our pies will be without crusts. We'll have to get a really loud buzzer, or a bell, or something like that."

"I've got that covered already. I checked with the gym teacher and the school has a big time clock they use for timed athletic events. We can borrow it and set it on the judges' table so everyone who's watching can see it, too. At the end of the time, it buzzes really loud. Then we'll have the judges inspect the pie plates and declare the winner."

"Perfect."

"I think we need three judges. Who do you think I should ask? Mother had some good ideas for the contestants, but I didn't ask her about the judges."

Hannah considered that for a moment before she gave her opinion. "I'm not sure, but it should be someone who'll draw a big crowd. Since you're selling tickets to the contest, you should decide that today and have Rod put it in the paper. Let's go ask Mother to see who she suggests. She's only a block away."

"Is she home?"

"We won't know unless we call her. And we're practically on her doorstep. Call her, Michelle. And ask her if she's receiving."

"Receiving?"

"Yes. She'll get a kick out of that. It means receiving visitors and that's what they called it in Regency days. You dropped by the manor and the butler brought out a silver salver for your calling card. He took it to the lady of the house and she either received you, or he came back to say that she was not available for callers."

"And now all we have to do is call on our cell phone and say, 'Hey, are you home?' "

"That's right. Everything's a shortcut in today's world."

"I know," Michelle agreed. "Mother would argue that the old world was more civilized."

"Perhaps, but I don't think she'd enjoy using the *convenience* in the backyard of the manor house."

"Is a *convenience* an outhouse?"

"Yes, and it probably wasn't as convenient as the one Grandma Elsa had on her farm."

Michelle laughed out loud. "You're right. I remember going out there before they got indoor plumbing. Grandma Elsa's was heated in the winter."

"And she had a fan in the summer," Hannah reminded her. "I remember tripping over that extension cord she ran from the house and skinning my knee."

"And I remember how cold it was to walk out there in the winter. But I really loved to go to the farm. Grandma Swensen always baked cookies for us and let us help her. Do you think that's why we enjoy baking so much?"

"I think that has a lot to do with it. Call Mother and we'll leave the truck here. It's not too cold today and we can just walk over there if she's home."

# CHAPTER TWENTY-ONE

Thirty minutes later, Hannah and Michelle walked in the back door of The Cookie Jar. After they'd hung their coats on the rack, Michelle headed straight for the kitchen coffeepot, and Hannah grabbed the thick, plastic-coated recipe book and took a stool at the workstation.

Michelle walked over with a cup of coffee and placed it in front of Hannah. "Drink this. You're looking tired."

"I am," Hannah admitted, "but I got more sleep than I usually do. I just don't understand it."

"It's taking a while to solve this murder. Maybe that's it. Do you feel that you're spinning your wheels?"

"Yes. That could be it, Michelle. I'm doing everything I can, but I'm not catching a break anywhere."

"It could also be because Ross isn't here. I'm sure you must miss him."

"I *do* miss him. It's probably mostly because we were together twenty-four seven for a solid week. And now it's like I'm back to being single again."

There was a knock on the back kitchen door and Michelle began to grin. "Just what you need . . . a diversion of some sort. Shall I go let it in?"

Hannah laughed. "Yes, but don't call it *it*. It's got to be someone we know and they might take offense."

"Yes, Mother," Michelle said, giving Hannah a saucy look. "I'll go see who it is."

"Norman!" Hannah said a few moments later when she saw who Michelle was ushering into the kitchen. "Sit down and have a cup of coffee with us."

"I could use a cup of coffee now that I'm through for the day," Norman told them. "Two root canals, a broken crown, and an impacted wisdom tooth make for a long afternoon." He sat down next to Hannah and gave her a little pat on the shoulder. "How are two of my favorite Swensen sisters?"

"We're fine," Hannah said noticing that he hadn't used her married name. Of course, Norman was technically right. She was still a Swensen sister, married or not.

"Change that to *I'm* fine," Michelle told

him. "Hannah's tired and depressed."

"About your investigation?" Norman asked her.

"Yes." It was the easy answer and Hannah took it. "Except for Tori's business manager, and that's really a long shot, I'm fresh out of suspects."

"How about the man with the black tennis shoes?" Norman asked her. "Did you find out any more about him?"

"Only that he was involved with Tori, but we already knew that since he broke into her apartment to find the love letter, or note, or whatever it was that he'd written to her."

"But you don't think he did it, do you?" Michelle asked Hannah.

"No, I don't." She turned back to Norman. "Remember how he almost talked to her as if she were still there in the bedroom with him?"

"I'll never forget it," Norman said. "It was one of the saddest things I've ever heard. I think he was genuinely grieving for her."

"That's part of it. And he didn't sound guilty when he talked to her. He didn't say, *I'm sorry,* or, *Please forgive me,* or anything that would indicate guilt. I just don't think he acted or sounded like the kind of man who could walk into her condo and shoot her in cold blood."

Norman gave a nod. "I think you're right about that."

"Yes, you've definitely got a point," Michelle agreed. "Usually murders between two people who have loved each other are done in the heat of passion and not premeditated."

Hannah turned to her younger sister in surprise. "You sound like you've been reading up on violent crime."

"Guilty as charged," Michelle admitted. "I took a night class last semester."

Norman looked shocked. "Don't tell me you're thinking of going into law enforcement!"

"Oh, no. I'm definitely not considering that as a career choice. This class was taught by a psychology professor and it was called Why People Kill. It went into motives and things like that, and I was hoping it would give me something to talk about with Lonnie."

"And did it?" Hannah asked her.

"Yes, it did. Lonnie was really interested in the psychology of murder and he even sat in on a couple of classes with me."

"Did you learn anything that would apply to Tori's murder case?" Norman asked.

"Not really. But I did learn something

about myself that I hadn't known before."

Hannah winced slightly. "That you're capable of murder?"

"That certainly. Everyone is, given the right circumstances. But I also learned that I don't want to understand a killer's mindset." She stopped and gave a little shiver. "It's really frightening. I hoped that by taking the class, I'd learn something that could help Hannah in her next investigation." Michelle turned to Hannah. "Where are you now, Hannah? Maybe if we talk about it, Norman and I could help you."

Hannah pulled the shorthand notebook from her purse and flipped to the suspect page. "Two suspects left," she told them. "One is Tori's business manager and the other is the man with the black tennis shoes and silver laces. That's it. I've eliminated everyone else."

"You always do that," Norman pointed out.

"I know, but I haven't found any new suspects to replace them."

"Dig deeper," Norman advised.

"Dig deeper?" Hannah repeated, wishing she could do exactly that. "But there don't seem to be any other suspects on the horizon."

Her cell phone rang, interrupting her

thoughts, and Hannah glanced down at the display. Ross was calling!

"I have to take his call," Hannah said, getting up with more energy than she'd exhibited all day, and heading for the pantry. "I'm . . . uh . . . I'm going to see if we've got any dried cherries so we can try those Cheery Cherry Cookies."

"Hold on, Ross. I'm here." Hannah said, ducking into the pantry for privacy. "Did you get a chance to go over to the business management firm that Tori used?"

"I just came from there, Cookie." Ross said, sounding very far away.

"Where are you?" Hannah asked, noticing the hollow tone in Ross's voice.

"I'm in the subway. The connection's not that good so let me tell you fast before I lose you. His name is Roger Ainsley and he didn't do it."

"Really? How do you know that?"

"Because I got in to see the head of the firm. Roger is his second in command and he's in the Bahamas for his oldest daughter's wedding."

"You're sure?"

"I'm positive. He showed me a photo that Roger's wife sent of Roger walking his daughter down the aisle. The photo was time stamped and it was a night wedding at eight o'clock last Saturday. And that was the night that Tori was killed, wasn't it?"

"Yes, it was." Hannah sighed heavily.

"Even considering the time difference, Roger couldn't have been in Lake Eden. It's impossible."

"Thank you, Ross. I'll put Roger Ainsley's name on my suspect list and cross him off immediately. I really appreciate this. I want you to know that."

"Anything you need, Cookie, and I'm there for you."

"And I'm here for anything you need," Hannah said quickly.

"That's great, but what I'm thinking about can wait until I get back home."

Hannah started to blush, even though she wasn't precisely sure what Ross was thinking about. But his next comment set her back on her heels.

"I want one of those Banana Cream Pies. Will you bake one for me and have it ready when I come home?"

"Of course I will!" Hannah felt like laughing at the direction her mind had been taking. "It'll be right there in the refrigerator."

"I can hardly wait. I should be home tomorrow night. P.K. and I have to get a clip of Michelle's pie eating contest on Saturday for the evening news. I ran it past the president of the station and he said it was a go."

"Wonderful! I've missed you, Ross."

"And I've missed you."

"Is there anything else I can do for you?"

"Yes. I overnighted some footage to you. Feel free to watch it if you want to, but be sure to keep it for me."

"Okay. I'll watch it and keep it for you."

"I sent it FedEx and it should arrive at the condo by ten tomorrow morning. Will you alert one of your neighbors to take it in? I wouldn't want to lose it."

"I'll stay home and wait for it. Michelle can take my place at The Cookie Jar."

"Are you sure? I could always get someone from the station to drive out and sit on the steps until it comes."

"It won't be a problem, Ross. There are some things I need to do at home anyway, and that'll give me a chance to get them done."

"Okay, then. I'll see you on Friday night, Cookie. It'll probably be eight o'clock or so when I get there."

"That's okay. I'll be at the condo with your pie."

"I love you, Cookie."

"I love you, too." Hannah listened to the click as Ross hung up and suddenly she felt bereft. She missed him so much. She brushed a tear from her eye and then she squared her shoulders and snatched a bag of dried cherries from the shelf.

When Hannah emerged from the pantry, she found Norman and Michelle deep in conversation at the workstation.

"Ask her," Michelle prompted.

"Okay," Norman said, turning to Hannah. "I have a proposition for you, Hannah."

"What's that?" Hannah took a sip of her coffee, which was lukewarm, and munched one of the cookies that Michelle had just brought to the workstation.

"I'd like to take the Swensen sisters out to dinner tonight. Andrea and Michelle have already accepted."

Hannah smiled at him. "Then so do I. Thank you, Norman. That would be lovely."

"I'll drive," Norman offered. "Then you'll all get a real night out. I told Andrea that I'd pick her up at seven, so shall I pick you and Michelle up at six-thirty?"

"That'll be perfect!" Hannah said, still smiling at the thought of a night out with Norman and her sisters.

After Norman left, Michelle picked up the bag of dried cherries. "Are you going to plump these?"

"I think we should. They'll be juicier that way. I considered using bourbon, but if we're going to serve them here in the coffee shop, maybe we'd better use maraschino cherry juice. I was planning to put a maraschino cherry half on top of each cookie anyway."

"That's always pretty," Michelle agreed. "Let's come up with a recipe and try it right now. And if it works, we can give some to Norman and Andrea tonight."

"Okay." Hannah glanced up at the clock. "We've got two hours before the coffee shop closes. We could probably finish one batch and test them out on the customers that are here."

"That's a good idea. They love to test recipes for you. Let's bake, Hannah! This is going to be fun!"

# CHEERY CHERRY COOKIES

Preheat oven to 350 degrees F., rack in the middle position.

1 cup dried cherries **(or cherry-flavored Craisins)**

large jar of maraschino cherries without stems

1 cup white **(granulated)** sugar

1 cup brown sugar **(pack it down in the cup when you measure it)**

1 cup salted butter, softened to room temperature **(2 sticks, 8 ounces, 1/2 pound)**

1 teaspoon baking soda

1 teaspoon salt

1 teaspoon vanilla extract

1 teaspoon almond extract

2 large eggs

2 and 1/2 cups all-purpose flour **(not sifted — pack it down in the measuring cup)**

1/2 cup finely chopped blanched almonds **(those are the white ones without brown skins)**

1/4 cup maraschino cherry juice

2 cups Cheerios

1 to 2 cups white chocolate or vanilla baking chips

Place the dried cherries in a microwave-safe bowl.

Drain off the juice from the jar of maraschino cherries and pour 1/4 cup of it over the dried cherries in the bowl. Reserve the rest of the cherry juice for later.

Place the bowl in the microwave and heat the dried cherries and juice on HIGH for 90 seconds. Let the bowl sit in the microwave for an additional 90 seconds and then take it out and set it on the kitchen counter.

Stir the dried cherries so the juice is evenly distributed. Then cover the bowl with aluminum foil and let it sit on the counter.

**Hannah's Note: You can mix this cookie dough by hand, but it's a lot easier with an electric mixer.**

Place the white sugar and the brown sugar in the bowl of an electric mixer. Mix them together on LOW speed until they're a uniform color.

Add the softened butter and beat on MEDIUM speed until the sugars and the butter are thoroughly combined.

Increase the speed of your mixer and beat for another minute.

Add the baking soda, salt, vanilla extract, and almond extract. Mix them in thoroughly.

Add the eggs, one by one, beating after each addition.

Add the flour, a half cup at a time, beating after each addition.

Mix in the finely chopped almonds.

Feel the bowl with the dried cherries and juice. If it's not so hot it'll cook the eggs, drain off the juice and throw that juice away.

Measure out 1/4 cup of the rest of the reserved cherry juice and add it to your mixing bowl. Mix it in until it's thoroughly combined.

Place the 2 cups of Cheerios in a Ziploc plastic bag. Crush them with a rolling pin or your hands until the pieces resemble coarse gravel.

Add the crushed Cheerios to your bowl, along with the white chocolate chips. Mix everything up thoroughly.

Scrape down the bowl and take it out of the mixer. Then give the bowl another stir by hand.

Pat the cherries dry with a paper towel and add them to your mixing bowl. Mix them in by hand.

Let the dough sit on the counter for a minute or two to rest while you prepare your cookie sheets.

Spray your cookie sheets with Pam or another nonstick cooking spray. Alternatively, line them with parchment paper.

Form the dough into walnut-sized balls

with your fingers and place them on the cookie sheets, 12 to a standard sheet.

Cut the maraschino cherries in two and press one half, rounded side up, on the top of each unbaked cookie.

Bake one test cookie at 350 degrees F. for 10 to 12 minutes or until nicely browned on top. If the test cookie spreads out too much on the cookie sheet, either chill the dough in the refrigerator before baking, or turn the dough out on a floured board and knead in approximately 1/3 cup more flour.

When the dough is the proper consistency, bake your cookies at 350 degrees F. for 10 to 12 minutes. Remove from the oven and cool on the cookie sheet for 2 minutes, and then remove the cookies to a wire rack until they're completely cool. *(The rack is important — it makes them crisp.)*

Yield: approximately 5 to 6 dozen delicious, crunchy cookies, depending on cookie size.

# Chapter Twenty-Two

*There was a light on in her bedroom. She could see it despite the fact that her eyes were closed. Someone had turned on the light . . . but there was no lamp on that side of the bed. There was only the window and . . .*

Hannah woke up with a start to see sunlight streaming in her bedroom window. She felt herself begin to panic. What time was it? Was she late for work? Where was Michelle?!

One glance at the alarm clock on her bedside table confirmed that she had, indeed, overslept. It was seven in the morning and she should have been up at four!

Hannah jumped out of bed, thrust her arms into her robe, and pulled on her slippers. There was a delicious smell coming from the kitchen, something that reminded her of Thanksgiving. Michelle must be baking. But why hadn't she come in to wake her?

Hurrying down the carpeted hallway, Moishe at her heels, Hannah arrived at the origin of the delicious scent quite breathless.

The kitchen was deserted. Michelle was nowhere in sight. There were, however, at least a dozen aromatic scones resplendent on a wire rack on her kitchen counter. Michelle had been there. Michelle had baked. But where was she now?

A note was propped up by the sugar bowl. Hannah poured herself a quick cup of coffee and carried it to the kitchen table. When she got there, she sat down and grabbed the note.

Glad you got some sleep, Hannah, *the note said.* Lisa picked me up and we're down at The Cookie Jar. Take your time. Everything's under control. I know you're expecting a FedEx package from Ross this morning, so Lisa and I won't expect you until noon or later.

The scones on the counter are pumpkin with cinnamon glaze. I thought they'd be great to serve to your customers right before Thanksgiving. Let me know what you think. I put two in the microwave when I took them out of the oven. Unless you sleep until noon, they're probably still warm.

See you when you get to work. I love you. *And the note was signed,*

Michelle

Hannah folded the note and put it back on the table. She had a sip of coffee, took a deep breath of the sweet-smelling air, and smiled. Michelle was amazing. She had more energy than Hannah ever remembered having in her entire life. And that last sentence was the nicest part of the note. Michelle had written, *I love you.* Her sister's affection made Hannah feel both blessed and very grateful.

The delicious scent of the scones drew Hannah like a magnet to the microwave where Michelle had said that there were two scones waiting for her. She opened the microwave door, took out the scones, and gave a big smile. They were still nice and warm.

There was a dish of butter on the table, so Hannah wasted no time in breaking open the scones and buttering them. She took the first bite, made a little mewling sound of intense delight, and sighed in enjoyment. Michelle's scones were delicious, a perfect combination of spice and sweet with the fresh, almost nutty flavor of pumpkin.

After her third cup of coffee, Hannah was ready to start her day. She was about to go into the beautifully remodeled master bathroom when she realized that it was already ten minutes before eight. What time did they start to deliver FedEx packages? Hannah wasn't sure. She was certain, however, that she wouldn't hear the doorbell ring if the package from Ross came while she was in the shower. What if she had to sign for the package? She hadn't thought to ask Ross about that. Ten minutes before eight would be ten minutes before nine in New York. She couldn't call him now. He was probably in the middle of one of the interviews he was doing today.

It was decision time for Hannah. She could rush through her shower and be dressed in ten minutes. She'd showered that fast before. But if she did that, she wouldn't have time to enjoy the incredible massaging jets that would erase the ache in her back and ease the tension in the back of her neck. It would be better to wait until she could enjoy the full benefit of the wonderful new shower.

Feeling a bit like a lazy housewife, Hannah decided to wait to shower and dress. She carried a fresh cup of coffee to the couch, set it on the coffee table, and sat down in one of the rocking and reclining leather chairs that were part of their new group of sofas.

The morning inactivity seemed very strange to Hannah as she sat there, sipping her coffee. It was comfortable and it was nice, but she felt as if she should be doing something productive. She supposed she could bake, but what if the package came at the exact time her cookies were ready to come out of the oven? The cookies might burn in the time it would take her to open the door, sign for the package, and bring it inside. She'd be better off just sitting and waiting . . . but that was something she was loathe to do. There just had to be something she could do with her time that would be useful and constructive.

She was just debating the wisdom of cleaning out the refrigerator when the doorbell rang. She jumped up and came very close to running to answer its summons. She opened the door without bothering to look through the peephole, expecting to see a uniformed FedEx delivery person, and she gave a little cry of surprise when she saw who was standing on the landing. "Mike!" Hannah gasped. "What are *you* doing here?"

"That's not exactly a welcoming greeting," Mike said, but the corners of his mouth were twitching with humor. "I thought I'd come by to keep you company since Michelle said you were home waiting for a package."

"Uh . . . sure. Come in, Mike." Hannah was acutely aware that she was still in her nightclothes and robe. "I just made a fresh pot of coffee if you want some."

"Wait a second," Mike said as Hannah turned and headed for the kitchen. "If you're waiting for FedEx, I saw a truck pull into the guest parking lot while I was walking up the stairs."

The words were no sooner out of Mike's mouth than Hannah's doorbell rang again.

She rushed to answer it, but Mike stopped her. "The peephole, Hannah. You've got to get into that habit."

"Right," Hannah said, looking through the peephole with its fisheye lens to see a highly distorted figure in a FedEx uniform. "Coming!" she called out, releasing the deadbolt and opening the door.

"Hannah?" the deliveryman asked after glancing down at the electronic device he was carrying.

"Yes, that's me. Is it from Ross Barton in New York?"

"R. Barton, yes," the deliveryman confirmed, turning the device around and pointing to a box that had appeared on the screen. "Sign here, please."

Hannah took the stylus he handed her and signed, remembering to use her married name, *Hannah Barton.*

"Barton?" the man questioned her. "This package is addressed to Hannah Swensen."

Hannah laughed. "That's me. And Ross Barton is my husband. We were married less than two weeks ago and I guess he forgot to use Barton when he filled out the paperwork!"

The deliveryman laughed. "It happens to the best of us. When my wife and I went on our honeymoon, I checked her in under her maiden name when I registered at the hotel. She still laughs about that."

Hannah accepted the package he handed her, thanked him for delivering it, and carried it inside. The package wasn't that large and she was surprised. "My package is here," she said to Mike.

"I see that. Do you want me to open it for you?"

"Yes, please. I'll get your coffee while you're opening it."

When Hannah came back from the kitchen, Mike had the package open and was holding a note. "Thanks, Hannah," he said, accepting the coffee with one hand and handing her the note with the other. "This must be for you, Hannah. It was right on top."

Hannah glanced down at the note.

*It read,* Here you go, Cookie. You can watch it on our big screen if you want to.

"That's for you, right?" Mike asked her.

"Yes."

"He calls you Cookie?"

Hannah nodded. "Ross started that in college. I took Ross and Linda cookies when they moved into my apartment building and he's called me that ever since."

"Appropriate. Do you want to watch this?" Mike pointed to the DVD cases in the package.

"Yes, but first . . ." Hannah stopped in mid-sentence, wondering if what she'd been about to ask was inappropriate.

"But what?"

"Uh . . . I didn't get a chance to take a shower this morning because I got up too late and I was afraid I wouldn't hear the doorbell in the shower. Would you mind if I took a quick one right now?"

"I don't mind. I know where the coffeepot is if I need a refill. Go for it, Hannah. And take your time. I'll be right here."

"Thanks, Mike. If you're hungry, help yourself to the pumpkin scones on the wire rack in the kitchen. There's soft butter in the dish on the kitchen table."

"Sounds good. I'll do that."

Hannah came close to regretting her offer as she hurried back to the master bedroom. She'd told Mike to help himself to the scones and she hoped he wouldn't eat them all. As she closed the door, she thought about racing back to the kitchen to put some scones away, but she decided that wouldn't be very hospitable. Instead, she immediately headed for the shower. If she hurried, perhaps there would be some scones left on the rack when she came back.

Fifteen minutes later, Hannah came out of the shower, feeling that all was right with her world. Her back no longer hurt, the kinks were gone from her neck, and she felt better than she had all week. She towel-dried her hair, dressed quickly, and was back in the living room in time to see Mike slipping the first disk into the DVD player.

"Those scones are great!" he said. "Did you make them?"

Hannah shook her head. "Michelle did. She was thinking of selling them Thanksgiving week at the coffee shop."

"Why not? I think everybody would like them. And it'll remind them to order one of your pumpkin pies for Thanksgiving dinner."

"I didn't think of that! You could be right, though." Hannah went into the kitchen, poured herself another cup of coffee, and glanced at the wire rack. There were a few scones left, thank goodness! She carried her coffee back to the living room, and found Mike waiting for her on the couch. "Do you want to watch this now?"

"Yes. Ross is working on a retrospective of Tori's life on the stage and he sent some footage to me. Would you like to stay and watch it with me?"

"Yeah. Maybe I'll learn something about Tori Bascomb that I don't know." Mike cleared his throat. "And speaking of Tori Bascomb, how is your investigation coming along?"

"You asked me that yesterday, Mike."

"I know. I just thought you might have discovered a new clue."

"I wish I had, but I didn't," Hannah said quite honestly. "I'm stumped, Mike."

"Join the club. We've followed every lead and we've gotten exactly nowhere. The one thing I do know is that her killer was probably someone she knew."

414

"What makes you think that?"

"Tori opened the door. And there's a peephole." Mike gave a little laugh. "Unless, of course, she was like you and forgot to look through the peephole."

Hannah sighed. Mike was right. She did forget.

"I'll have to talk to Ross about that, and impress on him how important it is to get you to use that peephole. It's there for a reason, Hannah."

"I know. I just forget, that's all."

"And that's exactly why you have to develop the habit. Even if you are *sure* that you know who it is, look first and *then* open the door."

"Okay. You're right," Hannah conceded. "Let's watch the footage, Mike. I want to see what Ross has been filming."

As Hannah watched the footage and discovered the path that Tori's acting career had taken, she was amazed at the number of Broadway performances that the mayor's sister had given. Tori had been multi-talented. She was an accomplished singer, dancer, comedian, and actress. She'd even had a one-woman show at one point in her career.

Ross had interviewed a number of Broadway actors and actresses who had known and worked with Tori and they had all agreed that she was highly talented and had performed her roles to perfection. But not one of them had said anything about her personally, and no one had said that she was a friend.

"Did you catch the fact that all those co-workers admired her, yet no one said they liked her?" Mike asked as he ejected the first disk and put in the second.

"Yes, I noticed. I'm surprised that Ross didn't interview any of Tori's theater friends."

Mike shrugged. "Maybe she didn't *have* any theater friends. The only real friend she had here in Lake Eden was your mother. And that was probably because they were neighbors."

"Right," Hannah said, deciding to think about that later.

"This disk is labeled EARLY YEARS," Mike told her.

"Good. That should be interesting. I was curious about how Tori got her start on Broadway."

"In a Broadway musical. That was her first role, Tori was the understudy and the actress playing the lead got the flu. Tori took over the role on opening night and got rave reviews."

416

"Interesting," Hannah said, mentally kicking herself for not researching that bit of information. "On opening night," she repeated what Mike had told her with a sigh. "That was a lucky break for Tori, but it makes me feel sorry for the actress who was scheduled to play the part."

"Laine Warner."

Hannah frowned slightly. "I don't know the names of that many Broadway actresses, but I've never heard of her."

"Neither has anyone else. This musical was supposed to be *her* big break."

"And she got the flu," Hannah repeated what Mike had told her. "What happened to Laine Warner?"

"She had some small parts on Broadway for a while, and then she became a character actress in the movies. I looked her up. She worked a lot and was very successful, but she never got to play the lead actress."

"Do you think that could be a motive for murder?" Hannah asked him.

"It's a possibility, but it's unlikely. Laine was successful in her own right. She made a lot of money before she retired. She hasn't done anything for the past ten years or so, but she made a very good living for a long time and probably has a nice big retirement income."

"Do you know where Laine Warner is now?"

Mike shook his head. "She dropped out of sight. No driver's license, no new social security information, nothing in the records about her."

"Do you think she's dead?"

"She could be. A lot of people fall through the cracks as far as the records go. But, it's also possible that she moved out of the country, or married someone and didn't bother to change her name on the records."

"So she's not one of your suspects?"

"No, but she could be if I knew more about her. For instance, does Laine Warner think that Tori somehow caused her to get sick just in time for opening night?"

"Would Tori have done something like that?"

"It doesn't matter if she did, or if she didn't. The important factor is if Laine Warner *believes* that Tori did it. Then that's a motive for murdering Tori."

"How do you find out what Laine believes without locating her and questioning her?"

"That's just it. I don't. Let's watch the disk and see if Ross managed to find her. Or if he interviewed someone who can give me a lead."

*Give* us *a lead*! Hannah changed the

418

personal pronoun in her mind, but she didn't voice it. All the same, she was going to watch the second disk very carefully to see if she could spot anything.

"Ready?" Mike asked her, picking up the control.

"I'm ready. Let's see what Ross found out about Laine Warner."

Less than thirty minutes later, Hannah and Mike had their answer. Ross hadn't been able to locate Laine Warner, either. And no one he'd interviewed had known where she was. He had, however, managed to locate some clips of her performances as a character actress and both Mike and Hannah had watched those carefully.

"So what did you think?" Mike asked her when the entire disk had played.

"Laine Warner was a very good actress and I wish Ross had found her. And . . . this may sound a little crazy, but she looked slightly familiar to me."

"Did you see her on Broadway? She was in a couple of other productions before she landed her first lead."

"I've never seen a Broadway play, so that can't be it."

"Then maybe you saw her in one of those old movies you like to watch."

"Maybe." Hannah thought about that for a moment and then she gave a slight nod. "That's probably it."

"Thanks for showing me those interviews, Hannah. Your guy is really good at getting people to talk. If he ever gets tired of lugging around all that equipment, I could sure use someone like him at the station."

"I'll tell him you said that," Hannah said, but she thought, *I doubt it! Ross loves what he does and he wouldn't do anything else for the world!*

"There's a few of those scones left," Mike said, standing up to retrieve the disk from the DVD player. "Do you think I could have a couple more to take with me to the station?"

Hannah gave a fleeting thought to the possibility of refusing. She wouldn't mind eating another pumpkin scone herself, but then decided it was best to be charitable. Mike had been very forthcoming about his investigation and he hadn't asked her that many questions about hers. He deserved some kind of positive reinforcement for that and more scones would give it to him.

"Sure, you can have them," Hannah said. "Wait for just a second and I'll pack up the rest for you."

Mike followed her to the kitchen and

watched as she wrapped the scones in foil and put them in a plastic bag. She knew he was counting how many were there and wondering if he could eat one on his way to the station, so she left one out of the package she was making.

"Is that last one for you?" Mike asked her.

"No," Hannah told him. "That last one's for you to eat on your drive to the station."

"Great!" Mike gave her the grin that always made her heart beat faster. Perhaps that was disloyal of her, now that she was married, but she excused it as an involuntary reaction. "Here you are," she said, handing him the scones.

"The guys at the station will go crazy over these. And . . . oh! I forgot to tell you. Your mother called while you were in the shower."

*Uh-oh!* Hannah's mind shouted a warning. *If I know Mother, and I do, she's going to think the worst!* Hannah was almost afraid to ask, but she had to know for purposes of damage control. "Did you tell her why I couldn't come to the phone?"

"Sure. I said you'd just gone to the bedroom to take a shower. And I told her you'd given me coffee and pumpkin scones for breakfast. I promised her that I'd tell you she called and that you'd call her later, after you got dressed and everything."

Hannah came close to groaning out loud, but Mike had no idea the size of the can of worms he'd opened. She had to call her mother right after he left and attempt to explain.

"That's okay, isn't it?" Mike asked her.

"Oh, yes," Hannah hurried to reassure him. He had no idea the ramifications his words could cause. "I'll call her back just as soon as you leave."

Several nervous minutes later, Hannah was punching her mother's number into the phone. It rang only once before Delores answered.

"Hannah? What's going on there anyway? Mike answered your phone and told me that you were in the shower. And then he said that you'd given him breakfast! You're a married woman, Hannah! What was Mike doing at your place for breakfast? And why did you take a shower while he was there?"

Hannah came close to laughing out loud. Her mother clucked and scolded like a biddy hen. "It's okay, Mother. Ross sent me some footage he'd shot in New York and I was here, waiting for the FedEx to arrive. Mike dropped by The Cookie Jar, Michelle told him I was at home, waiting for a package from Ross, and Mike came over so I took advantage of him."

"You *what*?!" Delores sounded even more like a hen in distress and Hannah laughed.

"Sorry, Mother. I shouldn't have used that particular word. I didn't have time for a shower earlier because I thought I might not hear the doorbell with the water running. I asked Mike if he'd stay in the living room while I took a quick shower and get the package if it came in."

"Oh." Delores sounded slightly relieved. "But I don't understand why you asked him to stay if your package from Ross had already arrived."

"Because I thought there might be some kind of a clue that would lead us to Tori's killer. And if Mike watched it with me, two sets of eyes would have to be better than one."

"Oh." Finally, Delores sounded completely relieved. "Tell me, dear . . . did you discover any clues?"

"Maybe, but we're not sure yet. We're both working on it, though." Hannah didn't want to go into detail, so she changed the subject. "Did you find any good judges for the pie eating contest, Mother?"

"Yes, I did!" Delores sounded very pleased with herself. "I called Bill and he agreed to be one of the judges. I thought having the

423

sheriff on the judging panel would prove that the contest was legitimate."

"Good thinking, Mother. Did you get anyone else?"

"Of course. Ken Purvis was delighted to be asked. He agreed to be a judge the moment I asked him. You do know what that means, don't you, dear?"

"We get the high school crowd?" Hannah guessed, since Ken Purvis was the Jordan High principal.

"That's right. But my third judge is the icing on the cake."

"It's pie, Mother."

Delores sighed so heavily, Hannah could hear it on the phone. "I didn't mean it *that* way, Hannah!"

"I know," Hannah said quickly. "It was just a little joke. Who's the third judge, Mother?"

"Stephanie Bascomb. I invited her over yesterday afternoon and asked her if she'd be a judge. And once I'd told her how very important it was and how everyone would love to see her in that exalted position, she agreed to take part. She's even going to act completely shocked when she sees pie on her husband's face."

"You told her it was going to be televised on KCOW?" Hannah guessed.

"Of course. It was a selling point, dear. And Stephanie ran with it, thanks to my persuasive rhetoric."

Her mother was waiting for praise and Hannah wasted no time in giving it to her. "Thank you, Mother. You did a superlative job choosing the judges. They're just perfect."

"Of course they are, dear. I'm very good at this sort of thing, you know."

After several more compliments to her mother's intelligence, wisdom, and social awareness, Hannah managed to end the conversation. She hung up and spotted their local paper on her dining room table. Mike must have heard it arrive and brought it in for her.

Hannah glanced at the first page and gave a little gasp of surprise. There was a gorgeous photo of a slice of her Banana Cream Pie with the caption, *Hannah's Banana Cream Pie.* The first line of the article below it, all in caps, read *EVER WISH YOU COULD EAT THE WHOLE PIE?*

The article below it started off with a bang.

Three locals from Lake Eden will get the chance to do just that in a timed pie eating contest on Saturday at 1:00 PM at the Jordan High auditorium. Tickets are available now and there will be a bake sale to benefit the Lake Eden Players right after the contest. One of the judges is Stephanie Bascomb, who told me she's bringing baby wipes with her in case the mayor, who's one of the contestants, gets pie on his face!

The article went on to name the local businesses that were selling tickets. Hannah stopped reading and reached for the phone. She had to call Rod at the newspaper office.

"Hi, Hannah," Rod greeted her once she'd identified herself. "What did you think of the article?"

"It's brilliant, Rod! Thank you for the great article!"

"Don't thank me. Your mother wrote the copy. And it certainly did the trick. Rose McDermott called me a few minutes ago from the café and said that they sold over fifty tickets this morning."

"That's fantastic!"

"I sold over twenty right here," Rod told her. "They're going like hotcakes, Hannah. Everyone wants to watch Stephanie's reaction when the mayor goes facedown in a pie plate."

"But he won't go facedown," Hannah told him. "Michelle promised the mayor that the contestants could use spoons."

"Did she tell him what kind of a spoon?"

"Well . . . no, but . . ."

"They give the contestants those big spoons they use for dishing up stew," Rod interrupted. "Since KCOW is going to show it on the news, it'll be a lot funnier."

"But what if Mayor Bascomb backs out when he sees the size of the spoon?"

"He won't dare. That would make him look bad. It's a winner, Hannah. Do it and I'll get some great photos for the paper."

"Done!" Hannah promised, making up her mind instantly. Delores would love to see Ricky-Ticky with a whipped cream mustache and so would everyone else in Lake Eden. Stephanie would probably think it was funny, too.

Hannah hung up the phone with a smile on her face. This was going to be fun and she was really glad that Ross would be home to capture it all on video!

# PUMPKIN SCONES WITH SUGARED CINNAMON GLAZE

Preheat oven to 425 degrees F., rack in the middle position.

**Pumpkin Scones:**

1/2 cup salted butter *(1 stick, 4 ounces, 1/4 pound)* at room temperature

1/2 cup brown sugar *(pack it down in the cup when you measure it)*

2 teaspoons cream of tartar

1 and 1/2 teaspoons cinnamon

1/2 teaspoon nutmeg *(freshly ground is best)*

1 and 1/4 cups plain canned pumpkin *(not pumpkin pie mix)*

1 large egg, beaten *(just whip it up in a glass with a fork)*

3 cups biscuit mix *(I used Bisquick — just fill the measuring cup and level it off with a table knife)*

1 cup white chocolate chips or vanilla baking chips

In the bowl of an electric mixer, combine the butter, brown sugar, cream of tartar, cinnamon, and nutmeg.

Beat this mixture at MEDIUM speed until it is smooth and creamy.

Add the pumpkin and mix it in until it's

well combined.

Add the beaten egg and mix that in until it's well combined.

Mix in the biscuit mix, one cup at the time, beating after each addition.

Shut off the mixer, scrape down the bowl, and take the bowl out of the mixer.

Add the cup of white chocolate chips or vanilla baking chips by hand.

Prepare two baking sheets by spraying them with Pam or another nonstick cooking spray, or lining them with parchment paper.

Divide your dough in half. Each half will make 9 scones.

Working with the first half of the dough and using a large spoon, drop 9 scones on the baking sheet.

**Michelle's Note: I just eyeball it and add or take away dough from the scones to make all 9 the same relative size.**

Use the second half of your dough to make 9 scones on the second baking sheet.

Once the scones are on the cookie sheets, wet your impeccably clean fingers and shape them into more perfect rounds. Then flatten them with your moistened palms. They will rise during baking, but once you flatten them, they won't be too round on top.

Bake the scones at 425 degrees F. for 10 to 12 minutes, or until they're golden brown on top. *(Mine took the full 12 minutes.)*

While your Pumpkin Scones are baking, make the Sugared Cinnamon Glaze.

**Sugared Cinnamon Glaze**
This glaze is made in the microwave.

1/4 cup water
3/4 cup white *(granulated)* sugar
1/4 teaspoon ground cinnamon

Right before your scones are ready to come out of the oven, mix the water, white sugar, and cinnamon together in a small, microwave-safe bowl.

Heat the mixture on HIGH power for 30 seconds. Leave it in the microwave for 1 minute and then stir.

Set the resulting liquid mixture on the counter along with a pastry brush.

Brush the tops of the scones with the glaze right after they come out of the oven.

Cool the scones for at least five minutes on the cookie sheet, and then remove them to a wire rack with a metal spatula. *(If you used parchment paper, all you have to do is position the cookie sheet next to the wire rack and pull the paper over to the rack.)*

When the scones are cool, or nearly cool,

you can cut them in half lengthwise and butter them for breakfast.

**Hannah's Note: These scones reheat beautifully if you wrap them in a paper towel and heat them for 20 to 30 seconds in the microwave.**

Yield: Makes 18 delicious scones that are guaranteed to remind you of Thanksgiving dinner.

# CHAPTER TWENTY-THREE

It was the most beautiful dream in the world. Hannah Swensen rolled over in the early dawn on Saturday morning and cuddled up close to her husband. His arms were around her and she felt so loved and cherished, she never wanted to wake up from the dream.

Reality reared its ugly head when her alarm clock began to beep with an irritating electronic tone. She opened her eyes, realized that part of her dream was not a dream at all since her husband was holding her tightly, and she reached out to do something she'd never done before. She punched the snooze alarm, giving them five more minutes to enjoy the morning.

"Good morning, Cookie," Ross said in a sleepy, very sexy voice. "We don't have to get up yet, do we?"

Hannah's arm shot out and hit the snooze alarm another three times. "No, we don't," she told him. "We can stay here as long as we want. Lisa's opening the shop this morning and I don't have to rush."

"Neither do I," Ross said, smiling as he looked down, into her eyes. "I love you, Cookie."

"And I love you." And that was the last thing Hannah had time to say to him until the snooze alarm began to beep nineteen minutes later.

"The pies are ready," Hannah said, carrying two to the walk-in cooler.

"Good." Michelle looked up from the bowl of cookie dough she was mixing. "Are they the real ones, or the contest ones?"

"Both. I made the real ones yesterday afternoon before we left for the day. And the ones I just put in the cooler are the contest ones."

"With no crust?"

"Right. Did you find enough big spoons or do we have to stop at CostMart?" Hannah asked.

"I found three red ones. I thought they'd look good on television."

"Great! All I have to do is make a couple of pans of bar cookies and we're ready for the bake sale."

"What kind are you baking?"

"Multiple Choice Bar Cookies. Everybody loves those. I think they'll sell really well, especially since I talked to Edna Ferguson and she said we could use the school coffee pot. She's bringing it up from the school kitchen for us."

Michelle smiled. "That's not all Edna's doing. She's making the coffee and selling it for us. She says she loves the fact that Lake Eden has a theater group and she wants to help support us."

"Edna's always a big help at things like this. And she's a great school cook. Jordan High would be lost without her."

"I know. I used to love her chili."

"It's a shortcut recipe," Hannah told her. "Edna gave it to me and I'll copy it for you. It's one of the reasons I call her the queen of shortcuts." Hannah glanced up at the clock. "I'll get those bar cookies in the oven and then I'll start packing up the cookie truck."

"Okay. I'll just finish this cookie dough and tell Aunt Nancy that it's in the cooler. If they need it before the end of the day, one of them can come back here and bake it."

It didn't take long to accomplish everything, and Hannah and Michelle arrived at Jordan High at noon. They'd expected to be the first ones there, but when they opened the lobby door, they saw that Edna was there and she'd set up all the tables for the bake sale. She'd chosen the table on the far wall for herself and she'd brought the large thirty-cup coffee pot the school used for social events.

"You're early, Edna," Hannah told her. "No one else is due to arrive for an hour."

"And you set up the tables," Michelle commented. "I thought we'd have to do that."

"I didn't do it, Freddy Sawyer did. He dropped by my place last night and told me he wanted to do something to help."

"Well, please thank him for us," Michelle told her.

"I will," Edna replied, plugging an extension cord into the wall outlet in back of the table she'd chosen. "I still have to run up to the teacher's lounge to get their coffee pot."

"Do you really think we'll need two?" Michelle asked her.

Edna nodded, setting her tight gray curls bouncing. "We'll need two," she said emphatically. "It's cold out today and everyone'll want coffee when they come in."

"You could be right," Hannah agreed.

"Of course I am. And after I get that pot hooked up, I'm going to Mrs. Baxter's

Home-Ec room to get her coffee pot. I'll heat hot water in that for those who want tea."

"I'd better run and get some tea," Michelle said.

"I've got it. I stopped by the Red Owl on my way here and Florence donated a whole bunch of herbal tea bags along with the coffee she promised me yesterday."

Hannah and Michelle exchanged glances. Edna had everything under control. "I suppose you got sugar, creamer, and spoons, too?" Hannah asked her.

"Of course I did. And disposable coffee cups and napkins."

"You're a real wonder, Edna!" Michelle complimented the older woman.

"I'm not a wonder. I'm just a pro. I've been doing this sort of thing for years."

Michelle and Hannah went back to the cookie truck to carry things in and within the space of twenty minutes or so, the tables were set up and filled with the baked goods they'd brought.

"Here you are, girls," Edna brought over two cups of coffee. "You both take it black, don't you?"

"Yes," Michelle answered for both of them. "Did you make a whole pot of coffee?"

Edna nodded. "I figured the Lake Eden Players might want some when they came in with their baked goods."

"Where is the closest refrigerator?" Hannah asked Edna. "I really should chill the pies."

"We've got a big one in there." Edna pointed to a door set into one of the walls. "That's where they chill the sodas for the basketball games. I've got the key. I'll unlock it for you. We'll just move a couple cases of sodas. They won't need them until next Friday night anyway. I can put the sodas back after everyone leaves."

All three of them were surprised when the first Lake Eden Players arrived at one o'clock sharp and ten minutes later, the whole cast and crew were there. Everyone had brought something, even the young man playing Tricia's husband, who told them that his mother had baked eight loaves of her special blueberry tea bread.

While Michelle talked to her Lake Eden Players, Hannah and Edna went up on the stage to prepare for the pie eating contest.

"It's perfect!" Hannah said when she saw that the contestant table and the judging table were exactly where she would have placed them.

"Thank you," Edna said. "I told Freddy where to put them. And he'll be here ten minutes before the contest starts to open the curtains. I used a plastic tablecloth on the contestant table because I thought it might get messy."

"Good thinking."

"And the judging table has a real table-cloth. It's three chairs behind each table, isn't it?"

"That's right. And you even have the podium for the announcer."

"I didn't think we needed name tags since everyone in town knows everyone else. Was I right?"

"You were right."

"I thought I'd put a full water glass in front of each contestant. They might need to wash the pie down."

"Good."

"How long is the contest going to last, Hannah? The paper said it was timed, but it didn't say how long."

"Michelle and I think ninety seconds is long enough. What do you think, Edna?"

"Ninety seconds should do it. After that they might start to slow down and it wouldn't be as funny. The paper didn't say who was going to announce the contest. Someone is, aren't they?"

A lightbulb began to shine brightly in Hannah's mind. Michelle had asked her to announce it, but there was a much better choice. She turned to grin at Edna. "You are! If you'd like to, that is."

"Me?" Edna looked properly astounded. "Are you sure you want me? I'm not a celebrity or anything like that."

"We want you. Both Michelle and I have seen you handle rowdy kids in the school lunchroom. You'd be the perfect announcer, Edna."

"Well . . ." Edna hesitated, but Hannah could tell she was immensely pleased. "Of course I'll do it if you need me."

"Great! I'll tell Michelle you agreed."

"And I'll get a pitcher of water and three glasses for the contestant table."

Hannah found Michelle talking to the woman who played Tricia's mother.

"Hello," Hannah greeted her. "I caught a little of your performance in rehearsal yesterday and I want to compliment you. You're a very good actress."

"Thank you," the woman said graciously, and then she turned back to Michelle. "Would you excuse me, please? I'm sorry I can't stay for the contest and bake sale, but I have a previous engagement."

"No problem, Vivian," Michelle told her.

"I have plenty of other people here to help. Please don't forget. We have dress rehearsal in full makeup tomorrow at three."

"I'll be there."

Michelle waited until Vivian had left and then she turned to Hannah with a puzzled expression on her face. "Vivian's a strange lady."

"How so?"

"She's always polite, but she doesn't say much. And she doesn't really talk to the rest of the cast. She just keeps to herself, performs her part, and leaves. For everyone else, rehearsal is like a social occasion when they're not on the stage. They exchange news, make plans to meet for coffee or whatever, and kid around."

"Maybe Vivian doesn't have a sense of humor."

"If she does, I sure haven't seen it!" Michelle gave a wry smile. "She's been with the Players for a while now and she's been cast in a couple of plays, but no one really knows her. One of the women said she'd heard that Vivian had a sick husband at home, so maybe that's why she doesn't feel like socializing."

"That could do it, I guess. She did seem a bit preoccupied today."

"Vivian's always that way. It's almost like

she shuts down when she's not on the stage. She's polite, and she smiles, and interacts in a minimal way, but she has no real connection with anyone in the group."

"She keeps her emotions hidden?" Hannah suggested a possible explanation.

"Maybe. Either that, or she's just what Dad used to call a *cold fish*. But, once the lights go on and she walks on stage, she comes to life. She's a talented actress and I'd like to find out more about her, but she doesn't encourage that sort of thing."

"You're right about that. She was polite when I complimented her on her performance, but she was aloof without actually being rude. Perhaps her husband needs a lot of care and attention, and she doesn't have the time or the energy left to connect with other people. Taking care of someone you love who's very ill could drain your emotions to the point where you'd have nothing left for anyone else."

"That could be it. But I wish she'd unbend a bit and be friendlier. I had the cast do their makeup before the first rehearsal because I wanted to see how long it would take them and decide if I needed to recruit more makeup people to help them."

"How did Vivian do?"

"Perfectly. And she did it faster than

anyone else. I think she must have been practicing at home, but I can see why everyone thinks she's standoffish. Vivian waited to go into the dressing room until everyone else had finished."

Hannah thought about it for a moment. "There's another possibility."

"What's that?"

"She could be pathologically shy. Some people are so afraid of making a mistake, they don't want to interact with other people at all."

"Crippling shyness," Michelle said. "My psychology professor talked about that. That could be it, Hannah. Vivian is so uncomfortable trusting in her own reactions to people that she chooses not to engage with them at all. And she's only comfortable when she's on stage, because everything she says is scripted for her."

"Right. It's not really her, it's someone else she's pretending to be when she's up there on the stage."

The two sisters were silent for a moment, thinking about that, and then Hannah remembered why she'd come into the lobby to find Michelle in the first place. "I almost forgot to tell you. I asked Edna to be the announcer for the contest and she said she'd do it."

"But I thought you were going to be the announcer."

"I was, but Edna will be better. You remember how she used to maintain order in the Jordan High lunchroom if things got out of hand, don't you?"

Michelle gave a little laugh. "She could calm us down in a couple of seconds by just standing there with her hands on her hips and giving us a disapproving look. And if that didn't work right away, she'd call out somebody and dress them down. Edna's got a really sharp tongue."

"And she knows everyone in town," Hannah added.

"Right. Not only that, she's very filmic with her sharp features and bouncing gray curls. She's a really good choice, Hannah. But . . ."

"But what?"

"But you're not disappointed that you're not going to be the announcer, are you?"

"Heavens, no!"

"But if Edna's the announcer, you won't be on television."

"Sure I will. And so will you. I'll hand out the spoons and you'll put Bertie's beauty shop capes on the contestants. We won't have speaking parts, but that's fine with me."

"It's fine with me, too. Is everything set up on stage, Hannah?"

"Yes. Edna's taking care of that." Hannah glanced at her watch. "Ross and P.K. should be here any moment. Before he left this morning, he told me that they were going to set up their equipment early. Ross said that if they hurry back to the station to edit and do whatever else they have to do, they can get us on the five o'clock news *and* the evening news. And he promised to do a voiceover with a bumper card that tells people when the Thanksgiving play opens and how they can get tickets to the performances."

"That's great advertising for us!" Michelle looked very pleased. "I'll tell the cast before we start the contest so they'll be sure to watch the KCOW news. And I'll pass out tickets to the play for them to sell at dress rehearsal tomorrow."

"Isn't it early for a dress rehearsal?"

"Yes. The main concern with the cast seems to be their costumes so Trudi asked me to do an early run-through. She said that way, if there's anything about a costume that doesn't work well, she'll have time to fix it before opening night."

"You all know that in most pie eating

contests, the contestants have their hands tied behind their backs, don't you?"

There was a roar of laughter from the audience and Edna clapped her hands. "That's right! But this contest is different. You don't really want to see our esteemed mayor go facedown in one of Hannah's Banana Cream Pies, do you?"

There were several shots of "Yes, we do!"

Edna laughed. "When Michelle Swensen, the interim director of the Lake Eden Players, asked Mayor Bascomb to be a contestant, she promised him that the contestants could use spoons."

There were several shouts of "boo!" coming from the audience, but then Edna held up her hand for silence.

Hannah came very close to laughing out loud when the audience quieted immediately. There was no doubt in her mind that Edna must have been the head cook in the Jordan High lunchroom when *they* were in school, too.

"Don't worry," Edna told them. "Just wait until you see the spoons we're going to give them! Hannah? Please pass out the spoons. But first, hold them up high, so everybody can see them!"

Hannah held up the huge red spoons and there was another roar of laughter from the audience.

Edna let it continue for a moment and then she held up her hand for silence again. "To prevent public embarrassment — and a massive dry cleaning bill — Bertie Straub, from the Cut 'n Curl beauty shop right here in Lake Eden, has donated three of her best capes which Michelle will now drape over our contestants."

While Michelle was draping the capes and Hannah was passing out the spoons, Edna motioned toward the table of judges. "I've already introduced you to our judges and most of you probably know that Stephanie Bascomb is our mayor's wife. Your husband looks pretty dapper today, *Judge* Bascomb. Is that a really expensive suit he's wearing?"

Stephanie laughed. "Of course it is, Edna. The mayor wouldn't be caught dead in a cheap suit!"

There was another roar of laughter from the audience, and Hannah noticed that while Ross was capturing footage of the contestants and the judges, P.K. was documenting the audience reaction and panning their faces. It was a great maneuver to have one camera trained on the audience. Everyone who was here at the contest would watch the news programs tonight to see if they would be on KCOW television.

Once Hannah and Michelle had delivered the pies, the timer was set for ninety seconds and the contest started. There was uproarious laughter coming from the audience continually, as the contestants did their best to try to lick pie from the bowl of the huge spoons. Hannah found herself hoping that Ross was getting plenty of footage of Mayor Bascomb dribbling whipped cream down his cape and tipping the spoon this way and that to try to get the pie filling into his mouth.

By the time the klaxon on the timer sounded and the contest had ended, Bertie's capes were covered with banana slices, whipped cream, and pie filling. The contestant table was also a mess and Hannah was glad that Edna had thought to use a disposable tablecloth.

Michelle and Hannah donned the bright yellow kitchen gloves Edna had provided from the school kitchen and brought the pie plates to the judging table. Ross got a good shot of the pie plates they placed there, along with the little stand-up card with each individual contestant's name. Mayor Bascomb had eaten his first pie, and had started in on the second. Al Percy had almost finished his first pie, but his second was untouched. And Rose McDermott had gotten more pie on her cape than she had in her mouth.

When Hannah and Michelle had delivered the pies to the judging table, they removed the capes from the contestants, collected the big red spoons, and took off the disposable tablecloth. Then they were free to watch the judging while Edna continued to speak.

"Well? What do you judges think?" Edna asked the three judges huddled together to deliberate.

*This was an obvious setup between Edna and the judges,* Hannah thought to herself, *but it was a good one.* And Edna had obviously cued Ross in on it because Hannah noticed that his camera was pointed directly at Stephanie again.

"It's clear to me, and the other two judges agree, that my husband, the mayor, won this pie eating contest." Stephanie paused and smiled sweetly, directly at Ross's camera. "I always said that Richard had a big mouth!"

Norman, who had taken over stagehand duties, pulled the curtain to a huge roar of laughter. Even Mayor Bascomb was laughing right along with everyone else, although Hannah suspected that his laughter was forced so that he could prove he was a good sport. She highly doubted that Mayor

Bascomb thought his wife's quip was really funny.

"Hannah!" Norman called her from the wings. "Come here a second before you go out front!"

Once the spoons and pie plates were stashed in the same cardboard box Hannah had carried in earlier, she told Michelle that she had to talk to Norman and headed for the side of the stage where Norman was waiting. "What is it, Norman?"

"Did you happen to notice Al Percy's shoes?"

"No, not really. I didn't see the contestants file in, and I was standing in back of them most of the time. What about Al's shoes?"

"I'll show you. I took a photo with my phone from the other side of the stage. The tablecloth doesn't go all the way down to the floor, or I never would have noticed. I enlarged and enhanced the part of the photo that I wanted you to see."

Hannah was thoroughly puzzled until Norman handed her his phone. "Those are his feet, but . . . Oh!"

"Do his shoes look like the ones that the intruder was wearing when we were hiding under Tori's bed?"

Shock and disbelief had set in as she stared at the photo and Hannah had to swallow before she could speak. "*Exactly* like that," she said. "It's him, Norman! He's the intruder! But do you think that Al would . . ."

"No," Norman cut her off before she could finish her thought. "He didn't do it, Hannah. Al has an airtight alibi."

"How do you know that?"

"I know because I'm his alibi. Al's wife had a dental emergency on the night that Tori was murdered. I was already at home when Al called me to ask me if I could come back to the office. I got there at seven-thirty, and Al and his wife were waiting at the door. She had an abscessed tooth."

"And that gives her husband an alibi?"

"Yes. He brought her into the office and sat in the examining room with her the whole time."

"How long did it take?"

"From seven-thirty until quarter to nine."

"That long?" Hannah was surprised.

"That long," Norman confirmed.

"Then that clears him," Hannah said. "And I'm fresh out of suspects again."

"How about the unidentified suspect with the unknown motive? You still have him, or her."

"I guess," Hannah said with a sigh. "But that doesn't do me much good if I don't know who the suspect is and I don't know the motive."

"You're tired and depressed and you need chocolate," Norman said, reaching out for her hand and pulling her toward the steps that led down from the stage.

"But I thought you didn't believe in endorphins."

"I don't, but they've got brownies for sale out there and I love brownies. Let's go get some before they're all gone."

"We got some great footage!" Ross said when he came in from the parking lot. "P.K. and I went over it in the truck. Edna was very good, and we captured the shock on Mayor Bascomb's face when Stephanie said he had a big mouth."

"That's great, Ross!" Hannah was pleased. "Michelle was really happy when I told her about the voiceover and bumper card you're doing to advertise the play."

"KCOW reaches a lot of viewers. It should be good advertising for her. I just came back in to tell you that I'm going back to the studio, but I'll probably be home by four-thirty. What time do you get out of here?"

"The bake sale ends at four unless we run out of food before that. There's not much packing up to do and Edna says she'll have

Freddy take care of the tables and chairs. Unless there's some kind of a snag, I should be home by five at the latest."

"Perfect. We'll watch the news together and then I'll take you girls out for dinner tonight."

Hannah laughed. "Only one girl. And she's married to you. Michelle won't be back at the condo until later. Her friend, Tricia, isn't working tonight and they're driving out to the mall to do some shopping and take in a movie."

"You mean we'll actually be alone?"

Hannah nodded, but a little seed of worry began to grow in her mind. "I know you like Michelle, but is it becoming a little . . . uh . . . restrictive having her stay with us?"

"Oh, no! I told you before, Hannah. I *like* having her there. And it's not restrictive at all. There are always closed doors, you know." He gave her a grin.

Hannah knew she was beginning to blush because her cheeks felt hot. "Yes, I know," she said.

"Don't cook tonight, honey. I have to drive past Bertanelli's and I'll pick up a pizza for dinner. What kind do you want?"

"Anything with sausage or pepperoni. And you already know that I love anchovies."

"Then it's a done deal. We'll eat it while

we're watching the early news. And then"
— he gave her a look that made her cheeks
feel even warmer — "who knows what
might happen?"

"You do," Hannah said, moving closer to
him and putting her arms around his waist.
"And I think I know, too." And then she
buried her face in the front of his shirt so
no one could see how furiously she was
blushing.

# CHAPTER TWENTY-FOUR

It was close to eleven on Sunday morning when Ross pushed back his chair at the Corner Tavern and stood up. "I'll see you when I get home, Cookie. Where are you going now?"

"Back home, I guess. I need to wash a load of clothes. And then Michelle and I are going to Jordan High for the dress rehearsal of the play this afternoon. Do you have anything you want washed?"

"Not a thing. What time is the rehearsal?" Ross asked her.

"Michelle wants to start by three-thirty. It's full dress and makeup so we have to get there by three." Hannah turned to Michelle. "What time do you think we'll be through?"

"When we finish the rehearsal, we have to do a couple of photos for Rod at the paper. And after that, we're going to rehearse the curtain call." Michelle took a moment to think about it. "We'll only run through everything once, so I'd say seven-thirty at the latest. And if everyone's on time, we might even be through earlier than that."

"Okay." Ross smiled at Hannah. "P.K. and I have to edit some of the footage we shot on our last day in New York, but that shouldn't take too long. Do you want me to pick up Chinese for the three of us?"

"Count me out," Michelle answered him. "Lonnie's picking me up after rehearsal. It'll be just you and Hannah again."

Ross turned to look at her and Hannah knew she was beginning to blush, remembering what it had been like the previous night when they'd been alone. "Chinese would be good," she said, hoping that Michelle wouldn't notice the blush.

"Okay. I'll see you when you get home, Cookie." Ross leaned down to give her a kiss.

The kiss lasted a few seconds longer than just a casual good-bye and Hannah was smiling when Ross released her and turned to go. "See you later," she said.

"More coffee?" Michelle asked Hannah.

"No, thanks. Let's head out, Michelle. I have a few things I want to do before the rehearsal."

"Me, too. I have to write up some notes and make a few calls."

They were about to get up from the table when their waitress came by with the coffee pot "Want another cup?" she asked them.

Hannah glanced at Michelle, and Michelle nodded. "Sure. That way we won't have to put coffee on at home."

The waitress refilled their cups and then she turned to Michelle. "My sister told me that you came back from college to direct the Lake Eden Players."

"That's right. The college gave me time off to fill in for Tori Bascomb."

"What happened to her was just terrible!" The waitress sighed deeply. "Is there any chance you might take over as director of the junior play at Jordan High while you're here?"

Michelle looked surprised at the question. "I don't think so. At least no one's asked me. Isn't there someone at the school who could do it?"

"My sister says no, and she probably knows. She has the lead and they haven't practiced all week. Do you think the college would let you do it if we all signed a petition or something?"

Michelle thought about that for a moment. "Maybe. When is opening night?"

"There's a Wednesday matinee the week following the Thanksgiving break. That's just for the school, though. The real opening, the one for everyone, is the following Friday night. You don't have to be back in school until the week following that, isn't that right?"

"That's right."

"Could you call the drama department at Macalester and see if they could arrange something? My sister and the rest of the cast would be really thrilled if you could direct them."

"Are you sure that there's no one at the school who wants to do it? I wouldn't want to step on anyone's toes."

The waitress shook her head. "There's no one. I asked my sister and she said they asked the English teacher, but she said she'd never directed a play before and she told them she didn't know the first thing about it."

"Okay, then. I'll call the college tomorrow," Michelle promised.

"Great! My sister will be thrilled!"

As their waitress hurried off with a smile on her face, Hannah turned to Michelle. "Do you have time to direct two plays?"

"Sure. I can do it, but I can't give you as much time at The Cookie Jar." Michelle looked a little flustered. "I'm sorry, Hannah. I should have asked you first."

"Don't worry about that! I love having you there, but I have plenty of help now that Aunt Nancy has decided to be there the whole day." Hannah gave a little laugh. "That waitress talked you right into it, didn't she?"

"Yes, she did. It made me remember what fun it was when we did our junior play. I'd hate to see this junior class deprived of that. It really shouldn't be too much work since Tori's already laid the groundwork and I'm just taking over for the last week or two."

"Three."

"Okay, three. But I'd really like to do it. I wonder if they have a drama class. I might be able to fill in there, too."

"You're willing to do that much work?"

"It's not really work."

"What is it then?"

"It's . . . research. I might really like to teach high school drama. And if I take over an existing class, I'll find out if I like it, or not."

Hannah was surprised. "Do you think you might like to be a teacher?"

"Maybe." Michelle gave a little shrug. "I don't know yet, Hannah. Maybe I'd like to settle down right here in Lake Eden and teach at Jordan High."

"I thought you were going to give acting a chance and eventually own and manage a little theater."

"I might do those things first. And if acting doesn't work out, and neither does the theater thing, I could come back here and teach. It could be a fallback position for me."

"I see." All sorts of things ran through Hannah's mind like flashes of lightning in an electrical storm. Michelle was young. She wasn't sure what she wanted to do with her life. What if she was considering coming back to Lake Eden, marrying Lonnie, and settling down right here in town?

"Don't worry. I won't," Michelle said.

"Won't what?"

"Just marry Lonnie and settle right here without trying anything else first."

Hannah blinked and stared hard at her sister. "You knew what I was thinking?"

"Yes." Michelle laughed. "It was probably that worried look on your face that tipped me off. I'm not going to 'settle' for anything, Hannah, but I'm not discounting the notion that ending up right here in Lake Eden might turn out to be exactly what I want to do with my life."

Several loads of laundry and five hours

later, Hannah and Mike applauded loudly. Mike had dropped by the condo just as Hannah and Michelle were leaving for rehearsal and decided to watch with them.

"What's next?" Mike asked Hannah.

"Rod's going to take some photos of the cast to put in tomorrow's paper," Hannah explained. "He thought it would be a good advertisement for the play."

"He's right. Lots of people read the paper, and not just people from Lake Eden. There are a couple of other towns around here that don't have papers of their own and they read the *Lake Eden Journal* to find out what's happening locally."

Rod beckoned to someone on the stage and Tricia and Vivian came forward. They stood in the center of the set and, at Michelle's direction, Vivian put her arm around Tricia's shoulders.

"Who's that?" Mike asked.

"Tricia Barthel."

"Not her. The older woman."

"Her first name's Vivian. Michelle says she lives way out in the country somewhere and one of the Players told Michelle she'd heard that Vivian's husband was very sick."

"Has she been in many plays?"

"Michelle said that Vivian had been in a couple of plays before. I've only seen her

460

twice and she's not very outgoing, so that's really all I know about her."

"She was really good in the play. I was surprised."

"Why? The Lake Eden Players usually put on a good show."

"Yeah, but their plays are almost always pretty amateurish. They can act, but you can tell they don't do it for a living. This Vivian's better than that. She had me believing that she was Tricia's mother. Has she been with the Lake Eden Players for long?"

"Not too long. A year or so, I think."

"After Tori took over as director?"

Hannah shrugged. "I don't know. You can ask Michelle if there's any record of when people joined. She may know, because she's using Tori's office. If there's some kind of a roster, it's probably there."

The curtains opened again to show the entire cast assembled at one side of the stage. Michelle was standing at a podium in the center and Mike turned to Hannah. "They're going to run through the play again?"

"No. They're rehearsing the curtain call. Mayor Bascomb and Stephanie are going to do Michelle's part on opening night."

"Then I guess I'd better head out. I've got a couple calls to make. Unless . . . is

461

Michelle using your cookie truck tonight?"

"No, Tricia's got her car and she'll bring Michelle back to the condo. They're going out to the mall first to do a little shopping and see a movie."

"Okay. Then you don't need a ride home?"

"No, but thanks for offering, Mike."

Mike stood up and saw that Rod was packing up his photographic equipment. "Good. Rod's done. I need to talk to him about something anyway."

Hannah knew that if she'd had ears like Moishe, they would have swiveled in Mike's direction. "Is it about your investigation?"

"No. I'd like Rod to run a few pictures of the deputies out at our station interacting with the community. Cops are getting a bad name in some of the press right now, and I'd like him to counteract that by publishing positive things about the Winnetka County Sheriff's Department personnel."

"Good idea. I'm sure he'll do it. Rod's a good newspaperman. He's probably got some ideas for you."

Hannah settled back to watch as Mike went off to intercept Rod. She half-listened as Michelle gave instructions to the actors.

"The mayor will give a short tribute to his sister before he begins the curtain call. I don't have his script for that yet, but I'll read it to you when I do. When the mayor finishes, I want you, Tricia, to come up to the podium and tell him, and the audience, that the night's performance was dedicated to his sister, Victoria Bascomb, your esteemed director."

Tricia nodded. "Will you write a script for me? Or shall I say it in my own words?"

"I think your own words would be better. And then, when you've gone back to your place in line, the mayor and Stephanie will begin to call people forward for the curtain call. That's what I want to practice right now. When I say your character's name, and then your real name, I want you to step out of line, take up a position on the far left of the stage, and form a line with the podium at the center. I'll divide you into two lines and arrange you in order now."

Hannah watched as Michelle divided the cast into two equal lines and positioned them, in order of importance, on both sides of the podium.

"These will be your positions for the curtain call. Remember them and take the same positions when we go through the cast roster. Is everyone ready?"

There were nods from everyone and Michelle continued. "Here we go then. When I call your character's name, followed by your real name, come forward, take your position, and bow or wave to the audience. Let's try it now."

A couple of the Players looked a bit nervous, but they nodded agreement.

"The part of Hugh Blackwell was performed by Barry Withers."

Hannah was surprised at Barry's appearance as he crossed the stage and took up a position on one side of the podium. She hadn't seen him since his senior year at Jordan High when she'd watched him win a speed skating competition. The gangly boy had turned into a handsome man and she hadn't even recognized him!

"The part of Lorena Blackwell was performed by Tricia Barthel."

Tricia walked forward and positioned herself on the opposite side of the podium. It was obvious that Barry and Tricia were the two principals and their supporting players would come next.

"The part of Mary Dumont was performed by Vivian Dickerson."

Hannah gave an audible gasp as Vivian crossed the stage and assumed a position next to Barry. Her mind was spinning so fast, she felt dizzy and light-headed. *Mary Dumont. Vivian played Mary Dumont. Could she be the M. Dumont that Tori had written as the last entry in her appointment book on the night that she was murdered?*

The rush of adrenaline that Hannah experienced at the sound of Vivian's character name was so intense, her legs began to shake. Her heart rate accelerated and her breath came in shallow gasps. Was she sitting here trembling, on a theater seat in the Jordan High auditorium, staring at Tori Bascomb's killer?

*Don't jump to conclusions,* Hannah's mind cautioned. *Even if Vivian did have an appointment with Tori that night, it doesn't mean that she kept that appointment. And even if she did, it doesn't mean that she murdered Tori.*

Hannah readily admitted her mind was right. Tori could have canceled Vivian's appointment. According to Doc's autopsy report, the window of Tori's death stretched from seven to ten, but Hannah knew that it was shorter than that. Delores had heard the shots at a few minutes past eight. And Tori could have cut Vivian's appointment short the way she'd done with Tricia.

Those were all possibilities that would clear Vivian of any wrongdoing. There were all sorts of questions Hannah needed to ask and the only person who could answer them was Vivian.

There was only one truly valid conclusion

465

Hannah could draw from the new information she'd gleaned. And that conclusion was that she had to talk to Vivian now . . . *tonight*! Perhaps nothing would come of it, but she needed to know if Vivian had met with Tori on the night that Tori was murdered.

# CHAPTER TWENTY-FIVE

Hannah stood outside the dressing room door, waiting for Vivian to come out. Just as Michelle had mentioned, Vivian had waited until everyone else had left the temporary dressing rooms set up against the back wall of the auditorium to remove her costume and makeup.

The ring of keys were heavy in Hannah's pocket. Michelle had given them to her when Hannah'd promised to lock up after everyone left. Of course, she hadn't told Michelle exactly *why* she'd volunteered to stay. Her conversation with Vivian Dickerson would probably amount to nothing useful, but it was certainly worth doing.

Hannah had decided that her talk with Vivian had to be private. Vivian might not be as forthcoming if she asked her questions in front of anyone else. She would wait until Vivian came out, and talk to her then.

■ ■ ■ ■

"So you'll do it, Rod?" Mike asked the older man.

"Of course I will. The *Lake Eden Journal* has always supported law enforcement. You know that, Mike. Let's get a really good setup for the first article. How about if one of the deputies talks to some kid on the street and helps him fix his bicycle?"

"That's good. I think we should use Lonnie for that. We should have a younger deputy who's a Lake Eden native. For the next one, how about Bill having coffee at The Cookie Jar with a whole table of ladies?"

"You mean ladies from the Lake Eden Gossip Hotline?"

Mike laughed. "That's right. You can get Delores to arrange it. She's really good at things like that."

As they watched through Rod's windshield, Barry Withers came out and walked across the parking lot to his car.

"Who's left inside?" Rod asked.

"Hannah and . . . I'm not sure," Mike answered. "The other car's a fairly new Buick. Hold on a second and I'll run the plate. Can you see the numbers from here?"

"Yeah." Rod grabbed a small pair of binoculars from his glove box and read off the letters and the number.

Mike punched in the information on his cell phone and listened for a moment. "This could take awhile. Why do you carry those binoculars anyway?"

"Just in case something newsworthy is happening and I don't want to get too close."

"That makes sense. You don't want to get too close, but you want to get photos for the paper. I noticed you had a long-range lens on that camera of yours."

"Oh, good!" Hannah said when Vivian Dickerson walked out of the dressing room. "I was waiting for you."

"Why?"

"Because I have the keys and I promised my sister that I'd lock up after everyone had left."

"I'm leaving right now."

"Wait a second. I'd really like to ask you something."

Vivian turned around and faced Hanna directly. "What did you want to ask me?"

"You're a very good actress. I told you that at the bake sale. And that made me curious about your background."

Vivian's eyes narrowed. "What about it?"

"I was just wondering if you had any professional acting experience."

"I never discuss my background," Vivian said, turning to go.

"No, wait!" Hannah reached out to grab her arm. "I didn't mean to pry. I just thought you were so good, that you must have acted somewhere else before. That's all."

"Thank you for the compliment, but that's none of your concern. I live here now and I'm with the Lake Eden Players. That's all your sister and you need to know."

"Of course it is." Hannah gave her a smile. "But there's one more thing."

"Yes?"

"Do you know that Tori Bascomb gave acting lessons in her home studio?"

"Yes, I heard that."

"Did you ever take an acting lesson from her?"

Vivian's eyes flashed with anger. "Of course not! Why would I?"

"No reason. I was just curious because she had you listed by your character name in the appointment book she used for her acting lessons. The appointment was for seven forty-five on the night she was murdered."

Vivian turned to face Hannah fully. "It wasn't an acting lesson. It was a personal matter."

"Then you knew Tori in some capacity other than as the director of the Lake Eden Players?"

"You could say that." Vivian moved a step closer and Hannah found herself backing up.

Warning bells went off in her head and she knew this wasn't good. "I'll bet you were in a play together, or something like that?" Hannah said, trying to cover her earlier question with some explanation that Vivian would find innocuous.

"You know better than that." Vivian's voice was hard as ice chipped from a solid block. "You figured it out, didn't you?"

*You're alone with her. You'd better backtrack as fast as you can,* Hannah's mind told her. And Hannah listened to that wise advice. "I figured *what* out? That you're a really great actress? Of course I did. And so should everyone who sees you on the stage."

"Thank you," Vivian said, but her eyes were still hard with a gleam of suspicion. "Have you ever seen me on the stage?"

"No, I don't get to attend many plays. I've seen a few things the Lake Eden Players have done, but that's it."

471

"Then perhaps you've seen me on the big screen."

"The *movies*?" Hannah pretended to be surprised and impressed. "I had no idea! I knew you were as good as a professional actress, but I don't think I've seen any of your movies."

"Really," Vivian said, and the expression on her face turned even colder.

*She doesn't believe you,* Hannah's mind told her. *You'd better think of some excuse to get away fast!*

Hannah knew that she had to escape and there was no time to waste. It was possible, even probable, that the same gun that Vivian had used to kill Tori was, even now, in the bottom of Vivian's tote bag, loaded and ready to kill Hannah!

The back door to the auditorium was directly behind her . . . Hannah knew that it was still unlocked, because when Michelle had given Hannah the keys, she'd reminded Hannah to make sure and lock up before she left! Hannah backed up another step closer to the unlocked door, trying to be as unobtrusive as possible. Even though her heart was pounding wildly and her knees were beginning to shake, she managed to keep the friendly smile on her face. It was time to get out while Vivian was still unsure what Hannah knew and what she didn't know.

Hannah glanced down at her watch. "Look at the time! I called my husband to tell him I had to stay at the school to lock up, but if I don't leave right now, he's bound to come looking for me."

"Of course he will. And he'll be the one to find you." Vivian's tone was flat and full of menace. "You know about me, don't you, Hannah?"

Mike turned to look up at Rod with surprise. "The plates came back as registered to a Vivian Dickerson."

"That's the woman who played Tricia Barthel's mother," Rod told him.

"So both of them are still in there."

"Yeah," Rod said. "And Hannah's probably still in there talking to Vivian."

"Why? Everybody else has left."

Rod shrugged. "I don't know. Why do women spend all that time talking to each other? Men will never understand that."

Mike nodded to acknowledge the comment, but his face took on a worried look. "It's odd."

"What's odd about it? Vivian's probably nattering away and Hannah has to stay to lock up."

Mike thought about that for a moment. "What do you know about Vivian, Rod?"

"Not much. She moved here a year or two ago and she lives way out in the country. She doesn't belong to any clubs that I know of and . . . I really don't know anything else about her."

"Was she a friend of Tori's?"

"Not that I know of."

Mike took a moment to digest that kernel of information and then he turned to look at Rod. "Does Vivian remind you of anyone you know? Or anyone you've seen before?"

Rod looked surprised at the question, but he thought about it for at least a minute. "In a way, she does. There was a movie I saw. Oh, it's got to be thirty years ago, but it had this woman playing a nanny. She was better than the actress that played the mother and that's probably why I remember her. If you took thirty years off Vivian's face, she'd look a lot like that actress."

"What was the name of the movie?"

"I don't know. It was something Gerda wanted to watch."

"Try to think of it, Rod. It's important."

Rod was silent for a moment. "It was something that was set in a foreign country, Mike . . . I think it was set in Paris, but I can't quite remember the name of the movie. . . ."

"Keep thinking. Maybe it'll come to you."

Rod thought for another minute. "Oh!"

"You thought of it?"

"Not exactly, but I think it was called *Interlude* or *Intermission* or . . . *Intermezzo!* That was it! *Intermezzo in Paris!*"

Mike grabbed his phone and typed in the name of the movie. It seemed to take forever to get an answer, but when he did, the search gave him a roster of the actors and actresses in the movie. Mike scanned it quickly and winced as he came to a familiar name. "Uh-oh!"

"What's wrong?" Rod asked him.

"I'll explain later. Stay here, Rod. And if I'm not back here in five minutes with Hannah, call Rick over at the station and tell him to get his . . . his squad car over here right away!"

"Is Hannah in danger?" Rod asked.

"I don't know yet. But I'm going in to find out!"

Just as they'd said in the old black and white gangster movie she'd watched with Norman a year or so ago, the jig was up. And Hannah knew it. All she could do was try to keep Vivian talking, stalling her as long as she could, in the hope that someone would see her car was still in the parking lot, and come in to find out what was taking her so long inside.

"So why did you kill Tori?" Hannah asked. "She didn't criticize your acting, did she?"

"Heavens no! She wouldn't dare! I'm better than she ever was, and I always have been."

"I've never seen Tori in anything, but I don't see how *anyone* could be a better actress than you are."

"Thank you, Hannah, but compliments won't save you now, you know. I'll have to kill you. I don't have any other choice."

"You could always lock me in somewhere until you got away."

Vivian shook her head. "Too sloppy. You're the only one who figured it out and I don't want you to tell anyone else. I'll leave Minnesota. You can bet on that. But I won't have to run as far or as fast."

"Are you sorry you killed Tori Bascomb?" Hannah asked, hoping to change the subject from a discussion of her fate.

"No. Why would I be sorry? She almost killed me! And she did kill my Broadway career."

"By taking over as the lead on opening night?"

"Yes. I would have gotten those rave

reviews. I would have been touted in all the papers, and been given starring roles for years after that."

Hannah nodded and backed up another step. "But you got sick, didn't you? And that's why Tori got the lead on opening night, instead of you."

"I got sick, all right!" Vivian's eyes began to gleam with intense emotion. "I got sick because she *made* me sick!"

Hannah hoped she looked as shocked as she felt. "*Tori* did that?"

"Of course, she did! She was my understudy, so we went out together to get lunch on our break. I ordered soup and went to make a couple of telephone calls. When I came back, my soup was there and so was Tori's."

"But . . . what does that have to do with . . ." Hannah stopped waiting for Vivian to continue. When she didn't, Hannah asked, "Did Tori put poison in your soup?"

"Of course not! If she had, I would have died. She put something else in my soup, something that gave me terrible stomach cramps that night. The cramps were so horribly intense that I couldn't even leave my apartment. And even though I tried to make it to dress rehearsal the next day, I was still too sick to go."

"Do you know what she put in your soup?"

Vivian shook her head. "No. If I'd suspected Tori right then, I would have gone in for a blood test and the doctors might have been able to tell. But I *didn't* suspect her, partly because she was so nice to me while I was sick. She fed me, helped me bathe and dress, and stayed over that night to take care of me. And she seemed so grateful and embarrassed that she'd gotten such a lucky break, that I didn't suspect her until I began to get better, and she stopped coming around to help me. It was only then that I realized that Tori had engineered the whole thing, just so she could play the lead on opening night!"

"Did you ever confront her about that?"

"Yes. She said I was crazy with jealousy because her performance was better than mine would have been. And she told me that she deserved the break she'd gotten."

"But she never admitted that she'd caused your illness?"

"Of course not! People like Tori never admit to anything."

There was a brief silence and Hannah knew her time was running out. She had to think of something else to ask Vivian, and quickly!

"There's one more thing I'd like to know," she said, hoping she could think of something in time. And that was when the idea hit Hannah and another line of questioning popped into her mind. "Did you call Tori and tell her you wanted to see her?"

"I called her, but I didn't ask for an appointment to see her. That was her idea. And that's the way I'd planned it."

"What made her ask you to come to see her?"

"Panic. Pure panic. I told her I wasn't sure I could be in the play, that my husband had taken a turn for the worse and I might have to drop out. And she asked me to come to see her at seven forty-five that night."

"Was your husband really sick?"

Vivian laughed. It was a throaty chuckle that contained no humor whatsoever. "I'm not married. I only came here because I'd heard that Tori was retiring and moving here. It was simple curiosity. I wanted to see if she'd changed over the years."

"What did you decide?" Hannah asked.

"She was the same person who'd put the drugs, or whatever it was, in my soup. She hadn't changed at all! Tori had always been a selfish, scheming person and she still had all those traits."

"Did you tell her who you were?"

"No. I wanted to see if she'd recognize me. But she never did. I acted in her plays right under her nose and she told everyone how good I was, but she never realized who she was complimenting." Vivian was silent for a moment and then she sighed. "And then it happened. The catalyst. The *denouement.*"

"The pivot point of the play."

"That's right. The climax. You're brighter than I thought you were."

"What was it? What happened to convince you to kill Tori?"

Vivian smiled a cold smile and her hatred for Tori was clear on her face. "The STAG lifetime achievement award."

Hannah could have kicked herself for not thinking of that, but this was no time for her to get distracted. "Tori won it and you didn't?"

"Yes. And Tori didn't earn it."

"But *you* did," Hannah said, hoping to soften the look of hatred that could be turned against her at any moment.

"Yes. I did. I was a successful actress on Broadway long before her, and even after Tori cheated me out of my starring role, I made a new, successful career for myself as a character actress. I deserved that award! And *she* was going to get it!"

"And you had to make sure she never got the satisfaction of attending the award ceremony and accepting it?"

"Exactly right. And now, that's enough talking."

As Vivian reached into her tote, Hannah knew that her time had run out. The last few grains of sand had dropped down to the bottom of the hourglass. She'd never make it out the back door of the auditorium, but . . . if she remembered correctly, there was a partially full sandbag attached to the scrim just over her head.

Hannah whirled, grabbed for the sandbag, and swung it forward as hard as she could. Since Vivian was looking down, into her tote bag, she didn't see the heavy bag coming directly at her head.

She spun around from the bag's impact, and Hannah was about to run forward to snatch the tote bag from Vivian's hands when she heard a voice from behind call out, "Hannah! Drop!"

*Mike!* Hannah dropped down quickly out of the way, as Mike ran past her toward Vivian. Mike left his feet, driving his right shoulder straight into Vivian's stomach and bringing her crashing down to the floor with a tackle worthy of one of the Minnesota Vikings linebackers. "Nice tactic with the sandbag," he said to Hannah, after first cuffing Vivian and hauling her back to her feet.

"Did you hear her confess?" Hannah asked.

"Yes. And any second now, Rick should be . . ."

"I'm here, boss," Rick called out, coming through the back door at a run.

"Don't forget to Miranda her and then take her down to the station. Lock her up, and book her for the homicide of Victoria Bascomb. She can cool her heels in a cell until I get there." Mike turned to Hannah and held out a hand to help her up from the floor. "Let's lock up and I'll walk you to your truck."

Hannah's whole body felt like jelly and she wondered if she could drive. She'd been terribly frightened and the physical reaction to that was setting in.

Mike realized that Hannah's legs were trembling, and he slipped his arm around her to support her. "You're in no shape to drive, Hannah. Leave your truck here and I'll take you home."

For once, Hannah didn't argue. She just watched Mike lock the doors to the auditorium, then she leaned on him as he walked her outside. Their breath came out in frosty puffs, and the cold night sky was filled with stars.

Hannah took a big gulp of the cold, night air, letting it out slowly. She was beginning to feel less shaky, but she still wasn't sure she could drive.

"Give me your keys," Mike said. "I'll have a couple of the deputies deliver your truck later."

Hannah leaned against Mike's squad car as he took her keys to Rick and gave him instructions. She wished that she could be magically and instantaneously transported home where Ross would be waiting for her. There was nothing she wanted more than to have Ross take her into his arms and hug her.

There was a flash which lit up the night, and Hannah realized that Rod must still be in the parking lot, and he was taking photos. Then there was another flash, as Rick helped Vivian into the back seat of the cruiser.

"No, no, no!" Vivian shouted at Rod. "Full face, yes. That's fine. But my profile can only be taken from the left. Do I look all right?"

Rod hesitated for a split second and Hannah knew he was wondering if Vivian's mind had become unhinged.

Then he said, "You look just fine, Vivian."

"Good! Then I'm ready for my close-up, Mr. Metcalf."

# CHAPTER TWENTY-SIX

"Ross is home," Hannah said, smiling as Mike pulled into her parking spot and she saw that Ross's car was parked right next to it.

"Good. You shouldn't be alone. I'll just walk you in, make sure everything's all right, and then I'll come back to take your statement in the morning."

"That's fine with me. And Michelle will probably have something for your breakfast. She's fixed something special every morning since she's been staying with us."

"You feel better, don't you, Hannah?"

"Yes, I do." Hannah said. She *did* feel better now that she was home. "You don't have to come up, Mike. I'll be okay, now that Ross is here."

"I'll come up, but I won't stay," Mike said, as he walked around the cruiser to open Hannah's door. "Ross is going to ask you a bunch of questions and I want to assure him that you're not hurt and everything's okay."

"That's nice of you," Hannah said with a smile, getting out of the cruiser and walking toward the steps that led up to ground level.

"I can be nice on occasion," Mike said.

Hannah gave a little laugh. "Yes, you can be. Thanks for everything, Mike. I really don't know what I would have done if you hadn't come in when you did."

"We'll talk about that tomorrow. Come on, Hannah. Can you make it up the outside stairway by yourself? Or do you want me to help you? Your legs are still shaking."

"I know, but I can make it." Hannah began to climb the staircase. It was true that her legs were still shaking slightly, but she managed with a good grip on the railing. Normally, she wouldn't have held the railing at all, but she was still just a bit weak in the knees and she didn't want to fall on her way to the landing.

"Here's my door key," Hannah told Mike when they reached the landing, pulling it out of her purse. "You unlock it and I'll catch Moishe."

"No problem. I'll unlock it, and *I'll* catch Moishe. He's too much for you to handle right now."

Mike inserted the key in the lock, but the door inched open before he could turn the key. "Whoa," he said, turning back to Hannah. "Stay right here."

"What's wrong?" Hannah felt her heart begin to pound at a rapid pace again.

"I don't know. Maybe Ross just didn't close it all the way and it failed to latch, but I'm going in to check it out anyway. Don't come in until I tell you it's clear, Hannah. And if I'm not back here in five minutes, go down to the garage and call the station. You got that?"

"I got it, Mike." Hannah leaned against the rail of the landing because her legs had begun to shake again.

"I need a promise, Hannah."

"I promise. Just go in, Mike. I'm getting really nervous." Hannah shivered and attempted to tell herself that it was because it was cold outside, but she didn't really believe it. Had someone broken in? Was Ross all right? How about Moishe? He'd always hurtled out the door to greet her before. Had someone hurt Moishe?!

Hannah stood there in the cold night air, clutching her cell phone in her hand and watching the seconds tick off on the display. One minute went by, much slower than it ever had before. Two minutes seemed to take an eon, and three minutes made her wonder if the clock on her phone was broken. She began to pace back and forth on the landing to keep her legs from locking in place. The four-minute mark finally came, and that was when the door opened.

"Come in, Hannah," Mike said, taking her arm.

"Ross is here, and everything's okay?" Hannah asked quickly.

"I don't know."

"What do you mean, *you don't know*?"

"I mean Ross isn't here. He was, but he's not now. Does Norman have Moishe at his house?"

"No! Not unless Ross took him there for some reason. But why would he do that? And why isn't Ross here?"

"You'd better come in and sit down, Hannah." Mike took her hand and pulled her inside. And then he hugged her tightly.

Something was wrong and it had to be bad. Mike looked almost as upset as she was.

"You think something's gone wrong, don't you, Mike?" she asked him, even though she really didn't want him to answer her question.

"Yeah. But I don't know what it is. I was thinking that maybe Moishe got sick and Ross took him to the vet. And he just didn't pull the door all the way closed when he left. Or Moishe got out somehow, and Ross is out there somewhere on the grounds, looking for him."

"Oh, no!" Hannah gasped. "Sometimes the coyotes come down here at night. And we had a bobcat once! We're way out here in the country. And . . ." Hannah stopped and her eyes widened. "Did you hear that?"

"Yeah. It sounded like a . . . a cat."

"Moishe!" Hannah called out. "Where are you Moishe?"

"Come here, Big Guy," Mike coaxed, using one of his favorite nicknames for Moishe.

A moment later, Moishe poked his head around the corner of the living room. His ears were back and his fur looked matted, as if he'd been hiding in a small space.

"Were you in the closet, Moishe?" Hannah asked, rushing forward to pick him up in her arms.

"Rrrrowww!"

"I looked in the closet and I didn't see him." Mike reached out to scratch Moishe's ears. "Is he hurt?"

Hannah felt for broken nails, sore places, and the obvious signs of feline trauma. "I don't think so."

"Then what is it?"

"I think he's just . . . just frightened."

Hannah walked over to put Moishe on the back of the couch. "I'll be right back with the treats, Moishe."

"Rrroww!"

"He sounds better," Mike said. "But it's hard to tell with a cat."

"I know. Sometimes I wish he could talk . . . but if cats could talk, they probably wouldn't."

"He's purring," Mike said when Hannah came back with Moishe's favorite fish-shaped, salmon-flavored treats.

"Good." Hannah began to relax and then she remembered. "But where's Ross? His car is here and it's too late to go to the gym in the recreation room."

"Yeah." Mike sighed heavily. "Did you leave first this morning? Or did Ross?"

"We left together. Ross took Michelle and me out to breakfast at the Corner Tavern. Then Michelle and I drove back here to do a few things before we went to The Cookie Jar. As far as I know, Ross drove straight out to KCOW to do some editing."

"But his car is here, right?"

"Right."

"And he had it this morning?"

"Yes. We drove two cars. I took my cookie truck and Ross took his car."

"Does Ross know anyone else in the

complex? Someone he might have gone to visit?"

"Not really. We've only been back for a week and I haven't had a chance to make any introductions."

"Then you'd better come back to the bedroom with me, Hannah. I need you to tell me if anything looks different than it did when you left this morning."

When Hannah stepped into the master bedroom, she gasped. Dresser drawers were open, the bed was piled with clothing, and a suitcase with several articles of clothing inside was open on the bed. "What happened? It looks like a tornado went through here!"

"You didn't leave it this way this morning?"

"Of course I didn't!"

"That's what I thought, but I had to ask. Look at the cell phone on the dresser. I need to know if it belongs to Ross."

Hannah walked to the dresser and stared down at the iPhone sitting there. "Yes, that's his cell phone. I have a Samsung."

"It's not Michelle's is it?"

Hannah shook her head. "No. She has a Samsung, too."

"Okay. There's a billfold there, too. Pick it up and tell me if that's Ross's billfold."

Hannah's hands were shaking as she picked up the billfold. It was the eel skin billfold she'd bought him in Puerto Vallarta on their honeymoon. "Yes, that's his."

"Open it and tell me what's inside."

Hannah's fingers were shaking as she opened the billfold. "His driver's license, the photo of us taken on the ship, his blood donor card from the Red Cross, and . . ." She pulled the section for bills open and blinked in surprise. "No money?"

"There's a key ring over on the other side. Do you recognize those keys?"

Hannah walked over to retrieve the key ring. "Yes. There's his key for the front door at KCOW, the key to his office there, and . . . that's all."

"No key to the condo?"

"No. It's not on the ring." When Hannah turned back to face Mike, there were tears running down her face. "Tell me what this means, Mike."

"I don't know for sure, Hannah, but it's not good."

"What do you *think* it means?"

Mike looked as if he didn't want to answer, and was now staring down at the floor between his feet.

Hannah walked a bit closer to him. "Tell me, Mike. I need to know."

"Sit down." Mike sighed, and looked up at Hannah's face, then he pointed to the chair next to the dresser and waited until she sat down. "Every case is different, but usually, when someone leaves without their identification, their cell phone, or their car, it's because they want to disappear for a while and they don't want anyone to be able to find them."

"But . . . how could someone disappear without a car or a driver's license?"

"They use another name, an *alias,* usually set up in advance. And because they don't want to be found, they don't take any of their old identification or anything that ties them to their old life with them."

Hannah's whole body began to shake and she grabbed the arms of the chair to steady herself. "But . . . why would Ross want to disappear?"

"I don't know, but I plan to find out."

Hannah heard the determination in Mike's voice. "You think he left me, don't you?"

"I don't know, but he ran for some reason." Mike took one look at the tears that were still running down her face, and reached out to pat her shoulder. "That reason may have nothing to do with you, Hannah. Before I came outside to get you, I called P.K. first. He said that Ross got a telephone call and said he had to leave work right away. It was right after their lunch break at twelve-thirty. Where were you then?"

"Michelle and I were at The Cookie Jar. We decided to mix up some cookie dough for tomorrow, to get a head start on things. If Ross had some kind of emergency, why didn't he call me?"

"I don't know, Hannah, but. P.K. said Ross told him that he might have to be gone for a while."

"Did Ross tell P.K. why he had to leave?"

"Not really. He just said it was personal. P.K. thought that maybe you were sick or you got into an accident or something like that. He was relieved to find out that you were okay."

*Okay?* Hannah's mind shouted. *My husband left me and I don't know why. I'm not okay. Not at all!*

There was a knock on the door and Hannah turned toward the sound. "You're wrong, Mike! That must be Ross. He just left his things here and went out for a walk around the complex." It was difficult, but she managed to get up on her feet. "I have to go let him in!"

"It's not Ross." Mike reached for her

hand. "It's probably Norman. I called him. I have to go down to the station, but Norman's going to stay with you until Michelle gets home."

Hannah felt numb as she walked toward the door with Mike to let Norman in. Her mind simply wouldn't process the fact that her husband had left without a word, without a note, without any kind of explanation, less than two weeks after their wedding. She had only one ray of hope, one thing to hold onto so she wouldn't slip into deep despair.

Ross had taken their condo key with him. And that meant he planned to come back to her.

# BANANA CREAM PIE MURDER
# RECIPE INDEX

# BAKING CONVERSION CHART

These conversions are approximate, but they'll work just fine for Hannah Swensen's recipes.

*VOLUME*

| U.S. | Metric |
|---|---|
| 1/2 teaspoon | 2 milliliters |
| 1 teaspoon | 5 milliliters |
| 1 Tablespoon | 15 milliliters |
| 1/4 cup | 50 milliliters |
| 1/3 cup | 75 milliliters |
| 1/2 cup | 125 milliliters |
| 3/4 cup | 175 milliliters |
| 1 cup | 1/4 liter |

*WEIGHT*

| U.S. | Metric |
|---|---|
| 1 ounce | 28 grams |
| 1 pound | 454 grams |

## OVEN TEMPERATURE:

Degrees Fahrenheit          325 degrees F.
Degrees Centigrade          165 degrees C.
British (Regulo) Gas Mark 3

Degrees Fahrenheit          350 degrees F.
Degrees Centigrade          175 degrees C.
British (Regulo) Gas Mark 4

Degrees Fahrenheit          375 degrees F.
Degrees Centigrade          190 degrees C.
British (Regulo) Gas Mark 5

Note: Hannah's rectangular sheet cake pan, 9 inches by 13 inches, is approximately 23 centimeters by 32.5 centimeters.

Here's a special treat from *New York Times* bestselling author Joanne Fluke! Find out what happened later in this exclusive epilogue, along with a bonus recipe!

# DAYS LATER

They were all gathered at the penthouse condo, sitting in the living room around Delores and Doc's flat screen television. Although Hannah hadn't wanted to go, everyone had urged her to do something besides work hard, come home, and sleep. Hannah had reluctantly agreed that she had to get out, that sitting at home on the same sofa she'd shared so happily with Ross and waiting for the sound of his key in the lock was having an adverse effect on her life. She knew he might never come home, might not even be *able* to come home, but she didn't want to think about that. Instead, she'd rushed home every night, pretended to be cheerful for Michelle, and fell into an uneasy sleep with one ear listening for any sound that could mean her husband had come home to her at last.

There had been no calls, no texts from new cell phone numbers, no contact at all.

He had simply vanished from Lake Eden and her life. She knew that somehow she had to cope with that, and tonight was her first attempt to reclaim her normal life.

The doors to the garden were open and both Moishe and Cuddles were enjoying a game of kitty hide-and-seek among the lush plants and colorful blossoms. They had all eaten dinner at the table in the garden, and Hannah had to admit that she had enjoyed the tropical warmth of the garden juxtaposed with the lazy snowflakes that had fallen gently on the climate-controlled dome over her head.

"Right after the break, we'll be presenting the STAG Lifetime Achievement award," the announcer said, and the camera panned the audience, settling, for the space of a second or two, on the mayor and Stephanie Bascomb, who were sitting in the front row.

"Look at Stephanie's dress!" Delores said, staring at the screen in awe. "There must be hundreds of mirrored beads on it."

"Several thousand," Hannah told her. "Claire mentioned it to me. She even showed me the photo of Stephanie that Rod's going to run in the paper tomorrow. Stephanie posed for it in her new dress before she left town."

"I couldn't really tell what the mayor was

wearing," Michelle said. "The camera just panned by him and then it zeroed right in on Stephanie."

"I wonder how much that dress cost," Delores said.

"Do you want one like that?" Doc asked her.

"Heavens, no! I was just wondering, that's all."

"I can ask Claire," Hannah said, trying her best to take part in the conversation, even though she wasn't really interested in Stephanie's dress. "Claire would probably tell me."

"And then you could tell me," Delores said with a smile.

Hannah nodded in a way she hoped was noncommittal. Delores was the co-founder of the Lake Eden Gossip Hotline. Hannah knew that if she told her mother the price, it wouldn't take more than five minutes for everyone in town to know it.

"Is P.K. in New York?" Mike asked.

"He's there and we're watching his live feed," Michelle answered.

"How do you know?" Lonnie asked her, and Hannah realized that he looked slightly jealous.

"I know because P.K. called Hannah and told her he was going. And he asked her to call him on his cell right away if Ross came back."

Hannah smiled. P.K. had taken over most of Ross's duties at the station and he was good about keeping in touch with her. She'd known that he was going to New York to film the award show before he'd even left town.

Ever since they'd taken seats and turned on the large flat screen, Hannah had watched carefully every time P.K. had panned the audience. She didn't think that Ross would be there. There was no reason for him to be there. But she watched all the same, hoping that she might catch a glimpse of him that would tell her he was still alive.

"He won't be there," Norman said in a low tone that the others couldn't hear. And then he reached out to give her hand a reassuring squeeze. "It'll all be explained, sooner or later, Hannah. I'm convinced that Ross really loved you. Don't listen to anyone who tells you anything else. There's no way Ross *wanted* to leave you."

"Then why did he?" Hannah asked, the pain clear in her voice even though she replied in the same low tone that Norman had used. "He took the time to pack. He could have taken the time to call me or at least write a note."

"Maybe he was afraid that someone else would find it and if it was made public, it might put him or you in danger. I really believe that Ross was forced to leave."

"Do you think someone broke into the condo and forced Ross to leave with them?"

"Maybe, but not necessarily. Ross might have been forced to leave because of a compelling reason that we don't know."

"That we won't know *yet,*" Mike, who was sitting on the other side of Hannah, corrected Norman. "I'm working on that, Hannah."

Hannah sighed. "Will you promise to tell me what you discover, even if it's not good?"

Mike thought about that for a moment. "Is that better than not knowing?"

"Yes! I'm imagining the worst and if you confirm that, it'll be a relief to know the truth. And if it's not the worst, it'll be a relief to know that, too. Either way, the truth is better than not knowing."

"Okay then," Mike said, reaching out to pat her shoulder. "I promise I'll tell you."

"Thank you."

"Good heavens! Where did he get that tux?"

Delores sounded genuinely shocked, and Hannah turned back to the screen. Mayor Bascomb was walking up to the stage and he was wearing a tuxedo that was so outrageous, Hannah couldn't keep from giving a little gasp. "It matches Stephanie's dress!"

"Do you think Claire ordered it for him?" Doc asked.

"That depends on how much she hates him," Hannah quipped.

"But where would Claire find something like that?" Michelle looked puzzled. "Claire doesn't carry any men's clothing."

"Maybe Ricky-Ticky found it at a costume shop in the Cities," Delores said, and then she began to laugh.

"Or the mayor has a connection to a circus that went out of business," Bill suggested.

Andrea looked as if she couldn't believe what she was seeing. "Stephanie must have picked it out for him."

"His and her outfits?" Mike asked, and everyone laughed as they nodded.

Mayor Bascomb began to give an acceptance speech for his sister. It went on and on until the background music began to grow louder.

"They're going to cut away in a minute if he doesn't stop," Lonnie predicted. And no more than a second or two later, a commercial for coffee began to air.

"That's a good idea," Michelle said, get-

508

ting up from the couch. "Just sit here and relax, Mother. I'll put on the coffee."

"And I'll get the dessert," Hannah added.

"What is it?" Mike asked as Hannah got up and turned toward the kitchen.

"Milk Chocolate Cupcakes with Butterscotch Frosting," Hannah told him.

"Butterscotch!" Doc repeated in a tone he usually reserved for references to the deity. "Hurry, Hannah. I think I have a butterscotch deficiency."

"You always have a butterscotch deficiency," Delores said, smiling at him.

"I'll help you," Norman said, standing up to walk to the kitchen with Hannah and Michelle. When they got there, he patted Hannah's shoulder. "He wasn't there, Hannah."

"I know." Hannah said. She knew that Norman was referring to Ross.

"Are you okay?"

"Yes," Hannah said, realizing that she *was* okay. She still missed Ross, but forcing herself to go out tonight had helped her more than she'd realized it would. Being with her family and the people who loved her was exactly what she needed to do while she waited to find out the answers to the questions that were firmly etched in her mind.

"These look great, Hannah!" Norman said, as he lifted the cover on one of Hannah's distinctive bakery boxes and peeked inside. "Do you want me to put them on a platter?"

"Yes, please." As Norman began to arrange the cupcakes on a platter, Hannah realized that she was looking forward to dessert. She hadn't eaten much in the time that Ross had been gone, and now, surrounded by her family and friends, her appetite for food had returned right along with her appetite for being a part of Lake Eden life again.

"Shall I carry them out?" Norman asked her.

"Not yet. Let's wait until the coffee is ready. If you take them out too early, Doc and Mike will eat them all and there won't be any left for us!"

# MILK CHOCOLATE CUPCAKES WITH BUTTERSCOTCH FROSTING

Preheat oven to 350 degrees F., rack in the middle position.

1/2 cup salted butter *(1 stick, 4 ounces, 1/4 pound)*

1/2 cup vegetable oil *(not canola — I used Wesson)*

2 and 1/4 cups all-purpose flour *(pack it down in the cup when you measure it)*

3/4 cup unsweetened cocoa powder *(I used Hershey's)*

2 cups white *(granulated)* sugar

1 and 1/2 teaspoons baking soda

1 teaspoon baking powder

1/2 teaspoon salt

1 cup chocolate milk

3 large eggs

8-ounce container sour cream *(I used Knudson)*

1 teaspoon vanilla extract

Line two 12-cup muffin pans with double cupcake papers.

**Hannah's 1st Note: This recipe makes 24 cupcakes. If you don't have a second muffin pan, you can spray a round layer cake pan with Pam or other nonstick**

**cooking spray and then flour it. Or you can spray it with baking spray, which already contains flour.**

Place the butter in a microwave-safe bowl and heat it for 30 to 45 seconds to melt it. Take the bowl out of the microwave and set it on a kitchen towel on the counter.

Measure out 1/2 cup of vegetable oil. Add it to the melted butter and stir. Leave it on the counter to cool while you begin to make the batter.

Place the flour, cocoa powder, sugar, baking soda, baking powder, and salt in the bowl of an electric mixer. Mix them together on LOW speed until they are combined.

Feel the sides of the bowl with the melted butter and vegetable oil. If you can touch it comfortably, add it to the ingredients in the mixing bowl. Mix on LOW speed until it is combined. Then add the chocolate milk and mix it in.

**Hannah's 2nd Note: You can make chocolate milk by measuring out a cup of whole milk and adding enough Hershey's syrup to achieve the right color.**

With the mixer running on MEDIUM speed, add the eggs, one at a time, mixing after each addition.

Scrape down the bowl to make sure all the ingredients will be mixed. Then turn the mixer up to MEDIUM-HIGH speed and beat for 1 minute. Then mix in the sour cream and the vanilla extract.

Turn off the mixer, take out the bowl and give it a final stir by hand.

Fill the cupcake papers three-quarters full. Distribute the batter as evenly as possible.

**Hannah's 3rd Note: Lisa and I use a 2-Tablespoon scooper at The Cookie Jar to add the batter to the cupcake papers in our muffin tins. If you do this at home, do one scoop for each cupcake paper and then use half-scoops to distribute the rest as evenly as you can.**

Bake your cupcakes at 350 degrees F. for 17 to 20 minutes. *(Mine took 18 minutes.)* To test to see if they're done, insert a toothpick in the center of one cupcake and pull it out. If it comes out clean without any batter clinging to it, your cupcakes are ready to come out of the oven.

*If you made the cake layer instead of the second muffin pan, it should bake an additional 5 or 10 minutes.*

Cool the cupcakes by setting the pans on cold stovetop burners or wire racks.

**Hannah's 4th Note: Cold cupcakes frost better than warm ones. You can even cover the cupcakes loosely with foil and let them cool overnight on your**

kitchen counter. This method, of course, could cause a reduction in the number of cupcakes by the time you are ready to frost them.

When your cupcakes are completely cool, make the frosting.

## Butterscotch Frosting:

2 cups butterscotch chips *(11-ounce or 12-ounce package — if your package is 10 ounces or less, add more chips until you reach a total of 2 cups)*

14-ounce can of sweetened condensed milk *(NOT evaporated milk — I used Eagle Brand)*

1/4 teaspoon salt

powdered sugar to add if frosting is too thin

24 cupcakes, or 12 cupcakes and 1 round cake layer, cooled to room temperature or below.

## Optional Ingredients for Using Leftover Frosting:

Chocolate cookies

Salted soda crackers, Ritz crackers, or Townhouse crackers

Marshmallows and toothpicks

**Hannah's 1st Note: If you use a double**

**boiler to make this frosting, it's fool-proof.**

**Double Boiler Directions:**
Fill the bottom part of the double boiler with water. Make sure the water doesn't touch the underside of the top.

Put the 2 cups of chips in the top of the double boiler, set it over the bottom, and place the double boiler on the stovetop. Turn the burner to MEDIUM heat and stir occasionally until the chips are melted.

Stir in the can of sweetened condensed milk and the salt. Cook the mixture approximately 2 minutes, stirring constantly, until the frosting is shiny and of spreading consistency. Add powdered sugar if needed.

Remove the top portion of the double boiler and place it on a potholder or folded kitchen towel on your counter, next to your cupcakes.

Turn off the stovetop burner.

**Hannah's 2nd Note: You can also make this frosting in the microwave, which is much easier.**

**Microwave Directions:**
Put the chips in the bottom of a quart Pyrex measuring cup or any microwave-safe bowl of a similar size.

Open the can of sweetened, condensed milk, pour it over the butterscotch chips, and set it in the microwave.

Sprinkle the salt over the top of the sweetened, condensed milk.

Heat the mixture in the microwave for one minute on HIGH. Let it sit in the microwave for an additional minute and then attempt to stir it smooth with a heat-resistant spatula. If you cannot stir it smooth, heat it for another 20 seconds, let it sit for an additional minute, and then try to stir it smooth. Repeat as often as necessary.

Stir in powdered sugar if needed and set your frosting on a towel or potholder on your kitchen counter. Use a frosting knife to spread the frosting on the cupcakes *(and on the cake layer if you made it)*.

**Hannah's 3rd Note: Since this is a soft frosting and not too thick, one easy way to frost cupcakes is to dip them in the frosting up to their cupcake papers and twist them to cover the entire top. Then pull them out of the frosting, set them on a rack to let the frosting "set", and you're done. This takes a lot less time than using a frosting knife to frost cupcakes.**

**Hannah's 4th Note: Unless you really pile on the frosting, you will have some**

left over. **This is where the optional ingredients come into play.**

## Yummy Uses for Leftover Frosting:

You can spread leftover frosting on top of chocolate cookies, or make frosting sandwiches with 2 cookies.

You can spread leftover frosting on any of the crackers. This is best if you turn the crackers salt side down and frost the unsalted side. Place them on a sheet of wax paper and let them cool to room temperature until the frosting is "set".

Alternatively, you can stick toothpicks into the bottoms of the marshmallows and use the toothpicks as handles.

Reheat the frosting in the microwave until it is liquid again. Place the frosting on a towel or potholder on the counter and use the toothpicks to dip the marshmallows into the reheated frosting. Let them cool on wax paper and remove the toothpicks after the frosting has "set".

If you like, you can also reheat the frosting again until it's pourable, and pour it over vanilla or chocolate ice cream for a tasty dessert.

# ABOUT THE AUTHOR

**Joanne Fluke** is the *New York Times* best-selling author of the Hannah Swensen mysteries, which include *Double Fudge Brownie Murder, Blackberry Pie Murder, Cinnamon Roll Murder,* and the book that started it all, *Chocolate Chip Cookie Murder.* That first installment in the series premiered as *Murder, She Baked: A Chocolate Chip Cookie Mystery* on the Hallmark Movies & Mysteries Channel. Like Hannah Swensen, Joanne Fluke was born and raised in a small town in rural Minnesota, but now lives in Southern California. Please visit her online at gr8clues@joannefluke.com. Her website is http://www.joannefluke.com

The employees of Thorndike Press hope you have enjoyed this Large Print book. All our Thorndike, Wheeler, and Kennebec Large Print titles are designed for easy reading, and all our books are made to last. Other Thorndike Press Large Print books are available at your library, through selected bookstores, or directly from us.

For information about titles, please call:
(800) 223-1244

or visit our Web site at:
http://gale.cengage.com/thorndike

To share your comments, please write:
Publisher
Thorndike Press
10 Water St., Suite 310
Waterville, ME 04901